# SPARKS FLY...

She watched Ben sip his champagne. His eyes left hers only long enough to make his new, young admirers think he was actually listening to their conversation. Just as quickly, he slid his gaze back to Isabel, and though no smile came to his lips, she would swear that his eyes were glittering. It might have been a trick of the chandeliers that blazed overhead, she reminded herself. Or the spark in his eyes might have been a result of the quantity of champagne he'd no doubt already consumed. It might even have been amusement she saw there.

Or it might have been something else.

It was the kind of look that communicated even across a crowded room, and suggested an invitation so bold and so completely inappropriate, it could make a woman's stomach flutter and her cheeks grow hot. Isabel knew that as well. It was something she'd learned from Ben, and remembering it caused heat to warm places that had been cold too long—or not nearly long enough.

Not, Isabel told herself, that she cared. . . .

# Diamond Rain

## Constance Laux

A TOPAZ BOOK

**TOPAZ**
Published by the Penguin Group
Penguin Putnam Inc., 375 Hudson Street,
New York, New York 10014, U.S.A.
Penguin Books Ltd, 27 Wrights Lane,
London W8 5TZ, England
Penguin Books Australia Ltd, Ringwood,
Victoria, Australia
Penguin Books Canada Ltd, 10 Alcorn Avenue,
Toronto, Ontario, Canada M4V 3B2
Penguin Books (N.Z.) Ltd, 182–190 Wairau Road,
Auckland 10, New Zealand

Penguin Books Ltd, Registered Offices:
Harmondsworth, Middlesex, England

First published by Topaz, an imprint of Dutton NAL,
a member of Penguin Putnam Inc.

First Printing, April, 1999
10  9  8  7  6  5  4  3  2  1

Copyright © Connie Laux, 1999
All rights reserved

 REGISTERED TRADEMARK—MARCA REGISTRADA

Printed in the United States of America

Without limiting the rights under copyright reserved above, no part of
this publication may be reproduced, stored in or introduced into a
retrieval system, or transmitted, in any form, or by any means (electronic,
mechanical, photocopying, recording, or otherwise), without the prior written
permission of both the copyright owner and the above publisher of this
book.

BOOKS ARE AVAILABLE AT QUANTITY DISCOUNTS WHEN USED TO PROMOTE
PRODUCTS OR SERVICES. FOR INFORMATION PLEASE WRITE TO PREMIUM
MARKETING DIVISION, PENGUIN PUTNAM INC., 375 HUDSON STREET, NEW
YORK, NEW YORK 10014.

If you purchased this book without a cover you should be aware that this
book is stolen property. It was reported as "unsold and destroyed"
to the publisher and neither the author nor the publisher has received
any payment for this "stripped book."

*For the world's best writing buddies:
Bonnie, Cheryl, Claire, Emilie,
Leigh, and Mary*

Dear Reader,

*Diamond Rain* is my sixteenth book, and I have to let you in on a secret—of all the heroes and heroines I've written about, I've had the most fun with Ben and Isabel.

At first it seemed odd to write about a hero and heroine who'd known each other before the book began. I've never done that. My heroes and heroines have always been strangers to each other who meet in the pages of my books.

But I knew Ben and Isabel had to be different. There had to be a certain tension between them, an antagonism that was so strong, there had to be other reasons for it than simply the fact that their companies were in competition.

A previous acquaintance was the perfect answer. And the perfect setup for a relationship that's as incendiary as the fireworks these two are providing for Queen Victoria's Diamond Jubilee!

And speaking of fireworks . . .

Doesn't it make your blood sizzle just to think about fireworks? They light up our most festive occasions. They put the exclamation mark on our holidays. As I found out when researching *Diamond Rain,* they have a long, glorious history.

There really was a famous family of fireworks manufacturers in England at the time I've set *Diamond Rain.* They were the Brock family, and from what I've read about them, their fireworks shows were every bit as spectacular as Ben's and Isabel's.

Some of the incidents I've mentioned in the book are based on fact. There really was a lancework of Queen Victoria that winked at the crowd. (I can't help but think she would not have been amused.) And there really was a daredevil who slid down a wire at the Crystal Palace. His name was Bill Gregory though, to add a touch of the exotic to the festivities, he was known as Signor Geregorini. He got stuck partway down the wire, and because his crew was busy, they had no choice but to leave him there for the remainder of the show. The audience soon discovered he wasn't Italian; he swore a blue streak in plain old English!

As always, my thanks to everyone who helped with this book and who cheered me on through writing it: my husband, David; my children, Anne and David; and an assortment of friends who listened to me plot and plan and whose suggestions and support are always appreciated.

# Chapter 1

*London, 1897*

There were worse things in the world than being stared at by Benedict Costigan. Isabel De Quincy was sure of it.

It was a pity that at the moment she couldn't think of one of them.

"Apoplexy. Ague. Consumption. The Black Death." Below her breath, Isabel recited as many of the world's ills as she could name, desperately searching her mind for at least one that might compare. She failed miserably.

Plague and pestilence were no match at all for the cool blue gaze of the man who lounged at the far end of Sir Digby Talbot's ballroom. A champagne flute in one well-shaped hand, Ben kept up an easy conversation with two debutantes who had clearly fallen under his spell.

But he never took his eyes off Isabel.

Damn the man! He was as subtle as those fireworks they called octopus shells and as bold as the one known as a red-hot trio. Not, Isabel told herself, that she cared.

She returned Ben look for look, her own pale gaze colliding with his cornflower blue. Let him stare. And remember. Let him take a good, close look and see that the girl he'd last laid eyes on four years earlier had grown into a woman. One who, if Isabel did say so herself, was poised, polished, and world-wise enough to refuse to let so simple a thing as a man's blatant scrutiny bring a blush to her cheeks or a flutter to her stomach.

Not any longer.

Nonchalantly, she adjusted the train of her slim skirt and ruffled one gloved hand across the flounce of silk that edged the plunging neckline of her ivory gown. She fingered her three-strand necklace of pearls and decided to fight fire with fire. Isabel raised her chin a fraction of an inch and assessed Ben as openly as he was examining her.

He had changed very little in the years he'd been away, though he did look taller than she remembered. There was a glint of gold in his honey-colored hair that she supposed must have come from the sun in one of the southern European countries she'd heard he'd been visiting. There was a bronze cast to his skin that might have been appealing had he been any other man. But other than that he was the same Ben Costigan, with the same devilishly handsome face and, if the smitten expressions of the young ladies he was talking to meant anything, the same devastating charm.

It was a dangerous combination—Isabel knew that all too well—an alchemist's brew that could mysteriously transform even the most level-headed woman into a weak-kneed and all-too-willing conquest.

She watched Ben sip his champagne. His eyes left hers only long enough to make his new, young admirers think he was actually listening to their conversation. Just as quickly he slid his gaze back to Isabel, and though no smile came to his lips, she would swear that his eyes were glittering. It might have been a trick of the electric chandeliers that blazed overhead, she reminded herself. Or the spark in his eyes might have been a result of the quantity of champagne he'd no doubt already consumed. It might even have been amusement she saw there.

Or it might have been something else.

It was the kind of look that communicated even across a crowded room, and suggested an invitation so bold and so completely inappropriate, it could make a woman's stomach flutter and her cheeks grow hot. Isabel knew that as well. It was something she'd learned from Ben, and remembering as much caused heat to warm places that had been cold too long—or not nearly long enough.

Not, Isabel told herself, that she cared.

She snapped open her silk and ivory fan and waved it in front of her burning face, feeling the press of the crowd and wondering how a room that had been so comfortable only a minute ago could suddenly feel as stuffy as a glasshouse.

"The Black Death." The crisp movement of her fan kept time to each word she snarled from between clenched teeth. "The Black Death must have been worse."

"What are you talking about?" At Isabel's side, the Duchess of Fenshaw, Lady Margaret Thorlinson, raised an eyebrow and gave her a quizzical look. "You're mumbling to yourself, Belle, and I can't imagine why. I—" Her eye caught by the scene going on across the room, Margaret pulled in a breath and leaned nearer. Her voice dropped to a conspiratorial whisper.

"Benedict Costigan! I heard he was back. And though I know there is no love lost between you, I have to say, unless my eyes are playing tricks on me, he is more handsome than ever."

"Really?" Isabelle flicked an imaginary speck of lint from her elbow-length gloves. "I hadn't noticed."

"Well, you really should pay more attention." When Margaret realized Ben was looking their way, she couldn't help but smile. Thankfully, she was a veteran of the marriage mart and canny enough to disguise her reaction behind a well-timed cough. She covered her mouth with one hand and turned her back to Ben, and the shiver that trembled through her nearly caused her champagne to spill. "Oh, those shoulders! And those eyes! If I wasn't a married woman . . ."

Isabel snorted. It was an unladylike sound at best,

but she hardly cared. "Go right ahead," she said, and try as she might, she couldn't keep the acid taste from her mouth or her words. "I hardly think as insignificant a matter as your marital status will make one bit of difference to Ben Costigan."

As if Isabel had just insulted one of her beloved children, Margaret's dark eyes widened. "Surely not! I've heard a great deal about Benedict Costigan, but that is one thing I have never heard to be true." She scowled and dared another look in Ben's direction. "Unfortunately."

"Honestly, Margaret!" With a shake of her shoulders, Isabel cast away the unnerving spell of Ben's gaze. She had had enough of his impertinence. Enough of the queer, slightly drunken sensations that filled her head for some reason she could not explain, and she turned and set her own, untouched glass of champagne on the nearest table. There was no way she could ever put enough distance between Ben and herself, but she would have to make do. She headed toward the French doors that led into the garden, and when Margaret fell into step beside her, she glanced at her friend out of the corner of her eye.

"You're perfectly happy with Richard, aren't you?"

Margaret laughed and wound one arm through Isabel's. "Of course I am! And you're a dear to care. I'm only teasing. You know that, Belle, for you know I'm as madly in love with my husband as a woman can be. As madly in love as you'll be once you listen to reason and make up your mind to marry my brother-in-law, Peter. You don't think I'd really—" At the sound of Ben's familiar laughter rumbling through the room, she looked back over her shoulder. "Well," she admitted with a sigh, "I might be tempted. What woman in her right mind wouldn't be?"

"What woman in her right mind would be!" Isabel untangled her arm from Margaret's and stepped over the threshold and out onto the terrace. It was nearly dark and far cooler than it had been under the heat of Ben's gaze. Isabel pulled in a breath of air and leaned against the marble balustrade, her back to the gardens that surrounded this portion of the house. It was a pleasant evening, and mild for April. Many of the party goers were already strolling there, and in deference to the others who were still in the house by inclination or obligation, the ballroom doors had been thrown open. From where Isabel stood, she had a perfect view of the room.

She was just in time to see Ben's two new admirers rescued from his clutches by a pair of rather flustered mamas. The ladies had, Isabel imagined, sent their daughters to practice the art of innocent flirtation with decent gentlemen. How horrified they must have been to find their offspring in the questionable company of a man whose reputation was as scandalous as his fortune was large!

To his credit, Ben exchanged the appropriate pleasantries, and to Isabel's unending wonder, by the time the mamas left with their daughters in tow, all four females were giggling like schoolgirls. Even before they withdrew, Ben was joined by two gentlemen, and for the life of her, Isabel could not have said which of the two surprised her more.

"Simon?" Amazed, she watched the scene unfold before her. "Simon, my own brother. Talking to that . . . that . . ."

Margaret laid a restraining hand on her arm. "Now, now, it's nothing to get upset about. You know how it is with men. They are all hale and well met when the occasion requires, even if they are not sincere. And your brother is as good at the game as the best of them. No doubt, he and Ben are old friends and—"

"Friends? Ben?" There was a curl of ashen hair arranged artfully over one of her shoulders, and Isabel pulled at it fitfully while she watched her brother act the traitor. "The two words can hardly be spoken in the same breath. Ben doesn't have any friends. Only worshipers."

"Yet Sir Digby seems friendly enough."

Isabel tossed her head. Margaret was right, as usual.

If she didn't know better, she would think that Ben and their host, Sir Digby Talbot, were old friends, indeed. They put their heads together, and when Ben spoke, Sir Digby nodded knowingly.

Sir Digby Talbot was one of those English statesmen who was more an institution than an individual. He had served Queen and country since long before Isabel was born, and for all she knew, he would go on like the Empire itself, flourishing long after the rest of them were gone. With his startling crop of white hair and a face as rumpled as a child's favorite blanket, he reminded Isabel of a beloved uncle, and that is exactly how she thought of him. Sir Digby had been a close friend of Isabel's family for as long as she could remember, and his visits, though infrequent, were grand occasions that were highlighted by the sweets and books and trinkets he brought for both her and her brother.

As she watched, Simon took his leave, and Ben was left alone with Sir Digby. Isabel shook her head. "I really don't understand what he's doing here." She didn't have to point out which of the men she was talking about. "This is supposed to be a reception for those of us involved in planning the Queen's Jubilee celebration."

Suddenly, there seemed nothing in the world as important to Margaret as the roses growing near the shallow steps that led into the garden. She gazed at them intently, her hands clutched at her waist. "You mean you don't know?"

There was something about Margaret's tone of voice that Isabel didn't like. She swung her gaze from Ben to her friend. "Know what? It can't possibly have anything to do with the Jubilee, or with the meeting I am to have tomorrow with Sir Digby and the committee planning the ceremony. I know that for certain. Costigan and Company? Purveyor of Penultimate Pyrotechnics?" She gave a cynical laugh and might have rolled her eyes if years of training at all the right schools had not taught her to control so ill-bred a behavior. "Ben can't possibly think he has a chance to—"

As if it had been derailed, the train of Isabel's thoughts broke in two. Margaret was quiet. Too quiet.

"He's hoping to get the contract for the Jubilee fireworks?" Isabel listened to her own question echo back at her, her voice sharp with astonishment, her words honed with the edge of impossibility. Ben and Sir Digby shared a laugh, and Isabel twirled away from the scene. "It isn't possible!" She slapped her palms against the cool marble balustrade. "He doesn't have a feather's chance in hell!"

"Really, Belle!" Margaret made the appropriate tsk-tsk noises of disapproval and offered a glance of apology to the people around them who'd overheard Isabel's unseemly remark.

Isabel didn't bother following Margaret's lead. Let Margaret offer apologies for her. As far as she was concerned, the only thing she had to apologize for was forgetting to add that she was sure the hottest fires in perdition had been earmarked especially for Ben. And that she would like nothing better than to see him roasting over them for all eternity.

For now there were more important things to worry about than apologies, and Isabel concentrated on them. She fastened her gaze to Margaret and refused to back down. Not until she got some answers.

"Richard is on the Jubilee committee," Isabel said. "What do you know?"

Though Margaret tried her best, she was a poor actress. And an even poorer liar. Her laughter rippled the night air. "I don't know anything. I assure you! You know how men are. They never share any information with their wives that is truly useful. They say it is none of our business and that we shouldn't fill our pretty heads with—" Margaret was less than convincing, and if she didn't know it, one look at the expression on Isabel's face must have told her as much. Her laughter died. Her smile vanished. Her shoulders sagged.

"He's been invited to the meeting," Margaret said.

"Ben?" Isabel could hardly believe her ears. "How? Why? He must know he'll never get the contract. De Quincy and Sons is the oldest fireworks establishment in the country! And the most distinguished! He can't possibly think that he can compete against us with those theatrical affectations he tries to pass off as fireworks! It's incomprehensible. That's what it is. Of all the arrogant, vain, disdainful—"

"Now, Belle." Isabel hadn't even realized she'd started back toward the house until Margaret grabbed her arm to hold her in place. "You can't march in there and take the man's head off!"

"Can't I?" Isabel shook herself out of Margaret's grasp. She might have continued on straight into the ballroom if common sense and business acumen were not as much a part of her personality as was her aversion to Ben Costigan. She reminded herself that Ben's melodramatic proclivities were legendary. He was known for fireworks displays that were as far from the tasteful shows that De Quincy and Sons produced as the earth was from the moon.

De Quincy shows were beautiful and elegant. Well considered and perfectly executed. Flawless. Artistic. Refined.

Costigan and Company shows were not unlike Ben himself. They were gaudy. Garish. Too loud and too flamboyant, and altogether too melodramatic.

"There isn't a chance Sir Digby will let Costigan and Company near the Jubilee celebrations," Isabel said, but whether she was trying to convince Margaret or herself, even she wasn't sure. Holding on to the thought, she pulled herself up to her full height, lifted her chin, and walked back into the ballroom.

But even by the time she had secured another glass of champagne and refused the offer to partner an especially drunken peer with a roving eye and a heavy foot for the next waltz, Isabel hardly felt better at all.

So, Ben would be at the committee meeting in the morning.

She let her gaze glide to where he stood and was relieved to see that he wasn't paying the least bit of attention to her. He was deep in conversation with a circle of young men. But not too deep. When a ravishing dark-haired woman sauntered past, Ben laid one hand on her arm and whispered in her ear. The woman was enough of a lady to blush to the roots of her hair, but apparently not enough of one to resist Ben's infamous allure. She smiled as if she knew a rather delicious secret, and before she walked away, Isabel swore she saw her wink at Ben.

Not, Isabel told herself, that she cared.

With one final glare she left the ballroom.

She could handle whatever feeble attempts Ben might make at winning the lucrative contract for the Queen's Jubilee fireworks, she assured herself, just as she could handle Ben himself.

Still, his presence at the next day's meeting was bound to make for some tense moments. After all, it was sure to be awkward coming face to face with a man she hadn't spoken to in four years. Especially when four years ago Ben had abandoned her at the altar on the day of their wedding.

"I once met a cobra in Delhi, who crawled through the dirt on his belly."

Ben Costigan raised his voice over the strains of a Strauss waltz at the same time he lifted his champagne glass. He looked over the heads of the men gathered around him, fully prepared to offer a salute in Isabel's direction, and was crestfallen to realize she was no longer standing where he'd seen her last. He searched the room, but there was no sign of her, and he lowered his glass and frowned.

"Go ahead, Costigan. Get on with it!" Someone in the small assembly offered encouragement. The request was echoed by others in the crowd.

"Finish the poem!"

"Give us the ending!"

Reminded of both the occasion and the company,

Ben shook off his momentary, inexplicable disappointment and grinned.

"Sorry!" He pulled a face. "I can't seem to remember the rest of it!"

There were groans all around, but fortunately, it was late enough in the evening and the champagne was flowing freely. No one really cared; no one would really remember. When the young, very drunk Earl of Haverness began the recitation of another limerick, Ben's companions were more than happy to turn to him, anxiously waiting to see if his state of inebriation would have any effect on either his elocution or his choice of subject matter.

"Cobras, eh?" Edward Baconsfield moved closer to Ben's side, and when a roar went up in response to whatever the squiffy young earl had the nerve to say in public, Edward tugged Ben farther from the crowd. "All that talk of cobras . . ." He scanned the crowd himself, and smiled over his champagne glass at a buck-toothed young lady who was all too eager to smile back. "That didn't have anything to do with the fact that Isabel De Quincy is here, did it?"

Ben grumbled an oath. "You know, I did once meet a cobra in Delhi," he said. "One of those snake charmer chaps kept it in a basket. He let me take a look. And I swear, Edward, the damn thing had a friendlier gaze than did Isabel when I saw her a moment ago. Cobras are congenial when compared to that one."

Edward laughed. "You don't blame her, do you?"

"Blame her?" Blame was not a subject Ben liked to consider. Not when it came to his past, his business, or his women. He dismissed Edward's question with a lift of his shoulders and headed toward the refreshment room to find a servant who might refill his glass.

Edward was not the kind of man who gave up easily. It was one of the few characteristics they shared. Edward Baconsfield was a political creature, one who seemed always to be embroiled in some crusade. He was the kind of man Ben usually found tiresome, and he might have been as dreary as was every other eccentric Ben had ever met if not for his love of good food and fine spirits and the fact that he was as ready to embrace a new mistress as he was a new cause.

Now he followed along. "You didn't expect her to welcome you back with open arms, did you?" Edward asked.

Ben didn't need to ask who he was talking about, but still, the fates and his own bad luck seemed to conspire against him and offer a reminder. No sooner had they stepped into the refreshment room than he saw Isabel over near the buffet table. She was talking to a handsome dark-haired fellow Ben recognized as Peter Thorlinson, Viscount Epworth, the younger brother of the Duke of Fenshaw. Young Lord Epworth was fairly fawning over Isabel, and from the love-smitten look on his face, he was enjoying every minute of it. He helped her decide which dishes she wanted to sample from the buffet. He carried her plate. He found her a seat. Usurping the duties of a servant who stood at the ready nearby, he pulled a chair away from a table, and once Isabel was settled, he sat across from her.

It was as flagrant a display of infatuation as any Ben had ever seen. And enough to make him queasy.

Not, he reminded himself, that he cared.

Isabel caught sight of him the moment she sat down, and the carefree smile on her face vanished. She set aside her knife and fork, and shot him a look that was as fully disagreeable as those she'd given him in the ballroom.

"Perhaps I am being too kind." Ben spoke to Edward with not the least concern that his voice was loud enough to be heard throughout the crowded room. "Not a cobra. Rather a modern-day Medusa. You know, that woman in the Greek myths. The one with snakes where her hair should have been." He wriggled his fingers above his own hair while he headed in the direction of the buffet, but he never took his eyes off Isabel. "Any man foolish enough to dare a look at her turned instantly to stone."

A gentle poke in the ribs reminded Ben that Edward was far more easily cowed by a lady's malevolent looks than he, and far less inclined to offend a guest of Sir Digby Talbot's. "Will you try some herring?" Ben pulled his gaze from Isabel's and found Edward holding out a serving spoon piled with fish.

"Damn, and why not!" Ben dismissed the subject with a tight smile and nodded to a servant who scooped up a plate and loaded it for him, and when it was full, he looked around for a place to sit. He found the perfect spot, right next to Isabel's table.

He sensed that Edward might have objected, but by the time Edward realized where they were headed, it was too late. Ben nodded a brief acknowledgment to Lord Epworth. He ignored Isabel completely.

With dubious looks at Ben, the table he'd selected, and the company nearby, Edward dropped into the chair next to his. Fitfully, he arranged and rearranged his cutlery. He glanced from Ben to Isabel and back again. He ran his tongue over his lips. Ben was reminded of a condemned man standing before a firing squad, waiting for the first shot.

Ben waited for it, too, every sense on the alert, every muscle tensed. The way he waited to see what would happen to the blind firework shells that sometimes fell to the ground without exploding. At the same time he wondered which of them would be the first to breech the fragile truce, he was reminded that if four years had taught him nothing else, they had taught him that Isabel's was a face he couldn't easily forget—no matter how hard he tried. He was surprised and more than a little dismayed to see that his memories, persistent though they were, did not accurately match reality. This close, he realized just how much Isabel had changed.

The features were the same: the same slightly upturned nose and delicate cheekbones, the same eyes, as icy and blue as diamonds. But four years had refined Isabel's face and form. Enhanced them. Perfected them.

The lips that had once been merely luscious were now generous as well. The eyes that had once seemed so innocent flickered with the shimmer of sophistication. Her hair was the same flaxen color, fairer than his, and luxuriant enough so that part of it was pulled back from her face and piled atop her head and the rest was left to cascade over one shoulder.

The body . . .

Ben dared to drop his gaze from hers long enough to take a better look.

Isabel was no taller than she'd ever been; he could tell that much even though she was seated. She was no rounder, either, except for certain portions of her anatomy that were, as fashion dictated, emphasized to attract a man's attention. Her gown was off her shoulders and cut low over her bosom. Rather than detract from the creamy perfection of her skin with its sprinkling of freckles, the pearly gown enhanced it. It flowed like liquid silk over her breasts, emphasizing their shape and size just enough to hint at the fact that there were treasures beneath the virginal fabric. Treasures that might be revealed at the right time. To the right man.

Not, Ben reminded himself, that he cared.

"Well . . ." Desperate to fill the clumsy silence, Edward dug into his food. "Here's something about England you must surely have missed on your travels abroad, just as I did when I did the grand tour of Russia recently. Caviar is all well and good, I dare say, but there's nothing like good, hearty English food."

"No. Nothing at all." Hoping to lull Isabel into a false sense of security, Ben toyed with a lamb cutlet he had no intention of eating. "But I must be honest, sir." He looked up from his plate, over Edward's shoulder, and straight into Isabel's daunting eyes. "There's nothing about England I missed. Nothing and no one."

Color flooded Isabel's cheeks and her jaw tightened.

She snapped her gaze from Ben's and concentrated instead on her dinner plate. It was a victory of sorts, albeit a small one, and it gave Ben a perverse sort of pleasure and a surge of satisfaction the likes of which he hadn't felt since he'd persuaded Sir Digby into letting him attend the next day's meeting of the Jubilee committee. Buoyed by his achievement, encouraged by the small signs that he might yet get a rise out of the frosty Miss De Quincy, and no doubt spurred on by the volume of the champagne he'd already downed, he decided to try again.

"No. I didn't miss a soul, and I'll tell you why." Ben leaned back, his arms crossed over his chest. "One meets the occasional unscrupulous character when one travels abroad, but in all, I find that people on the Continent are generally honest, especially in Italy, where I stayed for some time. They were only too eager to please. But here in England . . ." He let go an exaggerated sigh. "I'm sorry to say it, Edward, but my experiences have not been nearly so positive. The country is thick with deception, and I don't mean just the politicians. It seems everywhere you turn, you run into charlatans, frauds. Woman who are bold enough to carry on after a man when all they are really interested in is the color of his banknotes and the size of his—"

Before Ben could say another word, Isabel's cutlery rattled. Her china clattered. She bounded from her chair. The action was as involuntary as the blush that betrayed her, and she was obviously as surprised by it as were the people around her. She stood as still as a stone, her breaths coming and going rapidly, her hands flat against the table, her eyes fiery.

"Finished so soon?" Whether he knew it or not, it was Lord Epworth who saved the scene from escalating into either melodrama or farce. He touched his serviette to his mouth and pushed away his half-eaten meal. He rose from his chair and stood back to let Isabel by him and on toward the door, and it was only when Epworth did that he noticed the men at the neighboring table.

"Edward!" Epworth moved forward, his hand extended. "How good to see you again!" He pumped Edward's hand and nodded toward Ben. "Peter Thorlinson," he said, and added "Lord Epworth," almost as if it were an afterthought. "Edward and I were at school together. And you, sir, are . . .?"

Because Ben had no choice, he rose. He introduced himself, watching for the shudder of recognition that was sure to come once Epworth heard the name. But it seemed the viscount's manners were as impeccable as his looks. He smiled politely and offered his hand.

"And this . . ." Epworth reached around and gently piloted Isabel to his side. "This is Miss Isabel De Quincy." He pivoted his gaze from Edward to Ben. "But I do believe you two are acquainted."

"Are we?" Ben paused long enough to make his point. "Ah, yes, Miss De Quincy." He offered his hand and was surprised at how cool Isabel's felt, even encased in its satin glove. "Our families are in the same business," he said, turning to Epworth. "Fireworks, you know. I do believe Miss De Quincy and I have that in common."

Isabel extracted her hand from Ben's and pulled it to her side. "Only to a point," she said. "I'm afraid Mr. Costigan's idea of a fireworks display is not necessarily in agreement with mine."

Poor Epworth looked genuinely confused. "Fireworks? I knew about the fireworks, of course, but I thought . . . That is, I rather . . . That is, weren't you two once . . ." He never realized what he was into until he was well into it. The viscount's cheeks darkened, and he tripped over his words. "Wasn't there some sort of . . . relationship?"

"That was a very long time ago!" Ben's hearty reply cut Epworth off before he could get himself in deeper and well before Isabel could get a word in edgewise. "And I'd hardly use the term *relationship,* would you, Miss De Quincy?" He paused considering, and watched with no small sense of satisfaction as anger flushed through Isabel's ivory skin.

"Let me see . . . how can I explain? I know!" Ben beamed a smile. "In the fireworks business, we have shells we call *maroons*. They're the ones we send up as a salute at the beginning of a show. Lots of noise and no color. I do believe Miss De Quincy would agree. Our relationship was a great deal like one of those maroons." He fastened his gaze to Isabel's. "A good deal of noise and no color at all."

Ben had to give Isabel credit. Most of the women he knew would have been at him with claws extended. Not Isabel. She smiled a perfectly icy smile and laughed a laugh that could only be described as silvery.

"No doubt Mr. Costigan is misremembering," she said. "Or thinking of someone else. Honestly, though our families are in the same business, we hardly know each other at all. As a matter of fact, I'm not sure we've ever been introduced, have we?" Like a farmer who is thinking about purchasing a particularly unhealthy-looking dobbin, she looked him up and down, and for a moment Ben had the distinct and quite uncomfortable impression that she might ask to take a look at his teeth.

Isabel sighed. "I'm so sorry to admit it, Mr. Costigan, for it is rude to be so blunt, especially with a stranger, but you are hardly extraordinary. I really can't recall if we've ever met."

"Now that I think of it, neither can I." Ben stepped aside to allow Isabel by. "One little blond woman is so much like any other. Perhaps we will have a chance to meet again in the future."

"If we're lucky," Isabel purred.

"If we're lucky," Ben agreed. He waited until Isabel and Epworth were halfway across the room before he added, "And by the way, Miss De Quincy . . ."

She stopped and turned to him, and Ben had the small satisfaction of realizing her hands were clenched at her sides.

"Fortune," he said. "It was *fortune* I was going to say. That some women are interested simply in the color of a man's banknotes and the size of his fortune."

She smiled, a wintry, brittle smile. "Of course. I thought so all along. I can't imagine that any true gentleman would ever dream of saying anything else." She turned away from him. "Although . . ."

Isabel turned around and looked Ben up and down, her gaze skimming its way over his shoulders, across his chest, to his stomach and lower still, in a familiar sort of way that in the bedroom might have excited him no end. In the refreshment room of Sir Digby Talbot's elegant town house, and with an audience of bored aristocrats just waiting for the next delicious scandal they might chew on, it made him damned uncomfortable.

"It is little known to men, but quite a true fact," she said, "that no matter the size of a man's fortune, it's the size of his other attributes that really matters most to a woman. And all too often, the man with the biggest fortune and the largest ego is the one who is trying in some desperate way to make up for his obvious inadequacies in other areas."

And with that, she left the room.

Ben watched her go. "A scowl that could stop an eight-day clock and a temper to match."

"And the face of an angel." Edward was not usually inclined to sentimentality, and Ben forgave him, but only because they'd both had too much to drink. "It ought to be an interesting meeting in the morning."

Ben was about to sit down and start in on his dinner, but Edward's comment brought him up short. "What are you talking about?"

Edward clapped him on the back. "Don't you know? She's the power behind De Quincy and Sons these days."

"Isabel?" Ben stared at the now empty doorway. "You don't mean that she's—"

"In charge. I'm afraid so, old man. Not officially, of

course. Officially, the company's being run by that no-good brother of hers. But he's more interested in chasing skirts than running a business and everyone knows it. The company is his by all rights, but he leaves the day-to-day operation of it to Isabel."

"Which means she'll be at the meeting in the morning." It was a sobering thought, and it deserved to be drowned, but not, Ben thought, with anything as delicate as Sir Digby's champagne. He left behind his meal and headed toward the card room, where there was sure to be a game and a bottle of whiskey or two. Before he ducked inside, he looked back over his shoulder toward the ballroom and saw Isabel waltz by in the arms of Lord Epworth.

"You know, they say he's going to ask her to marry him," Edward told him.

Ben mumbled a word he should not have used in public.

Not, he reminded himself, that he cared.

But the fact that Isabel was managing De Quincy and Sons, and that she was nearly engaged to another man, could make for some sticky moments at the next day's meeting.

After all, it was bad enough running into the woman you'd been engaged to yourself four years earlier. It was worse still when he thought about the fact that four years ago, Isabel had left him waiting at the altar on their wedding day.

# Chapter 2

"The color of a man's banknotes and the size of his fortune!"

Isabel grumbled the words and punctuated them with a contemptuous snort. It was a sound she had made all too often in the twelve hours since she'd encountered Ben at Sir Digby's, and, not for the first time, she reminded herself that it was unladylike and unbecoming.

She didn't need to remind herself that she didn't care a fig.

"Despicable, detestable, damnable man. The size of his bloody fortune, indeed! As if I'd be interested in the size of anything else!" She tossed her handbag on her desk and, pulling off her gloves, dropped them down beside it. She was thankful it was early and she was the only one in the offices of De Quincy and Sons. She shouldn't like the staff to hear her swearing like a fishwife, and she was very much afraid that even if they had been present, she would not have been able to restrain herself.

The anger that had bubbled through her the night before and kept her from getting a wink of sleep still roiled in her blood.

And who could blame her?

Seeing Ben after four years was bad enough. Learning that he thought he could compete against De Quincy and Sons for the Jubilee contract was even worse.

"Loathsome. Contemptible. Vile man." Muttering, Isabel headed in the direction of the huge iron safe that dominated one corner of the office, her footsteps pounding against the Axminster carpet. "If he thinks he'll catch me off my guard, he can think again." She knelt on the floor in front of the safe and grumbled under her breath while she twirled the lock. "Oh, no, not this time. He may think me easy prey, but he'll find he's wrong. Just as he did last time. He may think he can flatter and cajole his way back into my heart but—"

The sound of her own words brought Isabel up short.

What Ben had done last night could hardly be classified as flattery. Cajoling her was the furthest thing from his mind. The things he'd said . . . The looks he'd given her . . .

"And isn't it just as well." Isabel set her jaw and went to work on the safe. "Twenty-four," she mumbled, repeating the combination aloud as she always did when she opened it. "He's wretched . . . thirty-nine . . . that's what he is. Too wretched for words. And if he did think I'd be swayed somehow by those lips or those eyes—" With a start she realized she'd gone right past the last number in the combination. She cursed herself and her errant thoughts.

"If he thinks he can come back after four years and . . ." Isabel spun the lock anti-clockwise and started again. "Well, he's wrong, that's for certain. Just because a girl is foolish enough to once . . . twenty-four . . . doesn't mean she can't come to her senses. It doesn't mean she spends all her time thinking about the feel of his . . . thirty-nine . . . or the size of his—Blast!"

"Belle! Who are you talking to?"

Startled by the sound of a voice from the doorway, Isabel sucked in a sharp breath and sat back on her heels. "Simon!" She pressed one hand to her heart and fought to catch her breath. "What are you doing here at this hour of the morning?"

It seemed that Simon was just as surprised to see her as she was to see him. For what seemed too long a moment, he stood frozen in the doorway. He was dressed in the same formal clothes he'd been wearing when Isabel saw him at Sir Digby's: black trousers, black jacket, white waistcoat, shirt and tie, but while last night he'd looked every inch the dandy, this morning he looked much the worse for wear.

There were smudges of sleeplessness under Simon's eyes, and his toast-brown hair was uncombed. It stood up as straight as a pound of candles at the crown of his head and drooped into his eyes at the front. As if he could feel Isabel's appraisal, he made to sweep it back with the same hand in which he held a piece of paper. He looked from Isabel to the paper, then folded it and tucked it away into the breast pocket of his dinner jacket.

"I might ask you the same thing," he said, strolling into the office. He set his silver-tipped walking stick on the desk and leaned back, his arms crossed over his chest. "Do you always show up this early so you can swear through a double deal board and hope no one will hear?"

As usual, Simon's easy manner and his sense of humor brought a smile to Isabel's face. She offered him her hand, and when he'd helped her to her feet, she brushed off her dove gray skirt and straightened her matching jacket. This close, he smelled of cigars and a good deal of liquor, but Isabel pretended not to notice. It was an issue they had discussed before, and it was not one she was willing to face this early in the morning and with so much else on her mind.

"I stopped by to check on some business matters before my meeting with Sir Digby this morning," she explained. "And I wouldn't have been swearing at all if it hadn't been for that bloody—" She caught herself and cleared her throat. She couldn't deny that her language was inappropriate, but the last thing Simon needed to know was the real cause of her frustration. It was far more circumspect to glower at the safe than it was to think about Ben, so that is exactly what she did.

"We really must have someone in to look at that lock," she said. "It's impossible to open."

Simon didn't reply. He was too busy brushing off the sleeves of his coat and checking his snowy cuffs.

It shouldn't have surprised Isabel. For all too long she'd known that Simon wasn't the least bit interested in the daily operations of the company. Ledger books. They were more to Simon's interest. Not because they represented a simple way to track both the company's successes and failures, but because they gave him an idea of how much money he had to squander.

The thought settled in Isabel's stomach at the same time she remembered the bit of paper she'd seen Simon slip into his pocket.

"Simon . . ." Her voice trailed away on the end of a sigh, right along with the momentary hope that this time things might be different. "You've written yourself another cheque, haven't you? That's why you're here before anyone else has arrived. You've—"

She was interrupted by Simon's good-natured laugh. He swept one hand through his hair. "Belle, Belle, Belle." He wagged his head. "Whatever are we to do with you? You sound just like Father."

It was a congenial enough comment, but Isabel rankled beneath it. "Of course I sound like Papa," she told him, her words tight in her throat. "I am as concerned about the business as Papa ever was. Perhaps more so, for Papa never knew that you are spending our money nearly as fast as we are making it. It would have worried him to death to know that you—"

"The man is already dead. What difference would it make?"

The smile never faded from Simon's face, but his tone of voice warned her he wanted nothing more than to put an end to the conversation. No matter. He was treading on thin ice, whether he knew it or not. He was threatening the very survival of De Quincy and Sons, the one passion she had left.

"For all his faults, you cannot deny that Papa cared about the company. It was his father's. And his father's before that. If poor Papa ever really knew how awful our debts were . . ." The very thought was painful, and Isabel shook it away. "It was just as well he wasn't able to attend to business as much as he liked in the months before he died. It made it easier for me to make sure he never really knew that you were—"

"That's enough!" Simon's face hardened into an expression Isabel had seen before. It was the same stony look he gave her each time she brought up his intemperate spending habits. The same one he used when she dared to mention he was drinking far more than was wise, just as her father had done in the months before his death.

Simon was not a tall man, and his eyes were nearly on a level with Isabel's. He held her gaze, his eyes penetrating even though they were shot through with red.

"Why shouldn't I spend the money?" Simon asked. "It was Father's company. And his father's before him. And his father's before that. Just as you said. Now it is mine. I am the eldest. I am the son. I can do whatever I like. I am not accountable to anyone." As if the thought was too ridiculous to even consider, he whirled away from her and went to stand behind the desk. "Especially a spinster sister who had her chance to save the company four years ago and decided she would rather keep her precious De Quincy pride than marry Ben Costigan's fortune."

It was an insensitive remark, even for Simon, and for a full minute Isabel could not bring herself to respond to it. She clutched her hands at her waist and swallowed the impulse to try and reason. Or explain.

There were no words that might explain to Simon what Isabel couldn't even begin to explain to herself.

"Yes. Of course. You can do whatever you like." With a cough she cleared the tightness from her throat. There was only one way to appeal to Simon. Isabel knew that well enough. She didn't feel the least bit guilty about using it.

"I am merely reminding you that I am trying as

hard as I can to preserve what our family has worked so long to build," she told him. "I'm not complaining, Simon. You know I'm not. You know there's nothing in all the world that I'd rather be doing than this. I have black powder in my blood, surely, just as Papa always said he did. But one of us has to be hardheaded, and it looks as if that job has fallen to me. If you continue spending our profits, sooner or later there won't be any money left to support the lavish lifestyle you so love."

Simon hung his head. "Consider me duly reminded." He turned back to her, but refused to meet her eyes. "I'm sorry, Belle," he said, and she knew he meant it. Simon was always sorry for the things he did. Pity it never stopped him from doing them again. "It was rather cold-hearted of me to remind you of everything that happened four years ago. I saw Costigan yesterday. I suppose that is why his name jumped into my mind." He gave her a sheepish grin. "I don't suppose you'd reconsider and—"

"No! I won't marry Ben Costigan!" It was so outrageous a statement, it dissolved Isabel's anger, just as Simon intended. She laughed. "The biggest fortune in the world couldn't change my mind. The man is contemptible. He proved that well enough, didn't he?"

Simon didn't agree or disagree, and Isabel didn't care. She didn't need Simon to tell her she was right.

And he apparently didn't need to take the chance that she might actually challenge him on the subject.

"I'll be on my way and leave you to your work." Simon picked up his walking stick and headed for the door. "And, Belle. . . ." He stopped in the doorway and patted his pocket. "Don't worry about the money. Please. My luck is changing. I can feel it in the air. I won a game or two of cards last night. That proves it, surely. Soon enough, I promise you, you'll never have to worry about money again." He took one step into the passageway, stopped, and threw a mischievous look over his shoulder at her.

"Now the only thing you need to worry about," he said, "is the fact that Ben is back in London."

No sooner was Simon gone than Isabel knelt again on the floor and got back to work on the safe. This time she concentrated on the job at hand, and before she knew it, the heavy door opened with a satisfying thump. She reached inside and pulled out a sheet of paper covered with neat columns of figures and the names of chemicals such as sulphide of antimony, sulphide of arsenic, and camphor. She read the recipe over to herself and nodded, impressed as she always was both by its simplicity and its pure brilliance.

Satisfied, Isabel creased the paper in half, then folded it again. She had brought a small pink silk pouch with her from home, one that had been given to her years before when her father presented her with some small token of jewelry, and she pulled it out of her pocket and set the recipe into it. Unbuttoning her white linen blouse, she slipped the pouch down into the front of her corset.

"Ben is back in town," she said to herself while she rebuttoned her blouse and gathered her gloves and handbag.

"And that," she said, placing one hand where the pouch lay against her heart, "is exactly what I am worried about."

Touching one hand briefly to the front of her crisp linen blouse, Isabel stood back so that Sir Digby's special assistant might open the door to his office for her. Though she was early, she hoped that at least some of the members of the Jubilee committee might already be gathered. She rather fancied a few minutes alone with them, and the opportunity to chat them up. Though she was not the least bit vain, she was, for all intents and purposes, eminently practical. She knew that she was very good with people.

De Quincy and Sons customers valued her unassuming manner and her ability to explain the fireworks business to them simply and effectively. They were sometimes surprised that a woman knew so much about explosives, but they were, on the whole, polite enough not to point it out and interested enough in what she had to say to take her seriously.

And make no mistake about it, she reminded herself, though the committee was made up of two dukes, a viscount, three captains of industry, and a representative of the Church of England, they were customers. Customers who would need the same assurances as any others. Customers she was sure she could lead gently but firmly to the final realization that De Quincy and Sons was the only fireworks company in the world qualified to produce a show as special as the one required for the celebration of the sixtieth anniversary of the Queen's ascension to the throne.

Eager to get to it, Isabel prepared her best smile and her brightest greeting.

The door opened and her smile faded. The greeting strangled in her throat.

Ben was the only other person in the room.

It was small comfort to realize he wasn't any happier to see her than she was to see him. He stood against the windows that filled the far wall of the room, his face shadowed with the light at his back. Not that it mattered. Isabel would have known him anywhere. There was no mistaking the line of his firm, square jaw or the confident tilt of his head. There was also no mistaking the fact that the instant he saw her, he tensed, and the smile that had brightened his expression in the moment the door opened disappeared completely.

He was wearing one of the new, terribly stylish lounge suits that Isabel had read about in the Paris fashion magazines, a well-cut charcoal gray jacket and matching trousers that were creased up the front and cuffed at the bottom. His jacket was not buttoned up the front as were so many of the ones she'd seen in the magazines, but worn open to best show his soft-fronted shirt of the palest blue, his stiff white collar, and his striking red tie.

For the space of a dozen heartbeats, they stared at each other across the vast expanse of a massive mahogany table, Ben's piqued expression an exact mirror of Isabel's own.

As if he could feel the pall that suddenly hung in the air, the clerk who'd shown Isabel to the office departed as swiftly as he could. The door closed behind him with a soft, rather sinister click of finality.

The silence seemed even more terrible once the man was gone.

Because Isabel didn't know what else to do, she nodded a curt hello and walked to the table. She set down her handbag and drew off her gloves. She didn't wait for Ben to pull out a chair for her. In fact, she hurried to do it herself, before he could get it into his head to play the gentleman and get so close as to assist her.

She needn't have worried.

Ben stayed precisely where he was, his eyes following her every movement, and it was only after Isabel was seated that he pushed away from the windows and strolled toward the head of the table. "You aren't surprised to see me."

Isabel answered with a muffled *hurumph*. "Should I be?" she asked. "I thought we had agreed last night, we are perfect strangers. I can't imagine why I should be surprised to encounter a stranger in so public a building."

It was as good a hit as she was likely to get in so early in the game, and Isabel congratulated herself for it. It was especially gratifying to see that Ben recognized it for the small victory it was. He winced, a reaction he covered instantly and neatly with an indolent smile.

"Touché, my dear Miss De Quincy." He nodded, acknowledging her triumph. "You heard, of course. It's the only thing that can account for your supreme indifference. You knew I'd be here."

"Of course I knew." Isabel met his gaze with as matter-of-fact an expression as she could muster. "I may once have been a neophyte in this business, a woman who was naive enough to trust that others were as honest as I am . . ." With a graceful lift of her shoulders, she dismissed whatever else she might have said, but not before she paused long enough to make it clear that she was not mentioning it because it was, quite simply, not worth mentioning.

"I know my business," she said. "And part of knowing my business is knowing my competition. If I may use so imaginative a word to describe Costigan and Company." Isabel sat back and forced herself to give Ben the kind of look she'd seen him use so effectively so many times. Sublimely unconcerned. Supremely confident. "I do hate to sound presumptuous, Mr. Costigan, but you don't actually think that you—"

"Have a chance at this contract?" As if actually thinking about it, Ben pursed his lips and cocked his head. "Why, yes," he said finally. "I do believe I do. After all, the committee is interested in a fireworks show worthy of the occasion. One of epic proportions. One that has more style than stodginess." He gave her a meaningful look, spurred on by the anger Isabel could feel heating her face. "It seems Costigan and Company isn't simply the best choice. It is the only choice."

"Stodgy?" Isabel could no more keep to her seat than she could siphon the exasperation from her voice. She knew it was a mistake the moment she was on her feet, and if she didn't, she need only take a look at the satisfied expression on Ben's face. He had won this round, that was for certain. He had tricked her into an outburst. She swore to herself it wouldn't happen again.

Swallowing her anger, she turned away from the table and paced the length of the room. "So, you think my work stodgy and unoriginal?" When she got to the head of the table, she stopped and faced Ben. "I'm surprised to hear it. You didn't think so four years ago. As a matter of fact, you rather admired the new effect I'd developed. You remember, the shimmering green firework I called Emerald Mist. A little nitrate of baryta, some chlorate of potash, nitrate of copper, acetate of copper." She brushed her hands together, as if mixing the chemicals.

"The right blowing charge and the precise compound. It was quite spectacular. And original. And the way I remember it, you were willing to do anything to get your hands on the formula. Even if it meant marrying me."

Much to Isabel's disappointment, Ben didn't rise to the bait. Instead, he clutched both his hands to his heart. "The ultimate sacrifice!" Like one of the actors Isabel had seen recently in a particularly melodramatic performance at the Olympic Theatre in the Strand, he leaned heavily against the table as if in a swoon. "Some men were destined to suffer for their art. Fortunately, your brother saved me from suffering too much. He presented me with the formula as a wedding gift, you remember, and thus rescued me from a fate worse than death."

Isabel threw him an acid look. "Your mind is surely playing tricks on you again. The way I remember it, you hardly suffered at all. As a matter of fact, you always looked quite happy to me."

"Did I?" As if the statement were a surprise to him, Ben stood up straight. "You must be thinking of someone else. Some other lovesick swain. I was never happy with you. Not for a moment. I wanted the Emerald Mist formula. There. I admit it. But—" He held up one hand to stop her when he saw that she was about to emit a crow of triumph.

"You were just as guilty. You agreed to marry me because you wanted my money. You needed it to save your company."

It wasn't the first time he'd accused her of the sin. Isabel didn't need a reminder. The night before their scheduled wedding, he'd hurled the same accusation in her face. Then she'd been too upset by his betrayal to explain herself or argue her case. Four years later, it hardly seemed to matter, especially when he was staring at her, his eyes shining with condemnation.

As much as she despised Ben Costigan, she found she could not disappoint him.

"Of course I wanted your money." Isabel surprised herself. She could sound as cold as he did melodramatic. She turned her back on him and strolled all the way to the other end of the table, trailing one finger over its perfectly polished surface as she went. When she got there, she tossed a casual look over her shoulder at him. "By all accounts, you have quite an overblown imagination, and your conceit is, of course, legendary. But I doubt if even you could possibly think there was any other reason I'd want to marry you."

Isabel knew it was a mistake the moment she'd said it. Even from across the room she could detect the hint of devilment that flickered in Ben's eyes in response to her remark. He looked her up and down, his gaze resting longer than was necessary on her lips, and her breasts, and her hips, and when he spoke his voice was deeper than it had been. More intimate. It wrapped around her like the arms of a lover. It stroked her and caressed her and left her feeling slightly light-headed and far hotter than was natural in a room that was as comfortable as was Sir Digby's office.

"You're wrong. I can imagine quite a few reasons you might have wanted to marry me." The smile in Ben's eyes traveled to his lips. "There was that night at your father's country estate. And that afternoon we spent in Oxford. You remember, Bella." His pet name for her rolled off his tongue. It was a name she had hoped never to hear again, especially from Ben's lips, and Isabel braced herself against its unwelcome effects. Tiny tremors of anticipation sparkled through her body the way they always had when Ben whispered the name. Like one of the chaser fireworks that swooshes along the ground, whistling its exaltation for all the world to hear, they burned her skin and fizzed through her blood.

"We went to Oxford to talk to the chaps at the university about a fireworks show," Ben continued, "and instead of conducting business, we spent the entire afternoon—"

"Hardly a reason to marry a man." Though Isabel tried her best to keep her temper as well as her pride, the words jumped out of her before she could stop them. She drew in a deep, painful breath and willed herself to keep the mortification she felt from showing in her face or blossoming into her voice. "That is . . ." she said. "What I mean is . . . is that fortunately, I came to my senses. I suppose that if nothing else, I owe you a debt of gratitude for demonstrating to me that my instincts were, as usual, unerring. I supposed your true character was that of a cad, and you proved me right. Only a scoundrel would leave his bride waiting at the altar."

"Me? Left you waiting?" It was the first time Ben let down his guard and allowed his anger to surface. Isabel supposed she should have felt a certain sense of satisfaction. She might have if not for the fact that she was just as angry. Through a red-hot haze, she watched Ben stalk the length of the table and position himself across from her. "The way I remember it, madam, you left me waiting. You are the one who never arrived at the church."

"Me?" The single word choked against the tight ball of outrage in Isabel's throat. She flattened her hands against the tabletop and leaned forward. "You, sir, were the one who never arrived! And if you had—"

"If I had," Ben growled, leaning forward, "I would have found that you weren't there."

"And if I had been there, I would have found that you never—"

"No, you never—"

"It seems as if I have arrived just in time."

As if they'd been snipped away in mid-sentence, Ben's words died and Isabel's anger dissolved into chagrin when Sir Digby came into the room. Like a general surveying battlefield casualties, he paused inside the door and shook his head. One look was enough to make both Ben and Isabel stand up straight and pull their hands to their sides.

Without another word Sir Digby marched into the room and took his place at the head of the table. As if he'd forgotten about them altogether, he didn't glance at them again until he was settled in his chair. "Perhaps I am the only one who is really qualified to give an account of what happened on the day of your supposed wedding. Or what didn't happen. After all, of the three of us, I am the only one who truly knows. Of the three of us, I am the only one who was there. I wasn't the only one you kept waiting, of course. There were four hundred other guests, including, may I remind you, Her Majesty the Queen. The way I remember it, neither of you ever bothered to arrive at the church."

"But if I had, he—"

"But if I had, she—"

Sir Digby was famous for his ability to negotiate with pashas and czars. He was as well known for his political savvy as he was for his ability to hammer out a treaty from the basest of beginnings, one that was always favorable to the empire.

Now Isabel knew why.

He had a frown that could only be described as monumental.

Sir Digby turned the full power of his displeasure on them, effectively putting a stop to both their protests. "It is not an affair that concerns me in the least," he said. "And it is hardly an appropriate subject to discuss here. Let me remind you, sir, madam . . ." He looked from Ben to Isabel, and it was clear that he was not the least bit pleased. "Her Majesty's Jubilee is a matter very near and dear to my heart. It is a notable and historic occasion. I will not have it ruined by personal squabbles, nor will I tolerate petty bickering." He flipped open the leather portfolio set on the table in front of him. "Ah!" Sir Digby's gaze moved to the door, and as quickly as it had surfaced, his annoyance was hidden beneath a veneer of efficiency. "Here is the committee. Let's get to work, shall we?"

There was nothing more Isabel could say, and her only consolation lay in the fact that there was nothing for Ben to say, either. Duly chastised, she dropped into the nearest chair, and it was only when it was too late that she realized Ben had taken the chair directly opposite. She paid him no mind, concentrating instead on the members of the committee who filed into the room, each in his black morning coat and stiff white collar more dignified and serious-looking than the last. Richard, the Duke of Fenshaw, Margaret's husband and Peter's brother, was at the head of the line, and she nodded a hello and offered her best smile to the rest of the committee members.

Sir Digby was a man of business, and he didn't waste any time. He introduced each of the committee members, told them a bit about both Ben and Isabel and their respective companies, and proceeded to cut to the chase. "That gentlemen . . . and madam," he added with an apologetic look at Isabel, "is the heart of the matter. A fireworks presentation befitting Her Majesty's status and her sovereignty, celebrating her sixty years on the throne. Miss De Quincy, what have you to say for yourself?"

Isabel had expected that he would ask, and she was ready. In precise detail she laid out her plans for the festivities. "Gentlemen." Convinced he was in no way entitled to the designation, she stood and nodded to the rest of her audience, ignoring Ben completely.

"I know many of you and you know the reputation of De Quincy and Sons, so I will not waste your valuable time recounting either my background or that of my company. I have worked with some of you on family festivities." She smiled at Richard, who had the good grace to smile back. "I have designed many fireworks shows for . . ." She made the mistake of glancing at the man seated next to Richard. He was the elderly Duke of Wycombe, and apparently the stories of his lecherous eye were not apocryphal. The man wiggled his bushy eyebrows at her and gave her a wink. Isabel lost her place in her presentation. She wasn't sure if she wanted to laugh or retch, and trying to convince herself neither was appropriate, she stared straight ahead instead.

It might have been an acceptable solution if Ben hadn't been staring back. He'd seen the whole thing, of course, and he chuckled quietly.

Knowing him to be far less boorish than the old duke and far more polite than Ben, Isabel focused on the representative of the Archbishop of Canterbury, who sat at the end of the table. She scrambled to get her presentation back on course. "We have also handled many Church celebrations," she said. "Those of you whom I have not had a chance to meet personally must surely know my company's reputation. We are the oldest and finest fireworks manufacturer in the nation. My ancestors provided fireworks for the coronation of Queen Elizabeth. We helped our country celebrate the arrival of William and Mary, and we heralded Victoria's accession to the throne sixty years ago. For his role in the Golden Jubilee celebrations ten years ago, my father was honored by the Queen with a knighthood. Now it is my turn to have the honor to serve Queen and country."

It was a pretty speech and prettily said, and all but Ben seemed impressed. He covered an outraged snort with a cough and excused himself politely.

Isabel pretended not to notice. Her lips aching from the smile she forced, she went right on. "As you know, the Queen's Jubilee is a momentous occasion. As such, it must be celebrated solemnly and in a dignified manner. Dignity is surely a quality you'll find embodied in De Quincy and Sons. A quality you will find nowhere else in the Empire." This time she turned her gaze full on Ben, long enough for there to be no mistake what she meant.

She began again when she was certain the committee had taken her meaning. "I am planning a variety of fireworks suitable for daytime along the parade route and another thirty full minutes of fireworks over Buckingham Palace after sunset. That would, of course, include a full aerial show that would feature not only the fireworks produced here in this country by De Quincy and Sons, but some we've imported from other parts of the globe. Her Majesty's colonies, like India, will be represented. So will other exotic lands, like Japan and China. I assure you gentlemen, it will be a night to remember. By the whole of the Empire."

Her piece said, Isabel sat back down.

A buzz of approval met her from around the table, and she raised her chin and glared at Ben, daring him to deny that she had done her job and done it well.

She did not have long to bask in the committee's admiration. Sir Digby shuffled through the papers in his portfolio. "And what about . . .? What about this new firework you've developed? The one you call . . ." He ruffled through another stack of papers and, finally finding what he was looking for, he sat back and looked to Isabel for an answer. "The one you call Diamond Rain."

The smile froze on Isabel's face, and it was only with the utmost restraint that she kept herself from placing one hand on her heart, the place where the precious recipe for her newest firework was safely hidden. She dared a glance at Ben, only to find him leaning forward, like a terrier on the scent of familiar game. It was a look she'd seen before. The same look he'd always given her back in the days when he'd first heard about Emerald Mist and was champing at the bit to get a look at the formula.

"I would rather not say too much about Diamond Rain, Sir Digby," she said. "There is the matter of company confidentiality." She looked toward Ben, then back at Sir Digby. "But I can assure you, the effect is astonishing. It has taken me many months to perfect, and it is truly befitting Her Majesty's grandeur. I promise, it will be the highlight of the festivities."

Sir Digby nodded in understanding. "Very well." He looked toward Ben. "Mr. Costigan, it is your chance to speak up. What have you to say?"

Ben leaned back. "Say? Not a thing." As casually as if he were passing the time of day with his drinking cronies, he rose from his chair. "Unlike Miss De Quincy," he said, tipping his head in Isabel's direction, "I am not a man—or should I say, a person—of many words. I would rather let my work speak for itself. And that, gentlemen, is exactly what I intend to do."

Without another word Ben went to the door and threw it open, and along with everyone else in the room, Isabel caught her breath.

It was the most incredible thing she had ever seen. And the most astonishing demonstration of Ben's arrogance she could have imagined.

There outside the door was a woman, a beautiful woman, with hair as black as night and eyes that reminded Isabel of a cat's, sleek and foreign-looking. She was seated on a kind of raised table that looked like one of the marble altar stones Isabel had seen displayed in the British Museum. The woman's brow was adorned with a circle of greenery. Her hair flowed over her shoulders and spilled onto breasts that were barely concealed beneath a gown of some gauzy fabric that was draped to look like a toga. All around the base of the altar, scantily clad women tossed rose petals and held onto silken white ropes that they used to pull the apparatus into the room.

"Behold!" Ben intoned with a flourish. "The Oracle of Delphi!"

The committee broke into spontaneous applause. Too astounded to do anything but gape in wonder, Isabel watched the device roll to the head of the table. They passed the Duke of Wycomb, who fairly drooled and could not keep his eyes off the goddess on the altar. And the representative of the Archbishop of

Canterbury, who seemed to appreciate the sight every bit as much as the more worldly members of the committee. And even Richard, who for all the fact that he was madly in love with Margaret as she was with him, obviously appreciated the goddess's all-too-apparent charms.

They stopped at the head of the table, and Ben gave Sir Digby an exaggerated bow. "You have the honor, Sir Digby," he told him. He pointed toward a tall vase set on the table next to the goddess-like creature. There was a bouquet of fantastic purple flowers in the vase, and Ben pointed at one long, thin green leaf. "Pull that leaf."

"Pull it?" Sir Digby did not look so sure of himself.

"That's right, sir," Ben urged. "Go right ahead." He pulled back Sir Digby's chair for him, and when the old man rose, Ben nudged him closer to the altar and to the extraordinary woman who sat on it. "She doesn't bite," he told Sir Digby, and added quietly, but not too quietly, "Unless you'd like her to!"

Sir Digby reddened to the eyebrows, but that didn't stop him from going along with the scheme. As eager as a child on Christmas morning, he approached the altar and grabbed hold of the shiny green leaf.

"It's a cracker." Isabel spoke her amazement below her breath. She saw exactly what Ben was up to, though it was clear the others didn't know what to expect. The vase contained a kind of cracker, though on a much larger scale than the ones children so enjoyed. And like a child's paper-wrapped cracker, when a string was pulled . . .

Sir Digby pulled the leaf, and a deafening pop resounded through the room. A stream of silver glitter erupted from the vase along with a folded piece of paper that Ben caught in midair.

"Here you are." He bowed and presented the paper to Sir Digby. "Your fortune, sir. Directly from the Oracle at Delphi."

Grinning with delight, Sir Digby opened the paper. His grin turned into a smile. It erupted into a laugh.

"My fortune," he said, showing it all around. "My fortune says, 'Soon you will have the very good judgment to work with the company that can produce a Jubilee celebration that will be every bit as fantastic as this demonstration. Soon, you'll be working with Costigan and Company!'"

The committee members cheered and applauded, and Isabel sank farther into her seat. The sounds still pounding through her head, she waited for the commotion to settle. It took some time. Like comrades in arms, the members of the committee slapped Ben's back and pumped his hand, and the Duke of Wycomb insisted on meeting the goddess, whom he promptly pinched on the bottom and who, no surprise to Isabel, did not look the least bit put out.

It was, in short, as disgusting a display of male camaraderie as any Isabel had ever seen, and she could only sit quietly and bide her time and wait for the excitement to die down. Once the ladies, if Isabel could call them such, were ushered from the room, the sensation subsided and Sir Digby got back to business.

Seeming to remember himself, he swept a flurry of silver sparkles from his hair and sat back down. "That was quite impressive, Mr. Costigan. I'm sure the committee would agree. I was not aware that so spectacular an effect could be achieved inside a building. It must take a great deal of skill. And imagination."

A study in modesty, Ben waved away the flurry of compliments. "It is nothing," he said, but it wasn't enough of nothing to stop him from looking in Isabel's direction and offering her a wide smile. "Nothing at all. You should see what I'm doing at the Adelphi Music Hall. There's a production opening tomorrow and—" He caught himself, and if Isabel had not known him better, she might actually have believed his stammer of humility. "No-no. That is not what we are here to discuss. The fantastic effects I've designed for the Adelphi, the dauntless and courageous Italian daredevil who is to perform in my show at the Crystal

Palace . . . those are topics for another day. For today, we have the Jubilee celebration to discuss."

They did, indeed, and Isabel had the distinct impression that they were all too ready to discuss it while the excitement of Ben's so-called presentation was still hot in their blood. Along with his continued hints at dazzling effects and incredible shows, it was the last thing she wanted, and she spoke before any of the others could.

"You will, no doubt, wish to discuss your decision in private." She rose from her seat, and everyone present was obliged to stand. Isabel looked at Sir Digby, silently conveying her fondest wish that dignity would win out over sensationalism. "Mr. Costigan and I will gladly wait outside," she said. She moved toward the door and smiled with some small sense of satisfaction when Ben had no choice but to follow.

It was a desperate move, but Isabel was pleased to see that it had worked. There was only one problem with her plan, of course.

It meant that she would be compelled to wait outside, alone, with Ben.

# Chapter 3

Isabel should have known better.
She would never have the chance to be alone with Ben. Not while there were women anywhere about.

No sooner had the door of Sir Digby's office closed behind them than Ben was besieged by the gaggle of giggling goddesses, each competing for his attention and one of his smiles.

"Yes. Yes. You were all wonderful. Really." He waded through them like Moses, not through a Red Sea but a sea of scarlet women, dispensing pats on the behind, kisses on the cheek and, finally, gold sovereigns to them all.

There was nothing for it but to get safely out of the way, and that is exactly what Isabel did. She went to stand beside the desk of the clerk who'd shown her into Sir Digby's office earlier. Try as he might to keep his fingers busy and his eyes on the sheaves of paper he was filling with small, neat writing, the poor fellow could not help but stare. His gaze was drawn again and again to the thighs and hips and breasts that were so provocatively displayed beneath yards of filmy fabric. When he realized Isabel was watching, he reddened all around his stiff white collar and got back to work.

"There you are, Lola my girl!"

Across the room, Isabel saw Ben throw open his arms to the woman who was still seated on the altar. She climbed down, her movements rather unsure, her footsteps faltering, and it wasn't until then that Isabel realized the woman was thoroughly and completely drunk. That didn't stop Ben from enveloping her in a ferocious embrace. He draped an arm casually over her shoulders and, grinning from ear to ear both in appreciation of her performance and her physical perfection, he pulled Lola close. "You were magnificent! Wasn't she, girls?" He saved the last of both his kisses and his sovereigns for her, and was rewarded by Lola with a prize of her own, a kiss full on the mouth that lasted long enough to make the giggles of the girls all around them dissolve into sighs.

"Magnificent!" Grumbling the word, Isabel spun away from the scene. There was a window in front of her, and she stared out of it steadfastly, her fingers drumming against the sill, tapping out seconds that for some unfathomable reason seemed all too long.

Not, she reminded herself, that she cared.

Still, she held a tight breath of annoyance deep inside her, and didn't let it go until she heard the girls applaud and Ben's laughter ring through the room.

"Thank you all. You were all wonderful. You are adorable creatures. Too beautiful for words. I'll see you all at rehearsal at the Adelphi tonight. You, too, Lola. Don't forget. That sovereign is for paying your rent, my girl, not for drinking away at the King's Head." He kept up a running commentary that faded bit by bit, and Isabel could only imagine that he was ushering the women out of the room and into the passageway beyond. He returned far more quietly than he left. Before Isabel knew it, he was standing at her side, holding out a gold sovereign in front of her nose.

"Oh! You're not one of the girls!" Ben grinned in mock embarrassment and tucked the coin back into his pocket. "I saw you standing there, and I thought you were one of my Adelphi beauties. Pity you're not. You would look splendid in one of those—"

Isabel whirled to face him. With the girls gone, the clerk was back at his books in earnest, but she fought to keep her voice low nonetheless. Theatrics might be to Ben's liking, but they did not appeal to her. "You really are a despicable man," she told him.

Ben's grin widened, and he quirked his eyebrows in a most maddening fashion. "Lola doesn't think so."

Isabel's lips thinned. "I dare say she doesn't know any better."

"Perhaps someone should tell her."

"Perhaps they should."

"Perhaps that someone should be you."

"I think not." She dismissed the notion with a toss of her head. "She needs to find out for herself, poor little squit, and I dare say she will sooner or later. Your true colors will show, and she will know you for the man you really are."

Ben's smile vanished, and he laid a hand on her arm, not so much to hold her in place as to command her attention. "Do you?" he asked.

It was not a question Isabel was expecting, not one she was sure she could answer, and for a moment she stood dumbstruck and confused. In this light Ben's eyes were the blue of a Highland loch, bottomless and ever changing. They were fired with flecks of green that shimmered in the early morning light. Every trace of his laughter was gone, drained from his voice and from his expression. He held Isabel's gaze, his fingers tightening ever so slightly against her gray linen jacket, his eyes demanding an answer.

It was a look she'd seen before, though even in the days of their courtship and engagement, it had surfaced all too infrequently. Ben saved it for those rare private moments when he abandoned the brash persona he wore like a suit of armor and showed another side of himself. Try as she might, Isabel had never been able to discover if this facet of his personality—thoughtful, intense, sincere—was any more genuine than the other. She'd had four long years to think it through, and she was no closer to an answer now than she had been then. The problem was, Ben hid behind so many facades, she was convinced that even he didn't know which man was the real Ben Costigan.

And if he didn't, she certainly wasn't about to try and puzzle it out.

"I know you're the kind of man who isn't above using devious methods to sway the committee's opinion."

Her words were enough to break the spell. Though he didn't remove his hand, Ben's hold on her loosened and a smile played again in his eyes. "You call that devious?" He glanced toward the door where only minutes ago his bevy of women had departed. As if he could still picture them and all their all-too-clearly displayed charms, he smiled with real appreciation. "I'd say it was anything but devious. It was outrageous, yes. It was flagrant, I admit it. It was damned brilliant, and you know it. I wasn't trying to be the least bit devious. It was perfectly apparent what I was up to. I was appealing to the members of the committee. Not as you did with your well-said and quite moving piece about Queen and country. I was appealing to their prurient interests, plain and simple."

"Well, you certainly appealed to Wycomb's. I have no doubt he is in there right now extolling your genius and urging the committee to put you in charge of the Queen's sixtieth anniversary festivities, and her seventieth, eightieth, and ninetieth as well. You have Wycomb's support. That is for certain. He was fairly drooling all over your charming Lola."

"And I assure you, she didn't mind one bit. She'd rather fancy an old fellow like Wycomb. You might have had his vote, you know." Dangling the obvious in front of her, Ben cocked his head and waited for her to admit it, and when she refused, he continued.

"You might have played up to him a bit more. You know, when you were reminding us all that without De Quincy and Sons, the Empire would have collapsed years ago. Old Wycomb was goggling you as if he were a starving man and you were a very juicy leg of mutton."

"Really!" Isabel shuddered.

Ben laughed. "You might have given the old boy a wink. What could it hurt? One thing's for certain, it either would have assured you of his vote or stopped the old fellow's heard mid-beat!"

Isabel bristled at the very thought, and showing far more compassion than was usual, Ben amended it. "Too conspicuous for you, eh? Too sensational? All right, then, if it's subtlety you're after . . . you might have flashed him that famous smile of yours." He turned his own smile up a degree and moved a step closer. "I haven't seen much of it lately, but I assure you, I remember it well. As I recall, it could dazzle the stars out of the sky."

And his could make a woman forget herself.

Isabel shook away the thought and the feel of Ben's hand against her arm, and retreated as far from him as she could, as fast as she could manage. Her escape was apparently a bit too fast. It was the only thing that could account for the fact that by the time she got to the other side of the room, her breathing was ragged and her face felt as if it were on fire.

She was saved from trying to think what it might all mean when the office door snapped open and Sir Digby peered outside. "We are ready to give you our decision," he said.

Eager to get on with it, Ben rubbed his hands together and smiled. Isabel didn't share his enthusiasm. She didn't need to remind herself that the future of De Quincy and Sons depended on what Sir Digby was about to announce. Her encounter with her brother earlier that morning had etched the importance of the committee's decision on her heart. Simon, with his intemperate spending habits, his endless gambling, and his indiscreet womanizing, had depleted the company's coffers and backed her against a wall.

And of all people, it was Ben Costigan who was firmly standing in the way of her success. Yesterday, before she knew Ben was back, she'd looked on the opportunity to obtain the contract for the Jubilee fireworks as a source of pride.

Today, she knew it was more. Much more.

It was a matter of survival.

The one thought pounding through her head, Isabel lifted her chin and glided back into the committee room. She would very much have liked to stand at the doorway so that she might flee quickly when the committee announced, no doubt in far more diplomatic terms, that they had succumbed to Ben's theatrics and Lola's charms and decided to award the contract to Costigan and Company. She couldn't. To a man, the members of the committee rose when she walked in, and etiquette demanded that she be seated so they could sit, too.

Hoping against hope for some small reassurance or some sign that her imagination had gotten out of hand and overruled her common sense, Isabel looked to Richard Thorlinson. He firmly refused to meet her eyes.

She glanced at the archbishop's representative and found him staring down at the paper on the table in front of him.

She braved a look at the Duke of Wycomb, but the only encouragement she got from him was a wiggle of his bushy eyebrows that told her the last thing on his mind was fireworks.

It was hardly a sign that she should be optimistic.

Her mood plummeting by the second, Isabel dropped into the chair across from Ben's and forced herself to meet his eyes with an expression every bit as blasé as the one she expected to find there. For once, he didn't disappoint her. Ben leaned back in his chair and chatted with the fellows on either side of him, eminently confident, supremely unconcerned.

"You are surely interested in our decision, and I won't keep you in suspense." At the head of the table, Sir Digby called the meeting back to order. "We have considered all aspects of the situation, and, I must say, you've left us with a pretty problem. On the one hand, we have De Quincy and Sons"—he looked toward Isabel—"as distinguished and well respected as any company in the Empire. On the other . . ." Sir Digby ran a hand through his shock of hair, and silver glitter rained down on the table.

"On the other hand, we have Costigan and Company, and though I must admit, I was skeptical when you first contacted me, Mr. Costigan, you have proved yourself a very clever and resourceful young fellow indeed. So you see . . ." Sir Digby slid his gaze from Ben to Isabel. "You've given us a choice and left us with no choice, if you get my meaning."

Isabel was very much afraid she did. She clutched her hands together on her lap, bracing herself against the words she was sure were to come.

"We have decided . . ." Again, Sir Digby looked around, this time at the other members of the committee, as if giving them one last chance to change their minds. When no one spoke, he went on. "We've decided on a rather unorthodox solution to the problem," he said. "A kind of contest."

"Contest?" Across the table, even Ben could not keep his surprise to himself. Curious, he leaned forward, his eyes narrowed, his jaw tensed.

Isabel leaned forward, too. "What kind of contest?" she asked Sir Digby.

"Why, a fireworks contest, of course!" Sir Digby smiled, and she knew it was his way of telling her he had championed her through the meeting and had won this compromise against the wishes of the committee. "Six weeks. I trust in that time both your companies will be producing a number of fireworks shows." He didn't wait for either of them to answer. He knew it was true. "There will be members of the committee in attendance at each of your productions. We'll be watching. Rating your performances. Seeing whose is the most spectacular. The most fitting for the occasion. And at the end of six weeks . . ." He rose, effectively putting an end to the meeting. "At the end of six weeks we will decide which company will be awarded the Jubilee contract."

Isabel wasn't sure if she should feel relief that De Quincy and Sons had not been excluded from the running, or anger at the fact that had it not been for Ben, none of this would have been necessary.

The anger won out.

Calling on every one of the lessons she'd learned through school and an endless procession of governesses skilled at teaching young ladies regal bearing and manners to match, Isabel rose from her chair and gave Ben as coolly calculating a look as ever there was.

"A contest." She murmured the words as slowly as she drew on her gloves. "This should prove quite interesting."

"It should, indeed," Ben agreed. He waited while the members of the committee gathered their belonging and left the room, and when they were gone, he walked to the end of the table and waited there for Isabel. "Especially interesting now that I know about Diamond Rain."

Isabel smiled. It was not the smile Ben had mentioned earlier, a girl's smile, the one that could dazzle the stars out of the sky. It was a woman's smile, one that could freeze a man at twenty paces, and she aimed it full at him and was disappointed to see that he was too much of a man to be chilled by it, and not enough of a gentleman to care.

"I wondered when you'd get around to that." She pretended not to notice when Ben offered her his arm, but headed out the door before him. "It's a pretty problem, don't you think? I have in my possession the recipe for the most superb firework ever produced. Diamond Rain, a sky full of brilliance so spectacular, it is sure to impress the committee far more than anything you could show them. Even Lola's bosom."

"I don't know." When they got to the door that led into the passageway, Isabel stopped and Ben opened it for her, but he didn't step aside to allow her through. He turned to her, his face angelic. "Lola's bosom is quite impressive."

Isabel's smile hardened. "No doubt," she said, "you have firsthand knowledge."

"No doubt," Ben countered, "I do. Hands-on experience, you might call it."

"I might. If I was so coarse as to mention it. Or so feeble-minded as to care."

"But you are neither."

"That's right." Tired of waiting, tired of smiling a smile that was getting tighter and more uncomfortable by the second, Isabel pressed one hand to Ben's chest and pushed him gently out of the way. She maneuvered through the doorway and headed down the long passageway that led to the building's front door.

"I could always ask you to marry me again."

Ben's words echoed out in the marble-floored passageway and froze Isabel in her path. She thought to ask him to repeat what he'd said, just to be sure she'd heard him correctly, but decided against it. It was bad enough hearing the words once. Another time might be her undoing.

Isabel pulled back her shoulders and turned again to face him. "You could, of course," she said. "I certainly can't stop you. But what do you suppose my answer might be?"

Ben laughed. He strode out of the office and over to where she stood. "You might say *yes,*" he ventured, and when she did not respond, his smile tilted and his expression soured. "Or you might not. Damn me, I'm not sure which is the lesser of the two evils." He recovered as quickly as ever, and his eyes filled with mischief. "But if you did agree to be my wife, Simon might present me the formula for Diamond Rain as a wedding gift, just as he did with Emerald Mist."

"And you might take it and run. Just as you did with Emerald Mist. Then you might leave me waiting at the altar again just as you did—"

"I never left you waiting," Ben cut through her argument with one swift movement of his hand. "If I'd shown up, you would have left me waiting."

Isabel could have gone on with the debate. She might have if they hadn't been attracting the attention of everyone who passed. Instead, she decided to be, as was usual in all her doings with Ben, the lone voice of reason. "Then it seems as if we are even," she said.

## DIAMOND RAIN

"Hardly." Ben was not ready to capitulate. He looked down at her, his eyes dancing in the light of the overhead lamps. "There is still the matter of our contest, and we are hardly even there. You may have Diamond Rain, m'dear, but I've got the Adelphi Music Hall. They've asked me to work with them, you see. To develop some special fireworks effects that can be used inside the theater. I've got one that's sure to astound the world. And I've got it on good authority," he said, leaning nearer, "that Sir Digby himself will be there in three days' time to see it. Then there's the Crystal Palace . . ." As if he'd said too much already, Ben waved away the rest of his words.

Isabel could not help herself. Too curious to keep silent, to vexed to care what he thought, she had to know more. "The Italian daredevil? The one you mentioned at the meeting? What are you planning, Ben?"

He held up a hand, stemming the tide of her questions. "There is the matter of company confidentiality," he said, echoing her words at the meeting. "I wouldn't want to give too much away. But I will tell you that your Diamond Rain will be nothing compared to what I have planned. A handsome young hotspur from Italy, Signor Francesco. A volley of fireworks the likes of which London has never seen. It is a combination that is sure to entrance. And certain to impress the committee more than anything you can come up with." He gave her a wink and headed down the passageway and out the door. "You like surprises, don't you?" he called over his shoulder. "I hope so. For the next six weeks I'd say you're in for a few."

"And you are in for a few of your own." Watching him go, Isabel grumbled beneath her breath. She might have gone right on mumbling away if a young clerk who hurried past hadn't looked at her as if she was an escapee from Bedlam. Instead, she collected herself and her self-control and headed out the door, but not until she peeked through the front glass to make sure Ben was well and truly gone.

He hailed a hansom, and she watched him speak to the driver and hop in. She stared at the cab until it was out of sight, and found herself correcting an earlier thought.

This was no longer a matter of either pride or survival, she told herself.

This was war!

All wars required sacrifices.

Isabel gritted her teeth against the certain knowledge and the scream of frustration that threatened to escape her.

She thought she had been ready to make the sacrifices, to fight the good fight and press on, her upper lip and her resolve as stiff as the Union Jack in a rigorous breeze. She thought she was ready to scrum with the best of them, to lie, cheat, and steal if she had to. All in the name of De Quincy and Sons.

She hadn't figured on Lola.

Through the smoke-clouded air of the King's Head tavern, Isabel took a long look at the woman seated across from her. Her determination disintegrated, and like a bad pudding, her stiff upper lip fell. Like it or not, her resolve was replaced by another emotion, an uncomfortable sort of feeling that crawled through her stomach, eating away at her confidence bit by bit and reminding her, in no uncertain terms, that Lola was a woman who seemed to have it all.

Lola was not beautiful, but she was striking, the kind of woman who turned men's heads and ensnared their hearts. She had hair the color of ebony and almond eyes that were green, like a cat's. She had a complexion that was, quite simply, perfection. It was as smooth and as white as alabaster and completely free of the unsightly freckles that marred Isabel's own cheeks and nose. Even though she was more modestly dressed than the last time Isabel had seen her, Lola's high-necked gown did nothing to conceal the fact that she was more than sufficiently endowed, and proud enough of her figure and the impression it seemed to create on the male population in general that she preened before every man who walked by and gave her a second look.

Lola had that certain air about her that theater people do, an atmosphere of the exotic that enveloped her as surely as did her overpowering perfume. She had intensity, color, and, Isabel very much feared, more than her share of passion.

She also had Ben.

The thought crept up on Isabel and left her feeling as if the five forty-five out of Victoria Station had just cannoned into her. It was unworthy of her, not to mention completely illogical, but try as she might, she couldn't banish it from her mind. It churned through her along with the envy she suddenly felt toward Lola, and made her insides feel the way they had the time she'd had dyspepsia over the winter and had spent the best part of an entire week in bed.

Or perhaps she was queasy from watching Lola down glass after glass of cheap gin.

Isabel held on to the thought. It was less uncomfortable than thinking herself small-minded and jealous. And far less mystifying than wondering why she cared about Ben.

Her mind made up, her resolve once again firmly in place, she watched Lola tip back her head, toss down her sixth glass of gin, and slam the empty tumbler on the table.

"Ooh! And ain't this lovely, you bein' such a brick as to buy me a nerver!" Lola's full lips curved into a smile, but her eyes were guarded. "What you haven't said is why you asked to meet me 'ere tonight."

"Yes, I did say. Or at least I tried." Isabel muffled a grumble of annoyance. More than once in the two hours they'd sat together in the dingy pub, Isabel had asked Lola about her act at the Adelphi. And more than once—six times to be exact—Lola had demurred, promising they'd talk as soon as she'd had just one more drink. Isabel's patience was dwindling along with the coins in her handbag. "I told you, I wanted to talk to you about the firework. The one you—"

Lola laughed. It was a deep, throaty sound, the sound of disbelief. She leaned back, her arm draped with great effect across the back of the empty chair next to her, and winked at a fellow who staggered by and gave her an appreciative look. She smiled her sleek, cat-like smile and waved away Isabel's words along with a trail of foul cigar smoke that wafted by. "That's not what you want to know."

"But of course it is!" Isabel clamped her jaw tight around the words. "I want to know about—"

"You want to know about Mr. Costigan."

"Ben?" It was not a topic Isabel wished to discuss, especially not with Lola, and she twitched her shoulders as if dismissing it. "I certainly do not want to know about Ben. I care neither what he does nor who he does it with." It was a slip of the tongue that revealed more than was wise, both to Lola and to herself. Fortunately for both Isabel's pride and her peace of mind, Lola wasn't listening. She was too busy trying to attract the attention of the barman so that he might bring her another glass of gin.

"There's nothing about Ben Costigan I want to know," Isabel assured her, paying for the spirits when the man brought over the glass. "I am a woman of business in a world that very much belongs to men. As such I have found it is sometimes difficult to compete and remain fair. Conducting business with men can be quite challenging."

"Don't I know it!" Lola didn't look at all embarrassed at the admission. She sipped her gin. "But challengin' ain't exactly what I'd call it. Why, I remember once, there was this fellow. Some nob from the blinkin' Bank of England, he was. Hoity-toity as you and the rest of your kind." Her top lip curled, and she gave Isabel a look that made it clear that whatever kind those were, she did not approve of them. It was the first time during the evening that Isabel realized Lola was feeling all the same jealousy as Isabel was, for all different reasons, and if nothing else, it brought Isabel's confidence back in full force.

"There he was," Lola said, "all dressed to the nines and stinkin' of fine cigars. And can you imagine what he wanted of me?"

Lola fully intended to shock her, and had Isabel been more fainthearted or less determined, she might have accomplished her goal. As it was, she refused to play the fragile English rose. "Yes, I can," Isabel said. "I can imagine quite well. But I am not here to spend my time imagining about you and your bed partners, and you . . ." She glanced down at the watch pinned to the yoke of her lavender-blue gown. "You don't have much time. Your performance starts at nine o'clock precisely, or so I've heard, and it is eight thirty-five already."

"We've got plenty of time." Lola took another sip of her gin, and not for the first time Isabel wondered how on earth she could take in so much strong drink and remain so sober. "Now, what was you sayin' about Mr. Costigan?"

"I wasn't saying anything about Mr. Costigan. I was talking about his firework. The one, if I am not very much mistaken, you are to light in approximately twenty-five minutes' time on stage at the Adelphi."

Lola sniffed. "Didn't know you two was friends. You and Mr. Costigan. Been real thoughtful lately, has that one," she added, almost as an afterthought. "Ever since that meeting what 'e had us appear at over at that there posh office. Haven't seen very much of him, and I was just wonderin' . . ."

Isabel curled her fingers into her palms. "Very well," she conceded, barely containing the anger in her voice. "If you insist. If you'd rather talk about Ben than about a way you can easily earn ten pounds, that is exactly what we'll do."

"Ten pounds!" She had Lola's attention now, and Isabel congratulated herself and wished she'd thought to mention the money earlier. "You said in that note you sent to ask me here, you said as how there was somethin' in it for me. But ten pounds? That's more than I make in a month at the Adelphi." Lola's excitement dissolved, replaced by suspicion. "What do you want me to do?"

Isabel got down to business as quickly as she could, before Lola could manage to take the conversation off in another direction. "Not much of anything at all. Really. I want you to tell me about the firework."

"Come see it for yourself and find out."

Isabel stifled a word that would not have been out of place either in the low-class pub or in the situation she found herself in. "I don't want to come see it," she admitted. "By the time you shoot the firework tonight, it will be too late. I want to know about it before the show. Well before Sir Digby sees it and Ben's the talk of London and—"

She stopped herself before she said any more. There was no use letting Lola know how desperate she was. Instead, she set her handbag on the table and ran her hand over it, a gentle if none too subtle reminder.

It was enough to make Lola remember herself, and the promise of the ten pounds inside the bag. As if thinking about it very hard, she closed her eyes. "It's a big thing," she said. "That there firework. Half again as tall as me. Looks like one of them fountains in Hyde Park—you know, all fancy like an urn with greenery all around, except as how it ain't real greenery but is made of paper and such."

"And the firework, it's concealed inside the greenery?"

"No." As if it were the most ridiculous thing she'd ever heard, Lola washed away Isabel's suggestion with another drink. "It's in the fountain!" she said. Showing far more enthusiasm than she had earlier, she popped out of her chair. She staggered a bit but not so much that she wasn't able to recover.

"This," Lola said, pointing at her glass on the table. "This'll be the fountain. And 'ere I am." She laid one hand against the shelf of her bosom. "The star turner of the performance. I dance out onto the stage . . ."

She managed a couple of almost graceful steps on the tips of her toes. "Dressed like a fairy princess, I am, in a gown that's pink and lacy and short enough to show my calves and cut low enough . . ." She leaned forward and drew one hand lazily across her breasts. "Low enough to make them blokes in the front seats drool."

Isabel didn't care about low-cut dresses or drooling theatergoers. She cared about fireworks, and about what she could do to make sure Ben's weren't any better than hers. "So you dance out onto the stage and toward the fountain. Then what do you do?" she asked.

"Well, I got this fairy wand, you see, and it spits out sparkles all around." Demonstrating, Lola waved her arms above her head. "And the music plays and I dances around a bit. And then I take the wand and I touch it to this one blue leaf on that there fountain."

"It's a flare!" It was so obvious, yet Isabel couldn't help but be pleased with her deduction. Satisfied, she slapped the table. "The wand is a flare. Like the batons we use to light outdoor fireworks."

"Don't know what you call it," Lola said. "Only know that when I do, the whole thing goes up bang!" She dropped back into her chair. "And all these here chatsbies come flying out."

"Like the fortune from the Oracle at Delphi?"

"That's right, only nothin' as simple as that. Thousands of things come pourin' out of that fountain, for minutes on end. By the time it's all over, the whole stage is covered. And if the dress rehearsal we done is any indication, the audience will be standin' and cheerin' like never before."

Leave it to Ben to design an effect that could bring a rowdy music hall audience to its feet.

Isabel wasn't sure if it was admiration or envy she felt at the thought. It didn't matter. Whatever her feelings, the source was the same. Ben and his firework. The one Sir Digby was to be in attendance to see that night. The one she had to do something about.

"I will pay you right now if you will agree to follow my instructions." Isabel blurted out the offer before her conscience could remind her that it was the least honorable and the most underhanded thing she'd ever done. "Is there an intermission before the firework?" she asked. "Some time when the curtain is down and you can go out on the stage without anyone seeing?"

Lola nodded.

"Wonderful! Then this is what you must do. Before the curtain goes up again, wad up some fabric." Isabel demonstrated, winding a piece of imaginary fabric around an imaginary baton. "Wet it. And when the curtain is down, go out onto the stage and get the fuse good and wet. That way, when you dance out there as part of your act—"

"It won't go off."

"Exactly." Isabel reached into her handbag and drew out a handful of pound notes. "Ten pounds," she said, and she slid the money across the table toward Lola. "Right here. Right now. Will you do it?"

"Cor!" Lola ran the money through her fingers. "You're damned right I'll do it."

"Excellent!" Isabel decided to act before Lola could change her mind. She stood. "Then we'd better get to the theater," she said. "You have only a few minutes to change." She headed for the door. She was halfway there when she realized Lola hadn't followed.

More irritated than surprised, Isabel turned. Her mouth dropped open, and a very unladylike curse escaped her lips.

It seemed six glasses of gin were enough. And seven too many.

Lola's face was on the table. She was sound asleep.

"Good heavens!" Isabel hurried over. She shook Lola's shoulders. She slapped her cheeks.

"Ain't no use even tryin'," the fellow at the next table told her. "Seen her like this more times than I can remember, and I'll tell you what, miss. She ain't movin' an inch until tomorrow morning."

"Tomorrow morning?" Isabel's hopes dissolved in

# DIAMOND RAIN

a haze of gin fumes. Her shoulders sagged and she looked toward the door, picturing the excitement that must undoubtedly be building at the Adelphi Theater across the way.

Surely, Lola must have an understudy. And just as surely, as soon as there was no sign of Lola, that woman would soon be donning the pink lacy costume, dancing to the middle of the stage and lighting the firework that would make Ben the talk of all London.

"Not if I can help it," Isabel decided. She yanked the pound notes from Lola's hand, and before she could talk herself out of a plan that was surely as risky as it was insane, she marched out of the pub and into the Adelphi.

# Chapter 4

By the time Ben got to the Adelphi, it was raining at a steady pour. He turned up the collar on his mackintosh and hopped out of his cab, dodging raindrops and a group of rather shabby-looking young men who were going into the theater, and headed toward the stage door at the side of the building.

He splashed through a puddle that spattered the legs of his trousers, but instead of cursing, he laughed.

He was a bloody genius.

Like a drug, the awareness sang through his veins and quickened his step.

He was clever. No, more than clever. He was resourceful. No, not resourceful.

"Damned, bloody brilliant." He made the announcement to the fellow who stood sentry at the stage door, huddled beneath a large black umbrella. "You, Thomas, are looking at a damned, bloody brilliant man."

"I 'ave no doubt of that, sir." Thomas chuckled, and it might have been from honest amusement or from the fact that before the night was over, he knew Ben would slip him a shilling or two, as he always did. "You with your bleedin' fine fireworks! Always said as how you was one of the true wizards of the world, sir." Thomas tipped his hat. "Only would you mind tellin' me what's made you just finally realize it?"

"It's raining!" Ben threw back his head and looked up toward the lowering skies. Raindrops patted his cheeks and plopped in his eyes. He whisked off his

# DIAMOND RAIN

hat and laughed when the cool water tickled his brow. "It's raining! And I'm shooting off fireworks!"

"Yes, sir." Thomas didn't look the least bit reassured, either by the words or by the fact that a man he'd always respected was cantering about in the rain like a madman.

"Don't you see?" Ben asked. "I was resourceful enough to invite Sir Digby Talbot to be here tonight. And clever enough to devise a firework that can be shot off indoors. The rain can't stop me. Not the way it would stop one of Belle's la-di-da aerial shows."

Thomas gave him his due with a bow and a smile. "A gent'lman and a scholar," he said. "Only, what bell is it you're talkin' about, sir?"

"Not a what bell, a who Belle," Ben told him. "And I swear, Thomas, she is the most maddening woman on the face of the earth. But not nearly as clever as me, eh, what?"

"That's right, sir!" Thomas moved forward and opened the door. "Give 'er 'ell, sir. If anyone can do it, you can."

He could, indeed.

Ben stepped into the Adelphi and shook the water from his hair. It was not quite as easy to shake thoughts of Isabel out of his head.

It was perplexing to think that her name could slip so effortlessly from his lips. He had hardly thought of her at all in the three days since their meeting at Sir Digby's. Oh, there was the time that morning when she had crossed his mind as he downed his second cup of coffee. And the time the previous night when he sat in a box at the opera at Covent Garden, bored and desperate for distraction. The way he remembered it, the tenor couldn't hit a note square on if it was a target and he, William Tell. It was no wonder Ben's mind had taken off in search of diversion.

The only puzzle of the thing was why it had headed in Isabel's direction.

Then there was the night following the meeting at Sir Digby's. The night Ben had been alone in his bed and wondered where Isabel was and what she might be about. Was she with Peter Thorlinson? What were they saying? What were they doing?

Even with the gas jets of the Adelphi winking around him, Ben felt as uncomfortable with the thought as he had when he lay in the dark.

And discomfort, like self-awareness, was one of the things he tried his best to avoid at all costs.

He shrugged away the thoughts of Isabel at the same time he slipped out of his coat. He had not meant to say Isabel's name aloud to Thomas or anyone else, fearing, he supposed, that like the Israelites of old who didn't dare mention Yahweh's name, doing so might put him at some great peril.

But there had been no crack of thunder. No flash of flame from the sky. He'd spoken the dreaded name. And lived to tell the story. He was a damned, bloody genius, indeed. And a lucky one at that.

Holding on to the thought and the buoyant feeling that went along with it, Ben hung his coat on a peg near the doorway and did his best to keep out of the way. It was nearly nine o'clock, and the curtain would be going up soon, and as always, there was a flurry of activity backstage that when compared to the sack of ancient Rome would put the Vandals and the Visigoths to shame.

The Adelphi Theater was one of the largest music halls in London and, to Ben's mind, one of the most merry. The singers and dancers and musicians who populated its maze of passageways and enlivened its stage were a colorful and lively mix of harlots, drunkards, and bona fide artistes who never failed to fascinate and amuse. When the theater had requested a firework—something astonishing and flashy enough to satisfy the sometimes rowdy crowd—he'd been only too eager to accept the commission. He loved the smell of greasepaint that hung in the air like perfume in a tart's bedchamber. He delighted in the taste of earthy excitement that resonated through every inch of the place. He enjoyed the humor of the performers and found a certain poignancy in the drama of their lives.

And then there were the women.

Ben nodded a greeting toward three pretty young things who happened to walk by.

Theater women were everything he had hoped they would be, easygoing and indulgent and accommodating when the gentleman they were accommodating was accommodating enough in return. They weren't at all demanding, or intractable. They weren't set in their ways and utterly vexatious. They weren't hard-headed, and they certainly were not hard-hearted.

They weren't at all like Isabel.

The thought crept up on Ben with all the delicacy of a left hook thrown by a bare-knuckled pugilist. He twitched it aside, but try as he might, the notion would simply not go away.

He hadn't meant to let thoughts of Isabel intrude on the night's triumph, and here he'd found them mucking up his mind not once but twice in the last few minutes. Isabel was a rival, nothing more, he reminded himself, one whose reputation would be naught by the time the performance was over and the whole of the city was crowing his name. He had not meant to think about her hard head or her harder heart, or the fact that she was as far from accommodating as Piccadilly was from Peru.

It was a damned nuisance to find that his intentions were so excellent and his ability to carry them out so flimsy.

Uneasy with the thought, Ben decided there was only one antidote.

Fireworks.

His cure for everything from failed love affairs to hangovers.

Eager to get to it, Ben rubbed his hands together and went in search of his firework and of Lola.

He excused his way between two magicians arguing some arcane point of legerdemain and skirted the chorus practicing its so-called ballet steps. He ducked just in time to avoid being struck square in the forehead by a piece of scenery that was being carted by. All the while he kept his eyes open for the flash of brilliant pink that would tell him Lola was dressed and ready to go on stage.

There was no sign of her, and Ben felt his stomach tighten.

Lola was a dear girl, but not very bright. Only that morning he had given her a long and, in retrospect, probably an overloud lecture about the importance of paying careful attention to what she was about tonight. He wanted to talk to her before the curtain went up. He wanted to make sure she remembered the procedure, step by step.

It also wouldn't hurt to make sure she was sober.

If Lola was drunk in her dressing room . . . If she was worried that her hair didn't look just right or her costume didn't hug her curves in all the right places . . . If she was so eager to earn an extra pound or two that she'd welcomed into her dressing room some high-stepper with a big role of banknotes and a bigger . . .

A glitter of pink caught his eye, and Ben breathed a sigh of relief. Lola stood in the deep shadows across the stage, her back to him, and he zigzagged his way through the crowd, headed in her direction. He stopped at center stage long enough to check on the fountain that was really a firework and talked to John, his chief loader, who had helped him design the fountain and who was in charge of making sure the firework was put down into its mortar safely and correctly. Satisfied, Ben continued across the stage, his gaze wandering over Lola.

It was a lazy glance. An appreciative glance. He paid little attention to the pink satin slippers on her feet, but let his gaze drift upward. Whoever had designed Lola's costume was as much of a genius as Ben was himself, he decided. The short-cropped gown with its pinched waist and low-cut neckline allowed a tantalizing look at those parts of a woman that were usually and quite foolishly hidden beneath yards of wool and layers of crinolines.

The costume showed off Lola's small waist. It caressed her hips and flowed like a pink dream over a nicely rounded backside that was even more appealing than Ben remembered it. It displayed calves that were not long but were shapely as hell, and alluring enough to make him feel the hot rush of desire.

Lola had added her own touch to the outfit, a long pink shawl that covered her head, and though Ben wondered what earthly purpose it might serve, he did not disapprove. It added an air of mystery, a touch of the exotic, and he imagined the men in the audience would find it as alluring as he did. He knew Lola's decadent imagination well enough, and he could envision what she might do with the length of silk. He could picture her whisking it from her head and draping it around her hips. Already, he could feel the tingle of electricity that was sure to fill the Adelphi from floor to rafters when she slid it back and forth over her buttocks. Every man in the place would watch it move from side to side. Everyone would wonder how it would feel to glide his hands over the same path, and swear he'd risk his reputation, his fortune, and even his soul for one touch from Lola that was half as enticing.

The thought burst through Ben's veins like the trail of fiery stars that chased after a Roman candle, but he damped it before it had a chance to lodge firmly in his gut.

It was nearly time to shoot the firework, and that meant he needed his wits about him and his passions focused on a very different kind of flame.

As Ben neared, he saw Lola turn to peer at the stage, and in spite of his warnings to himself, he couldn't help but anticipate yet another visual delight. He knew the costume was cut low and tight around Lola's breasts, wickedly so, and he braced himself for another delicious pang of desire.

He was very much surprised to find his only reaction was one of utter disbelief.

Though the woman in pink was nicely rounded, she was hardly extraordinary. Not in the way Lola was extraordinary. The gauzy fabric of the costume hung down rather forlornly over breasts that were not at all unattractive. They simply weren't monumental.

They were, instead, small and high and firm, the kind of breasts a man could cup, one in each hand. The kind that were soft to the touch, and sweet to the tongue, and glorious because of it. The kind that—

"Isabel!"

The realization hit Ben full force, and his voice echoed in the vast confines of the stage like thunder. The woman in pink—the woman he thought was Lola—swung around and her mouth dropped open. If he'd had any doubts as to her identity, they were erased once and for all when he saw her face.

It was Isabel, sure enough, impossible though it seemed. Isabel who stared at him from the shadows that collected in the wings of the Adelphi Theater like dusky lamb's wool. Even though her eyes were shaded, they were wide enough for him to read the emotions that raced through her. Horror first of all. Horror at having been discovered. Just as quickly horror turned to panic. Panic mutated to absolute embarrassment.

She was holding something in her right hand, and as soon as she saw Ben, Isabel hid it behind her back.

"What the hell—" Ben pounded across the stage. He stopped inches from Isabel and clamped his hands over her shoulders, his fingers pressing tightly against her bare flesh. "What the hell are you doing here?"

Isabel managed a smile that trembled over her expression in much the same way as her shoulders quaked beneath his fingers. Yet somehow she kept her chin steady and her gaze level with Ben's. "Why, I am watching the show, of course," she said. "I have heard so much about this wonderful firework of yours that I—"

"You decided to damp the fuse." The truth of the

thing fell into place, and before Isabel could utter another word or move an inch, Ben shot one hand around her and grabbed the hand she held behind her back. Just as he suspected, she was holding one of the batons that were usually used to light fireworks. Only this one was tipped with a wet cloth.

"That is unworthy, even of you." Ben snatched the baton from her hand and cast it into the deepest shadows. His disbelief bubbled into anger. He glanced over his shoulder toward the fountain. "You didn't—?"

Isabel shook her head. "Your John is a conscientious lad," she commented, but there was no satisfaction in her voice. "I haven't had the chance to get close enough. I thought if I waited . . ." She didn't give him chapter and verse of her plan. She didn't need to.

"Of al the devious, deceitful, dishonorable . . ." The words wedged against the anger that blocked Ben's throat and played havoc with his heartbeat. Too angry to keep still, he dropped his hand and spun away from Isabel. "I can't believe you—"

"You're only sorry you didn't think of it first."

Isabel's words froze him in place, and in spite of himself Ben smiled. "You're damned right," he admitted. "Though I doubt that even you, Miss De Quincy . . ." He made her an elaborate bow. "Even you wouldn't be shooting off fireworks on a night like this. The rain would damp your fuses sure enough. Far better than you've been able to damp mine."

Isabel answered him with an exasperated *hurumph*. She crossed her arms over her chest but to no avail. The movement made the pink costume sag. It dipped off her shoulder and drooped even farther over her bosom, revealing the top of Isabel's sensible and quite formidable-looking corset.

Ben couldn't help but chuckle. She looked rather like a pink flower, its petals demolished by a high wind. Taking pity on her, he stepped forward and slipped the short, capped sleeve of the costume back where it belonged. He was close enough to see down the front of the costume, and pragmatic enough to know he'd be a fool to pass up such a golden opportunity. Stepping even closer, Ben let his gaze drift, over shoulders dotted with freckles, down to where a warm, soft shadow showed inside the front of her corset.

He swallowed hard, barely controlling the incomprehensible urge to dip his tongue between her breasts. "I rather think," he said, "that you are not meant to wear something so awkward as a corset beneath that pink confection of a dress." He cleared his throat and collected what little was left of his reason, laughing to cover the fact that his voice was far more ragged than he liked. "It's flesh the men in the boxes pay to see," he told her. "And flesh the fellows up in the cheap seats want to imagine."

"Not my flesh, certainly." Isabel blinked rapidly, her voice, for some odd reason, breathy. "It looks as though they will have to ogle someone else tonight." She stepped away from hm, and might have fled into the shadows if Ben hadn't grabbed her.

"Oh, no!" He held on tight, his fingers encircling her wrist, her skin soft against his. "You won't just run off. I won't allow it." Another thought struck him, and he looked at her hard. "What have you done with Lola?"

Isabel did her best to wiggle away. It didn't take her long to realize that the more she fidgeted, the more tightly Ben held on and the more her costume crept up and down in all the wrong places. With a mumbled curse and a look of disgust, she gave up. "I haven't done anything with Lola," she snapped. "She's drunk. And from what I've been told, it isn't the first time. She's passed out on a table over at the King's Head."

Ben bellowed an expletive. The word might have caused a stir, even in the dissolute atmosphere of the Adelphi, if anyone had heard it. No one did. At that precise moment the orchestra started into the opening strains of Lola's dance. The raucous music was met with a deafening cheer from the crowd out front, and the curtain began its slow rise.

Ben stepped back and looked Isabel up and down. "So you came to take her place."

She dismissed the notion instantly, just as Ben thought she would. "Of course not! I only put on her costume so that no one would notice me. I thought to damp the fuse and leave. You can't possibly think I would want to—"

"There's nothing for it, my girl." His mind made up, Ben tightened his hold around Isabel's wrist. He whirled her around so that she was facing the stage, and watched her eyes widen in what could only be described as terror as the curtain inched upward and the faces of the men in the first few rows were revealed. Every countenance glowed from the heat of the moment and the anticipation of being part of what was promised to be a sterling theatrical event. Mustaches twitched. Hands applauded. Whistles and bawdy shouts filled the air.

In one small corner of his mind, Ben supposed he should take pity on Isabel. Hers was a jolterheaded plan, but he'd been honest enough when he admitted he wished he had thought of it first. He had to give her credit for trying. And for looking so pink and delicious in Lola's costume.

Not, he reminded himself, that he cared.

Ben leaned over Isabel's shoulder and whispered in her ear. "Sir Digby's out there somewhere. As well as half of London. And I would not disappoint them for the world." He signaled to John, who, as instructed, handed him a flaming baton. He slapped the baton into Isabel's hand and closed her fingers around it.

"Break a leg!" he said, and flattening both hands against her back, he shoved Isabel out onto the stage.

The lights were far brighter than she'd ever imagined. The noise was far louder.

Grappling with the flaming baton, grabbing her drooping costume, and tripping over her own feet, Isabel stumbled out onto the stage. She skidded to a stop twelve feet or so from where she'd stood hidden in the wings and righted herself, squinting against the lights that blazed around her like a thousand fireworks shells all gone off at once.

In one breath she prayed that her eyes would become accustomed to the blinding light. In the next she was sorry when they did. The searing light hurt less and less, and Isabel opened her eyes and looked out beyond the footlights.

A thousand faces stared back at her.

Isabel's stomach flipped. Her head whirled. Her knees felt no more steady than they had when she'd stood in the dark shadows with Ben and he grazed a look over her that somehow robbed her of her breath and caused her heart to beat an uncertain rhythm.

Her heart wasn't just beating uncertainly now. It was banging out a cacophony that was nearly as loud as the hoots and whistles that billowed from the audience, so loud they drowned the music. The orchestra had no choice but to surrender. The music stopped. The shouting didn't.

"Hey! You ain't Lola! Where's Lola?"

"Get to it! Where's the music? Where's the dancin'? We came to see dancin'!"

"Better hold up that dress, girl. Your frillies is showin'!"

The voices lapped over Isabel like waves, sucking her breath away. She darted a look around. Up in the balcony the audience was on its feet, whooping and cheering. Music hall crowds were notoriously boisterous, and already, down in the cheap seats at the back of the theater, at least three fistfights had broken out. Obviously deciding a little mayhem was far more interesting than a dancer who wasn't dancing, half the crowd was engrossed in the brawls.

Unfortunately, the other half was still watching her.

Trying to swallow around the lump of panic in her throat, Isabel moved her gaze farther toward the front of the house. Even in the expensive boxes where the men wore evening clothes and drank champagne, things were turning ugly. A tall top hat sailed onto the stage. Someone else threw a bouquet of roses, but the ribbon tied to them with the name LOLA in large gold letters spelled out on it told her the flowers were anything but a tribute.

Through it all, only one person remained calm.

Sir Digby Talbot sat in the first row at center stage, his head tipped to one side as if he were thinking very hard. His hands were folded on his lap in front of him. His face was an impassive mask.

Ice formed in Isabel's stomach. It filled her veins. Shame and embarrassment congealed inside her, like a fist slammed right below her heart. In her mind's eye she saw her reputation slipping away along with her chances at the Jubilee contract. Gone forever in a pink haze.

All because of Ben.

Isabel tossed a look over to where he stood watching from the wings.

As she might have expected, Ben was surrounded by a bevy of chorus girls who seemed just as interested in the proceedings as he did. One arm hooked around the waist of each of the girls at his side, Ben watched Isabel with growing amusement. A smile played around his lips and lit his eyes. A laugh rumbled through him. The girls around him chattered and giggled and added their own raucous comments to those of the crowd.

And Isabel's humiliation melted into white-hot anger.

Always observant, Ben caught the change in her mood instantly. He lifted his shoulders, an elaborate gesture that proclaimed his innocence to all the world. His arms still curved around the girls at his side, he wiggled one finger at Isabel, indicating the right shoulder of her dress, which was hanging precariously. His voice carried even over the din.

"Need help?" he asked.

"Not from you," she yelled back, hoisting her sleeve. "Never from you."

Ben nodded toward the front row. "Sir Digby might think so. He might think you are not as clever a businesswoman as you pretend to be."

"Damn you." Isabel bit the words off between clenched teeth, but it seemed that in addition to his many other talents, Ben was a lip reader as well. He laughed.

"Come back in," he called, waving her toward the wings. He patted the backside of the girl closest to him. "One of these little beauties will get the job done far better than you ever could."

"And I'll see you in hell first." Her anger fueling her every movement, Isabel gritted her teeth and set her jaw. Keeping the sparking baton at arms' length, she whisked the shawl from her head with one hand and looped it around her shoulders. An audible groan of disappointment went up from the crowd.

Not that she cared.

She shot them a look that silenced them to a man and signaled the orchestra conductor to start playing.

The conductor looked dubious, to say the least, but he was not insensitive to the fact that the longer they waited, the more chance there was of an out-and-out riot. He tapped his podium, raised his arms, and brought down his baton, and the music rose all around. Isabel listened for a moment, trying to catch the cadence.

"Wonderful," she grumbled. "Utter embarrassment in four-four time."

But she wasn't about to let that stop her.

Her movements were not quite a dance. They were part waltz step, part hop, and she was very much afraid she looked just as ridiculous as she felt. But ridiculous or not, it was enough to catch the attention of the audience. Before she'd gone more than a dozen steps, they had assumed, to a man, that it was all part of the act. Their skepticism dissolved, and they decided the awkward woman in the pink costume was part of the grandest comedy any of them had ever seen.

Their catcalls turned to laughter. Their hoots became cheers.

Isabel did her best not to notice. It wasn't so easy to ignore the fact that, in the wings, Ben had loosened his hold on his devotees. He stepped forward, and the smile that lit his face conveyed his disbelief and, damn him, more than a hint of admiration.

Isabel shot him a look of utter venom that did nothing at all except make his smile widen. Ignoring it, ignoring Ben, the noise, and the mind-numbing certainty that she was ruined, she favored the audience with her most dazzling smile.

Then she touched the flaming baton to the fuse.

Years of experience told Isabel exactly how long she would have to wait before anything happened. But the audience didn't have the same knowledge. She heard a collective intake of breath and watched as two thousand eyes focused on the fountain.

There was a familiar *plop* and a loud enough *pop* from inside the fountain to let Isabel know exactly what was going to happen.

She stepped back out of the way just as a geyser of flaming golden stars issued from the fountain. The effect was certainly beautiful, and even a little picturesque, but it wasn't at all unusual. Isabel had seen the same sort of firework a hundred times. She'd designed similar ones for her own shows, and she knew Ben had, too. She watched the shower of golden stars and listened while some of the better behaved members of the audience applauded politely. The rest were not so easily indulged. A rumble went around the theater, the general tone of which echoed the sentiments of a fellow in the balcony who hung over the rail and screamed, "Is that all the bloody hell there is?"

It was all there was.

The realization left Isabel feeling remarkably pleased at the same time she scolded herself for being so taken in by Ben's boastful claims. It seemed she'd been forced to make a fool of herself for no good reason. The fountain of golden stars was pretty but hardly remarkable. And if it was this gold Ben was counting on to gild his reputation, she was afraid he would be very much disappointed.

She tossed a look over her shoulder at him. "Is that the best you could do?" she asked. "Golden stars. Hardly the stuff legends are made of."

"Hardly," Ben agreed. He cupped one ear in an exaggerated gesture. "But listen, Miss De Quincy, is that another shell I hear?"

It was.

Isabel heard a muffled *thunk* and, surprised, she looked toward the fountain just in time to see the front of it fall away. A series of loud reports echoed through the theater. The polite applause stopped. The catcalls from the balcony were lost in the noise made by the half dozen shells that broke high over the heads of the audience. Every last man looked up. Every last mouth was open in surprise.

And wonder rained down from the rafters.

Thousands of glittering paper snowflakes. Hundreds of colored paper streamers. Dozens and dozens of tiny Union Jack flags floated through the air, and audience members scrambled to snatch them up like so many fireflies. One flag landed directly in front of Sir Digby, and he scooped it up before anyone else could and waved it enthusiastically, a huge grin smoothing his rumpled face.

Awash in a pool of sparkling snowflakes, Isabel watched it all. This was no ordinary firework. A lifetime of experience told her as much. With one effect Ben had accomplished every firework maker's dream.

He had made magic.

She knew it was the kind of firework that would be talked about for days. The kind that sparked men's imaginations as well as their applause. The kind that would be described over and again in countless pubs and countless parlors and, if the rapturous look on Sir

Digby's face meant anything, countless boardrooms as well.

It was the kind of a firework of which legends—and legendary fireworks manufacturers—are made.

Isabel snatched a red streamer from her hair and cast it to the floor, and with the cheers of the audience ringing in her ears, she left the stage as quickly as she could. It was a poor ending, she told herself. A poor ending, indeed, to both her turn on the stage and to her career as the director of De Quincy and Sons.

Had she been thinking more clearly, she might have looked for another way off the stage. Instead, she headed the way she'd come and was very much disheartened to find Ben and his girls waiting there for her.

"Go on. Out of here!" Ben smacked his palm against the backside of one of the girls. She didn't seem to mind at all. Giggling, she scampered past Isabel and into the passageway beyond, a column of dancing girls following, wagging their behinds for Ben's benefit.

He didn't seem to notice. His head to one side, he kept his eyes on Isabel. Finally, he stepped back and applauded. *"Brava!"* he said. "A stellar performance, and one that is sure to go down in the annals of London history! Perhaps you might consider a career on the stage when I am awarded the Jubilee contract and you are reduced to selling Christmas crackers on the street corner."

"Christmas crackers, indeed!" Isabel slammed the still flaming baton into a nearby bucket of sand and skewered Ben with a look. She was no more in the mood to spar with him than she was to be the recipient of his smug smile or his questionable sense of humor. She sidestepped her way around him and headed for the door.

What she found waiting for her was no better.

Performers lined the passageway. They cheered and applauded and urged her to join the show. Isabel didn't dare respond. She kept her head high and her eyes straight ahead, and when she finally arrived at the stage door, she banged it open and made to step outside.

It was only then that she realized that Ben had followed her.

He grabbed Isabel's arm and spun her around to face him, his eyes filled with mischief. "You're not leaving, are you?" he asked. "Listen." He bent his head. The sounds of the audience's cheers still echoed from out front. "You can't chuck your stage career now. They love you!"

Isabel glared at him. She wanted to tell him she knew they didn't love her. They loved his firework. But she refused to give him the satisfaction. "I don't want to be loved simply for my legs and my bosom," she told him instead. "You of all people should know that."

Ben's eyes lit. Standing this close, he could not possibly see all of her, but he made the effort. He skimmed a look from the top of her head to her waist. "You've got it all wrong. I never loved you simply for your legs and your bosom."

Isabel's breath caught in her throat. Ben was not comfortable expressing his feelings. She knew that well enough. The idea that he might choose this inconvenient time and this very inopportune place to confess to some ancient and long-dead emotion caused her heart to skip a beat.

Ben stepped nearer. "Bella, Bella, Bella." He skimmed his thumb down her cheek. "How can you think that of me? Of course I didn't love you simply for your legs and bosom." He bent even closer and whispered in her ear. "I loved you for all those delicious parts in between!"

Isabel barely contained a shriek of frustration. Flattening her hands, she pressed against Ben's chest and pushed him out of the way. He might not have given up so easily if he wasn't so busy laughing.

Isabel ground her teeth and turned back toward the door.

"You're not going out there like that, are you? It's still raining." Wiping tears from his eyes, Ben made another grab for her. He caught her shoulder and held her in place. "You'll catch your death."

"Good. Then I won't have to face the rest of the world in the morning."

He did not seem at all sympathetic to her plight. His smile inched its way up until the corners of his eyes crinkled and his face shone with delight. "By then there'll be even more to talk about. Once that frothy fabric gets wet . . ." He stepped back to get a better look, his gaze skimming the costume and Isabel's curves beneath it. "I do declare, Miss De Quincy, I believe if that fabric gets wet, it will be completely transparent. How delightful for the cabman who finally snatches you up off the street!"

"Damn you, Ben Costigan." Isabel gritted her teeth. "My clothes . . ." She looked back in the direction of Lola's dressing room, where she'd left her clothes. The passageway was crowded with performers who were all too eager to goggle at her, hanging on every word Ben said and every one of her answers. "I am leaving," she said, jerking away from Ben's grasp. "Now."

Ben shook his head in wonder, but he knew better than to argue. He reached for a macintosh that hung on a peg near the door. "Here, take this." He draped the coat over her shoulders. "And this." He pressed a sovereign into her hand, and when she opened her mouth to refuse it, he silenced her, one finger to her lips. "I doubt there are pockets in that costume of yours," he said. "And if you don't have the wherewithal to pay for your cab, you may have to earn your way home." With one finger he nudged aside the front of the coat and took a good look at her. "The legs aren't bad," he declared. "They ought to earn you a shilling or two. And the bosom—"

Isabel didn't wait to hear his opinion of her bosom. With a final withering look she turned her back on him and, clutching his coat around her shoulders, she hurried out the door.

# Chapter 5

"Belle?"

The voice was muffled by the closed door of Isabel's bedroom, but she had no doubt who it belonged to. It wasn't the first time that morning that Simon had tried to talk to her. This time, like the times before, Isabel ignored him. Bundled in her oldest dressing gown, she sat on the chair in front of her dressing table, her arms wrapped tightly around herself, her head pounding. She hadn't bothered to open her curtains, and the room was as dark as her mood.

"Belle?" Simon tapped on the door. "You have to come out sooner or later. You can't spend the rest of your life in your bedchamber."

"Can't I?" As if she could see her brother through the door, Isabel glowered at it. The look might have been considerably more comfortable if her vision wasn't clouded by tears and her eyes weren't swollen from lack of sleep. "Go away, Simon. Just leave me here to die."

The door snapped open, and Simon poked his head inside. "No one's ever died of embarrassment," he told her.

Isabel wasn't so sure. She glanced at her mirror. Even through the gloom she could see that her eyes were an unsightly shade of red and they were ringed with black. Her skin was pale and her hair was a fright. Because of the inclement weather, it had taken her more time than usual to find a cab the night before, and the rain had chilled her through to the bone. She could feel the cold still, and she was grateful—as grateful as she could be—for the coat Ben had given her. "I feel dead," she told her brother. "And I look dead."

Simon chuckled. He came up behind her and rested his hands on her shoulders, bending to peer at her in the mirror. "You do look rather dreadful," he admitted. "And from what I heard last night from the fellows at my club, it's no wonder."

Whatever small hopes Isabel had that her adventure of the night before was over and forgotten were dashed completely. Her heart sank. She propped her elbows on her dressing table and stared into the mirror. "The fellows at your club! Do you mean to tell me that they knew the story already? Last night?"

"You're the talk of London, I'm afraid." Simon gave her an encouraging pat and headed across the room. He pulled open the draperies, and the morning sunlight flooded in.

Isabel squinted against the brightness.

"Don't worry." Simon's voice came to her from the other side of the room. She heard him open the draperies on a second window, then a third. "No one's being critical. At least not too critical. They say you were a real brick. And a real stunner in that little pink costume."

"Excellent!" Isabel turned away from the sight of her own miserable expression. She could do nothing to disguise the bitterness of her words. "So I am the talk of the town. Ben must truly be enjoying this. He said I'd end up on the street selling Christmas crackers." Isabel sighed. "I'm afraid he might be right. Well . . ." She grasped at what little cheer she could find in the situation. "At least if everyone is busy talking about me, they can't be waxing rapturous about Ben's firework."

"Oh, they're doing that, too." Simon opened the French doors that led out to a small balcony, and a wave of cool air invaded the room. "They say it was quite spectacular. Far more inventive than anything—"

"Stop!" Isabel hoisted herself out of her chair. There was a bell pull on the other side of the room, and she dragged herself toward it.

"I've already ordered coffee for you," Simon said before she could get there. "I left instructions that it is to be served downstairs in the drawing room."

"No." Isabel shook her head. "I'm not going down. Not today. Maybe never. I don't want to face anyone. By now even the household staff must know the story of what happened last night. I won't have them snickering behind my back."

Simon did his best to look solemn, but Isabel could not fail to notice that there was a hint of a smile in his eyes. "I've strictly forbidden snickering," he said. He went to the door and opened it, but before he left the room, he turned back to Isabel. "You will want to come down," he told her. "You'll want to see what's waiting for you." And with that, he left.

Isabel knew he was wrong. Whatever was downstairs, it couldn't possibly make her feel any better. Nothing could do that.

Except for one thing.

For all too brief a moment an image flickered through Isabel's brain.

Ben Costigan's head on a platter. Silver, of course.

Even that wasn't enough to make her feel much better.

In spite of the fact that she told herself she didn't care, Isabel found herself staring at the door, looking at the place where only moments ago Simon had been standing. He knew she could never resist a mystery, damn him, and by the time another fifteen minutes had passed, she had changed into a plain but presentable dress, run a brush through her hair, and marshaled enough courage to venture out of her room and down the stairs.

She smelled the roses even before she got there.

Halfway down the staircase that led into the imposing foyer of the De Quincy home, Isabel paused and drew in a deep breath. The air was heavy with the

# DIAMOND RAIN

scent of summer roses, though she couldn't say why, and curious, she continued on her way.

With each step, the flowery aroma intensified. So did Isabel's curiosity.

When she got to the bottom of the stairway, she could hardly believe her eyes.

The foyer was filled with roses. Dozens of roses.

There were vases of yellow roses on the table where calling cards were usually kept, and vases of red roses on the floor next to the front door. There was one spectacular bouquet of white roses on the table right outside the door to the drawing room, and just as Isabel got there, the butler came into the hallway carrying another.

"Willoughby?" Isabel stopped the man and examined the bouquet. There was a full dozen roses in it all told, each more perfect and beautiful than the next. She looked from the white roses to the vase of red roses at her feet. "Willoughby, where on earth have all these flowers come from?"

"I really can't say, Miss De Quincy." Willoughby stood back and allowed Isabel into the room ahead of him. "They've been coming all morning."

They had, indeed. From wall to wall the drawing room was filled with roses. Isabel stood wide-eyed, staring about the room.

There were red roses and yellow roses and apricot roses and wonderful bicolored combinations that reminded her of fireworks crackling high overhead. There were tiny roses and lush cabbage roses, roses in crystal vases and roses in Chinese porcelain urns and roses nestled in pottery tureens. There were roses on the tables and the floors, roses spilling out onto the veranda. More roses than Isabel had ever seen anywhere.

And the scent . . .

Isabel pulled in a deep breath, and in spite of her misery, she found herself smiling. She twirled around, taking in the blur of color that whirled with her.

"Simon?" She looked toward her brother, who was

standing on the other side of the room, surrounded by potted rose trees. "Simon, where have they all come from? Who's sent them?"

Simon shook his head. "No card saying who sent them. Not on any of them. But I can tell you one thing, they are all for you."

"Me?" It was the most outrageous thing Isabel had ever heard, and she laughed. She hurried over to examine an exquisite spray of red and white variegated roses. "They can only be from Peter," she said. "Though he is apt to use Tuthill's, the florist on Wigmore Street, and these are from Barneighs."

"From Barneighs and Tuthill's and Memorlards and from every other florist in London." Simon went from bouquet to bouquet, reading the names on the cards. "There isn't one florist in all the city that would stock this many roses in any one day. He must have gone to them all."

Isabel's heart warmed at the thought. "He's heard, of course," she said, bending to inhale the aroma of the apricot roses that had been left on the piano. "He's heard about the terrible fiasco last night, and he is trying to make me feel better. It really is very sweet, don't you think? Chivalry is not dead, Simon!" She plucked a single white rose from the bouquet nearest her and tucked the flower behind the pin of the brooch she wore on her dress. "There isn't another man in all the world who is so very romantic."

Before Isabel had a chance to say any more, the door snapped open and Willoughby entered carrying yet another spray of flowers. There were at least three dozen roses in it, so many that poor Willoughby could hardly see his way around them, and he stepped gingerly into the room, balancing the flowers and the stunning French crystal vase in which they were arranged. The vase was exquisite. Like diamonds, it winked at Isabel. The roses were lush and dew-kissed. They were gorgeous.

Except that they were pink.

The exact pink of the costume that lay even now in

a sodden heap in her bedchamber. The costume she'd worn at the Adelphi.

The realization settled in Isabel's stomach like the remnants of a bad meal. The effervescence that had bubbled through her all but fizzled. It was a coincidence, surely. Nothing more. A coincidence, or Peter's idea of a joke.

But Isabel did not believe in coincidence.

And Peter was far too considerate to play perverse jokes.

An uneasy suspicion pounded through Isabel's head along with the headache that was suddenly back in full force. She took a closer look at the roses on the piano and the tables and the sideboard. She stepped back to allow Willoughby by, and when he finally set the prodigious bouquet on the table closest to her, she narrowed her eyes and looked it over as if she expected something—or someone—might be concealed deep within the pink petals.

"This one has a card, Miss De Quincy." Willoughby's words snapped Isabel out of her fantasies. She scolded herself and, dashing her suspicions aside, she accepted the envelope Willoughby held out to her.

Isabel turned the envelope over in her fingers. MISS ISABEL DE QUINCY, it said on the outside, but the hand was not familiar.

She ripped open the envelope and drew out the card. "Thank you." She read the simple message out loud, and looked at Simon as if he might help her make some sense of it. "What do you suppose that means? Why would Peter be thanking me for anything? Why would anyone . . .? Anyone but—"

Before Isabel could speak the name, the coachman, the groom, and the gardener marched into the room. Three of them carried vases of pink roses. The fourth had a large parcel in his hands.

"There's a message 'ere for ye, ma'am." The gardener reached around the vase he was carrying and presented an envelope to Isabel. It was marked with a large number *1*.

"And this 'ere one, too," the coachman said. The envelope he gave her had a *2* scrawled on it.

"And this." The footman handed her the parcel. There was a *3* written across the envelope attached to the brown paper wrappings.

"And this." The groom handed her a final envelope.

Wonder-struck, Isabel set the parcel on the divan and started in on the envelopes in order.

"You were spectacular." She read the first message aloud, and the suspicions that had been only inklings bloomed until they were as abundant and as well colored as the flowers that surrounded her. She opened the second envelope with less enthusiasm.

"Now . . ." the message said.

More sure than ever, she tore into the third envelope, the one that had arrived with the parcel. "Here are your—" The words caught on the gurgle of outrage that climbed up Isabel's throat.

"Here are your what?" Too curious to wait for her to calm down, Simon crossed the room and grabbed the parcel. He ripped open a corner of it without bothering to undo the string. "Clothes," he said, looking at her in wonder. "The gown you wore yesterday when you—"

"Yes, yes." Isabel tossed the third card to the floor. She tore into the fourth envelope and read the card, and when she finished with it, she crumpled it into a tight ball and held it in her fist. She looked from Simon to Willoughby and from him to the others of her servants who stood nearby. "Get them out," she said.

"What?" Even Willoughby, usually the soul of discretion and the height of decorum, could not help but be surprised. He looked at Isabel as if he hadn't heard her properly. "What's that you say, Miss De Quincy? Get them out? Get who out?"

"The flowers." Isabel clenched her teeth until her jaw ached. Her voice was muffled beneath the weight of the anger that pressed against her chest and drove the breath from her lungs. "I want them out of here, and I want them out of here now."

Willoughby didn't bother looking at Simon for approval. Along with his wife, who was the housekeeper, Willoughby had spent thirty-five years serving the De Quincy family, and he knew that when Isabel made a request, there was no arguing with it, just as there was no second-guessing her intent. He bowed from the waist. "Yes, ma'am." He hoisted a vase into his arms and looked at the others, instructing them to do the same.

Isabel didn't move. Not until every one of the vases had been taken away. The last of them in his arms, Willoughby backed toward the door. "What shall I do with them, ma'am?"

Isabel had a very good idea what Willoughby could do with the flowers. Her suggestion had to do with loading them into a dray and carting them back to a certain so-called gentleman, and with certain portions of that so-called gentleman's anatomy she knew it was better not to mention in front of the servants. She bit her tongue and kept her ideas to herself.

"One vase for each of the maids, I think," she told Willoughby. "And one for Mrs. Willoughby, of course." She glanced out the doorway at the vases that were being cleared from the foyer. "Simon . . . You no doubt know a woman or two who would appreciate flowers. You may as well send some of these. It will save me the trouble of paying for the ones you might order yourself."

"Indeed!" Simon took up the offer instantly and went out of the room to supervise the delivery of the flowers he chose.

"The rest . . ." Isabel glanced at Willoughby, who was still waiting for further instructions. "A church. A hospital. I hardly care. Do what you will with them, Willoughby. Only do it quickly. I do not want to see them. Not even one. Especially the pink ones."

"Yes, ma'am." Willoughby backed out of the room and closed the door behind him, and it wasn't until after Isabel had heard it click shut that she allowed herself the luxury of a completely crestfallen groan.

She sank onto the divan and dropped her head into her hands. That's when she realized she still was clutching the fourth card in her fingers. She pried it out and smoothed it flat and read the message.

"Please," it said, in a hand that was all too familiar, "can I have my coat back?"

"I came as soon as I could, of course." Peter Thorlinson, Viscount Epworth, slipped out of his greatcoat and handed it to the footman who waited near the door, his dark eyes filled with sympathy and the telltale signs of the ardor he had no choice but to bridle with the servants watching. He took Isabel's arm and stepped aside so that Willoughby could lead them up the stairs to the first floor.

"I'm sorry it took so long," he said. "With Richard back at Briarcliffe, there are certain family matters that must be attended to here in town and—"

"No need to apologize." Isabel stopped outside the door to the drawing room and allowed Willoughby to open it, and when he had, she went inside and stood by the small fire that had been started in the grate to chase the chill of the spring evening.

Peter had sent a message earlier in the day saying that he would call upon her at eight, and knowing she would see him was the only thing that had made the balance of Isabel's day bearable. After personally supervising the disposal of every last one of Ben's roses, she had forced herself to get enough sleep so that she might look far more presentable then she had that morning. She had fortified herself with a good deal of coffee and a leisurely bath, and had dressed in one of her best at-home evening dresses, a concoction of yellow silk and lace that made her look far sunnier than she felt. With the help of her maid, Isabel had swept her hair up and back and crowned it with a layer of soft curls that she'd adorned with flowers cut from the garden.

Not roses.

Isabel shivered. She cast the thought aside and concentrated instead on Peter.

There was no spark of mischief in Peter's burnt-almond eyes, and for that Isabel was grateful. There was no hint of a lecherous grin on his lips, either, and for that she was relieved. Peter was as handsome as any man in London, and if he was not as exciting as some, or as devilish, or as unpredictable, or as mercurial, he was also not as irritating and as fiendish and as impulsive and as volatile.

Not that she was comparing Peter to anyone else. The very thought was unworthy of her, and Isabel dismissed it. As soon as Willoughby left the room and closed the door behind him, she went to Peter, her hands extended.

He took them in his. "I can't tell you how outraged I was when I heard what went on at the Adelphi last night."

It was enough that he had tried. Isabel rewarded him with a kiss. It was meant to be nothing more than a friendly greeting, but Peter deepened it and she didn't resist. There was comfort in Peter's arms, especially after the disaster of the last twenty-four hours, and Isabel allowed him to draw her nearer and hold her close.

"Oh, Isabel!" He nuzzled her cheek, his voice heavy with longing and soft against her skin. "I've missed you these last days. I've—" He sniffed. "I say, is that a new perfume you're wearing? I smell roses!"

"Roses!" Isabel pulled away. Roses were the last things she wanted to talk about. Not tonight. She'd had her fill of roses and the thoughts of Ben that seemed tangled up in them, like beautiful rose petals nestled in treacherous thorns.

Grumbling her displeasure, Isabel paced to the other side of the room and did her best to change the subject. "You said Richard's already gone to Briarcliffe. I suppose he is there putting the last touches on the costume ball he and Margaret are planning.

Margaret has asked for a fireworks display, and I couldn't say no. I've done a good deal of research, and we shall have a show that will rival Versailles. I've even got an appropriate costume. Marie Antoinette!"

Peter didn't respond, and Isabel couldn't help but wonder why. He was usually an easy conversationalist. "You're still going as a musketeer, aren't you?" she asked.

"Yes. Yes. Of course." Peter went to the sideboard and poured himself a whiskey and soda. He knew how Isabel liked her liquor, and he poured one for her as well. But he didn't hand it to her right away. He stood in front of her, shifting slightly from foot to foot, refusing to meet her eyes.

"What is it?" Isabel didn't wait for his answer. She commandeered her whiskey and soda and took a drink. "You're very quiet suddenly. Ever since I mentioned the costume ball."

"Well . . . The ball. Yes." Peter huffed and puffed and took a sip of his own drink. "That's what I've come to talk to you about."

The words were innocent enough, but Isabel didn't like the sound of them or the queer, shivery feeling that made its way over her shoulders when he said them. A premonition of doom. "What's he done?" she asked.

"He?" Peter's dark brows rose. "You mean that Costigan fellow? How did you know—"

"It has to have something to do with Ben." Annoyed even before she knew what she had to be annoyed about, she deposited her glass on the nearest table and turned away from Peter. "Everything lately has something to do with Ben," she said, and the chill in her stomach told her it was the absolute truth. Wherever she turned, there he was, standing firmly in the way of the success of De Quincy and Sons. "What's he done this time?"

Peter sighed. "He's talked Richard into—"

"Not the ball!" Isabel spun around. "He hasn't persuaded them into letting him—"

"I'm afraid so." Peter took her hands in his. "Costigan has offered to provide his services to the family for free. You know how concerned Richard is about looking good in front of his peers. He couldn't turn down the opportunity. Yours won't be the only fireworks at Briarcliffe that night, I'm sorry to say."

"Fireworks!" Isabel sniffed, but it was far too genteel a sound to contain her anger. "If that's what you call one of Ben's tawdry displays. Mine will outshine his, surely. They will be better. Brighter. Far more impressive. They will be—"

"Isabel?"

She didn't realize she was clutching Peter's fingers quite so tightly. She saw him wince. She curbed her fury and released his hands. But instead of looking relieved, Peter only looked agitated.

"Isabel, this has to stop!" He closed his eyes and drew in a deep breath, bridling the displeasure that edged his every word. "You are far too taken with the man!"

The very idea was ludicrous, and Isabel let Peter know as much with a disdainful laugh. "I'd hardly call it taken. I think a better word might be enraged or exasperated or antagonized beyond all tolerance. But not taken, Peter. Not with Ben. Never taken with Ben."

"All right, then," he conceded. "Preoccupied. You're far too preoccupied with this Jubilee contract nonsense. Let Simon worry about it, darling Isabel. Business is no place for a woman. Look what it's done to you. You spend a good deal of your time worrying about Ben Costigan, and I don't think that's healthy at all." Peter hauled in a long breath. "That's the other thing I've come about."

"Oh?" Isabel could not imagine what he meant. Not until Peter scooped her right hand in his and got down on one knee in front of her.

Her heart skipped a beat. She had been waiting for this moment for a good long time. She had been expecting it. But now that it was finally here, she found herself feeling more panic than anticipation. She held a breath deep in her lungs and waited for Peter to say more.

"Isabel . . ." He twined his fingers through hers and looked up into her eyes, and if he noticed the flutter of trepidation that caused her breath to rise and fall erratically and her pulse to pound, he was enough of a gentleman not to point it out. And enough of a man to think that it was a reaction to the situation. And his nearness.

"Running a fireworks company is certainly no job for a lady." It was a poor opening gambit for a declaration of love, but Isabel excused him. Proposing marriage was not something a man did every day, and it was quite possible he was just as nervous as she found herself to suddenly be. "You'll agree, no doubt, that if you weren't so involved in De Quincy and Sons, you never would have been a part of that debacle at the Adelphi last night. A woman like you needs to be free of the mundane worries of business. You should have better things on your mind. A home. Children. A husband." He adjusted his grip, squeezing her fingers tighter. His palms were damp.

"Isabel, you would make me the happiest man in the world if you would—"

"Where the bloody hell is my mackintosh?"

The drawing room door crashed open, and the question echoed through the room.

Startled, Isabel gasped and Peter's face went ashen. They both turned to stare at Ben, who stood propped against the doorway.

"I'm so sorry, ma'am." Behind Ben, Willoughby was the color of old candles. "I tried to stop him at the door, but you know how Mr. Costigan can be." He rolled his eyes, as if that one expression explained it all.

It did.

Isabel's face froze. Her lips thinned. "It's quite all right, Willoughby," she told the butler. "You may go.

And Mr. Costigan . . ." She swung her gaze toward Ben. "You may leave as well."

"Not yet." Ben ventured farther into the room. He was dressed as Peter was, in evening clothes, but while Peter's dark trousers and jacket made him look distinguished and aristocratic, Ben's made him look more devilishly handsome than ever. Or perhaps it was the gleam that lit his eyes when he saw Peter on his knees.

"I say . . ." Ben whistled low under his breath. "I'm not interrupting anything, am I?"

"Would you care?" Isabel untangled her hand from Peter's and helped him to his feet. "When you barge in on people—"

"I am hardly barging." Ben's gaze landed on the whiskey bottle and siphon on the sideboard, and he went over and poured himself a drink. "I am merely looking for my coat," he said. "It's damned chilly out there, woman. Don't you ever venture outside to check? I need my coat. She took it, you know," he confided to Peter while he took a sip of the rather generous drink he'd poured himself. "Last night. She was dressed in this little . . ." As if unable to describe it adequately, Ben pulled a face and sketched the shape of the pink costume over his own hips.

"Looked mighty delicious, too, I can tell you that much. But tiny costumes are not much for keeping out the rain. Did you get your clothes, by the way?" he asked Isabel. "I had to send them to her." He turned again to Peter. "She left them behind, you see."

Peter was a man of infinite patience, but Ben's ill-timed visit tried even his limits. "This is ridiculous." He grabbed his own drink and tossed it down. "And very rude. Miss De Quincy and I were discussing a very private matter, sir, and I—"

"Ah, young love!" Ben sighed. "Proposing, were you? This is the very room in which I proposed to Isabel. No, wait! It wasn't here, was it?" He looked at Isabel, his eyes sparkling sapphire. She didn't doubt for one moment that he was enough of a cad to tell Peter the whole story.

The summerhouse at her father's country estate. The thunderstorm that had trapped them there for an entire afternoon. The one experimental kiss that had exploded into a passion that had surprised and delighted them both.

Isabel caught her breath.

"I see you do remember." The spark in Ben's eyes softened until it was the color of the heart of a flame when it burns hot and bright. His voice carried its heat. As if remembering where he was, and who he was with, he snapped out of the moment as quickly as he'd succumbed to it. "I stand corrected," he told Peter. "This wasn't where I proposed at all. She might not even be the woman I proposed to. It's hard to remember, isn't it?"

"It isn't at all hard to remember." For all his virtues, Peter did not have an especially keen sense of humor. He didn't tease. And he didn't recognize when others did. He stood straight and stiff. "If a man truly loves a woman, he remembers everything. Every minute of their time together."

It was just enough of a challenge, whether Peter realized it or not. Isabel knew she had to change the subject or risk Ben saying far more than he should. Though her glass was still half full, she held it out to Peter. "Freshen this for me, will you, please?" she asked. She knew he wouldn't refuse.

Before Peter got as far as the sideboard, Ben swallowed down the rest of his drink and held out his glass as well. When Peter turned to make their drinks, Ben closed in on Isabel.

"Looks as if I got here just in time," he whispered.

Isabel fluffed her skirt. She refused to meet his eyes. "I don't know what you're talking about."

"Don't you?" Ben glanced over his shoulder toward Peter and stepped to his left, effectively shielding Peter's view of them. "I could stay all night if you need me. It might help keep some of that famous Lord Epworth devotion at bay."

"Really!" She tossed her head. "I don't need saving, thank you very much. I've told you that before. Especially not saving from Peter."

Ben snatched her hand. "Saving from yourself, then?"

His hand was warm, not soft and damp like Peter's but dry and strong, the skin toughened from their peculiar trade. His fingers were long and thick, and they curled through hers with the instinctive ease of remembrance.

Ben smelled of soap and the lime scent his valet splashed on after his shave. And something else.

Isabel sniffed. She leaned nearer and wrinkled her nose. "You've had more to drink than the whiskey you stole from my sideboard. Ben Costigan, I do believe you're drunk!"

Ben grinned, and for the first time she realized he was not as steady on his feet as he pretended to be. He looked up quickly and had to resettle himself because of it, and when he was done, he gave her a wink. "Only a little."

"A little too much."

"I had to get a little drunk to get up the nerve to come see you after what I put you through last night." Ben's voice dipped and his mouth moved dangerously near. It was a potent combination, and Isabel found she couldn't look away. She watched the fire in his eyes flare and felt an answering spark flame somewhere within her. It was not at all a comfortable warmth. Not like the glow she felt when she was in Peter's arms. This fire was hotter and far more dangerous. "Did my roses do the trick?" He looked around, searching for the flowers.

"What roses?"

"Got rid of them, did you? I am crushed by your disdain!" Ben laughed. "No matter. All that really matters is if you forgive me. Do you, Bella?"

Fortunately, she didn't have a chance to answer, and

it was just as well. She wasn't sure what she would have said. Peter returned with their drinks, and Ben let go of her hand. Isabel used it to fan her face.

"I'm glad I found you both together." Ben accepted the drink Peter held out to him and retreated a dozen steps, slipping as easily into his brash persona as some men slipped into their morning coats. "I can issue my invitation to both of you." He looked from one of them to the other. "You're coming, aren't you? To the Crystal Palace? Next week?"

"You mean the demonstration?" Peter's eyes lit, and with a sinking feeling Isabel realized he must have seen the handbills Ben had distributed all through London. He was just as taken with the promised excitement of the event as was the rest of the metropolis. "The one featuring that Italian daredevil fellow. Signor . . . Signor . . ."

"Signor Francesco." Ben supplied the name for him. "That's the chap. I wanted you to be there." He wasn't looking at Peter. His eyes were full on Isabel, but she pretended not to notice.

"I can't imagine why we should," she said. "It is, no doubt, just another one of your flamboyant demonstrations. More fluff than substance. More noise than imagination."

"Not this time!" Ben finished his drink and set his glass on the table. He fished into his pocket and pulled out two tickets, which he handed to Isabel. "You'll want to be there," he assured her. "I guarantee, you'll be as impressed as the Jubilee committee. They'll be there as well."

"And at the gala at Briarcliffe?" Isabel gave him an icy smile.

"I see you've heard about that, have you?" Ben wasn't the least bit embarrassed. Or repentant. Laughing, he headed toward the door. "It's a grand opportunity for you, Miss De Quincy. You can watch a real fireworks master at work."

His words still echoed in Isabel's head after he'd gone.

"A real fireworks master." She lifted a pillow from the divan and punched it, then tossed it back where it had come from.

"Don't worry." Peter came up behind her and planted a kiss on the back of her neck. "Remember, I told you. Don't worry. Not about the fireworks business."

Isabel looked down at the tickets clutched in her hand. A plan formed in her head, and a smile came to her lips.

"You're right." Smiling, Isabel turned to him. "I won't worry. Not any longer."

# Chapter 6

There had been fireworks shows at the Crystal Palace in Sydenham since 1865. Isabel knew that well enough. De Quincy and Sons had mounted most of them, or at least, she was certain, the ones that were the most spectacular and the best received. The others—inferior, lackluster, and undoubtedly secondrate—had been engineered by Costigan and Company.

Not by Ben, of course. Not in the beginning.

It was Ben's grandfather who had designed the first shows. From what Isabel had heard about him, she knew that Matthew Costigan was a crusty fellow who had at one time been an assistant to her own grandfather at De Quincy and Sons. They'd had a falling-out over the ownership of a fireworks recipe—Isabel knew it went without saying that the Costigans were in the wrong—and Matthew had gone on to start his own company. After Matthew's death, Ben's father took control. By all accounts, he was a poor manager and had even less common sense than he did business acumen. A scandalous affair with the youngest daughter of an earl destroyed his reputation and nearly ruined the company.

It might have. If Ben had not taken over.

Ben was the first of the Costigans who had the audacity to go head to head with De Quincy and Sons. He had amassed a fortune by catering to the nouveau riche and the theater crowd, and he used his money to make a name for himself and for his business. He might have redeemed the reputation of Costigan and Company completely had he married well.

Had he married Isabel.

The thought skittered over Isabel's shoulders like the touch of icy fingers. It settled inside her like a lead weight.

She had been trying her best not to think about marriage. But ever since the night Ben had interrupted what most certainly would have turned into a full-blown proposal from Peter, she had found it more difficult than ever to put the subject out of her mind.

It was an annoying predicament at best. And disturbing at worst.

Not because Isabel wasn't expecting the proposal from Peter, but because every time she thought about it, her mind went into a muddle. Images of Peter smeared with those of Ben. Memories of Peter's heartfelt if somewhat bumbling proposal blurred beneath other memories. Memories she had no business remembering. Emotions she had done her best to control. Sensations she had tried so hard to forget.

With a shake of her shoulders, Isabel banished the thoughts and held tightly to her determination.

She glanced up at the Crystal Palace. It rose in dazzling bubbles of glass and iron above the trees, an enormous building that had originally been constructed to house the International Exposition and was now used as a pleasure garden. There were footpaths all around, shaded groves of trees, band concerts on terraces. And at night there were fireworks.

Sometimes they were De Quincy shows.

Sometimes, like tonight, they were Costigan fireworks. And after tonight?

Isabel smiled. For the first time since the day she'd learned that Ben was back and that he had his eyes and his heart set on the Jubilee contract, she felt her spirits lighten.

Her arm was wound through Peter's, and sensing her contentment, he patted her hand. "You seem quite happy this evening, Isabel. I hope it's because you've finally decided to listen to me. No more worries about fireworks?"

"No more worries," she assured him. She glanced up, searching for a glint of the slender, nearly invisible wire she knew was strung from the top of one of the towers that flanked the front entrance of the building. Had she been a casual observer or simply one of the thousands who was gathered here this evening to watch the extravaganza, she might not have noticed the wire at all. But she was hardly a casual observer. She had spent a good deal of time here in Sydenham in the last week, watching Ben's workers, talking to them.

She had learned a great deal about what was going to happen here tonight. Not the least of which was that Signor Francesco, the Italian daredevil Ben had hired for the occasion, was a man who must be absolutely, thoroughly, and entirely mad.

Her eyes followed the path of the wire from the top of the sixty-foot tower to the ground. No man in his right mind would do what Signor Francesco was about to attempt. And only a man with Ben's flamboyant imagination would have designed such an effect.

There would be a flurry of fireworks to begin with. Then Francesco would appear at the top of the tower. He would be dressed in a light-reflecting suit, Isabel knew. With fireworks going off all around him, his body would look as if it was molded from pure flame.

To be in the middle of a barrage of fireworks was bad enough, but what Ben had Signor Francesco doing next was unthinkable.

After some theatrics, some music, and a good deal many more fireworks, Signor Francesco, daredevil and madman, would slide down the wire to the ground.

It was a difficult stunt and, if the height of the tower and the breadth of the wire meant anything, dangerous as well.

It was also sure to cause a stir the likes of which even Ben's fountain at the Adelphi had not.

If it worked.

Isabel's smile grew and her heart skipped with excitement. It wouldn't work. She had devised a well-planned scheme that would embarrass—and certainly not harm—the good signor. But not nearly as much as it was sure to embarrass Ben. That, and a well-placed fifty pounds to one of Ben's crew had assured her of success. Poor Ben was about to be disappointed. Poor Signor Francesco was about to be disappointed.

But neither would be nearly as disappointed as the crowd was sure to be when the effect Ben was calling the Descent of Jupiter failed miserably.

"Ah, I wondered if I'd see you here." Isabel's pleasant thoughts were interrupted by Sir Digby Talbot, who bowed a greeting to Peter and tipped his hat to Isabel. Always the diplomat, Sir Digby had the good grace not to acknowledge the fact that the last time he'd seen her, Isabel had been wearing nothing but a pink costume that covered too little and showed too much.

"Have you taken a look at this?" Sir Digby waved a handbill in front of Isabel's nose. It was printed on mustard yellow paper and featured fat black letters that proclaimed

*The Descent of Jupiter*
*The Incredible Signor Francesco*

right above a drawing accented with lurid shades of red that showed a man flying high over the Crystal Palace, flames shooting from his back and arms. "If the performance is half as excellent as this picture . . ." Sir Digby sucked in a breath. "I say, it's bound to be a ripping show!"

Isabel's smile tightened. It would be a ripping show, indeed. Especially if the man to whom she'd paid fifty pounds to sabotage Signor Francesco's flight had not done his job.

The thought damped the edges of her excitement, and Isabel glanced at the Crystal Palace and at the last rays of the sun that were turning the glass structure to orange fire. It would be dark enough to begin the show soon, and she excused herself, ignoring Peter's questions at the same time she headed toward the building, her eyes searching for the slender wire and the block that had been put on it ten feet or so above the ground that would bring Signor Francesco's flight—and Ben's dreams of the Jubilee contract—to a screaming halt.

Ben's workmen knew her, and Isabel had no trouble at all making her way over to where they were getting ready for the show, carefully inserting the flame cases into their mortars. A man or two stopped long enough to tip his hat or nod a hello, and the fact that she heard them whispering behind her back about "that De Quincy woman and what she might want and why she was 'ere distractin' Mr. Costigan when he had such important work to do" did not concern her in the least. She knew Ben had to be busy with preparations for the show, just as she was before every production, and with any luck, she wouldn't see him or John, his assistant, or the incredible Signor Francesco at all.

But it seemed that wishing for luck and getting it were two different things.

There was a makeshift tent set up at the side of the building for use by the workmen, and Isabel rounded it and crashed full force into what looked to be a tall, broad, man-shaped looking glass.

Isabel lost her balance. She might have gone down in a heap if the man she knew must be Signor Francesco hadn't reacted so quickly. In an instant he had his arms around her to steady her. The breath rushed out of her lungs, and she felt herself lifted up off her feet. The next thing she knew, her hat was down around her eyes and it, and her nose, were pressed flat against Francesco's odd-feeling, strange-smelling, light-reflecting suit.

"Thank . . ." Isabel struggled for a breath. Signor Francesco's arms were tight around her, and she attempted to lift her head. "Thank you," she said. "I'm fine. Really. You may release me now."

But instead of releasing her, Francesco brought one

hand up to the back of her head and clasped her even closer.

"Signor!" Isabel squirmed in his iron grip. "I am quite all right now."

"*Si, Si,* Signor Francesco, he know this. He is so sorry!" Francesco's voice was a strange combination of Italian accent and garbled words. It was muffled, or perhaps it only sounded so because his hand cradled Isabel's head and his thumb was against her ear.

"But, signor . . ." Isabel managed to turn her head so that her cheek, instead of her nose, was against his chest. It didn't help much. Her hat, a newer creation from one of the finest French haberdashers on Oxford Street, was hopelessly crushed. The brim blinded her. "Signor, really, you do not need to hold me . . . so . . . tightly." Again she tried to squirm out of his arms, and again the only consequence of her action was that Francesco tightened his hold. One arm still clamped around her waist, he let his other hand drift over the tight knot of hair at the back of her head.

The action was simple enough, and brazen beyond belief, yet it had a curious effect on Isabel. Warmth heated her blood and she held her breath, bracing herself, but she wasn't sure if it was against the feeling, or against the likelihood that all too soon it might be over.

Whatever the feeling, Francesco felt it, too. She could tell as much from his sudden intake of breath and the subtle change in the pressure of his arms around her. He softened his hold at the same time he adjusted his stance so that one of his legs was tucked ever so slightly between hers.

Magic.

It was the only thing that could account for the numbness that gripped Isabel's limbs and dulled her mind. There must surely be magic in Signor Francesco's hands. Or perhaps the magic was contained in the malodorous suit. It was the only reason Isabel relaxed against him. The only thing that made her bold enough to skim her hands over his well-muscled chest.

A strangely familiar-feeling well-muscled chest.

This time when Isabel froze, it had nothing at all to do with magic. An impossible notion sprang up in her head, and suspicions streaked through her like rocket fire.

She glided her hands over Francesco's broad shoulders, and her suspicions grew. They were shoulders she had never been able to get out of her mind.

She trailed her hands over his chest, and her suspicions intensified. Her fingertips remembered every contour, every muscle.

In the skin-tight suit, every inch of the good signor's body was well defined, and looking past the flattened brim of her hat, Isabel glanced down. There were certain parts of a certain man she would never forget—no matter how much she tried—and Isabel's suspicions were confirmed.

Her hands still flat, she pushed away from the light-reflecting suit and the man she'd thought was the great Italian daredevil. "Signor Francesco, I presume?" She yanked her hat off and set it flying.

She'd been right about the suit, she thought, looking up and down at the man in the curious creation. It did show every inch of its wearer's body to best advantage. But right now every inch of its wearer's body was not what Isabel wanted to think about.

She forced her gaze up over the chest. And the shoulders. The suit included a close-fitting bonnet that completely covered his hair, but there was enough of the man's face showing.

Blue eyes blazed down at her.

"Damn! You weren't supposed to know it was me!" Just as quickly Ben recovered and gave her a bow as exaggerated as the Italian accent he slipped into. *"Si. Si.* It is I, Signor Francesco. You are looking for me, yes?"

"I am looking for you, no!" Isabel stepped back, out of reach of Ben's arms and downwind from the odd-smelling suit. "Why are you dressed like that?" she asked. "Where's the real Signor Francesco?"

"It is me. It is I." Ben placed both his hands to his heart in a very Continental gesture. Just as quickly a cocky smile lit his face. "You don't think I'd ask anyone else to perform this fool stunt, do you?" he asked. "I'll be lucky if I don't break my head open!"

"You're Signor Francesco?" Isabel looked at him in wonder. "You can't be!"

"You are surprised?" Again the accent. As heavy as it was spurious. In Isabel's hurry to get rid of her ruined hat, she'd loosened a curl over her right ear, and Ben wound it around his finger and tucked it behind her ear. "Ah, Bella, Bella." The name escaped him on the end of a long, soft breath. "You did not seem so reluctant to believe Signor Francesco when his arms, they were around you. You did not mind so much, I don't think. You maybe enjoyed the feel of his embrace, the heat of his touch." He moved a step closer. "The warmth of his body against yours."

Isabel swallowed hard. "I was light-headed. From bumping into you. That's the only thing that might explain—"

Her explanation was interrupted by Ben's gentle laugh. "Yes," he said, very much Ben Costigan again. "I was a bit light-headed myself. Otherwise I would never have dared to get so close. You might have taken my head off!"

"I'm surprised to hear you're sensible enough to realize it." There was a buzzing in her ears that Isabel could not account for, and she stepped back, away from Ben's disturbing nearness and the uncomfortable feeling that was growing somewhere between her heart and her stomach. She smoothed her skirt. "You can't be the great Italian daredevil," she told him. "It isn't possible. You're not going to—" Against her better judgment, she looked back over her shoulder toward the sixty-foot tower. "You're not going to go sliding down that thin little wire, are you?"

"Oh, you know about that, do you?" Ben didn't look upset or surprised. He nodded and crossed his arms over his chest. "I heard there was a woman hanging about this week, and I thought it might be you. Jealous?"

"Of you?" The idea was preposterous. Isabel clicked her tongue.

"Of my effect. Imagine it, Belle. Not one, not two, not even three, but twelve two-hundred-and-sixteen-caliber rockets!"

Isabel made a mental note to use sixteen large rockets in her next show. Quickly, she did some calculations. Two-hundred-and-sixteen-caliber. That would mean rockets approximately two and one sixteenth of an inch in diameter. Twelve and a half ounces of composition. A flight rate of—

"They'll blast off in quick succession," Ben continued, oblivious to the thoughts swirling through her head. "And rise to a height of two thousand feet in six seconds. Four bursts of red. Four more of green. And then the purple."

One word cut through Isabel's thoughts. "Purple?" Her throat went dry. The chemicals used to create purple fireworks were among the most dangerous and volatile. The very thought of Ben being so near them when their bursting charges went off made the small hairs on the back of her neck stand on end. Not that she was about to let him know it.

She turned away, disguising her uneasiness by glancing toward where the work crew was still busy with shells and mortars. "Don't tell me you were foolish enough to mix sulphide of copper with a chlorate. You know how unstable those compounds are. If you're up there on top of that tower with—"

Ben leaned over so that they were nose to nose. "Worried?"

Is that what the feeling down deep in the pit of her stomach was? Isabel considered the thought, then discarded it. She stared over Ben's left shoulder to where the sun was about to slip over the far horizon. "Of course I'm not worried. Not about you."

"Are you sure? It's a very long way up." One hand up to shield his eyes, he gave the tower an exaggerated look. "Something could go wrong with the wire, and I could come crashing down. It wasn't too many minutes ago that you showed you were more than interested in Signor Francesco's body. You wouldn't want to see it damaged, would you?"

"Hardly interested." She corrected him before the wrong ideas he already had could take further shape in his mind. "Light-headed. Remember?" Isabel turned away. "I care no more for Signor Francesco than I do for you."

"All right, then. If not damaged, what about incinerated?" He leaned over, his chin brushing her shoulder, his lips grazing her ear. "You wouldn't want to see me incinerated, would you?"

It was on the tip of Isabel's tongue to tell him it would be just retribution. It would offer some redress for the fact that the whisper of his lips against her ear was causing an odd, burning sensation all through her. She decided against mentioning it. "You might as well be incinerated now," she told him instead. "You will be sooner or later. Take my word for it, Ben Costigan, with your reputation you'll eventually burn in hell."

Ben threw back his head and laughed. "You know, Belle, you're so damned sure of yourself, I nearly believe you." He stepped around her, adjusting the close-fitting suit. "Heaven or hell, I'll find out soon enough." He, too, looked to where the sun had all but vanished, and for a second his expression sobered. A flicker of doubt darkened his eyes.

Isabel had no intention of responding to the look. She didn't even realize she had until she'd already taken a step toward him, and by then it was too late. Ben was too canny not to notice her impulsive move. And far too cocksure not to make something of it, if only she gave him the chance.

Before he could, Isabel stuck out her hand. "Then I shall say good-bye and get back to where Peter is waiting for me," she said. "I would say good luck, but of course you know I don't mean it."

Ben looked at her hand and, apparently deciding

she was not laying a trap, he shook it rather formally. "Of course. No more than I wish you luck with that extravaganza you're staging at Briarcliffe. It's war, Belle. War between us."

She gave him a frosty smile, a perfect reflection of the chill that settled in her stomach at his words. "It always has been."

"Always?" The question was as soft as the long shadows that spread their fingers between them and as painful as the ache of regret that stabbed Isabel's heart. "I remember a time or two— "

"I don't." She didn't want to hear it. She didn't want to remember. As quickly as she could, Isabel pulled her hand to her side. "But then, my memory was always better than yours."

"Your memory, yes, but your ability to tell believable lies leaves a great deal to be desired." Ben closed the distance between them. He raised one hand, ready to touch her cheek, and Isabel had the absurd notion that he was about to kiss her.

Panic churned through her. It mingled with the heat that spread through her blood, and fused with the lengthening shadow of the impossibly tall tower, and the smell of Ben's strange suit and the stunning thought that if he did—if he kissed her—she wasn't at all sure how she would respond.

It was fortunate, she decided, that she never had a chance to find out.

The evening air was ripped by the blast of a trumpet, and Ben straightened and backed away. "That's my cue," he said. "I need to get up to the tower."

There was nothing she could say. Isabel turned to walk away.

"Belle?"

At the sound of Ben's voice she whirled to find him watching her carefully.

"It's not the most idiotic thing I've ever done," he admitted with another look at the tower and a wry, all too engaging grin. "But it's close. I may be sacrificing my life for the sake of my art! The least you can do is kiss me good-bye."

"No." Isabel answered automatically, before she had the chance to say something she knew she would regret for the rest of her life. "You are being melodramatic, and besides, I can't imagine why you might want a kiss from me. You think me hardheaded and stubborn and far too outspoken."

"And difficult and ambitious and irritating, yes. But it would be a pity to have to stare death in the face without the taste of you on my lips."

He was surely teasing her. Isabel knew that as well as she knew her own name. He didn't mean a word of what he said about facing death. He didn't care if she allowed him to kiss her. He couldn't. Not anymore.

"You are ridiculous." She managed to sound flippant, but just barely. "The last thing you want from me is a kiss."

He had no choice but to agree. It was the only rational response.

But Isabel should have known better. If she said the sky was blue, Ben would certainly say it was green. If she said the atmosphere was suddenly so warm as to make breathing quite impossible, he would no doubt comment about how pleasant the evening had turned.

A smile slid from his mouth to his eyes. "No, the first thing I want from you is a kiss."

Honeyed words. And intentions that were just as treacherous. Isabel reminded herself of as much at the same time she pressed a hand to her heart, hoping to stop its surprising, crushing beat. "You'd best get to your tower, Signor Francesco," she told him. "The crowd is waiting."

Ben moved a step closer. His words brushed her lips. "And if I say let them wait?"

"You won't. Not even for me." The truth of her words settled inside Isabel and the heat in her veins evaporated. "Especially not for me. Sir Digby is here. The Jubilee contract is at stake. So is your reputation and your chance to make Costigan and Company respectable once again. I've learned my lesson, Ben. I know when you have to choose between me and fireworks, it's the fireworks that win every time."

"And you don't feel the same way?" Ben's expression was transformed by complete exasperation. His question boomed above the sound of a second trumpet blast. He backed away. "Damn it, Belle, don't make me out to be the villain. You were just as responsible for that fiasco we called a relationship as I was. And you are the one who left me waiting—"

"I? I never left you waiting. You left me waiting. To your tower, Signor Francesco, and I hope you are incinerated. You are an awful man! You're hardheaded and incorrigible and—"

"And difficult and ambitious and irritating, just like you." Ben walked away, shaking his head. "But you'd be heartbroken if I went up in flames with the rockets!"

"I certainly would not! I wouldn't care a fig!" Ben was too far away to hear her mumbled reply, but Isabel didn't care. She watched him wave and bow to the crowd. She watched him walk toward the tower, toward certain danger and very probable harm, and she listened as her own last words echoed all around her, louder even than the cheers.

And she knew down deep inside her where she kept the emotions she refused to bring out and examine in the light of day that Ben was right about one thing.

She was a terrible liar.

He deserved to be incinerated.

It was only fitting that he be burned to cinders, or dashed to the ground at the end of the wire, or trampled by the crowd when they learned that the Italian daredevil they had paid their hard-earned money to see was really an imposter.

It was the only just punishment for his stupidity.

Pivoting right and left, Ben waved to the crowd. *"Grazie. Grazie."* He smiled and bowed, all the while cursing himself. He had done some idiotic things in his life—this stunt was as fine an example as any—but none was more foolish than flirting with Isabel. Flirting with disaster. How could be have been such a dolt? How could be have been so asinine as to succumb to Isabel's dubious charms?

He'd asked her for a kiss!

Hell, if that wasn't enough to prove him a madman, nothing was. He'd been careless enough to let her know how eager he was to kiss her, and jackass enough to be disappointed when she'd refused.

For that he deserved more than incineration. He deserved a good, swift kick in the pants.

Biting off a string of profanities that would surely give him away as an Englishman, Ben made a great show of stopping at the main entrance to the Crystal Palace and gesturing with a flourish toward the tower.

The crowd responded just as he'd hoped. They cheered in approval. They yelled in encouragement. They applauded and waved and chanted his name, "Signor Francesco! Signor Francesco!"

With a final wave Ben went into the building. "Damned suit!" he tugged at the spot over his stomach where the light-reflecting suit squeezed his muscles. "Everything ready?" he asked John.

His assistant nodded. "Right as rain, guv!" He stepped aside and allowed Ben into the caged elevator that would whisk them to the top of the structure. "Only if you don't mind my sayin' so, you don't look nearly ready."

"Don't I?" Ben looked down at the ridiculous suit that covered him head to toe. "I'm as ready as I'll ever be."

"Not the suit I'm talkin' about." John rubbed one finger under his nose. "It's that De Quincy woman. Saw her talkin' to you. She ain't good for you, if you take my meanin'. There. I've said it straight out. I don't trust the woman."

"Not trust Isabel?" The very idea was preposterous. Ben laughed. "Of course we can trust Isabel. Just because she abandoned me the day of our—" It wasn't something he wanted to think about. Not now. With a twitch of his shoulders, Ben cast the thought aside and started again.

"Just because she tried to sabotage the fireworks fountain at the—" Something else he didn't want to think about. Ben shook the words away.

"Just because I managed to get the best of her at the Adelphi and humiliate her in front of half of London—"

The elevator jerked to a halt, and John opened the door. Ben stood stock still.

"You don't suppose she's the kind of woman who holds a grudge, do you?" he asked.

John had the good sense not to answer.

It didn't matter. Ben didn't need John's answer.

The thought of how spiteful Isabel might or might not be settled squarely in his stomach, right where the suit pinched. Isabel might be devious and conniving. She might be ambitious and uncompromising and even a little cunning, but she would never do anything to sabotage a show as intricate and dangerous as this.

Would she?

The moment Ben stepped out of the elevator and onto the roof, he knew it hardly mattered. Cheers rose around the tower like thunder. On all sides of him and down below, he could see that his workers already had their batons lit, ready to touch them to the hundreds of fuses on the hundreds of fireworks that would serve to etch his name in the annals of fireworks history in pure, bright flame.

All that remained was for Signor Francesco to stride out on the roof and begin his descent.

And if he didn't?

Ben glanced down at the sea of upturned faces. He wondered where in the crowd Isabel might be and what she was thinking and what she might be waiting to see happen.

And he knew that if he hesitated, she would win.

He drew in a long breath and marched forward,

signaling his crew, and while the crowd was distracted by the first maroon that went up and exploded overhead with an authoritative *bang,* he slipped into the harness he would ride all the way to the ground.

He was as ready as he would ever be.

The first fuses were lit, and Ben heard the *harrumph* of the shells coming out of their mortars. It was a sound he'd always liked, a small, comforting noise, rather like the purr of a cat. He knew better than to be fooled. Once the shells were catapulted into the air, the launching site trembled, quite enough to remind him of the forces involved in igniting small containers filled with combustible chemicals and gunpowder.

Acrid smoke filled the air, and the first of the shells broke directly above him. Ben threw out his arms and jumped up onto the platform that had been constructed atop the tower, waiting while John attached the harness to the wire.

"Ready, guv?" John screamed above the explosions and the explosive cheers of the crowd.

Ben's suit caught the red light. It reflected it back and damn, if he didn't look as if he was made of fire!

He was ready.

Exhilaration bubbled through Ben's veins, nearly muzzling the niggling voices of doubt and suspicion that filled his head.

Where was Isabel?

As if he might actually see her there, he glanced down at the crowd.

What was she doing? What was she waiting to see happen?

The green rockets burst overhead, and Ben poised himself on the edge of the platform, waiting for the purple rockets, his signal to propel himself out into the night where nothing would hold him up at all but the thin wire and his own ambitions.

Where was Isabel?

The sky above Ben lit with purple, and the question burst through his head.

What was she doing? What was she waiting to see happen?

It didn't matter now.

Ben hurtled down the wire, headed for the ground at breakneck speed. And even with the wind ripping at his face and the heat of the fireworks that were bursting all around him, all he could wonder was what might happen to him on the way down and if he would live to touch the earth again.

"Damn it, Isabel!" he yelled, and his voice trailed behind him like the flaming tails of the rockets that burst all around. "This was supposed to be fun!"

# Chapter 7

"Damn it, Isabel! You can't leave me hanging up here all night!"

"Can't I?" Isabel backed up a step, allowing herself a better look at Ben. The light-reflecting suit was working admirably. Ben's body was ablaze with the reflected colors of the fireworks that burst overhead. Blinding white. Flashing red. Blue and gold and purple. But even the glittering lights were not enough to distract from the fact that his Descent of Jupiter had been less than a success. Poor Jupiter had never made it all the way to the ground. He was hooked into a harness that enveloped his shoulders and hitched under his arms. And he was dangling . . .

She bit her lower lip and calculated the distance. Considering the fact that the stop on the wire was approximately ten feet above the ground. And figuring Ben's height into the equation. And the extra few inches added by the length of the harness . . .

He was dangling a little less than four feet above the ground, she decided. Not enough to put him in any real danger. Just enough to be embarrassing.

As she watched, Ben tried again to free himself. He kicked his feet and flailed his arms. It didn't do any good; he simply swung back and forth. It was not the result he'd wanted, and he made his opinion of the whole thing more than clear by letting out a long and heartfelt string of invective.

All to no avail.

He was well and truly stuck.

Isabel cupped one hand to her mouth and yelled to

him above the sounds of the fireworks that popped high above their heads. "You may have to stay there all night. Your crew is quite busy at the moment. I doubt they have time to rescue you."

"My crew." Ben's eyes flashed flame that had nothing to do with the fireworks or the light-reflecting suit. "When I find the man who cooperated with you on this little humbug, I'll blacken both his eyes, and then I'll sack him!"

Isabel shrugged. Rather nonchalantly, she thought. "No need," she said. "I've already hired him for my crew. You should pay your workers better, Ben. Then they wouldn't be so tempted to earn an extra fifty pounds."

"Fifty pounds? Damn!" Ben's voice was louder even than the noise around them. The crowd had been kept back a reasonable and safe distance from the mortars where the fireworks were launched, and Isabel glanced that way. She was more than pleased to see that most of them weren't watching the fireworks at all. They were staring at the unfortunate daredevil who was hanging before them like a trussed goose, swearing like a sailor.

"Careful, Signor Francesco," she warned, and wagged one finger for emphasis. "Your command of the language will surely give you away. You wouldn't want the audience to know you're an imposter, would you?"

"As if I care!" Ben tried one more kick and, obviously deciding it was getting him nowhere at all, he gave up the fight. Instead, he concentrated all his energies on Isabel. The scowl he sent her way might have intimidated a lesser woman. It cheered Isabel no end.

A smile on her lips and her head tipped, she strolled nearer, looking him up and down in that careful, critical sort of way one judged livestock at a country fair. "It's a good thing I didn't waste a kiss," she told him. "It seems you didn't die, after all."

"I might have." He was boastful to the end, and

Isabel shook her head, amazed but not at all surprised. "I might have been incinerated. Or worse."

"Really?" She circled him slowly, glancing up and down, and when she was directly behind him, he craned his neck and did his best to look around the harness and over his shoulder to see what she was doing.

Isabel pretended not to notice. She took her time, ticking off his attributes one by one.

Fine, long legs. She let her gaze slide from his foot in its light-reflecting boot up to his thigh. Muscular. And a backside . . .

She allowed herself to assess that portion of his anatomy and decided that in spite of its peculiar smell, the skin-tight suit did have some advantages. She might have continued with her musings for quite some time had not an especially loud bursting charge gone off. Isabel's bones rattled. She shifted her gaze from Ben to the shell that broke in an orange chrysanthemum pattern high over her head. Bits of burnt shell casings drifted down on her, and smoke collected near the ground and drifted all around like morning fog. She breathed in the familiar scent of the gunpowder and continued her perusal, coming back around Ben's left side and stopping directly in front of him.

It was not a bad angle from which to view a man in a skin-tight suit.

The thought might have caught Isabel by surprise, but there was no denying it. With Ben hanging the way he was, at just the right height and just the right tilt, it was indeed an interesting angle from which to assess him.

Hiding her thoughts behind a look of supreme concentration, Isabel tapped one finger against her lips. She knew Ben was looking down at her and that his look demanded attention, but she refused to shift her gaze.

"You don't look at all incinerated to me," she told him. "It seems as if everything is . . ." She glanced up, her eyes wide and as innocent as could be. "Everything seems to be right where it is supposed to be."

His eyes sparkled, and this time it wasn't with irritation. It might have been a reflection of the silver tourbillion that just then snaked through the sky. Or perhaps the look was caused by some emotion, one Isabel did not have the time to try to name.

"Ah, but is everything in working order?" Ben grinned down at her. "Perhaps," he suggested, "you should get closer and make sure."

"I would rather not, thank you." Isabel stepped back to emphasize the point and to hide the blush she was afraid had crept into her cheeks. "I do believe I will wish you a good night instead." She had designed her departure to be swift and sure. It might have been had not another firework burst overhead.

She recognized it immediately.

Nitrate of copper. Verdigris. Aluminium.

She knew the recipe by rote.

The right combination of chemicals and the proper bursting charge.

It was all so sterile. So technical. So precise.

And yet when those chemicals were mixed correctly . . . When they were ignited and burst from their flame cases . . .

Isabel let out a long sigh.

High above the Crystal Palace, green flame spread as if by magic, until the entire sky above them was its palette and the glass building the mirror that reflected its brilliance. The burn was soft around the edges, an ethereal color that intensified toward the center where the shell had burst. At the very heart of the firework, the color was the pure green of a jewel, bright and clear. It hovered in the air one second, two, three, before it swirled and spread, raining from the sky in curls of emerald mist.

Emerald Mist.

The words soured inside Isabel's head.

It was her recipe. Her firework. And she listened to the audience applaud and cheer and gasp at the sheer marvel of it, and she wondered if Ben had cheered as loudly four years ago when he'd managed to obtain the formula without the inconvenience of marrying Isabel.

The thought tempered the edges of her triumph, and when she looked at Ben again, she found that no matter how hard she tried, she couldn't manage a smile. "I do hope they rescue you by morning," she said. She wasn't at all sure she meant it, and the way she bit off the words told him as much. "It can get quite chilly here in Sydenham, I'm told, and if you freeze, well . . ." She made a gesture that relieved her of all responsibility as clearly as did the fact that she turned her back on Ben. "Even if there are certain parts of you that are in still working order, I doubt they would be after a good freeze."

"You could warm them for me!"

She refused to rise to the bait or acknowledge the way her heart drummed at the very thought.

"You could get me down off this damned thing," Ben called after her. "And I could get out of this damned stinking suit and for that matter, you could get out of that damned prim and proper gown of yours and—"

He tried his best to persuade her. Or perhaps unnerve her.

Isabel told herself it didn't matter which. There wasn't anything in the world that could make her change the way she felt about Ben.

She was still telling herself that as she walked away.

Funny, she'd always thought that triumph would feel more . . . well, triumphant.

Isabel chewed over the thought along with the piece of toast she was nibbling halfheartedly.

There was no doubt at all that last night had been a triumph. She had effectively destroyed Ben's Descent of Jupiter. She had embarrassed him in front of thousands of people, and if the look on Sir Digby Talbot's face as she passed him when she left the grounds meant anything, she had thrown a spanner into Ben's plans for whisking the Jubilee contract out from under her nose.

Yet she didn't feel triumphant, and the realization disturbed her because she didn't understand it. After all, she'd gotten exactly what she wanted. She'd foiled Ben Costigan. She'd paid him back for everything he'd ever done to her: The humiliation she'd suffered at the Adelphi. His theft of the Emerald Mist formula. The day he never arrived at the church for their wedding.

And for the inexplicable fact that in spite of it all, each time she saw him of late, her heart beat a little faster and every inch of her body tingled.

Alarmed by the very thought, and more than a little disgusted with herself, Isabel pushed away from the table. She had a good many preparations to make for Margaret and Richard's costume party extravaganza, and she decided in an instant that she would spend the day in the country. She would go to the factory where De Quincy and Sons fireworks were produced.

Striding into the passageway, she resolved to set out immediately and spend the day up to her elbows in oxidizer and coloring agent. She would help in the cutting room, where the chemicals were mixed and pounded into the dough that made the exploding stars. She would assist in the spiking room, where the stars were loaded into the cardboard breaks. Perhaps she might even spend an hour or two in the black powder house.

Yes.

Isabel smiled a smile completely lacking humor.

A great deal of good, black gunpowder. Exactly what she needed to smother her disquieting thoughts of Ben.

She was thinking about the timetables for the trains to Surrey when she rounded the corner and turned into the main foyer—just in time to see two strange men carrying a large floor clock out the front door.

"Hey! You there!" Isabel called out to them, but

the men didn't stop. They went right on with what they were doing, inching the bulky clock out of the house. After a moment she realized why they hadn't listened when she called to them. Simon was there as well. He was standing against the far wall, his hands in his pockets, clearly directing the operation.

"Simon, what are they doing?" Isabel hurried over to where her brother was hunched against the wall. She stabbed a finger over her shoulder toward the men and the clock. "That's Papa's clock. Where are they taking Papa's clock?"

"It isn't Papa's clock any longer." Simon refused to look at her. His eyes as flat as his voice, he watched the men, and when they were finally out the front door, he turned and walked into the morning room.

Isabel followed right behind.

"Of course it's Papa's clock," she said. She would recognize the clock anywhere. It was the mahogany one that had until now stood in the corner of the library. The clock that played the Westminster chimes every quarter of an hour. It had a broad brass face plate and fat cherubs that stood guard over it, one upon each of its four finials. "It was the clock Papa received as a gift from Mama when he was knighted," she reminded her brother. "It will always be Papa's clock. Simon, where are they taking it?"

He didn't answer but instead turned toward the windows and pushed the draperies aside. Isabel looked that way, too. She was just in time to see the two men clump down the front steps and load the clock into a lorry. They snapped closed the doors on the back of the cart and jumped into the driver's seat, and the bigger of the two men cracked the reins and called to his team. The horses started up and the lorry rumbled away down the street.

"Simon?" Isabel's voice was small and sounded, even to her, as if it was poised precariously on the edge of tears. She refused to let them fall, just as she refused to let her brother know that the fact that he was ignoring her was just as painful as seeing the clock carted away. "Simon, that was Papa's clock."

Simon's eyes wavered and darkened. He let go of the draperies, and they swung back into place. "It isn't Papa's anymore," he said, turning from the window. "It belongs to someone else now."

"You sold Papa's clock?" It was absurd. Impossible. So impossible that it didn't take Isabel long to figure the thing out. She dropped into the nearest chair. "Oh, Simon. You gambled it away!"

If the accusation did nothing else, it at least caught Simon's attention. For the first time he looked directly at her, and Isabel realized that he was no more pleased with the situation than she was. There were dark rings around Simon's eyes and his face was ashen, as if he'd been awake all night, worried and restless.

Isabel might have felt sorry for him, she might even have done her best to understand, if he hadn't tried to make excuses. He lifted his shoulders, the movement more defensive than it was indifferent. "Don't be ridiculous! I didn't exactly gamble the clock away. I know better than that. Who in their right mind would accept a clock as a wager? But I did need to borrow some money to get into last night's game. And when I lost . . ."

The rest of the story was all too clear. Isabel knew his explanation was bound to do nothing more than aggravate an already infuriating situation, and she waved it away with an impatient gesture. "You should know better, Simon. You have no better luck with cards than you do with women!"

It was cruel but true, and the accusation hit its mark. Simon bit his lower lip, holding in the indignity he must surely have felt. He could not so easily disguise the fact that his hands shook and that his chest rose and fell to a ragged rhythm.

Isabel's heart broke at the sight. "I'm sorry." She got up from the chair and went to him. "I didn't mean it that way, you know I didn't."

He turned away from her. "Of course you did. And why shouldn't you? It's true." He kept his back to her, but Isabel could not fail to notice that there were tears in his voice. When he was certain he could face her without losing his composure, he turned. "It wasn't my fault."

Isabel had expected as much from him. With one finger on each hand she massaged her temples, willing away the tension that had collected there. "It's never your fault," she told him. "There's always someone else who—"

The careful face he had put on his distress cracked, and Simon slapped one hand against the top of the nearest table. "I don't need to be lectured like a schoolboy!"

"Then perhaps you'd better stop acting like one." Isabel's words crackled through the air. "It's time you took responsibility for your actions, Simon."

"I am taking responsibility." His voice rose, matching hers. He raked a hand through his hair, leaving it standing on end. "Believe it or not, I'm being careful about who I borrow money from. It's easy enough to fall in with the wrong crowd, I can tell you that much. I've been careful about that, Belle. I am paying my debts, as any real gentleman would. And if that means we have to lose every stick of furniture in this house—"

Isabel grumbled in frustration, "The next thing you know, you'll be wagering the company."

As quickly as it came, Simon's anger ebbed. His eyes stilled. His face grew solemn. He reached out a hand and touched it briefly to Isabel's cheek. "That would hurt you very much, wouldn't it?"

She couldn't find the words to answer. She nodded instead.

"Yes," he went on, and the words were as heavy as if they were crowded in his throat. "I know it would, and you must believe me, Belle, I wouldn't hurt you for all the world. I just can't seem to keep myself from the gaming table, no matter how hard I try. I tell myself that the night will be my last. My last game of cards. My last go at baccarat. But the next night, and the next, and the next after that—"

"Shhh." Isabel could not help but be moved. She grabbed Simon's hand and held it tightly. "You don't need to explain. Not to me."

"But I do!" As if her fingers were on fire, Simon pulled his hand away. "We're in a terrible mess, you see, and—"

"And there's nothing we can't take care of. As long as we're honest with each other. As long as you tell me what's going on."

"What's going on?" With his hair standing on end and his eyes wide, Simon looked more than ever like a hare startled from the underbrush. "No." He shook his head and, still shaking it, he headed for the door. "I'll take care of it. I promise, Belle. I don't know what I'll do, but somehow I'll take care of it all."

"So, are you happy with Lola?"

"Happy? How could a man not be happy with Lola? She's beautiful and thank God, she's not too smart. She doesn't ask for nearly as much as some of the others of her ilk, and she is very, very accommodating."

It wasn't often that Edward Baconsfield rhapsodized about anything except pointless political causes, and listening to him, Ben laughed. He clapped his friend on the shoulder. "I'm glad she's treating you so well."

"Then you don't mind?" Edward asked the question, but didn't look certain that he wanted to know the truth. He held his breath and waited for Ben's answer.

Ben didn't hesitate to provide him with it. "Of course I don't mind. Why should I?"

Although Ben was accepted into polite society, he was, for all intents and purposes, a tradesman. Edward was not. He had relations who were powerful—though for the life of him, Ben could never remember who they were—and he had been educated at all the best schools. He knew enough to look discomfited, and

Ben might have thought less of him for it if he didn't know the look was genuine. "Naturally, I assumed that you and Lola were . . ." For all his sophistication, Edward was not nearly as open about his thoughts or his feelings as were the theater people Ben knew. When the subject was economics or social reform, he could wax poetic, but he still retained that aristocratic chill when it came to talking about anything as uncomfortable as emotions or as intimate as a friend's private life.

"Well, you know what I mean. Lola thinks the world of you, and I thought you two were—"

"No." Ben jumped in with his answer a little too quickly, but Edward had the good grace to pretend not to notice. "I have other things to chew upon this trip to London. Women are not on the menu. At least not until I've got that Jubilee contract in hand."

At least not women like Lola.

Ben might have had an easier time casting the thought aside if every muscle in his body didn't ache like the devil. He gritted his teeth, and when he saw that he'd put Edward's fears to rest, he smiled. "I should have introduced you and Lola a long time ago. I should have known she was the kind of woman who could keep you satisfied."

"Indeed!" Edward scratched one finger behind his ear. He was not, certainly, a man in love. For all his rhetoric about the equality of the classes, Edward was a gentleman and Lola was not the kind of woman that gentlemen fell in love with. But Edward was bewitched enough by the delightful Lola to have that slightly bovine look in his eyes that all men got when they were in the early throes of infatuation. He grinned a good deal and laughed when there wasn't anything funny, and if Ben wasn't careful, he knew Edward would soon be lecturing him about the importance of a little less work in his life and a lot more pleasure.

Pleasure in the form of a woman.

Edward grinned. "And what kind of woman would keep you satisfied, Ben?"

Ben snorted. "Not the one you're thinking of." It was too early in the morning for a drink, but he was tempted to pour one nonetheless. One for himself. One for Edward. At least it might change the subject.

But it would do nothing to cool the burn of anger in Ben's throat.

"In case you haven't heard, I was made the laughingstock of London last night. Thanks to the lady you're thinking of." He went as far as the other side of the room, then thought better of the idea and bypassed the whiskey bottle. He turned and leaned back against the marble and rosewood sideboard, absently rubbing the sore muscles in his left shoulder with his right hand. "The little minx tried to murder me!"

"And nearly succeeded, if the stories I've heard are true!" Edward laughed even though there wasn't anything funny about the situation.

"Like laundry on a clothesline." Ben tried to shake his head. He might have succeeded if the muscles in his neck weren't so sore. He winced and grumbled and shot Edward an acid look. "That's exactly what I looked like. Laundry on a clothesline. Hanging out there for all the world to see. And Isabel?" Ben snorted. It was getting to be a habit. "Isabel didn't give a damn. She went her way as fine as la-di-da while I hung there for the better part of an hour. I might have died!"

"Of embarrassment perhaps." Edward grinned. Again. "You have to admit, Ben, you brought it all on yourself. If you hadn't embarrassed her at the Adelphi—"

It was too much to think that Edward would actually believe such nonsense. Ben shot forward. "If she hadn't shown up at the Adelphi to sabotage my work, you mean. I'm not the one who started this thing."

But he had tried to continue it. He'd teased her. And tempted her. He'd tried his best to upend her by asking for a kiss.

Ben didn't mention any of that. It wasn't pertinent to the conversation. It wasn't anything Edward needed to know. And besides, Ben didn't want to think about it.

It had upended him as well.

Too uneasy to keep still, Ben did a turn around the room. His house in London was nothing like his home in Surrey near his factory, and he vowed that as soon as the business of the costume party was over, he would go to the country and spend some time away from the noise and dirt of the city. And his disturbing thoughts of Isabel.

He didn't mention that, either. There was no use mentioning anything sensible to a man who was a slave to amour as was Edward, especially when he had that cat-that-ate-the-canary look on his face and a bee in his bonnet to lecture.

"You have to admit it, Ben." Edward flopped onto the overstuffed divan and stuck his legs out in front of him. "Isabel earned what little revenge she got last evening. It was a subtle sort of vengeance. A clever thing for her to do."

"Yes. Clever." It was Ben's turn to grin. "But we both just agreed, we don't like clever women."

"No." Edward caught him in the lie. He poked his thumb at his chest. "I said I didn't like clever women. You . . ." He jabbed a finger toward Ben. "You never agreed."

"Or disagreed." Ben didn't like the feeling of being put on trial in his own home. He clumped to the windows and looked out on the fashionable traffic outside his Mayfair town house. "I do know that the sooner I have secured this Jubilee contract, the happier I'll be. Then perhaps Isabel will leave me alone."

"Is that what you really want?" There was a note of amusement in Edward's voice that made the hairs on the back of Ben's neck rise in protest. "I dare say Isabel could make a man happy." His elbows on his knees, Edward leaned forward and dangled the words like they were tempting worms and Ben the fish. "I seem to recall there was a time when she made you very happy, indeed."

"Ancient history." Ben discarded the theory with an impatient motion of one hand. "And you are misremembering, surely. I wasn't happy. I was—"

"Content?"

"Who could be content with a termagant such as Belle?"

"Satisfied, then."

"Hah!"

"Chipper? Energized? Optimistic?"

Edward's appraisal was not worthy of a comment, but that had never stopped Ben before. He was about to let his friend know what he thought of his theories when there was a tap on the door. After the requisite polite few seconds, the door snapped open and a servant stepped inside. "There is a man at the door, Mr. Costigan. Not a gentleman." With a decorous lift of his upper lip, the London servant Ben had hired for the season made it all too clear what he thought of the visitor's unfortunate state. "He says his name is Goodich, sir. Harry Goodich."

"Ah!" Ben's mood brightened immediately, not only because of Mr. Goodich's arrival but because it brought about a welcome end to Edward's badgering. He sent the servant to fetch Mr. Goodich and rubbed his hands together in anticipation. "Stay," he told Edward when he made a move to take his leave. "And see just how energized Isabel makes me feel."

The servant returned in less than a minute with Mr. Goodich in tow. Ben had met the fellow twice before, and he wasn't the least bit surprised that Goodich looked even more meek and mouselike here in Mayfair than he did in the Oxford Street tailor shop where he worked.

Goodich toed the doorway, hat in hands.

"Mr. Goodich!" Ben moved forward and, taking Goodich's arm, he showed him farther into the room. "You'll have a whiskey?"

Goodich was middle-aged, a small man with gray

eyes and hair of the same color. He had hands as delicate as a woman's, and it was that, Ben was sure, which made him so skillful with needle and thread, cloth and buttons. He ran his tongue over chalky lips. "Mighty early in the morning for that, sir," he said, but his gaze honed in instantly on the bottle on the sideboard.

"Never too early for friends to share a drink." Ben abandoned Harry Goodich in the middle of the room and went to fix him a drink. He splashed a generous swallow of liquor into the glass and handed it to the man. "Now . . ." He watched while Goodich drank it down. "Tell me. Do you finally have news?"

"That I do." Goodich nodded, and the twinkle in his eyes and the sudden color added to his cheeks by the liquor made him look like a gnome from a children's story. He pulled back his shoulders. "A musketeer, sir," he said, the pride of the accomplishment shining off every word. "That is my news for you. A musketeer."

It was an appealing notion, if somewhat romantic, and Ben turned it over in his head. A musketeer. It would play nicely into his plan. Nodding his approval of a job well done, he asked Goodich, "Can you duplicate the costume? Down to the last detail?"

"My eyes . . ." Goodich shook his head and sighed. "My eyes are not as good as they once were," he said, but he didn't seem to be having any trouble seeing the whiskey bottle from where he stood.

Ben poured another glass for the man and waited while he drank.

Goodich drank every last drop, and his confidence restored, his memory fortified, he smiled. "I do believe I can do it, sir." He looked Ben up and down. "You're taller than he is by a bit and broader in the chest, too, if I'm not mistaken. But with one of them great, droopy hats and a wig—"

"You can get those for me as well?"

"Oh, yes, sir." His spirits bolstered by Ben's obvious approval, not to mention the courage of the bottle,

Goodich beamed. "Same as for Lord Epworth. Down to the last detail. Only . . ." He cleared his throat and looked away, his sheepishness back now that he was forced to mention something so boorish as business. "It's a complicated costume, sir. Lots of leather and even some lace. It may take a bit more, if you see what I mean. More than we originally agreed."

Ben expected as much. He fished into his pocket and pulled out a five pound banknote. "Will this be enough to begin?"

Goodich's eyes lit. As if he was afraid Ben might change his mind, he pocketed the money quickly and moved toward the door. "You'll have it on time, sir. Just as I promised. In plenty of time for the costume party at the Duke of Fenshaw's. And when I get done with you, sir . . ." Goodich paused and grinned, as if picturing the finished product. "Your own mothers won't be able to tell one from the other."

"What was that all about?" Edward's eyes were puzzled as he watched Goodich leave. "Why was that man jabbering about musketeers? And what did he mean to say you'd have the same costume as Viscount Epworth? What would be the purpose of that?"

The answer to his questions was really quite simple. "Revenge," Ben said. "Only this time Isabel is the one who will be taught a lesson."

"I see a scheme forming behind that thick skull of yours, and I'm not at all sure I like it." Shaking his head in wonder, Edward hoisted himself out of his chair and headed for the door. "Whatever your plan, don't claim it's all for revenge, Ben. You obviously thought of it long before last night or you wouldn't have made Goodich's acquaintance. What are you really trying to accomplish?"

It was a question Ben was still asking himself after Edward was gone.

What was he trying to accomplish?

The question rattled through his head while he went over some paperwork, finished the pot of coffee he had a servant bring in, and prepared to go out to the Adelphi to check his fountain firework.

What was he trying to accomplish?

He was honest enough with himself to know that he'd told Edward the truth, or at least part of it.

Revenge. That was certainly one motivation.

But he was too honest to deny that there was more to it than that.

His desire to avenge the humiliation Isabel had put him through had nothing at all to do with the burr of excitement that tingled through him when he thought about his plan. He would dress in the same costume as Lord Epworth. He would invite Isabel to meet him is some secluded part of the house or, better still, some shady hollow where it would be difficult for her to recognize him.

He would find out exactly what the relationship was between Isabel and Peter. When they were to be married. How much she really loved him. He would find out all there was to know, and once and for all he would put his foolish imaginings about Isabel to rest. He would be a free man.

Free of the fantasies that tickled his thoughts at the most inconvenient times. Free of the disturbing dreams that haunted his nights.

Of course, he might make it easier on himself and just ask Isabel.

Ben discarded the thought as quickly as it came.

He might ask Isabel what her relationship was with Peter. He might inquire as to the nature of Peter's intentions. And ask about Isabel's feelings for the man.

But that might lead Isabel to think Ben cared, and that wasn't just preposterous, it was out of the question.

Besides, that wouldn't be nearly as much fun.

Satisfied both with himself and with his plan, Ben clapped his hat upon his head and started out for the Adelphi, and in spite of the fact that his intentions were as firm as his resolution, there was one other thought he couldn't seem to get out of his head.

Maybe he'd even be lucky enough to steal a kiss.

# Chapter 8

"That's the last of 'em." Tommy Eagan, the burly chief of Isabel's work crew, crouched over the mortar that had been sunk into one of Briarcliffe's many pastures and checked the shell inside it. He nodded, satisfied. "All set to go," he told Isabel. "All we need is blessed darkness and fine, clear skies."

Isabel glanced up. Above her head the sky was a perfect sapphire bowl with not a cloud to mar its surface. "It looks as if the clear skies will be no trouble at all. The darkness isn't up to us," she reminded Tommy with a smile. "Another two hours ought to do it."

"And in another two hours they'll be ready as well." Tommy looked across the field to where Ben's crew was finishing its setup work. He cleared his throat and spat a stream of tobacco juice on the ground. "They're a rowdy lot," he said and if the tone of his voice wasn't enough to let her know exactly what he thought of the crew of Costigan and Company, the look he shot their way certainly was. Tommy had been with De Quincy and Sons as long as Isabel could remember, and being an Irishman, he was not a man who kept his feelings or his opinions to himself. Especially his opinions about fireworks.

"Settin' up like they was on a Sunday picnic. Don't they know this is serious work?"

Isabel didn't answer him. All fireworks crews knew their work was serious. They had to or they wouldn't be alive to do it. Ben's was no different, she supposed.

She saw that they were being careful enough, even if they were a bit noisy.

As she watched, the two men who looked to be directing the setup work yelled to each other and waved to the rest of the crew. They gathered around the men, and for the first time Isabel noticed that there was something large and flat lying in the grass at the far end of the field.

"Lancework." She didn't need to tell Tommy. He knew the business as well as anyone. Lanceworks were frames made of cane and wood, and as Ben's crew hoisted theirs in the air and secured it all around, she saw that this one was no different from the rest. She knew it would be studded with the small, bright-burning fireworks called lances and that after the first one was lit, the others would catch one by one. From where she stood, she could get little sense of what the shape of the thing might be, but she knew that by the time all the lances were all burning, they would draw a picture in fire.

Isabel's lips thinned. "I wonder what he's up to."

"No matter. Won't be nearly good enough." Another jet of tobacco juice hit the ground. "We got our waterworks, don't forget."

Isabel hadn't forgotten. There was a reflecting lake to one side of Briarcliffe, and she and her crew had claimed it as theirs. They had already set up the gerbes and fountains that would float along its surface, and Isabel knew it would be quite a sight: fire and water and rippling reflections. If that wasn't enough to impress Sir Digby . . .

She dashed the thought away.

It would be enough, she told herself. It had to be. This was her last chance.

In the past weeks, the Jubilee committee had attended a show she'd mounted in Hyde Park and another that she had designed to honor the shah of Persia when he visited the court of St. James's. Neither show had been without its complications, and she shuddered at the very thought. The Hyde Park show had been ruined by an untimely rainstorm and an onslaught of peasoup fog. The other show . . .

At the memory Isabel's fingers curled into her palms. She tucked her thumbs around her fists.

Before the show for the shah of Persia, she'd seen a member of Ben's crew lurking about and had done everything in her power to make sure the man kept his distance.

Even that, it seemed, was not enough.

Somehow, Ben had gotten to one of her lanceworks. Somehow, he'd managed to tamper with the lances. On cue, the first lance was lit, and for a few moments everything worked like a dream. One by one the lances caught, and in less than a minute there was the image of the shah, outlined in dazzling fireworks. Just as Isabel had planned, the fire jumped to the lancework that had been constructed next to the shah's. There, too, the lances caught. There, too, they drew a blazing picture, this one of the Queen. The crowd cheered in approval.

And then their cheers turned to laughter.

Isabel squeezed her eyes shut. Even now the memory made her head spin and her stomach turn sour.

Her Majesty's image looked out over the crowd. It was regal. Majestic. Dignified. Just like the Queen herself.

Until it winked.

"Childish." It was exactly what she'd told Ben when she ran into him after the show. The same words she mumbled now. "Childish. And disrespectful. Imagine vandalizing an image of the Queen, rigging the lances so that they blinked off and on."

"What's that you say?" Tommy Eagan's voice snapped Isabel out of her thoughts. She turned from Ben's lancework to find him watching her.

"Nothing." She dismissed her thoughts and her behavior with a shake of her head. "Just wondering what the committee will think. It's the first time our work will be seen side by side, you know. Mine and Ben's."

"No worry there." Isabel had the feeling that had

she been a man, Tommy might have given her an encouraging thump on the shoulder. "You can dress up a tart like the Queen herself, but she's still a tart underneath. Same with them Costigans." He emphasized the point with another geyser of tobacco juice. "I just hope them splits you hired do their jobs and keep them Costigan lads away from my fireworks, 'cause if they don't, there'll be hell to pay."

Isabel followed Tommy's gaze over to where the private detectives she'd hired—the fellows Tommy called *splits*—were patrolling the perimeter, making sure that none of the fireworks were tampered with. Though they were dressed like her workers, in dark trousers and white shirts, it was obvious they weren't really a part of the team. Not one of them had lifted a finger to help in the setup, and Isabel knew it was just as well. As Tommy had so ably pointed out, working with fireworks wasn't a Sunday picnic. It was serious. And dangerous. To their credit, the detectives realized it and kept their distance.

"You'd best get a move on it." Tommy nodded once toward the house, another time at Isabel. "Can't go strolling into a costume party looking like that, can you, now?"

Isabel glanced down at her attire. She was dressed in a plain dark-colored dress with long sleeves and a high neck. It was a perfectly appropriate outfit for the head of a respected fireworks family. And a perfectly inappropriate one for a guest of the Duke and Duchess of Fenshaw at what was sure to be one of the highlights of the social season. She headed toward the house.

"I'll be back in time to shoot the show," she told Tommy. "No worry there."

"None at all." Tommy touched the bill of his cloth cap. "Only you be careful, missy, and avoid that Costigan fellow. I don't trust the lad as far as I could throw him."

"No." Isabel couldn't argue the statement. "Neither do I."

The realization still drumming through her head, she stopped to speak to each of the detectives, and when she was satisfied that nothing was amiss and not one member of Ben's crew had been anywhere near her fireworks, she checked with her own crew. She talked to the loaders who'd set the shells into their mortars and with the shooters who would be working with her to ignite the fuses. Satisfied everything was ready, she made her way toward the house.

*House* was hardly a sufficient word.

Though Richard and Margaret called Briarcliffe their country house, Isabel always thought the word far too cozy and not anywhere near adequate enough.

Briarcliffe was not so much a house as it was a small, self-contained country. The manor had no less than fifty rooms and was surrounded by its own chapel, extensive stables, a gas house that provided the fuel for lighting, and glorious gardens, all of it arrayed like jewels in a splendid setting of three thousand acres. The house itself was one of those Gothic atrocities of heavy stone and square, stoic windows, but Isabel forgave Margaret for it. After all, it was a family seat, and Margaret could do only so much to change a house that had stood the test of four hundred years' time. She had added her own touches and made it as homey as possible, and for that Isabel was thankful. The room she was using for the night—and for the weekend if Margaret had her way and talked Isabel into staying—was luxurious and comfortable, and Isabel hurried up to it and, with the help of Margaret's own lady's maid, changed into her costume for the ball.

"Pardon my saying it, Miss De Quincy, as I know it is not my place or any of my business, but . . ." Margaret's maid looked Isabel up and down. "You do look fine!"

"Thank you, Anne." Isabel stepped back and took a long look at herself in the full-length mirror. Her dress was a classic style from a hundred years earlier, a sumptuous concoction of brocade and silk in a delicate blue that perfectly matched her eyes. The gown was nipped in close at her waist and held out by *paniers,* hoops that made it look enormously wide at the hem and made Isabel wonder how she would ever get through Briarcliffe's doors. The huge overskirt opened in the middle to reveal another skirt beneath, white silk printed with sprigs of delicate blue flowers.

The dress was cut low over Isabel's bosom, its bodice adorned with row after row of lace and silk ribbons. They matched the bows on the elbow-length sleeves and the simple blue bow tied around Isabel's throat. The dress was delightful, and to go with it, Anne had piled Isabel's hair high and powdered it carefully. Even as Isabel watched, she added a finishing touch, a garland of blue and white flowers that she carefully pinned at the back of Isabel's head.

It was altogether charming, if Isabel did say so herself, and she thanked Anne and started for the door. Before she got there, someone knocked, and Anne hurried to open it.

"A note for you, Miss De Quincy." The maid handed her an envelope and left the room.

Curious, Isabel ripped open the envelope. Inside it was a single piece of paper marked with the Thorlinson family's coat of arms. *"Darling,"* the note said. *"How tedious to have to share you with the rest of the company! Can't wait to see you alone. Meet me in the conservatory at eight o'clock."* It was signed, *"Peter."*

Isabel found herself smiling. How typical of Peter to be so considerate. And so flattering. She folded the note and made to place it in the bosom of her dress, then thought better of the idea. Since the day she had retrieved the recipe for Diamond Rain from the safe at the offices of De Quincy and Sons, she'd kept it in a tiny silk pouch tucked into the front of her corset. There was no room for Peter's note, and besides, she didn't need to remind herself of its contents. She set it down on the bed and left the room. "The conservatory at eight," she reminded herself, and headed down to the party.

The ballroom at Briarcliffe was as impressive as the rest of the place. By the time Isabel got there, it was ablaze with color and light. The music had already started, and she stood at the top of the wide, shallow steps that led down to the dance floor and watched couples swirl by to the strains of a Strauss waltz. There were harlequins and Turkish sultans, maidens who looked as if they'd just stepped out of fairy tales and even a Chinese emperor or two. Margaret was dressed as Elizabeth I to Richard's Henry VIII, and Isabel complimented them both, and offered her regards to Hilda, the dowager duchess, Richard and Peter's mother. She made small talk with Hilda, all the while remembering what Margaret had said about the woman earlier: "She won't be in costume. She doesn't need one. She's already a dragon."

Margaret was right. Hilda was civil, and as cold as an iceberg, and Isabel was polite in return, but as soon as she could, she made an excuse to leave. She was already on her way down the steps when she heard a burst of hearty laughter from the front door.

She didn't need to turn around and look to know who'd arrived.

A quick retreat was totally out of the question. It would be rude and altogether too obvious. Isabel stood her ground, and when Ben came into view, she realized she couldn't have left if she wanted to. She was too stunned to move.

While the rest of the crowd had selected costumes that were as aristocratic as the titles many of them held, Ben had chosen something less blue-blooded and far simpler. He looked like one of the pictures Isabel had seen in magazines and on the covers of the penny dreadful novels sold at the stationers'.

Only pictures didn't do the outfit any justice at all.

And Ben certainly did.

Isabel snapped open the blue and white silk fan she carried in one hand and waved it in front of her face, watching as Ben greeted his host and hostess and even managed to charm Hilda into a smile. If they were surprised by his singular choice of a costume, they were all too well bred to make it known, but even Margaret could not disguise the fact that, not once but twice, she allowed her gaze to run the length of Ben's body and both times she caught her breath.

Isabel could well understand why.

Ben was dressed in well-worn dungarees that, like the light-reflecting suit he'd worn at the Crystal Palace, clung to every inch of his long, muscular legs. The trousers were a soft blue color that was faded over the knees. They were slung low over his hips and hugged his backside.

Alarmed that someone might notice her interest in that portion of his anatomy, Isabel forced her gaze up to Ben's red and black plaid shirt and found that it was unbuttoned at the neck to expose an intriguing V of bare flesh. Not that she cared. She barely remembered the hard, flat planes of Ben's body, she reminded herself. No more than she remembered the intriguing feel of his muscled flesh beneath her fingertips, or the soft brush of the sprinkling of honey-colored hairs that dusted his chest and arrowed down over his abdomen.

And if she did remember, it wouldn't have mattered one bit. Or so she told herself. The sight wouldn't have affected her any more than did the realization that Ben's shirtsleeves were rolled to his elbows, displaying his powerful forearms. The outfit was made complete by the addition of pointed-tipped boots and a Stetson hat that was so old and dusty, it looked for all the world as if Ben had just come in from riding the range.

It was an authentic costume, right enough, and it made Isabel wonder if real cowboys in the American West ever got any work done, or if they were so busy being ogled by the women who lived there that work was the furthest thing from their minds.

It was, at the moment, the furthest thing from Isabel's mind. So was rational thought. Had she been thinking logically, she would have registered the fact that Ben was done greeting his host and hostess and he was headed her way.

"Howdy, Miss De Quincy." It wasn't a bad imitation of an American accent, though it sounded more like it belonged in a music hall than in the Duke of Fenshaw's ballroom. With a flick of his thumb Ben tipped back his hat. He turned a smile on Isabel.

"Howdy, indeed." She clicked her tongue. "Where on earth did you get that costume?"

"Like it?" Ben hooked his thumbs in the pockets of his trousers and rocked back on his heels. "Got it up at the general store."

"Really!" When Ben took a step closer, Isabel took a step back. "I hope you don't smell as much like a cowboy as you look."

Ben laughed. He took another step forward and raised his eyebrows in a silent challenge. "Dance with me and find out."

He was teasing. He didn't really want to dance with her. He couldn't. He cared no more for her than she did for him. Realizing it was the only thing that kept Isabel from running away as fast as she could. "By the time I agree to dance with you, it will be too late. If you smell like cows—"

"He doesn't!" Margaret stepped forward and sniffed the air, as if confirming her suspicions. "You have no excuse at all, Belle. You have to dance with him."

Isabel sent her friend a withering look. One Margaret firmly ignored.

Ben noticed the exchange, and it only made him bolder. "See? As sweet as a rose!" He snatched up one of her hands, and though the smile he gave her was meant for everyone to see, the words he murmured were for her ears alone. "Dance with me, Bella."

It was impossible for Isabel to say no. People were watching.

Her host and her hostess were watching. The dowager duchess was watching. Even Sir Digby, dapper as always in the garb of an Arabian chieftain, was watching from across the room.

It would be cheeky to refuse. An insult to Richard and Margaret. It would signal to the world that Ben could topple even the firmest of Isabel's resolutions, and she refused to do that. She refused to let anyone know that he had a way of taking her thoughts and turning them upside down. Especially Ben.

Isabel had no choice but to allow him to lead her to the dance floor.

As if he knew all along that she would surrender, Ben acknowledged his victory with a wry smile, and his fingers tightened over hers. A shock of awareness traveled through Isabel, and she braced herself against it. It was not so easy to steady herself against the feel of Ben's hand when he flattened it against the small of her back, or the odd, prickly sensations caused by the fact that his body was only inches from hers.

They fell into the rhythm of the waltz, their feet moving in an easy harmony that belied the look Isabel shot Ben's way.

His only defense was a merry laugh. "Admit it, Belle, this isn't so bad. We always were the perfect dance partners."

At least he wasn't trying to sound like a cowboy any longer. Isabel would give him that much. "Yes. But the way I remember it, the dance floor was the only place we ever got along."

"Was it?" He looked down at her, his eyes sparking a memory inside Isabel that caused heat to race up her neck and spread into her cheeks.

Ben was a lot of things. He was generous to a fault, and he could be civil when the spirit moved him. He was an astute businessman and a clever fireworks technician. He had even been known to be brilliant. What he was not was graceful in victory.

He must surely have seen the blush that betrayed her, and he wasn't about to let it pass without pressing his advantage. He let his gaze drift over her, from the top of her head to the china-blue bow at her throat, from the blue bow down to where her gown was cut square and very low over her bosom. For the space of a dozen heartbeats he kept his gaze there, and she saw his chest rise and fall and felt the nearly imperceptible tightening of his hand against her waist.

"The way I remember it . . ." He let his gaze glide up again, until he was looking into her eyes, watching for any flicker of emotion that would bare her soul to him. "There were a few other places we got along quite well. I could itemize them for you if you need the reminder."

"That won't be necessary." Fighting to hold on to her composure, Isabel looked over Ben's shoulder. They swung around the perimeter of the dance floor, and in a whirl Isabel saw Simon, who was dressed as a medieval knight, talking to Edward Baconsfield in the clothes of a Russian czar. At another turn, she saw Margaret at the top of the stairs talking to Peter. He looked elegant in his musketeer costume, and he was enough of a gentleman to offer Isabel a tiny wave as they whirled by. There was something about Peter's stolid good sense that made her feel more levelheaded, more in control. Some calm that counteracted Ben's intensity. Some balance that offset the capricious way her heart beat when Ben was anywhere near, and the way she fought to catch her breath, even when they weren't dancing.

"There's no use arguing with you," she said, switching her gaze back to Ben. "If I say I don't remember, you're certain to tell me I'm wrong. And if I tell you I do remember—"

"You will, for all intents and purposes, be admitting that you've never been able to forget me."

It wasn't what Ben said, it was the self-satisfied way he said it. Isabel gave him her most long-suffering look. "It isn't as if I haven't tried."

Ben chuckled. "As hard as I've tried to forget you, I dare say. It's a damned awkward situation, Belle. You must admit that much. I lie in bed at night and I think about what you're doing and who you might be with." His own gaze traveled briefly to Peter. "I wake in the morning and wonder what it would be like to find you there beside me." Emotion flickered through his eyes, but it was impossible for Isabel to tell whether it was passion or exasperation. She thought it must surely be the latter, especially when Ben sighed. "Do you suppose we were ever in love?" he asked.

It was not something Isabel liked to think about. She dismissed the question with a shake of her powdered head. "You haven't honestly been wasting your time thinking about that, have you?"

"Oh, yes." Ben agreed readily enough, and he didn't seem the least bit embarrassed by the admission. They whirled to the far side of the ballroom, and the light there must have been less dazzling. His eyes darkened to the color of the evening sky. "I think about it a good deal of the time. I wonder what would have happened had we gone through with it. Had you ever shown up at the church for our wedding."

"Had I shown up at the church for our wedding," she reminded him, "I would have found myself quite alone."

Ben's lips thinned. "And had I bothered to show up—"

"Two wrongs hardly make a right." Isabel's voice rose. "You are the one—"

"I am certainly not. You are the one who—"

It might have been the whirl of light and color that surrounded them, or the realization that they were dancing in the midst of sultans and carnival clowns. It might have been the heady feeling of being whisked around the dance floor in the crook of Ben's arm, or the fact that the night was young and promised to be filled with the exhilaration and glamour of fireworks.

Whatever the reason, Isabel could not keep herself from bursting into laughter. "You see? Now you know exactly what it would have been like had we married. We would have murdered each other for certain!"

Ben chuckled, his intensity disappearing beneath an

onslaught of good humor. "You're right, of course," he said. "Fireworks at twenty paces! You'd shoot me with a rocket, and I'd retaliate with my best shell."

"Flights of rockets, Katherine wheels, suns and stars and golden streamers!"

"And fiery serpents chasing each other across the night sky." Ben's laughter stilled and the smile fled his face. "It's not a pretty picture, is it?"

No, not when he put it that way. But there had been a time when Isabel thought it would be. A time when every minute with Ben was giddy and electrifying. A time when she dreamed of spending the rest of her life with him.

Her smile vanished along with his, and a hollow feeling she feared was regret established itself firmly where only moments ago she had felt her heart race at his every word.

As amazing as it seemed, Ben must have been feeling all the same things. Or at least he was enough of an actor to pretend it. He caught her gaze and held it, his eyes dark with longing. "Do you love Peter?" he asked.

"Love him?" It was a foolish question, surely, yet the moment Ben asked it, Isabel realized she didn't know the answer. She slid her gaze over his shoulder and searched the ballroom, but Peter was nowhere in sight and she felt suddenly like those acrobats she'd seen swing from their trapezes with no net below to catch them should they fall.

For a full minute Ben waited for her answer. Or perhaps it was longer. Too busy with her own thoughts, Isabel wasn't sure. She might never have responded at all had he not looked down at her, his eyebrows raised. "Well, he did ask you to marry him."

"He never had the chance." Isabel dared him to contradict her. "As you may recall, you interrupted us."

"I would say you owe me a debt of gratitude."

"You would."

"And you would not agree." It was more of a question than a statement, but it was obviously a question Ben was reluctant to ask. He let his words trail away, hoping, perhaps, that she would elaborate, and when she didn't, he looked at her expectantly. It must surely have been Isabel's imagination. She could have sworn that Ben looked relieved. "Then you're not going to marry him?"

"I didn't say that." Isabel was no more sure of her own reaction to the news than she was of Ben's. "I said he hadn't asked. We've both been quite busy. He hasn't had another opportunity. As a matter of fact—" Suddenly, the reasons for Peter's carefully planned tryst at eight o'clock became all too clear. She looked over at the clock that stood in one corner of the room and realized it was nearly eight o'clock. She had an appointment to meet Peter in the conservatory.

It was just the right time for the music to end, and that is exactly what happened. Ben guided Isabel through the last figures of the dance, then stepped back and bowed. Her glance at the clock had not escaped him.

"I see you have other places to go," he said. "So I won't detain you. I'll let you be on your way. Only, Marie Antoinette . . ." The emotion that pulsed through his voice caused Isabel to stop just as she was about to walk away. Ben reached one hand toward the ribbon at her throat. His fingers strayed to the bow, ruffling it. "Don't lose your head," he said, and gave her a wink.

This time she didn't hesitate to answer him. She looked him in the eye and if nothing else, her expression told him she'd learned a thing or two in the last four years. And she wasn't about to forget any of it. "Better my head than my heart," she told him.

Ben's only reply was a laugh. Still chuckling, he moved away, and Isabel set out for her meeting with Peter.

She was very much surprised to find him in the passageway outside the billiard room, speeding toward the front hall, precisely the opposite direction from the conservatory.

"Am I so late or so early?" she asked him.

Peter looked at her in wonder.

Isabel shook her head. It seemed that even the most dependable of men could be absentminded at times. "The conservatory? Eight o'clock?"

Her reminder was met with an expression as blank as any Isabel had ever seen.

Isabel's stomach went cold. Her skin prickled, but this time it didn't prickle with anticipation the way it did as she danced with Ben. It prickled with suspicion.

The stationery with the family crest. The reasonable facsimile of Peter's writing. She looked beyond the sweeping hat and long, curled wig Peter wore, searching his face for the truth.

"You didn't send me a note, did you? You didn't ask me to meet you in the conservatory at eight."

It was clear Peter didn't quite know how to respond. "Well, I wish I would have," he said. "It's a jolly fine idea. But . . ." He looked in the direction of the conservatory, then back toward the ballroom. But though he may have been torn, there was no question which choice he would make. With Peter, duty would always win out over temptation. "I really must help Mama. She's quite put out about the fact that the quail eggs have not been served on the buffet yet." He didn't wait for an explanation, or for Isabel's reply. His mind clearly more occupied with quail eggs than it was with romance, Peter hurried away.

And left Isabel very thoughtful indeed.

She was still deep in thought when she heard a voice she recognized as Edward Baconsfield's echo from the other end of the passageway.

". . . fool her this time, and that's for certain."

Isabel darted into the empty billiard room just as Edward came past. He was deep in conversation with a tall man in a musketeer costume, and for a moment Isabel thought it was Peter. Until she saw the man's blue eyes.

Her own eyes narrowed, her mind working over the curious turn of events, Isabel peeked around the half-closed door and took a good long look.

When she'd seen Ben only a few minutes ago, he was a Wild West cowboy. Now he was a musketeer. A very familiar-looking musketeer.

Ben's knee-high leather boots were the same as Peter's. Ben's baggy breeches were the same as Peter's. So was the long scarlet tunic that he wore over a white shirt with flowing sleeves. And his large, floppy hat. He even had a wig that looked for all the world to be a twin of Peter's. It was dark and full of curls, and it cascaded over Ben's shoulders.

Surely what Isabel was thinking was impossible! She was being fanciful, she told herself. She was being absurd. No one was that audacious. Not even Ben. Even he wasn't brazen enough to pass himself off as another man, or cocky enough to take advantage of a woman who was unaware of the switch.

But of course she knew he was.

Torn between indignation and disbelief, vacillating between keeping herself hidden and confronting Ben, Isabel watched the men say their good-byes. Edward ambled into the card room across the passageway. And Ben proceeded toward the conservatory.

The pieces to the puzzle fell into place, and Isabel's mouth dropped open.

Just as quickly a slow smile lit her face and a deliciously wicked plan formed in her mind. Isabel checked the mirror that hung to one side of the room. She ran a hand over her head, smoothing every last hair into place. She tugged the sleeves of her gown lower, exposing the sweep of her shoulders. She adjusted the ribbons at her bodice, loosening the one at the top, baring even more of her bosom.

She drew in a deep breath, lifted her chin, and headed for the conservatory, as ready as she would ever be to give the devil his due.

# Chapter 9

"Damn!" Ben grumbled and brushed a curl of dark hair away from his face. He scrubbed one finger under his nose. Whatever this bloody wig was made of, it was making his nose itch, and he cursed Lord Epworth for choosing such a ludicrous costume and himself for being curious enough about Isabel's relationship with Epworth to wear a replica of the damned thing in public.

Not that his plan wasn't brilliant. And foolproof. It was just that sometimes great art required great sacrifices. And this—he sneezed—was one of them.

He was tempted to let loose with another oath, and he might have done just that if the door hadn't opened. Isabel stepped inside the tile-floored conservatory and carefully closed the door behind her.

From where he stood in a shadowy alcove, Ben was to Isabel's left and roughly thirty feet from the door, and he could see, but not be seen. For a moment he simply watched. The light was not completely gone from the evening sky, and it seeped through the glass walls and ceiling that surrounded them, infusing everything with a glow that reminded him of the pink begonias that grew in profusion in pots all around his feet.

It was a dainty color, soft at the same time it was mysterious, and it heightened the flush of excitement that colored Isabel's cheeks and washed over her neck and the shelf of her bosom where it showed above her low-cut dress.

And what a dress it was!

In spite of the fact that the gown was old-fashioned

and that its absurdly wide skirt made it impractical as well, Ben found himself nodding in approval. The ladies of a hundred years earlier may have hidden the true shape of their hips beneath their immense skirts, but they more than made up for the blunder by baring a good deal of shoulder and bosom. Thank goodness, Isabel had not chosen demureness over authenticity.

If she had, Ben was certain that watching her would not be nearly so agreeable.

As if reading his thoughts, Isabel bent at the waist and looked to her right and left, and Ben had an even better view. Enjoying the brush of soft pink light against flesh he knew to be softer still should have been enough to occupy both body and mind. But try as he might, Ben found that he could not get one disturbing thought out of his head.

He wondered that as he twirled Isabel around the dance floor, he had not noticed that so much of her was so delightfully exposed.

It wasn't as if he hadn't tried. The enticing dress fairly invited a man to take a second look, and a third, and Ben was nothing if not a man who took advantage of his opportunities. But though he clearly remembered the sparkle of Isabel's eyes in the glow of the crystal chandeliers, and the ring of her laugh, and the delectable feel of her in his arms, he couldn't for the life of him remember her shoulders being so blatantly bared.

It was a riddle. One nearly as puzzling as the fact that though he had certainly noticed the hint of her breasts above her low-cut bodice, he hadn't taken note of just how much they showed above the confection of blue ribbons.

He must surely be a blind man or, worse, a complete fool. He must surely be losing his flair with the ladies and his appreciation for real beauty.

For that is how Isabel looked. She didn't look like some long-dead queen. She looked like a dream. Like a vision. Like every man's secret fantasy.

Ben drew in a deep breath. But whether it was to still the sudden pounding of his heart or to encourage it to keep right on pounding away and fuel the hot rush of blood within his veins, even he wasn't sure.

It didn't help matters to realize that he wasn't the only one breathing hard. The closer Isabel got, the easier it was to tell that her breaths were coming in small, short gasps. Her cheeks were flushed. Her eyes were wide. There was no question that she was excited, and after Ben thought about it another moment or two, he realized there was no question what she was excited about.

Isabel was excited about her rendezvous with Epworth.

The thought caught Ben off guard, and he sucked in a breath, this time to cushion what felt like a blow to his gut. He stepped back, an instinctive response to both Isabel closing in on the little alcove and to emotions he didn't even want to begin to explore.

The distance didn't help. As much as he warned himself to shift his gaze, he could not. He stood mesmerized, watching the way Isabel's lips were parted with what could only be interpreted as desire. He let his gaze drift over her, and he realized with a start that of course he would have noticed if Isabel had been in such a charming state on the dance floor. He would have noticed it the moment he walked in the door and, like a magnet, his eyes found hers.

It seemed his riddle was no riddle at all. The answer was as simple as simple could be, and as plain as the inexplicable twinge of disappointment that stabbed his insides.

This charming display was for Epworth to see and appreciate. Epworth and Epworth alone.

Ben narrowed his eyes and watched Isabel draw nearer, and he shook his head in amazement. "Lord Epworth," he grumbled. "You lucky devil, you."

He couldn't say if Isabel heard him, or if she saw some movement in the shadows where he stood, but she had some indication he was there. She smiled and headed straight for the alcove, raising her skirts above her ankles so that she might move more quickly.

At the last moment Ben remembered himself. He

tugged his floppy hat farther down on his head, arranged his wig so that it concealed a portion of his face, and stepped deep into the shadows created by the lush vegetation that surrounded him.

"Peter? Is that you?" Isabel's voice was as musical as the murmur of the fountain that bubbled away somewhere to Ben's left, beyond the sheltering pots of ferns and flowers. She peeked into the opening of the bower, and when she saw him, her face split with a smile. Holding her wide skirt close against her body, she slipped into the alcove, rushed toward Ben, and threw her arms around him.

It was the kind of moment men dream of, or at least the kind Ben had always fantasized about. A romantic evening. A secluded setting. A beautiful woman whose inhibitions were as unbridled as her passions.

He might actually have been enjoying himself if the impact of Isabel's enthusiastic embrace hadn't knocked him against the waist-high pot of rubber trees behind him and pushed both his hat and his wig farther back on his head. Ben steadied himself. With a grunt he tugged the hat and wig back into place, and automatically his arms went around Isabel.

"Oh, Peter!" Isabel's voice was breathy. Her words tumbled out, eager and excited. She tipped back her head at the same time she nuzzled closer and squeezed her eyes shut. "Don't wait. Not another moment, darling. Kiss me!"

Ben wasn't sure exactly what he had been expecting. But whatever it was, it wasn't this. He stared at her, more than a little taken aback. His gaze drifted from the sweet pout of her lips to the pastel glow of her skin in the muted light. He stared at the ribbon that caressed her throat and at the soft mounds of her breasts where they were crushed against his chest.

Great art demanded great sacrifice.

The words pounded through Ben's head in much the same way as desire suddenly pulsed through other, far more sensitive portions of his anatomy. Deception was apparently as much an art form as anything else, and this time it looked as if he might have to sacrifice all if he was to have any hope of keeping up his masquerade.

Resigned to his fate, Ben tightened his arms around Isabel's waist and lowered his mouth to hers.

It was not a perfect kiss. Not as kisses go. The damned wig had been knocked more askew than Ben realized, and strands of it stuck to his lips and tickled his nose. It was enough to ruin any man's concentration. Or it might have been, if Isabel had not been so very delicious.

Ben tightened one hand around her waist while with the other he yanked the hat and wig into a more agreeable position. Satisfied, he deepened the kiss.

Isabel's lips were as warm as he remembered them. They were as soft as when last he kissed her. The heady scent of her perfume combined with the musky smell of damp soil that hung in the air and the exotic fragrance of the flowers that grew all around. The aromas mingled together. They filled Ben's nose and sent his head into a spin that robbed him of his reason at the same time it made him feel more daring than ever. He touched his tongue to Isabel's mouth.

As if the feeling were fire, Isabel started and scurried out of his arms. She scrambled backward and collided with a pot of begonias. Steadying herself, one hand back against a tall pot of what looked to be orchids, she pressed her other hand to her heart.

"Peter!" Isabel swallowed a huge gulp of air. She blinked rapidly, and Ben watched her fight to calm the erratic breaths that were the echo of his own.

She couldn't have been surprised by the kiss. She was the one who'd initiated it. But she was surprised by something. There was no doubt of that. Perhaps it was the skill of Ben's touch, or the taste of his mouth on hers. Perhaps she was surprised by the sudden, startling passion that had engulfed them both.

It was an interesting thought, and it caused Ben's

smile to widen. Suddenly, he found himself standing a little straighter and taller.

It was just possible that Epworth wasn't a man to be envied.

Though it was certainly mean-spirited, the thought appealed to Ben.

Perhaps Lord Epworth wasn't much of a kisser, not much of a lover at all. Perhaps Epworth was a man who should be pitied.

Though he was at a loss to explain exactly why, the theory left Ben feeling uncommonly pleased. Eager to test the accuracy of his hypothesis, he stepped forward.

The movement was enough to snap Isabel out of her momentary shock. She lifted her hand from her heart and placed it on Ben's chest. The touch was intimate enough to send a shock wave through him, and firm enough to keep him at a distance.

A wobbling smile came and went over her lips, so quickly Ben was not sure he'd seen it at all. Especially when the next second Isabel was herself again. Supremely confident. Carefully controlled. She lifted her chin, and though she looked Ben in the eye, the light must have faded just enough to hide his identity. It was not, however, dimmed enough for Ben to miss the fact that her eyes, so recently heavy with desire, were now clouded with worry.

"Peter, darling, I'm so sorry." Isabel's touch relaxed. She skimmed her hand over the front of his linen shirt, "You know I am not usually so uncertain and not nearly so shy. Your kiss surprised me, that's all. I thought . . ." She hesitated, biting her lower lip, and glanced up at Ben with a look that might have been flirtatious if there wasn't so much concern in it. "I must admit," she said, "I am a little worried. Is something wrong?"

It wasn't a question Ben could even begin to answer. Not without giving himself away. Thankfully, before he could think what to do about the problem, Isabel pressed her fingers to his lips. "No, Don't speak. Don't try to explain." She touched one hand to the corners of her eyes. "I know something must be wrong. Otherwise, your kiss would not be so cold."

"Cold!"

This time Ben couldn't help himself. The word shot out of him. But fortunately, Isabel seemed too preoccupied with her own worries to pay any attention to his voice.

Not that Ben was sure he cared. Cold? What the devil did she mean, cold? The kiss had been enough to knock him off balance, that was as certain as can be.

Cold? She called that cold?

Ben's mood soured. His cocksure attitude dissolved.

For a moment he thought he saw a hint of a smile play over Isabel's face. He was wrong, of course. She was far too upset to smile. It was instead a distressed look, and as if to emphasize it, she clutched her hands at her waist. "I'm sorry, darling Peter. That was cruel of me. I'm nervous about the fireworks, no doubt. Nervous that things won't go right tonight and that the Jubilee contract will—" She discarded the thought with a shake of her shoulders and brought her other hand to Ben's chest. This time there was no mistaking the look she gave him. It was flirtatious, right enough, and as coy as can be. She stepped close enough for him to feel the blue ribbons at her bodice touch the front of his shirt. "Perhaps," she purred, "we should try again."

Perhaps they should.

Ben took the invitation as a personal challenge. Cold, was he? Awkward? Incompetent?

He'd teach her a lesson, that was for certain.

Without another thought to the matter or its consequences, Ben hooked an arm around Isabel's waist and yanked her against him. Her eyes went wide and a gasp escaped her, but he didn't give her a chance to say a word. He covered her mouth with his and kissed her long and hard.

If the first kiss had been simply adequate, this was anything but. Within a second or two Isabel had tunneled both her hands under the ridiculous wig. Her arms went around Ben's neck. Within another few seconds her lips parted, and this time she was the one who touched her tongue to his.

This kiss was fire, and Isabel's reaction to it was everything Ben remembered. She was soft at the same time she was insistent. Vulnerable at the same time it was clear that she was enjoying herself, and eager for more.

Ben didn't hesitate to give it to her. His mouth slid from her lips to her ear, and he nibbled his way down her neck, one slow, swirling kiss at a time. With one hand he found the ribbon at her throat. He loosened it, discarded it, and nudging aside the ribbons at her bodice and something that felt like a small silk purse and, no doubt, carried some love memento from Peter, he pressed a kiss into the soft, warm shadow between her breasts.

What started as a ecstatic moan came out of Isabel as a shriek and turned just as quickly into a sob. She spun away from Ben, so quickly he was left with nothing in his arms but empty air and nothing in his gut but a fire the likes of which would light every rocket, squib, and roman candle Costigan and Company had ever made.

Ben's first thought was to go after Isabel, to snatch her into his arms and continue right where he'd left off. His instincts warned against it. He kept his distance, gulping in swallow after swallow of humid air, fighting to make some sense of Isabel's behavior and her desires and what looked to be her very strange relationship with Viscount Epworth.

Because this time Ben knew there had been no problem with his kiss. Isabel couldn't accuse him of being cold. She couldn't wonder what was wrong.

Nothing had been wrong. Not a bloody thing. It had been magic. Perfect. Damn it, it had been just the way Ben remembered it.

"It's no good. No good at all." Isabel apparently didn't agree. Her voice was choked with tears. She kept her back to Ben, but he could see that she was wringing her hands. "Peter, darling, please tell me what's wrong. Your kisses . . . They remind me of—"

Whatever she was going to say, she caught herself, and when she turned back to him, there was an expression on her face that was half guilt, half pity.

"I'm sorry," she said. "I know you don't like to talk about it. I know you don't like me to bring up the terrible mistakes I've made in the past, but this time I really have no choice. Peter, dear, this time I must tell you. Your kisses are so unfeeling. So distant. So heartless. They remind me of Ben Costigan's."

Ben wasn't sure which of the emotions that smacked into him was the strongest, the anger or the shock. Maybe it was the humiliation. Whatever the cause, he was dumbstruck, too stricken to move or even think. He opened his mouth, then thought better of saying anything because he wasn't sure what he would say. He snapped his mouth shut, biting off a breath.

"It's too wicked of me to compare you to Ben. I know it." Isabel stepped closer. Her wide skirt swayed from side to side. "You're not at all like him, Peter dear. You know you're not. If you were, I wouldn't think so very much of you. No. No." Isabel lifted one hand, as if she expected him to make some sort of objection.

"Don't even say it. I know it's true. Ben Costigan is a coarse, contemptible man. There isn't a shred of honor in him and not an ounce of honesty. He always thought about himself first. Then his fireworks business. Then his fortune and his home and what few friends he had. I was at the bottom of the list, and I suppose I should thank my lucky stars that I realized it before I ever promised myself to the man for life." She shivered at the very thought.

"He is self-centered and self-indulgent. He is egotistical and arrogant and—" She caught herself again, and again a fleeting smile lit her face. "I'm sorry. I am carrying on. But you need to understand why your actions this evening upset me so. Ben is everything you are not, Peter my love. He isn't at all as intelligent as you are. As a matter of fact, there are those who say he is soft in the head, and I can well understand why. He isn't generous or kindhearted, either." Isabel sighed. "Perhaps that is why he was always so dreary a lover."

Ben didn't have to worry that his voice might give him away. As much as he wanted to defend himself, he wasn't able to utter a word. Nothing came out of him but a deep, guttural growl that echoed in the silence that filled the conservatory. A sound somewhere between a grunt of indignation and a groan of mortification.

Isabel rushed over to him, her voice pleading, her eyes glistening with tears. She grabbed one of Ben's hands. "Forgive me. I am overwrought. It isn't at all like me to be so emotional. You know that, dearest. Please, let's try to put it behind us. Will you forgive me? Will you kiss me again and tell me you love me?"

Ben didn't answer, he couldn't, and Isabel took his hesitation for uncertainty.

"Oh, Peter! You know I can't live without you. Darling, please." She lifted his hand and pressed it to her heart.

Ben closed his eyes against the wave of awareness that washed over him and the aching need that rekindled itself so quickly it surprised even him. Isabel's heart thrummed against his closed hand, and his own heart throbbed to the same rhythm. He spread his fingers through the blue ribbons, and even through the silk fabric he would feel her nipple harden instantly. Isabel closed her eyes.

"Oh, Peter!" The pleading in her voice softened to a moan. She tipped her head and arched her back. "Oh, Peter, I . . . That is, I . . . What I mean is, I . . ." Isabel's words were as erratic as Ben's breathing, and he didn't give a damn. He swirled his thumb over her breast, and when she slipped a hand along his thigh, he sucked in a sharp breath and held it deeply within his lungs, poised on the exquisite edge between anticipation and ecstasy.

Isabel glided her hand to the inside of his thigh, and Ben murmured his approval. She let it drift upward, her palm flat, and grazed it over the front of his breeches, and Ben groaned. She stopped, started again. Stopped.

Isabel's eyes flew open, and though she stepped back, she didn't remove her hand. Her ragged breaths stilled. She looked from the front of Ben's breeches into his eyes and back again. "Oh, Peter," she said, but this time there wasn't even a hint of passion in her voice. Disappointment dripped from her every word. "Now I know there's something wrong." Again, she glided her hand all around. Despairing, she shook her head. "This isn't at all like you, Peter. You've never been so . . ." She pulled a face, searching for a word that would suit the occasion, and apparently finding it, she looked Ben straight in the eye. "So small. I must say, now you are certainly just like Ben."

"Hell and damnation!" It was the final straw. The final insult. Ben whisked the floppy hat and the annoying wig off his head and flung them to the floor. He turned on Isabel, his fists on his hips.

And though he thought to find her aghast with surprise, he found her instead clutching her hands to her mouth, nearly doubled over with laughter.

"Hell and damnation." The words did not ring through the conservatory as they had the first time Ben bellowed them. They fell flat against the damp, close air, muffled by Isabel's laughter.

Ben's desire disappeared into bewilderment. His bewilderment crumbled into confusion. His confusion evaporated into white-hot anger.

"You knew! Damn it, Isabel. You knew it was me. All along. You knew I wasn't Peter."

Isabel wiped tears from her eyes. She leaned against the nearest pot of tropical plants, fighting to catch her breath. She pressed one hand to her heart, and remembering the loose ribbons, she tied them back into place and hiked her sleeves up onto her shoulders. "It wouldn't have mattered a jot if I knew it was you or not," she said. "One kiss told me all I needed to know. One touch." She gave the front of his breeches a pointed look, and in spite of the fact that it felt as childish as it must have looked, Ben tugged his long tunic tighter around himself.

"You're lying, of course." He defended himself automatically, his dignity and his vanity and what was left of his pride. "You just don't want to admit that—"

"Nonsense!" Isabel didn't wait to hear a word of what he had to say. Spying the discarded blue ribbon on the ground, she snatched it up and retied it around her throat, ignoring him with a haughtiness that would have done an empress proud. "There's nothing I won't admit," she said, daring him to differ. "I will admit mistakes when I make them. And I will admit, gracefully, of course, when I am right and you are wrong. And the only thing I will admit about this encounter, Mr. Costigan, is that it bedeviled you right enough. Just as I intended."

"Perhaps. I'll give you that much. I can hardly deny that I was titillated by the experience. You saw the proof yourself." Ben grinned. "You touched it."

Isabel clucked her tongue and tossed her head. He might have known she'd go all dignified on him. She did it every time he was charitable enough to remind her of her shortcomings. He also knew her well enough to know that her next move was sure to be a convenient retreat.

He wasn't about to allow that. When Isabel moved toward the opening of the little alcove, Ben sidestepped his way around her. Solid and unmoving, he stood in her path.

"Admit it, Belle," he said. "You may have started out with nothing more on your mind than teasing me, but you were tempted. After a while you were as tempted as I was."

She gave him a little grimace, distancing herself from the very thought. "Playacting. That's all it was. I must admit, I surprised even myself. I hadn't realized I was such a skilled actress. Or such a dutiful martyr.

It's amazing, isn't it, what one will put up with in the name of a good cause."

"Playacting?" It was Ben's turn to laugh. He bent to look her in the eye. "The way your lips softened against mine?"

Isabel sniffed disdainfully. "Dramatics."

He leaned nearer and skimmed one finger over her lower lip. "That seductive way you nibbled your lip between your teeth?"

"Histrionics."

Ben inched closer. "That little moan of pleasure?" He looked her in the eye. "You remember, the one you made when I nudged aside these frilly ribbons?" Demonstrating, he ran a finger through the blue bows. "That wasn't playacting."

"Of course it was." Isabel's voice was as tight as the expression on her face. "Playacting. All of it. Just as it all was four years ago."

It was too cruel a comment, even coming from Isabel, and while Ben was still trying to digest it, she scooted around him and hurried out of the conservatory.

He followed right behind. "It was never playacting. Not four years ago." Ben's voice boomed through the conservatory.

"Of course it was. How naive you must be if you think it was anything else." Isabel's words echoed back at him. She didn't turn around to confront him. She kept right on, her eyes ahead, her back ramrod straight. She didn't stop once. Not even when she got to the door. She wrenched it open and hurried out into the passageway.

Ben didn't bother to close the conservatory door behind him. He took up the chase, shadowing Isabel's every move as she zigzagged through the groups of people who stood outside the billiard room and near the card room door.

"I may be a lot of things, but I am hardly naive." Ben glared at one old fellow who dared to look at him askance as he walked by and at another who had the audacity to ask him to keep his voice down. "And I'm not gullible enough to believe that everything we did four years ago was nothing more than playacting!"

This comment attracted a good deal of attention. Conversations stopped. Heads turned. And automatically, the crowd parted to let Ben and Isabel through, then closed again around them. People stared and followed along, hanging on every word of what looked to turn into a delicious enough scandal to keep the Society gossips jabbering for days.

Ben didn't care. And Isabel looked not to even notice. She darted through the passageway and on toward the ballroom, and it wasn't until she got there that she bothered to stop at all.

Well aware that people inside the ballroom were already staring to see what the commotion was all about, Isabel drew in a breath and lifted her head. She ran a hand over her skirt, smoothing it, and wiped every trace of emotion from her face. She glanced from side to side and lowered her voice. "I had no choice tonight but to pretend that your kisses bedazzled me, just as I had no choice four years ago," she said, her voice a rough whisper that had those around them leaning forward to catch her every word. "But it is time you faced facts. You, Ben Costigan, are a mediocre lover."

Isabel had spoken quietly. But not quietly enough to discourage the curious and the gossips. A storm greeted her statement, and a rumble went around the room as her words were repeated—complete with horrified gasps—from one person to the next. She ignored the whispers just as she ignored Ben's sputters of outrage. She ignored the squeals of outrage from some of the ladies and the titters that came from behind the hands of a number of others. She ignored the quietly controlled laughter of the gentlemen Ben didn't know and the unbridled guffaws of those he did, and she glided into the ballroom as if nothing at all had happened.

Too angry to keep still, and far more hurt by her

cavalier attitude than he'd ever let her know, Ben was right on her heels. "I was not a mediocre lover!" His voice thundered through the room, so loud the musicians were obliged to stop their playing and the people who were out on the dance floor spun to a stop and turned to stare.

So did Isabel.

Disbelief and outrage stretched into a brittle smile, she pulled to a stop and spun to face Ben.

In that one instant he realized exactly what he'd done. With one sentence he had taken Isabel's reputation and his own and thrown them out the window. He had scandalized Society. And outraged his host and hostess. He had revealed what had surely been a secret (especially to Peter, who was looking a bit pale) and exposed to the public eye what most of the people in the room had no doubt done. And what none of them dared to talk about.

The absurdity of the whole thing goaded Ben further. The hypocrisy fueled his anger. He poked his thumb toward his own chest. "I was not a mediocre lover," he bellowed. "I was good enough to make you scream!"

Isabel's face paled, and she went deathly still. But he might have known she wouldn't stay stunned for long. No doubt as aware as he was that now, once and for all, their reputations were inexorably twined, and just as inescapably tarnished, Isabel lifted her chin. She was as mortified as Ben was. At least for a moment. Just as quickly the outrage that burned in her eyes turned into the sparkle of devilment. And the cold, hard light of revenge.

As if looking for witnesses, Isabel glanced all around. Satisfied that every person there was hanging on her every word, she looked Ben in the eye. "Of course I screamed." Her voice was as chilly as the look she shot his way. "I had no choice. I was so mightily disappointed."

# Chapter 10

The scream of the rocket that hissed into the night sky and burst overhead was enough to make Isabel cringe.

It wasn't as if she regretted her row with Ben; it was just that she didn't need the reminder. Something told her she never would. From the looks she was getting from the people she'd spoken with and passed since the incident in the ballroom an hour earlier, she had the uneasy feeling that no one would ever let her forget it.

Margaret and Richard had been kind enough. Peter had been outraged on her behalf, in his own, distracted, kind of way. Strangers, of course, were another story. Strangers had no qualms about talking behind their hands as she passed. As for Hilda . . . well, it seemed as if Isabel's potential mother-in-law was the type who didn't even try to hide her disapproval. To say she'd been icy was an understatement. To say Isabel didn't care three damns was not.

Let Hilda be caustic. Let strangers talk and whisper. Let them all gossip and grin. Isabel had had the last word. And the last word had wounded Ben's pride. It was all that mattered.

"Made me scream!" At the same time she touched her baton to the next fuse waiting to be lit, she grumbled the words, and with all the dignity she could muster, she sniffed her disgust. "I was right when I said he was soft in the head. The man's a lunatic."

He was. There was no doubt in Isabel's mind that

Ben Costigan was a madman. He was also a scoundrel. And a blackguard.

What he was not was a liar.

The very thought shot heat through Isabel's face. She was glad for the glare of the fireworks that flashed overhead. The colors that painted the sky helped hide the fact that her cheeks must surely be as bright. They felt just as hot.

She had been desperate to annoy Ben. It was the only reason she'd accused him of being a mediocre lover. It had been rash to bring up so explosive a subject, yet when he kissed her . . .

This time Isabel felt heat down to her toes.

When Ben kissed her, she had to say something to turn her thoughts from the fact that the taste of his lips made her heart melt, and the warmth of his touch made her feel his fire all the way through to her soul.

No, Ben was not a liar. But Isabel certainly was. Otherwise, the word *mediocre* would never have left her mouth.

It was not a comforting thought. Nor was it encouraging. It was nearly as disturbing as the fact that even now Isabel was tempted to press a hand to her lips, as if by touching them she could relive the heat of Ben's kiss. Instead, she briefly pressed two fingers to her heart, finding some small comfort in the tiny silk pouch that contained the recipe for Diamond Rain, the pouch Ben had been all too close to discovering in their encounter in the conservatory.

Chastised, her thoughts back on fireworks and, at least for now, away from Ben, she waved her baton, signaling Tommy Eagan, who stood across the meadow. With his own baton Tommy gave her a quick salute and started to fire the next portion of the program.

Rocket after rocket howled into the sky. Shell after shell popped. Even from where she stood near the bank of mortars that would throw the next volley into the air, Isabel could tell the crowd was impressed. She heard more than a fair share of *oohs* and *ahhs* and, when a particularly smashing shell broke, a burst of applause.

"Impressive."

The single word came from somewhere on Isabel's right, and she didn't have to turn that way to know who had joined her. Though she couldn't for the life of her determine if the tingling in her veins was the result of anger or desire, every inch of her was suddenly aware of Ben's presence. Disguising her uneasiness, measuring her time and her words, she kept her gaze on the next cannonade and nodded in approval when the report of its especially strong lifting charge vibrated through her bones and echoed against the ancient walls of Briarcliffe. Blinding white streamers filled the air, chased through the sky by golden sparks. Again, the audience applauded. Their approval gave Isabel courage.

"I wonder you have the nerve to even dare to speak to me."

She didn't look his way, but she knew Ben shrugged. She could hear the nonchalance in his voice. "Why not? I'm as annoyed with you as you are with me, but that's never kept us apart before. I thought you might need some help."

The offer was too ridiculous to even consider. "From you? We are quite capable of shooting our own show." Another thought occurred to her, and she dared a look at Ben. "You are talking about fireworks, aren't you?"

He replied with a grin. "Fireworks, yes. But I could help with a lot of other things as well. Our recent talk"—he gave the word an odd inflection—"in the house should have reminded you of as much." His gaze slid over her, assessing the outfit she'd changed into before the show began. Like her crew, Isabel was dressed in dark trousers, a white shirt, and boots that were sturdy enough to withstand the touch of the flaming ash that fell from the sky and the occasional piece of cardboard that had not burned completely and crunched underfoot. The outfit was unfeminine and it sometimes caused people to talk, but Isabel didn't care. It was practical and efficient, and once she'd blended in with her crew and the audience forgot it was a woman shooting the show, it was inconspicuous as well. That was enough for Isabel.

And, apparently, enough for Ben, too.

He looked her up and down, and his grin brightened. In its own way, his smile was as annoying as if he'd come at her swearing like a tinker. Perhaps more so. If Ben was angry, Isabel knew she would be just as angry in return. But when he was like this, when he was enigmatic and roguish, she was never quite sure how to respond.

He knew it, of course. It was why he acted that way to begin with.

Ben poked his hands into the pockets of his trousers. As had Isabel, he'd changed to work the show. He, too, was dressed simply, in tweed trousers and the kind of inexpensive white shirt workingmen wore, the kind with buttons up the front. Unlike Isabel, whose trousers were tailored so that they were loose enough to be comfortable and snug enough not to demand that she wear a belt, he was wearing dark-colored braces that skimmed his shoulders, emphasizing their width.

The change was subtle but effective. He was no longer a musketeer or a cowboy. He was simply Ben.

It might have been a comforting thought if not for the way Isabel's heart responded to it. Another rocket went off behind her, and automatically Isabel counted the seconds from the time it whooshed out of the mortar.

". . . three, four, five." She nodded, satisfied, when the first bursting charge went off, then again when a second, a third, and a fourth fired right on time. Flaming stars spread into the sky, changing the color of the leaves on the tree to Ben's back so that they looked to be gilded with gold.

He didn't notice. Or if he did, he didn't look impressed. He rocked back on his heels and drew in a mouthful of the smoky air. "We'll be the talk of the town, the two of us."

Isabel couldn't argue with him there. She motioned toward the members of her crew who were waiting beside the reflecting pond, and they nodded in return. "We always are," she conceded, watching as the first of the fireworks fountains was lit and pushed toward the center of the pool. It spouted stars, red, then orange, then brightest yellow. "It seems we always will be as long as you continue to act the way you do."

Like the sparks that flew from the fountain, the innocent—and quite accurate—comment was enough to cause Ben's temper to flare.

"Me?" His face went red in the reflection of the fireworks. "I am not the one who decided that the entire city of London needed to know about our love life."

"Hah!" There was a Katherine Wheel anchored at the center of the pool, and Isabel waited until it was lit. It shot sparks, slowly at first, then faster and faster, until the whole wheel was alive with them and spinning as out of control as her anger. "I was not the one who made that scene in the ballroom." As if he needed the reminder, she poked one finger back toward the house. "I am not the one who announced intimate secrets for all the world to hear."

"Like the fact that you were mightily disappointed in my lovemaking? That's not an intimate secret?"

"You made me say it. You goaded me. You pressed me far beyond my endurance and then you—" Isabel might have gone on if Ben didn't start to laugh.

As if he himself were surprised, he shook his head. "God, but it's good to fight with you again, Belle."

"Do you think so?" Isabel wasn't so sure. She thought, rather, that sooner or later they were certain to say something the likes of which no amount of defenses or excuses could ever make up for. Today, they had come close. As close as they'd come four years earlier when neither of them had bothered to attend their own wedding. One of these days they'd go too far and there'd be no turning back. She would lose him then. As absurd as it seemed to be, it mattered. Isabel knew it in her head. She felt it in her heart. That would be the day she lost Ben forever.

The realization left her feeling empty. She couldn't tell Ben, of course. He would turn it back on her somehow, and that was intolerable.

Instead, she sighed away the heaviness in her heart and held fast to both her composure and her pride. "I can't believe you came all the way over here just to badger me further," she said. "I thought you would have saved that for our meeting with the Jubilee committee later this week."

"I came to admire your fireworks." Ben held out his hands, palms out, the picture of innocence. "I came to tell you what a marvelous job you're doing. What an incredibly smart businesswoman you are."

"Uh-huh." It was time for the finale, and disregarding his sarcasm, Isabel lit three of the shells closest to her. They were answered by three shells from Tommy's direction, and three more from the lake. It was her signal to light the last of the shells in the mortars in front of her, and Isabel did. Green and silver stripes brightened the sky. Blue balls like full, ripe plums filled the air. There was a burst of red directly overhead. Another of green and a final, bone-shaking bang that left the audience breathless.

It wasn't until both the echo of the explosion and the thunder of applause died down that Isabel bothered to give Ben another look. "So, what do you really want?" she asked.

"The recipe for Diamond Rain?" He looked at her expectantly, honey brows raised, eyes bright with what was either challenge, amusement, or a little of both.

She didn't give him the satisfaction of an answer, but turned to leave the field.

"No." Ben touched her arm. "What I really want," he confessed, "is for you to watch my fireworks right beside me."

It sounded innocent enough, and that in itself was

enough to make Isabel suspicious. She was about to ask what Machiavellian thing he had in mind when a loud maroon announced the beginning of Ben's show.

"You're not shooting?" Isabel yelled the question above the noise.

Ben simply shook his head no. He stood at her side, watching the show as she was, commenting when he thought a firework was especially good, swearing quietly when his crew's timing was the least bit off or the firework effect not as spectacular as he anticipated.

All in all, it was as good a show as Isabel's. It was dignified, as the occasion dictated. It was restrained, which was, she decided, somewhat of a surprise when it came to one of Ben's shows. Volley after volley of fireworks lit the night sky, competing with the stars and outshining them, and when the last of them had faded, Ben nudged her with his elbow.

"Ah, here it is," he said. "Here is what I wanted you to see."

It was the lancework Isabel had seen being assembled earlier. Now it was fastened in the center of the meadow, a wooden frame that was at least thirty feet tall and another twenty across. Ben waved an arm over his head to signal the shooter, and the first lance was lit. The next caught, and the next, and it was clear that the picture was that of a woman.

Isabel.

"What!" Isabel's mouth dropped open. She had never even imagined to see her face drawn in fireworks, and for a moment she wavered between feeling embarrassed and flattered. If this was what Ben had wanted her to see so badly, it could only mean one thing.

It was his way of apologizing. His way of making up for all the beastly things he had ever done.

"You don't think I've made you look too young, do you?"

His question was enough to dissolve her illusions and renew her suspicions.

"Your nose may be a bit too long." His arms

crossed over his chest, he looked at the picture, then gave Isabel's face a critical stare. "And the chin isn't nearly stubborn enough. But it's a good likeness, I think."

So, apparently, did the rest of the audience.

Almost as soon as Isabel realized what the picture was, so did Margaret's guests. They applauded and called out Isabel's name, watching as she was as the lances continued to light, one by one. They continued to do so, even as the fire made its way down the frame and the rest of the picture came to life.

Isabel's stomach lurched. The heat she'd been feeling earlier drained completely, leaving her shaky and cold.

The lancework picture was of her, right enough, and though she was holding a large, rectangular-shaped object in front of her that covered her from the knees to the bosom, it was clear she wasn't wearing anything at all. Her legs were bare. So were her toes. Above the edge of the rectangle, her breasts swelled enticingly.

But even that was not the final indignity.

The lancework on the sides of the rectangle caught, and a message formed in fire.

COSTIGAN AND COMPANY the sign Isabel was holding said. NOTHING BUT THE VERY BEST.

It didn't seem possible that the last meeting of the Jubilee committee could be any more strained than the first.

But it was.

Anxiety flitted through Isabel's stomach. It damped her palms and made her shift uncomfortably in her chair.

It seemed that all around her the members of the committee felt the tension, too. Though Sir Digby had yet to arrive, the room was completely silent. Committee members sat with their arms at their sides, stiff-backed and tight-lipped. They refused to meet Isabel's eyes.

And who could blame them?

For weeks now they had been witness to the extents to which she and Ben would go to discredit each other. They had seen her humiliated, first at the Adelphi, then with the lancework in Margaret's garden. They had watched as she tried her best to retaliate. They had been in the audience the night Ben's stunt at the Crystal Palace ended in embarrassment. Most of them had been spectators to the spat that escalated into a full-scale war in Margaret's ballroom.

In the last weeks Isabel's name had been mentioned occasionally in the Society columns of the newspapers, a fact that members of the committee—or at least their wives—could not have failed to notice. In the last days the occasional mention had turned into a positive flood. One of the less reputable newspapers printed a picture of the infamous lancework. And though none of the gossipmongers had the audacity to report what they euphemistically called the Ballroom Episode word for word, there had been sly illusions and double entendres aplenty, tossed out like so many bread crumbs to lead their reader to their own conclusions.

As Isabel's reputation unraveled, so did her relationship with Peter. He came to call less and less often, and try as she might, she could find no fault with his actions. She could hardly blame him. The only thing that surprised her was that she didn't miss him in the least.

Her personal life was a mess. Her reputation was in shreds. Her mind was in a constant state of turmoil. And the fate of her company depended on what would be determined by the committee.

It was not a pretty picture. Not any of it. It was no more pleasant for Isabel to admit than it was for her to sit there waiting for the committee's final decision.

Fitfully, she drummed her fingers on the table and looked at the floor clock that stood in one corner of the room. Sir Digby was late. She glanced across the table toward the empty chair directly opposite hers. Sir Digby wasn't the only one.

Ben wasn't there, either.

The fact that he had yet to arrive for an important meeting might have had Isabel worried had she been feeling more charitable. But *charity* was hardly a word she associated with thoughts of Ben Costigan. Neither was *tolerance* or *mercy*, and for a few delicious moments she entertained herself with thoughts of him missing the meeting altogether and thus invalidating his chance for the Jubilee contract.

It was not to be, of course. Isabel knew it even before she heard the rumble of a familiar laugh outside the door. Ben was too astute a businessman to miss an opportunity such as this, and too cagey by half not to make the most of every advantage.

She was even more certain of it when the door snapped open and Ben walked into the room with Sir Digby Talbot at his side.

"A duck walks into a pub!" Marveling, Sir Digby shook his head and wiped tears of laughter from his eyes. "Most amusing, Mr. Costigan. Most amusing, indeed. A duck! In a pub!"

Still chuckling, Sir Digby took his place at the head of the table, and Ben settled himself across from Isabel. He had won the last battle of the war, the one in Margaret's garden, and Isabel supposed he had the right to look pleased with himself. But not this pleased.

Ben's smile was as bright as the sun that streamed in through the window on the far wall of the room. He either didn't feel the tension that crackled through the air, or he chose to ignore it completely. His manner was calm and assured. He looked cool and confident. Cheerful and carefree.

As if he knew something Isabel didn't.

The panic that had been crawling through her stomach all morning leaped into her throat, blocking her breathing. She looked from Ben's smiling face to Sir Digby, still chuckling and mumbling to himself about ducks and pubs. She glanced back at Ben and noted the optimistic tilt of his chin, the sparkle in his eyes, and her insides went cold with the certainty that he already knew the committee's decision, and that it was one he found very agreeable, indeed.

As if reading her thoughts, Ben nodded her way. Certain she'd noticed, and just as certain she wasn't going to respond, he turned to nod a greeting toward each of the committee members in turn. To a man, they nodded back.

It was far more of an acknowledgment than Isabel had gotten from any of them, even Richard, and she bristled at the implied insult. "Men!" She hid the comment behind a dignified little cough, and when Ben glared in her direction, she offered him a glare in return.

They might have gone on that way forever if Sir Digby had not convened the meeting.

"We all know why we're here." His face wiped clean of laughter, Sir Digby glanced at his fellow committee members. He flipped open the leather portfolio on the table in front of him and glanced through some papers, and now that the meeting had officially begun, it seemed, blessedly, that he was willing to forget Society scandals and focus on the business at hand. He shifted his gaze to Ben, then Isabel. "We've talked, the committee members and I, and we are all in agreement. Unfortunately, our most important consideration isn't what's right or fair. Our most important concern is providing Her Majesty with the kind of celebration she deserves. One that is impressive and memorable and dignified."

"Here, here." The murmur went around the table, and the gloom that had filled Isabel lifted ever so slightly. If the committee was talking *dignified,* they couldn't possibly be considering Costigan and Company. *Dignified* was not a word that had ever been used in the same breath as Ben's name.

"Miss De Quincy . . ."

The sound of Sir Digby's voice startled Isabel out of her thoughts. He turned enough in his seat so that he was looking directly at her, and Isabel's stomach clenched. She held her breath and slipped her hands into her lap. She latched her fingers together until her knuckles went white. "Miss De Quincy, I can't tell you how much I enjoyed your performance at Briarcliffe recently."

Isabel hoped to God he meant the fireworks. She didn't dare ask.

"Your fireworks are everything you promised they would be."

She took a breath. Managed another. Sir Digby's words were encouraging. Complimentary. Did he mean . . . ?

"The committee and I were especially impressed by the fireworks on the water," he went on. "Very well done. Very impressive. Your work has all the refinement, all the stateliness, we feel the occasion warrants."

The corners of Isabel's mouth twitched into a smile. She chanced a look across the table and found Ben looking a little stunned.

Isabel's smile widened. Her spirits lifted.

"Miss De Quincy, we are all in agreement, your fireworks are extraordinary," Sir Digby said. "However . . ."

Sir Digby turned in his chair so that he was looking at Ben, and suddenly Isabel's rising hopes were dashed to the ground. Ben's, on the other hand, were reawakened. He sat up a little straighter and darted a glance in her direction before he turned his attention full on Sir Digby.

"Mr. Costigan, your work is certainly . . ." Sir Digby searched for the word. "Well, I think if we say unique, it is not too much of an overstatement. The fountain you brought here the first time the committee convened, the display at the Crystal Palace."

With every word Sir Digby spoke, Ben seemed to puff with pride. By the time Sir Digby was done, Ben's eyes gleamed with satisfaction.

"However . . ."

Isabel watched Ben's sparkle fade around the edges.

"It simply wouldn't be fair," Sir Digby went on. "Not to the splendor of the occasion, or to her Majesty."

His piece said, Sir Digby sat back and exchanged looks with both Ben and Isabel.

"Begging your pardon, Sir Digby, but I don't quite understand." It was Isabel who dared the comment, though she knew Ben was just as confused as she was. She could tell from the twist of his brows and the way a tiny muscle jumped at the base of his jaw. "Are you telling us you want neither Costigan and Company nor De Quincy and Sons?"

Sir Digby's face went ashen with dismay. "Not at all. Not at all." He sat up and looked at Richard.

"What Sir Digby is saying," Richard explained, "is that those of us on the committee have enjoyed all the fireworks immensely. And we've noticed . . ." He looked away from Isabel. "Well, damn it," he muttered, "we couldn't help but notice how well you two work together."

"What!"

The word escaped from both Ben and Isabel at the same time. They leaned forward, hands on the table. The full realization of what was happening struck like lightning.

Ben jumped out of his chair. "You can't mean—"

Isabel slumped back in her seat. "You don't actually think—"

"Exactly. Exactly." Sir Digby grinned, and for the first time in all the years she'd known him, Isabel saw more in his smile than she ever suspected. There was poise and polish, surely, but there was also something of the devil in it. Something that sparkled with mischief and glimmered with humor. As if to prove it, Sir Digby rubbed his hands together.

"We have made our decision," he said. "The Jubilee fireworks program will be presented by both De Quincy and Sons and Costigan and Company. The two of you will work together to produce the show."

# Chapter 11

Simon brushed his fingers lazily over the ivory keys of the piano and, not liking the tune, punctuated it with a harsh chord. "I thought Sir Digby was our friend," he said.

"Seems he is." As much as she hated to admit it, Isabel couldn't deny the facts. She had a ledger open on the desk in front of her, and she glanced from the neatly written figures in it over to where her brother sat at the piano. "At least he got us half of the Jubilee contract. It isn't what I wanted . . ." Isabel's words trailed away along with her thoughts.

Letting her imagination run away with her was a dangerous diversion. She'd learned that in the last few weeks. But this time, like so many others, she couldn't seem to help herself.

What she'd wanted was peace of mind, and the chance to save De Quincy and Sons from bankruptcy at the same time she produced a Jubilee show so spectacular, it would be the talk of the Empire.

What she'd gotten was something else altogether.

What she'd gotten was irritation. And worries enough to make her question herself, her motives, and every single one of her scruples. What she'd gotten were sleepless nights and days filled with the sorts of disturbing fantasies she'd thought she put behind her four years earlier. She'd gotten a certain infamous notoriety as well. And a kind of unsettled feeling between her shoulder blades that stayed with her constantly and transformed, miraculously and inexplicably, into a sort of tingling hum every time Ben was anywhere near.

A strange, cacophonous noise sounded from somewhere outside the house, intruding upon Isabel's thoughts. It was just as well, she told herself with a shake of her shoulders. She had other things to think about. Things other than Ben.

"As I was saying . . ." She looked back down at the ledger. "Sir Digby has done us something of a favor. He could have chosen Costigan and Company exclusively. I almost thought he had the way he and Ben were chatting it up like old chums before the meeting. Half of the Jubilee contract is better than nothing, I suppose. The money we'll earn—"

Again, the odd noise blared through the usually quiet neighborhood.

"It sounds as if someone's skinning a cat!" Simon rose from the piano.

"Or stepping on a bagpipe," Isabel offered, looking toward the window.

"Or a bagpipe player!" His mouth pulled into a caustic smile, Simon went to look out the window. Whatever he saw, it had an odd effect on him. He pulled in a shallow breath and dropped the drapery back into place at the same time he spun around and headed for the door. "You don't need to worry about De Quincy and Sons anymore," he called to her over his shoulder.

Isabel nodded. "I know. Even though we don't have the entire contract, the money we earn from the Jubilee should be enough to at least start paying back the most pressing of your debts. It's not a perfect situation, but—"

"That's not what I mean at all." Simon stopped in the doorway long enough to poke his head out into the passageway and look all around. "I told you I would take care of it, Belle. Don't you remember? I have. I've taken care of everything. My gambling debts are paid and—"

"Paid?" Isabel shouted over the noise that seemed

to be coming from directly outside the De Quincy house. "How on earth did you—" She shrieked with frustration. "Oh, bother!" Slapping the desktop, she rose and looked toward the windows. "What is that awful noise?"

Like a large, startled bird, Simon flapped out into the passageway and was gone. She made to follow, but the noise sounded again, and she hurried down the stairway to the foyer and flung wide the front door. She stepped out onto the stoop, and her mouth dropped open in wonder.

Out on the street directly in front of the house was the most remarkable thing Isabel had ever seen. It was a horseless carriage, and its brass trim and yellow paint sparkled, rivaling the early morning sun.

Another blast of the vehicle's horn split the air, and Isabel covered her ears with her hands.

"What on earth . . .?" She started down the stairs, staring in amazement and wonder. Until her eyes fell upon the driver.

Isabel's surprise melted in a wave of fury. "What are you doing here?"

Ben didn't bother to return her greeting. He jumped down from the driver's seat, his stony gaze in direct contrast to the sunny color of his automobile. "I've come to collect you," he said. He gave the horn a final blast for good measure and, no doubt, because he realized how very annoying it was. "Needed to attract your attention first."

"It seems you've attracted more than just my attention." Up and down the street, heads peeked from doorways and faces pressed against windows. Already, a number of children had come running and gathered around the incredible machine, and even as Isabel watched, constable Lionel Cranley came huffing and puffing from around the corner, intent on seeing what the noise was all about.

"So, what do you think?" Ignoring the crowd, Ben gave the automobile an affectionate pat. "She's a beauty, isn't she? A Daimler Phaeton and the sleekest thing on the streets."

"Sleek, indeed." Isabel let her gaze glide over the car. *Sleek* it was. And impressive. There weren't many of the extraordinary vehicles about, but Isabel had seen other automobiles in London. Except that they had no horses to pull them, they looked no different from carriages. They were dark and plain, spindly and rather frail-looking contraptions of metal and leather that looked to be far too fragile for all but the most careful sort of driving over the most well-kept sorts of roads.

Ben's automobile was completely different.

The gleaming yellow two-seater was sturdy and substantial-looking, but it had no lack of style. Its curves were graceful and generous. Its lines were pleasing to the eye. It had running lamps on either side and a wood and brass wheel that the driver could steer. It had marvelous spoked wheels and tires with elegant white rims. In spite of the city's renowned bad climate, all of the automobiles Isabel had ever seen had no covering at all above the driver and passenger. This one had a black leather top that Ben had folded back in deference to the perfect weather.

"Petrol engine." For some reason Isabel did not even want to begin to understand, the fact seemed impressive not only to Ben but to Constable Cranley as well. The policeman's bushy eyebrows shot up at the very thought, and two of the young lads who had gathered around exhaled sighs of pure wonder.

"Not electric like some of the cabs they're using now," Ben confided to Isabel. "This one doesn't need recharging. And it can travel at more than thirteen miles an hour."

This statement was obviously too much for even Constable Cranley to believe. He waved his hands, dismissing Ben's words as nothing more than idle boasting, and shooed the crowd away.

With his audience of admirers gone, Ben seemed to remember the real reason he was there—whatever that might have been. He turned away from the automobile and grabbed Isabel's hand.

"Come on," he said, "Don't waste time. We've got a lot to talk about."

Automatically, Isabel tugged her hand back to her side. "We have nothing to talk about. And never will."

"Not even the Jubilee?" As Ben looked down at her, his eyebrows slipped up. "It seems to me, Miss De Quincy, that we'd better talk. And soon. We have only six weeks until the Jubilee."

"Six weeks! It might as well be six years. Or six days. Or six minutes." Isabel had guarded her anger carefully in the last days. She had put on a brave face for Sir Digby and the committee members. She had focused on the fact that half the Jubilee contract was better than none and taken comfort in the knowledge that the money she earned would make a start toward paying off Simon's debts.

But Simon had rejected her generous offer to pay his creditors. And the committee couldn't even begin to appreciate how difficult it was for her to keep her upper lip stiff while she played the faithful retainer who was willing to do anything for Queen and country, even if it meant working with a firm as notorious as Costigan and Company.

And it was all Ben's fault. He'd stolen half the contract just as he was sure to steal more than his share of the glory. He'd been as surprised as she was when Sir Digby announced his decision. But now it looked as if he was reasonably content with the prospect, and reasonably certain to treat Isabel like a child who needed leading through the planning process by the hand.

Isabel's anger burst out of her along with her words. "What difference will six weeks make?" she asked. "We'll never agree on a thing. Not from the start. You'll say red and I'll say blue. I'll say tasteful, and artistic and majestic, and you'll no doubt suggest—"

"Women in skimpy clothes. Yes, I was afraid you'd

object." Ben did his best to look guilty at the very thought, but it was clear he wasn't nearly as conscience-stricken as he was crestfallen at having to abandon the idea before it ever took bloom.

"We're smack in the middle of the biggest muddle of our lives," he admitted, and his guilty smile dissolved into an expression of real concern. "That's why we need to talk."

Isabel hated to admit it, but it was true. Somewhere in the back of her mind, she'd known this was bound to happen. Sooner or later they would have to sit down together and argue their way through the details of the program. "We do need to plan the Jubilee program. Come inside and we'll—"

"I thought you'd come with me instead."

It was an innocent enough invitation. And it really did make sense, from a business standpoint at least. They needed to talk and plan. They needed to communicate. What they didn't need was a ride in an automobile that was as sleek as sin, and a meeting in some out-of-the-way sort of place where their passions—for both fireworks and each other—might have even the remotest chance of getting the better of them.

No, they didn't need to be alone. Their disastrous rendezvous in Margaret's conservatory had proved as much. Isabel's skin burned at the very thought. Her lips tingled.

It was a disturbing reminder of all that had passed between them, and as much of a warning as any she was likely to get. Isabel tried her best to heed it. She scrambled to keep the conversation on business.

"Sir Digby had no idea what he was doing," she told Ben, sure it was the one thing he could never dispute. "I'm more convinced than ever. He's a dear and a dear friend, but I sometimes wonder if his age isn't showing."

"You're right." Ben nodded solemnly, and his eyes darkened with the kind of concern Isabel herself was feeling. It was a surprising show of compassion on Ben's part, and when Isabel realized it, her heart squeezed with affection, an emotion that was as uncomfortable as it was inopportune. She tried to ignore it. It wasn't safe for her mind or her body to start thinking of Ben as a gentle humanitarian. But it was difficult to pretend it wasn't happening, especially when he leaned nearer and lowered his voice.

"Sir Digby is getting old," he said sadly, "and he must be getting feeble-minded. It's the only thing that can explain why he would have even begun to think that this arrangement could work. Of course . . ." Ben's sensitivity dissolved beneath a healthy explosion of laugher. "He might have done it simply because he felt sorry for you!"

"Me?" Isabel tossed her head at the same time she discarded what she realized was the ridiculous notion that Ben might actually have a heart. "I am convinced Sir Digby did what he did only to be kind to you. It's the only thing that can even begin to explain why he would make a decision that's so . . . so very unsatisfactory."

"Unsatisfactory? Is that what you think?" She had hit Ben where it hurt. She'd wounded his pride and his inflated opinion of himself, and questioned his skill as a fireworks artist. The damage showed. He pulled himself up to his full height and glared down at her. "Unsatisfactory for me perhaps," he thundered. "The last thing I need is for you to be ruining my fireworks show."

"Your fireworks show?" The very words sizzled like rockets through Isabel's veins. She balled her hands into fists and propped them on her hips. "I think it far more likely, Mr. Costigan, that you will ruin my fireworks show."

"Hardly." Ben had a way of looking amused even when he was angry. It was one of the things that made him so thoroughly annoying. But this time even the sparkle in his eyes couldn't disguise the exasperation in his voice. "I can see it now," he barked. "My splendid shells filling the sky while your pitiful rockets—"

"I think it is rather that my splendid rockets will fill the sky while your pitiful shells—"

". . . tripping over my mortars, mucking with my lanceworks—"

". . . mishandling my delicate set pieces and ruining the dignity of the—"

". . . bungling the whole thing until it is as insipid—"

". . . boorish—"

". . . boring—"

". . . utterly inappropriate and—"

"And I told you we needed to talk!" Ben threw his hands in the air and sucked in a deep breath.

Isabel was glad when Ben surrendered. She was running out of breath, and patience, and arguments, just as he appeared to be, but she'd be damned if she was going to yield first. Taking some small comfort from the even smaller victory, she hitched up her skirts and turned to head up the stairs and into the house. "I do believe we've said all there is to say."

"No. You're coming with me." Ben reached for her arm, holding her in place.

With her anger still fresh and hot, it was not easy to think straight. The process was made no less challenging by that fact that Ben's fingers were pressed into her flesh. Isabel shook off his hand. "Come with you?" She looked over Ben's shoulder toward the automobile and curled her top lip. "In that?"

"Yes, in that!" It was obvious that to Ben the automobile wasn't merely a form of transportation. It was an object of art. And devotion. Clearly insulted, he pulled back his shoulders and his mouth thinned. "We'll have lunch," he said. "Just the two of us. We'll talk."

Isabel didn't bother to tell him that it was far too early in the morning for lunch. He wouldn't have listened in any event. Ben never listened to what he didn't want to hear.

As if to prove it, he stomped over to the automobile, opened the boot, and fished out a long chamois-colored dust coat. "Here." He didn't hold the coat as any gentleman would, so that she might slip her arms into the sleeves. He didn't even hand it to her (as anyone so churlish might be expected to) and let her fumble with it herself. He crossed the pavement to where Isabel stood, and seizing her right arm, he shoved it into one sleeve of the coat, then repeated the process with the other arm.

"Really!" Isabel did her best to stand stiff and unyielding, but it was a difficult enough prospect when someone was only inches from you and yanking your arms about. It was more difficult still when that someone was Ben.

He smelled of expensive soap, fresh air, and automobile oil, a combination that was as odd as it was uniquely male, and as masculine as it was intoxicating. Isabel pulled in a breath, as much to steady herself as to savor the aroma. She was successful at reveling in the scent. And not at all successful at steadying herself. Especially when Ben tugged the coat closer around her at the front and began to fasten the bone buttons.

Isabel slapped his hands away. "I am quite capable of doing that myself."

"No doubt." Deep in concentration, Ben went right on with the buttons. Unused to attacking buttons from that angle, his fingers fumbled and his expression was marred by the fact that he was so intent on getting it right. He bit his lower lip. "There." When he was done, he stepped back, satisfied. "Now a hat."

"Ben, no!" When he produced a wide hat with a gauze veil, Isabel ducked out of the way.

But Ben refused to be deterred. When Isabel parried to the left, he moved right. When she tried to avoid both Ben and the absurd hat by moving to the right, he danced to his left. They might have gone on that way forever if he hadn't made a drastic move. Timing his lunge with split-second accuracy, he pounced and jammed the hat on her head.

"Ben!" The hat came down nearly to Isabel's nose,

and she gave a muffled scream of protest. "I can't see! I—"

He adjusted the hat, but so begrudgingly, Isabel wasn't sure if he did it to make her more comfortable or to stop her complaining. "There." Looking far more satisfied than he had any right to look, Ben smiled in approval of both the hat and the fact that he had won this skirmish. He pursed his lips and tilted the hat to the right, pulled a face and tried it to the left. "Much better." He gathered the gauze veil on either side and tied it smartly under Isabel's chin. It may have been a trick of her imagination, but she thought his fingers lingered there rather longer than they should, and that he stood rather too close for a man who had nothing more on his mind than tying her hat.

"Are you quite done?" Isabel scooted back a step, away from the heady scents that surrounded Ben and the heat of his body. "I must surely look a fool," she said, wrinkling her nose. "And I haven't even agreed to go with you."

"Of course you've agreed." Completely undisturbed by her protests, Ben reached into the automobile and pulled out a pair of goggles.

"Oh, no!" Isabel backed up a step or two. She might have kept going if she hadn't smacked against the bottom of the front stairs, and she might have escaped up them if the wide, awkward dust coat hadn't hindered her every movement. "I am not wearing those things."

"Of course you are." Breezy and blasé, Ben held the goggles up in front of Isabel's face. They had long straps of notched leather on either side of them, rather like a belt, and he set them on the bridge of her nose and made to fasten them at the back of her head. It was not something he could accomplish without putting his arms firmly around her.

Ben seemed to realize it at the same time Isabel did. He hesitated for a second, and Isabel knew that in that one second she had a last chance to escape. She didn't take it.

She couldn't.

Not when Ben looked down at her and his smile ignited an answering heat. She had no choice but to smile back.

Ben inched closer, one careful step at a time. "You're damned pretty when you smile. Even when you're wearing goggles. You ought to do it more often."

"Smile? Or wear goggles?"

"Smile. Wear goggles. Either. Both." Ben didn't seem sure. Nor did he seem to care. His own smile brightening, he propped both arms over her shoulders, pulled Isabel close, and went to work on the goggles.

It was a simple process, and it should have taken no more than a second or two. It might have if Ben hadn't decided to take advantage of the situation.

He pressed Isabel's head to his chest, crushing her hat.

"Ben!" Isabel did her best to look up, or at least to gulp in a breath of air. It was no use. The more she tried, the tighter Ben held her, and the tighter he held her, the more she realized that being held by Ben was not at all an unpleasant sensation.

The awareness flushed her cheeks and quickened her pulse. Against her ear, she heard Ben's heartbeat speed up until it was every bit as fast as her own.

"I could do that myself." She offered one last protest. It was a feeble one at best, and Ben recognized it for exactly what it was. She felt the vibration of a chuckle rumble through his chest at the same time he adjusted his stance so that her hips were fit neatly against his.

Even the bulky dust coat wasn't enough to hide the fact that going out for a drive was suddenly the last thing on Ben's mind. And the first thing? Nothing Isabel had the fortitude to even think about.

"I can't go rushing off with you in your automobile." Isabel was breathless. Her words were muffled against the expensive fabric of Ben's own dust coat.

"I can't be seen in this ridiculous outfit. And I can't go to lunch. Not the way I'm dressed."

"What's wrong with the way you're dressed?" As if even he wasn't sure, he undid the top three buttons on the dust coat and pushed it aside. Thinking that she was going to keep to the house for the morning before she ventured to the De Quincy and Sons offices for the afternoon, Isabel had dressed casually. Her gown was lightweight muslin embroidered with sprays of pink carnations and adorned with white lace all along the scooped neckline and at the edges of the elbow-length sleeves. It was a charming enough dress for stay-at-home, but it was hardly appropriate for business.

Ben looked from what he could see of the dress to Isabel, and his eyes clouded with that typically male response to anything that had to do with female fashion.

"You look fine," he said, dropping the dust coat back into place and reaching for Isabel's hand. "Come on. Let's go."

"But, Ben, I—"

Taking her arm, Ben turned Isabel toward the automobile. He nudged her from behind until she was in the vehicle, and when she was, he pressed her into the passenger seat.

"But, Ben, I—"

Again she tried a protest and again he didn't listen. He donned his own goggles and went to the front of the automobile. He cranked it to life, and when it was purring contentedly, he climbed behind the wheel.

"But, Ben, I—" Isabel's final protest was lost in a rush of wonder. Ben gave the horn another resounding honk and started off down the street, and the air wafted by Isabel at the same time the gentle vibration of the vehicle's motor hummed through her blood.

Ben set an easy pace, carefully making his way around the hansom cabs in the street and honking the horn and waving to those on the pavement who watched and waved back. The automobile was comfortable and relatively quiet, and after a while Isabel relaxed against the plush leather seat. Motoring was quite pleasant, she decided.

Or at least it might have been.

If the moment they had turned from Isabel's quiet residential street, Ben had not pressed the accelerator all the way to the floor and taken off like a rocket.

Three hours later, Isabel hoisted herself out of the Phaeton on shaky legs.

"Dear God!" She slumped against the vehicle. "Do you always drive that way?"

Ben removed his goggles, eased out of his dust coat, and took a long breath of salty sea air. "What way?" he asked.

Isabel fanned her face with one hand. The goggles had ceased to be an inconvenience hours ago. Now they were simply unbearable. She tore off her hat, ripped off the goggles, and threw them and her dust coat into the vehicle. "There is a speed limit, you know," she said, smoothing her hair into place as much as she could. "Twelve miles an hour, if I'm not mistaken."

"Twelve miles!" Ben waved away her reminder as if it were a small, pesky insect. "If we drove that slowly, we never would have made the channel in three hours' time. Amazing, isn't it?" He patted the bonnet of the automobile, and when he saw something smeared on it, his expression crumbled into concern. It wasn't until he pulled his handkerchief from his pocket and wiped away the smudge that he bothered to look Isabel's way again.

"You know," Ben told her, "there's a fellow somewhere who swears that motoring is a wonderful form of exercise. Says it acts on the liver, whatever that means."

"My liver may never be the same." Isabel put one hand to the small of her back, kneading her sore muscles. "Your automobile is comfortable enough, but the roads ..." She shivered, remembering every bump and hole.

Ben laughed. "The same fellow recommends that when you finish a motoring trip, you should run two or three hundred yards. To restore the circulation in your legs." He glanced her way, his gaze gliding from her hips to her feet, and a smile tickled the corners of his mouth. "If you need some help getting your circulation started again, I could massage—"

"I'll run the three hundred yards, thank you." It was impossible to keep still with Ben looking at her as if he were a starving man and she, the banquet that had been set out on a table in front of him. This time the wobbly sensation in her knees had nothing at all to do with motoring, and eager to banish the feeling, Isabel walked to the edge of the high chalk cliff where they were stopped. Above her gulls reeled on the freshening breeze that blew over the channel from France, their bodies dark against the bright blue sky. Below, the aquamarine water lapped lazily against a strip of sandy shore.

It was not at all what she'd expected when Ben had come around to collect her that morning, but by now she knew enough to never expect the expected from Ben.

She had realized hours ago that he had something outrageous planned. Her first inklings came when they sped through London without ever stopping at one of the restaurants where he might have reserved a table for lunch. Her suspicions grew when they raced past every one of the quaint inns on the outskirts of the city. For a while she even thought that Ben might be taking her to Surrey, where he had both his country home and his fireworks factory, but she'd been wrong about that, too. The longer they dashed through the countryside, the more curious Isabel became. And the more she wondered where they were headed, the more Ben refused to discuss their destination.

Now she saw why.

Visiting the shore was one of the true pleasures of

Isabel's life, and a diversion she did not allow herself nearly often enough. She loved the feel of the damp air against her skin and the wind in her hair. She enjoyed the sounds of the waves licking the shore, and of the seabirds screaming their greetings. She liked the way the light seemed different here than it did in London, as if the sky itself was lit from the back, like a West End stage set. It seeped through everyone and everything it touched, until Isabel felt as if she were a part of it, moving and shimmering, brilliant in the sunshine like the tail of a roman candle, and grim as the report of a lifting charge when a storm washed over the coast.

"Beautiful, isn't it?"

Isabel didn't need to turn to know Ben had come up behind her. She felt a subtle warming in the air, and a shiver skittered over her shoulders. She hugged her arms around herself.

"So what do you think?" He stepped close enough to lean over her shoulder, his breath soft against her neck. "Was it worth the drive?"

"Yes." It was true. Isabel couldn't deny it. Three hours of bumpy roads might be uncomfortable, but even a glimpse of the sea was more than enough to make up for the inconvenience. And the simple fact that Ben had remembered how special the ocean was to her more than made up for the high-handed way he'd commandeered her to join the excursion.

Isabel's heart squeezed at the thought. Comfortable and content, she sighed. "You remembered."

"Did I?" Ben stood up straight. He darted a look left, then right, as if searching for something, and not finding it, he gave her a sheepish grin. "Of course I remembered," he said, rocking back on his heels. "You think I'm not a sentimental sort of chap, but actually, you see, I really am. I—"

If his actions weren't enough to give him away, the silly sort of way he was trying to rationalize certainly was. The momentary fantasy she'd had of Ben as a kindly, caring person vanished in a surge of vexation and another, even stronger wave of some emotion that felt far too much like disappointment for Isabel's liking.

She turned around and stomped back to where the automobile was parked. "You have no idea what I'm talking about, and don't pretend you do, Ben Costigan. Obviously, you've brought me here for your own nefarious purposes, though I am at a loss to see what those might be. We are supposed to be discussing the Jubilee program. And we are supposed to—" The rumbling of Isabel's stomach brought her up short. It was well past noon. She could tell as much from the position of the sun in the sky. Now that she thought about it, she realized she hadn't had a thing to eat since breakfast, and that was hours ago. She pulled to a stop and glared at Ben. "You promised me lunch."

"Lunch. Yes." Though he was saved from the uncomfortable difficulty of trying to talk his way out of a situation he didn't understand in the least, he didn't look happy about it. He glanced over the chalk cliff down to the shore. He rubbed one hand along the back of his neck. "I thought that we might talk first," he suggested.

"Talk?" Ignoring another, louder protest from her stomach, Isabel gave him as indulgent a smile as she could manage. She had learned long ago that when Ben's mind was made up, there was no use trying to change it, and she admitted defeat with a groan. "Very well. Talk. What do you think? We'll open the program with a maroon. A giant, bone-shaking *bang* that will make everyone sit up and take notice. We'll have to make it loud enough for Her Majesty to hear, for I'm told she is a bit deaf and—"

"And I really don't want to talk about the Jubilee program." In three long strides Ben covered the distance that separated them, and before Isabel could object or even react, he took one of her hands in both of his. "I want to talk about us."

This time the sigh that escaped Isabel had nothing to do with the contentment she'd felt while looking out over the sea. It was a deep and desolate sigh, as heavy as the weight that pressed upon her heart. She pulled her hand from Ben's.

"There is no *us*," she told him. "There never was. There's you, Ben. And there's me. That's all there is. There isn't anywhere we meet. Not anywhere we touch. I'm sorry for that. I suppose that is the one thing I've learned in the time you've been back. Once upon a time we thought there was *us*. We were wrong."

"Yes." He didn't look any more pleased by the realization than she was. His eyes darkened until they were the color of the sea when a storm approaches, and a muscle jumped at the base of his jaw. Still, he reached for her hand again, and this time he turned it over in his and brushed his thumb along her palm.

"I suppose I phrased that rather badly. I'm sorry. I didn't mean *us*, I meant *us*." He chuckled at the feeble sound of the explanation, and folding Isabel's fingers over her palm, he gave them a squeeze that was warm with affection. "I don't mean four years ago," he explained. "And I certainly don't mean what's happened between us in the last weeks. What I meant is today. Just today. We've got a good deal to accomplish in the next six weeks, Belle, and we'll never do it if we're sniping at each other at every twist and turn. I thought . . ." He looked away, collecting his thoughts, and when he looked back at her, his eyes shimmered with the reflection of the sun against the water. "I wondered if just for today we might pretend that we actually liked each other."

"That's absurd!" Brave words, but Isabel's voice hardly conveyed her resolve. It quavered somewhere on the thin line between incredulity and emotion that was too raw to even consider. "It's preposterous."

"Insane."

"Illogical."

"Impossible." A smile crept back to Ben's face. "All the more reason we might want to try."

He had a point, of course, but Isabel wasn't about

to admit it. She threw back her shoulders. She drew in a deep breath. "Very well. It's ludicrous, of course, but I can see your logic. If we must work together for the Jubilee—"

"And we must."

"Then we may as well—"

"We may as well."

"We might begin with you allowing me to take back my hand."

The smile in Ben's eyes traveled to his lips. He gave her a lopsided grin at the same time he tightened his hold on her hand. "Ah, Miss De Quincy, but if we liked each other, it is just possible that you might allow me to keep a hold of this hand."

"I might." Isabel was willing enough to join in the game, or she might have been if not for the fact that Ben's smile and the feel of his skin against hers was making her week-kneed all over again. She steadied herself, looking past him to still the sudden confused clamoring of her heart.

"And if we liked each other, I just might thank you for bringing me here," she said sweetly, returning her gaze to his. "You must surely have remembered how much I enjoy the seashore."

"Remembered? Of course I did!" Ben tripped over his words. "It's one of the things I like about you, your love of the seashore."

"Really?" The more he scrambled to redeem himself, the more Isabel enjoyed the silly game he'd invented. "Then tell me, what else do you like about me?"

"Like?" When confronted with so blatant a question, Ben seemed a bit unsure. He ran his tongue over his lips and cleared his throat. "You have very nice eyes," he said. Ben stood tall, shoulders back, chin steady, as if now that he'd proposed the game, he wasn't at all sure that he wanted to play. "Nice eyes. Lovely hair. You have the face of an angel, Belle, though there are times I think you are one of those avenging sorts of angels and not one of those pink and white fluffy angels one sees in children's books."

"Hmmm." Considering the flattery—if that's what she could call it—Isabel tipped her head and bit her lower lip. "It is quite fitting, I suppose, that the only things you like about me are physical. Shallow, Mr. Costigan." She shook her head sadly. "Shallow, indeed. If we are really to pretend we like each other, I would suggest that you try for something far more profound. You might expound on my multitude of talents. Or my business genius. You might even say something as to the transcendental nature of my soul and how it speaks to yours."

"I might." Ben pulled a face that told her it was not really much of a possibility. He slipped his hand from hers and up her arm until his fingers were nestled just below the lace that decorated her sleeve. "Or I might start all over again." He leaned closer and lowered his voice, and whereas before he'd sounded no more confident than a condemned man speaking his last words, now he sounded like a poet, his words shimmering with emotion.

"I might remind you, Miss De Quincy, that you do have the most beautiful eyes in all the world." He touched one finger to each of her eyes so that her eyelids drifted shut. "And lovely hair." He drifted one hand over her head, then cupped her chin in one hand.

"I might tell you that you do have the face of an angel. And that though I tried like the devil for four long years, I could never get it out of my mind." Her eyes still closed, Isabel felt him close the space between them. Tentative and experimental, and all the more eloquent because of it, his lips brushed hers.

Isabel's heart skipped a beat. Her pulse quickened. She held her breath and braced herself, desire mixing with the panic that pounded through her bloodstream and caused her stomach to pitch.

It was not so much the kiss itself that worried her. It was what her reaction to it might be.

It was easy for her to tell herself exactly how she

should act. She should be as chilly as the ocean waters. She knew that much. She should be calm and dispassionate, and as disinterested as Ben expected her to be.

A few weeks ago the advice might have been easy enough to follow. But that was before Ben had charged back into her life and began the slow but steady process of demolishing the walls she'd spent four years building around her heart.

Yes, Isabel admitted to herself, the advice was sound. The only problem was that she wasn't at all sure she had the self-mastery, or the inclination, to follow it.

And she knew she didn't have the strength.

Poised on the brink where bitter memories battled sweet desire, she felt herself sway back, widening the gap between them, then forward toward Ben. She tipped her head to share the kiss. She heard Ben take a sharp breath of air, a sound of delight as surely as it was one of surprise. His hand tightened ever so slightly against her chin, and she knew he was about to bring his mouth down full on hers.

He might have done just that if Isabel's stomach hadn't chosen that particular and very inopportune moment to growl its emptiness loud enough for the world to hear.

Still cradling her chin in one hand, Ben laughed and backed away far enough for Isabel to see his embarrassed grin. "I promised you lunch." He offered her his arm. "Miss De Quincy, would you care to join me for luncheon? Ah! But before you answer!" He held up one hand, stopping her words. "You must agree. Just for today. No quarrels. No conflicts. Just for today, we are the best of friends."

It was the best she could hope for.

"Yes. Just for today." Isabel put her arm through Ben's and allowed him to lead her along the ridge. She thought they might stop at the Phaeton and that he would produce a picnic basket from the boot, but she was wrong. He bypassed the automobile and continued on to a sloping path that led down to the shore.

Once there, he instructed her to close her eyes, and when she'd reluctantly complied, he spun her around twice and steadied her on her feet.

"You can look now."

Isabel opened her eyes, and she could not control herself. She laughed. There in the shade of a rocky cliff was a table set for two. It was complete with every luxury she might have imagined: wine goblets and fruit, silver and lace. It was breathtaking, and so astonishing she could not keep herself from clapping in approval.

"No. No." Ben waved away the applause. "I am not the miracle worker. My staff is. My country home isn't far from here, and I am, you'll agree, quite persuasive when I have a mind to be."

She couldn't deny that. After all, he had persuaded her to accompany him today. He had coaxed her into believing that for the few hours they lingered there at the shore, they might actually be civil to each other. He had reminded her that years before, there had been a magic to being with him, and he had shown her that in spite of all they'd said and all they'd done, the remnants of it had somehow managed to survive. It glimmered in the air all around them like the droplets of sea mist that sparkled over the water.

When Ben pulled a chair back from the table for her, Isabel sat down. She watched while he opened a bottle of wine and poured some of it into the two crystal glasses set on the table, and when he was seated, she raised her glass and touched it to his.

"This is all very impressive," she said, her laughter as clear as the sounds of the glasses clinking together. "Only tell me one thing, Ben. What would you have done with all this if I'd decided not to agree to like you this afternoon?"

# Chapter 12

It really was remarkable how little they had to say to each other when they weren't fighting.

Considering the thought, Ben swirled the last of his wine in his glass. He looked across the remnants of the cucumber sandwiches, potted shrimps, smoked salmon, and Madeira cake that had been their picnic lunch and over toward Isabel.

Her cheeks were flushed from the sting of the breeze and the afterglow of the wine. Her hair was delightfully disheveled. The short sleeves and low, rounded neckline of a gown that was meant to be worn in a warm and comfortable drawing room were no defense against the cool breeze coming off the water, and Ben had found a paisley shawl in among the paraphernalia left by his staff and thrown it around her shoulders. Embraced in the folds of the voluminous shawl, she looked nothing less than charming.

And Ben couldn't tell her as much.

He couldn't tell her anything. Now that they were supposed to be friends, now that their conversation wasn't filled with imputations and accusations, condemnations and criticisms, it seemed as if they'd run out of words.

"The weather is certainly fine for this time of year." Isabel did her best to try and sound interested, but her words had the hollow echo of the idle chatter Ben had heard at countless teas and interminable soirees. "With any luck—"

"Yes, with any luck it will stay fine." As if he really

cared, Ben took a long look up at the bright blue sky with its splashes of fleecy white clouds. "Last month wasn't nearly so pleasant, of course. But then it's not quite summer yet, and with any luck—"

"Yes, with any luck . . ." Looking as uncomfortable as Ben felt, Isabel hitched the shawl farther up her shoulders.

An awkward silence filled the air, punctuated only by the screams of seabirds and the unrelenting rhythm of the water lapping against the shore.

Ben drummed his fingers against the tabletop. He checked the wine bottle, and finding it empty, he set it down, moved it, settled it back right where it had come from.

"Lunch was delicious." Isabel offered him a smile that came and went quickly, like the shadows of the gulls that raced over the lace-covered table. "Your household staff must be very good. They've been with you long?"

"Not too long. My butler, of course. Been with me for years. But my chef I met in Italy. Masterful fellow. Talented."

"Very talented."

"He's adapted remarkably well to using local ingredients. The man's talented."

"Talented, yes."

Isabel cleared her throat. Ben shifted in his chair.

"We should—"

They spoke the words together and covered the untimely faux pas with uneasy laughter.

Ben nodded toward Isabel, urging her to continue. Isabel yielded with an answering nod.

"We should—"

They started together again, and this time their laughter was genuine.

"Damn!" Half in amazement, half in disgust, Ben shook his head. "I can't believe two people who have known each other for so many years can find little else to do than exchange meaningless pleasantries. There must be something we can talk about." Before he could even stop to think about it, he spoke the first words that came to mind. "Tell me about Lord Epworth."

It was a mistake. Ben knew it. It was a mistake to ask about something so private. A mistake to let Isabel know that her personal life was of any concern to him.

Surprisingly, she did not point it out. She looked straight ahead, her eyes reflecting the clear green-blue of the water. "Peter and I . . ." She hesitated, gathering her thoughts the same way she gathered the folds of the shawl closer around her. "He tried very hard. Really." She turned in her chair and looked at Ben, as if trying to convince him. "Peter is a dear, but he is not used to being associated with gossip of any kind and . . ."

"And we are providing a feast for the scandalmongers." Ben slapped one hand against the table. "It's none of their business."

"None at all," Isabel agreed.

"I'd like to rip out their tongues. Every one of them." Reminded of how angry he felt each time he saw their names mentioned in the newspapers, Ben shot out of his chair. His voice ricocheted off the cliff at their backs. "I'd like to ask every one of them how they'd feel if—"

"It's our own fault, of course."

Isabel's voice wasn't nearly as loud as Ben's. Her words weren't nearly as fierce. He pulled himself out of the fury that burned through him to find her considering him, her head tipped to one side. "The same thing happened four years ago when the wedding was canceled, you remember. They ate up every delicious piece of gossip they could find—"

"And regurgitated it for all the world to see."

"We should have known better. We should have been more controlled."

"But control was never one of the things we did well."

They both knew exactly what Ben was talking about. Isabel's cheeks colored, and even though she was wrapped in the folds of the shawl, he saw her take a quick, sharp breath. He was about to remind her of all the times and all the places where control had been the last thing on their minds—and passion the first—when he recalled their agreement.

Just for today.

Ben bit back the words that might have baited Isabel further. It was obvious she didn't need the reminder. Neither did he. The memory warmed him through and sent a rush of desire pooling in his gut.

"So . . ." As eager to hide his reaction as he was to scatter the memories that had no place in his head, he strolled over to where the waves lapped against the shore. "That brings up the subject of the wedding. We've been avoiding it, you know. But I suppose we have to talk about it sooner or later. It's time."

"There isn't a thing to talk about." For a moment a familiar note of irritation sharpened Isabel's words. She remembered herself just in time, and pulling in the rest of what she might have said along with a deep breath, she rose from her chair and went to stand near the water. As careful to keep her distance from Ben as she was to keep her gaze on the waves, she clutched her hands where the shawl was knotted over her bosom. "I thought I loved you."

"I thought I loved you, too." Feeling more the fool than ever, Ben laughed a laugh that sounded far more convincing than it felt. "Remarkable, isn't it, how wrong two people can be?"

"Completely wrong," Isabel agreed quickly. Too quickly. It was obvious she'd spent time thinking through the problem, and just as obvious she'd decided long ago that a romance he'd thought of as nothing short of extraordinary was simply a foolish mistake to her.

Eager to convince her she wasn't the only one who felt that way, hoping to convince himself, Ben clenched his jaw against a wave of emotion that tasted far too much like disappointment for his liking. "Totally wrong."

"Absolutely wrong."

"We're lucky, you know," he told her. "Lucky we realized it."

"Infinitely lucky."

"And luckier still that we were wise enough not to get into a situation we might never have been able to get out of."

"Very lucky, indeed."

"So that instead of cursing each other every chance we get, we should be thanking each other—"

"We should."

"And cursing Sir Digby instead." Ben came to the conclusion with a satisfied *hurumph*. "It really was outrageous of him to make us work together this way. If I didn't know better—"

"I know. I've thought the same thing." Mystified, Isabel shook her head. "If I didn't think him a man of utmost honor, I might actually think that Sir Digby—"

"Engineered the entire thing—"

"Just to throw us together."

"The question is, why?" Frustrated, Ben kicked the toe of his left boot into the soft sand.

Isabel poked the sand with her right foot. "I remember what Papa used to say. About Sir Digby. He said that he was a crusty old fellow on the outside. And on the inside he was a hopeless romantic."

"Sir Digby?" The very idea seemed out of keeping with everything Ben knew about Sir Digby Talbot. "You mean Sir Digby really might have had this whole thing planned from the very beginning? Seems rather ruthless."

"And more than a little devious."

"And hopelessly romantic." Ben wasn't sure he liked the sound of that. He wasn't sure he liked the way it made him feel, either. For some reason he didn't even want to think about, his blood suddenly buzzed through his veins and his heart beat in perfect time to the restless rhythm of the waves. "So . . ." He edged back into their original conversation the way he might have edged into the water had he been fool enough to dare its depths. Carefully. One step at a time. "So . . . you aren't seeing Epworth any longer?"

"No." Isabel untied the shawl. Retied it. There was a large boulder near where she stood, and she ran one hand over the moss that carpeted it. "We thought it best. Or at least Peter did. I thought . . ."

There was less wistfulness in her voice than there was self-awareness. The realization startled Ben, and he turned to her. "You thought what?"

Isabel tightened the shawl around her shoulders. She smoothed the skirt of her gown. She might have been considering her answer, or she might simply have been stalling for time. Finally, her mind made up, she turned to Ben. "I thought I would miss him," she said. "I find that I don't."

Ben was just as surprised by the rush of hope that quickened his blood as he was unsure what to do with it. It was a damned inconvenient sort of emotion, and not at all comfortable, and because he didn't know how else to respond to it, he laughed. "Poor Epworth! Gone and forgotten, all in one fell swoop." His laughter was a poor defense against the emotion that shone in Isabel's eyes. His words evaporated along with his laugh, their bravura fading beneath Isabel's intensity. Before Ben could stop himself or even think through the fact that it was the wrong thing to do, he had Isabel's hand in his. "Then what you're saying is that you are a free woman?"

"I assure you, sir, I have always been a free woman." For a moment the old Isabel was back in spades, full of spit and vinegar and angry enough to chew button sticks. Her eyes flashed. Her lips thinned. "There isn't a man anywhere who has a claim on me. And never has been."

It was as close as she'd come to reminding him that though they had pledged an afternoon's friendship, there were other issues that stood between them and always would. Chastised, Ben released her hand. "No. Right. Of course. I didn't mean to imply—"

"Of course you didn't." Embarrassed by the outburst, Isabel's face paled. She hurried to make amends at the same time Ben raced to accept her apology.

"It's just that—"

"Of course it is."

"I only thought that—"

"Of course you did." Isabel turned away to stare out at the water again.

Because Ben didn't know what else to do, he stared at the ocean, too.

Side by side they watched the waves lap the shore, and the awkward seconds turned to even more awkward minutes.

It was Isabel who made the first move. Poking the sand with one foot, she darted a look at Ben as if to gauge his reaction. "I might ask you . . ." Bolstering her courage, she bit her lower lip. "I might ask you much the same thing. I might ask about Lola."

"Lola?" It took a second or two for Ben to think what—or who—she might be talking about. The realization dawned with a flash. "Oh, Lola!" Ben laughed self-consciously. "That's different, isn't it? You and Peter were nearly engaged. You don't think that Lola and I were—"

"Weren't you?"

She pinned him with the question. And a look.

Ben shifted his weight from one foot to the other. The soft sand moved along with him, giving him the momentary, unsettling feeling of losing his footing. It was the same way he was beginning to feel about the conversation, and he planted his feet and turned to Isabel.

"Lola is Lola." It was a feeble explanation at best, and he capped it with an innocent sort of smile that was every bit as ineffectual. "She was and is nothing more than a sweet charmer with more of a body than a brain. She was a toy. A plaything. You can't blame me, Belle, and you can't condemn me, either. I really had no choice." Ben knew he sounded far too defensive to be convincing. And he didn't give a damn. Though their agreement had sworn them both to be cordial, there was nothing in it that barred him from speaking the truth. He raised his chin and met Isabel's crisp look head-on. "I had to do something to try and forget you."

She wasn't nearly as impressed by the confession as he'd hoped she would be. Skeptical and not above letting him know it, she gave him a one-sided sort of smile. "How flattering. Did it work?"

"No." There was little consolation in the admission, and less relief. Ben took out his frustration by stomping the few paces back to the table, then stomping back again.

"How could Lola make me forget you?" It was a rhetorical question. She wasn't meant to answer it. And even though she tried, Ben didn't give her the chance. He hurried right on with what he had to say. "It wasn't simply that she wasn't as beautiful as you. Hell, I haven't met a woman yet who is. But it's hard . . ." He drew in a breath, trying to put together the words that would explain his thoughts fully. "It's difficult to get close to a woman like Lola. For one thing, she drinks far more than she should. You discovered that for yourself that night you appeared at the Adelphi. For another thing . . . I said Lola wasn't very bright, but that isn't entirely true. She may not be intelligent, but she's damned clever when it comes to business. She knows how to make a man pay. For everything. Why, even that soulful kiss she gave me that day of the first committee meeting when we were out in Sir Digby's antechamber—"

"You paid her to kiss you?"

If Ben wasn't so busy explaining away his actions, he might have laughed at the expression on Isabel's face. Her mouth dropped open in astonishment, and her eyes went as round as saucers.

He pulled his earlobe. "I'm afraid so." he admitted. "Yes. It's true. As poor Edward Baconsfield is finding out even as we speak, Lola doesn't do anything for free. I did pay her to kiss me, but only because I wanted to see what your reaction might be. And I'll tell you what . . ." At the memory a smile crawled up Ben's face. "It was worth every shilling. You should have seen your face! You looked as if you'd bit into a lemon. You were upset, Belle, and don't say you weren't. You were as jealous as hell."

"I certainly was not." Isabel was as good as any at putting on airs when the situation suited her, and right now the situation more than suited. She lifted her chin, and her face took on that placid semblance of porcelain perfection that told Ben beyond a shadow of a doubt that he was right. But as masterful as Isabel was, even she was not adept enough to keep her astonishment at bay for too long. Her icy expression melted into one of complete disbelief. "You *paid* Lola to kiss you?"

Ben laughed. So, she was as worried about his relationship with Lola as he was about hers with Peter. It wasn't much, but it was enough to lighten his spirits. There were a few coins in his pocket, and he pulled out a sixpence and held it up for Isabel to see while he took a step closer to her. "I'll pay you, too. Interested?"

She gave him a glare of epic proportions. "I am certainly not."

He flashed her a smile and took another step nearer. "Then you'll do it for free?"

"I'll . . . you'll . . ." Caught on the horns of her own logic, Isabel shrieked in frustration. "You are putting words in my mouth."

"Not the only thing I'd like to put there." There was less than a foot between them, not enough to deter Ben. With one hand he reached out, and with one finger he brushed the full curve of Isabel's lower lip.

As if waiting for him, she stood as still as the ancient outcroppings of stone around them, her eyes suddenly dark with the same desire that pounded through Ben's veins.

"We are supposed to be nothing more than friends this afternoon." Isabel's words were brave, but her voice caught over them, stumbling over a breath she couldn't seem to catch.

"We are being friendly." Ben grinned. Another step brought him another few inches nearer.

Isabel's eyes wavered from his face to the coin he still held up between his thumb and forefinger: "Friends don't need to pay friends to—"

"Right you are!" With a flick of his wrist Ben sent the coin spinning out into the water. It splashed into the waves twenty feet from shore and disappeared with a satisfying *plop*.

"Friends don't let their friends get deep into a situation that is as foolish as it is dangerous, either." Even as Isabel spoke, she leaned into the caress of his hand and rubbed her cheek against his skin.

"Friends also admit when they've made a mistake." Ben grazed his thumb across her cheek. "They don't lie to each other."

A smile came and went over Isabel's face. It left her looking desolate. "They don't pretend at something that doesn't exist, either," she told him. She closed her eyes against the certainty but her lips grazed his palm.

Like lightning, the touch of Isabel's lips seared Ben's skin and sizzled through his bloodstream. He looped his free arm around her waist and pulled her to him. "Then we won't pretend. The last time you kissed me was in Margaret's conservatory," he reminded her. "You were pretending I was Peter."

"I knew you weren't."

"Yes, but I didn't know that." The memory of the frustration and humiliation he'd felt at the time rushed over Ben like the ocean waves. He fought his way clear of the emotions, the exquisite hunger that shone in Isabel's eyes a lifeline in a storm-tossed sea. "This time, we won't pretend. Not for a moment. It's just you and me, Bella. Not a man and a woman who were once engaged to be married. Not a man and a woman who are competing tooth and nail to outdo each other at the Jubilee. Just Ben and Isabel. A man and a woman."

His courage emboldened by the fact that Isabel's enthusiasm was every bit a match for his, Ben brought his mouth down on hers and kissed her thoroughly. His passion spiraled with each new touch of her lips, each taste of her tongue. He drew in a sharp breath of delight when her arms went around his neck, and she tickled her fingers through his hair.

"There. You see. It isn't so bad to pretend we're friends, is it?" He spoke the question against Isabel's ear, his voice rough with longing, before he outlined the shape of her ear with the tip of his tongue and glided his hands to her waist. Her gown was a light concoction of some summery fabric, delicate against his fingers, and light enough that he could feel her curves beneath it. Ben murmured in approval. He skimmed his hands up her ribs. He brushed her breasts with his thumbs.

Isabel dragged in a breath that was honed with pleasure. It pushed her breasts against his hands, and Ben nudged aside the shawl and pressed a lingering kiss to the hollow at the base of her throat. He smiled when she moaned.

It was the same sound he remembered hearing from her a dozen times before, soft at the same time it was sensual, dreamy as a whisper and as intoxicating as the finest wine, and it wasn't until the vibration of it registered in his brain and trembled against his lips that he realized how much he'd missed her.

"Oh, Bella!" His fingers far more clumsy than they should have been, Ben worked at the knot of the shawl. He tugged at it, fumbled it, loosened it finally, and with a whoop of triumph, he tossed it to the sand. He covered Isabel's neck with kisses and ran his tongue along the ridge of her collarbone. She tasted like heaven, exactly the way he remembered, and when she glided her hands from around his neck and slid them inside his jacket, he breathed a contented sigh against her skin.

"Oh, Bella!" Ben grazed a series of lingering kisses over her shoulders and down to where the neckline of her gown skimmed over the rise of her bosom. "It's been too long."

"Far too long." Isabel's voice broke over the words. They were punctuated by the quick, short gasps of breath that pressed her breasts provocatively closer to Ben's lips, underscored by the eager and delicious feel of her hands as they swept up his back and over his shoulders, across his shoulders and down to his waist.

"And we've been far too angry with each other."

"Far too angry."

"And we really should—"

"No, we really shouldn't, but—"

"But you want to as much as I do." Ben moved far enough away to look into Isabel's eyes. They were the same clear, bright blue as the sky and flecked with sparks that reminded him of the glint of the sunlight upon the water. Her pupils were dark and glassy, like onyx, and her lips were moist and swollen from his kisses. A single curl of flaxen hair hung over her shoulder, and he twisted it around one finger and tugged ever so gently, drawing her nearer.

"Tell me you want this as much as I do, Bella." Still watching her, he brushed a finger along the neckline of the dress. Back and forth and back again, and when she caught her lower lip in her teeth, he dared to venture even farther. He dipped his finger inside and brushed the curve of one breast, smiling at the silken feel of her skin against his and the look on her face that was a perfect and irresistible mix of wonder and yearning.

Ben bent and pressed a kiss into the shadowy softness between her breasts. It might have been infinitely more pleasurable, not to mention helpful, if his lips hadn't met with the small silk pouch he'd first discovered in their encounter in the conservatory.

"What's this, then?" Intrigued, Ben touched a finger to the pouch. "A love token? It can't be from Epworth, yet—"

As if his touch were fire, Isabel flinched and scrambled out of his arms. She clutched both her hands to her bosom, protecting the pouch. "It isn't anything," she said. Her voice was breathy with the remnants of their shared passion, but there was surely some other emotion in it. Some feeling that trembled through her hands as surely as it did through her words. It sounded to Ben like mistrust, or regret, and left him with the sensation that the sand had given way under his feet and left him to free fall into a place where sudden heart-stopping desire melted into frustration and hope dissolved into confusion.

"You don't have to tell me about it if you don't want to." As desperate to recapture the mood of unchecked passion as he was to understand what was going on, Ben took a slow step toward Isabel, one hand out in appeal. "You are surely allowed your secrets, Belle. I only thought—"

"Yes. Of course. I can hardly blame you." An apologetic smile fluttered across Isabel's face. Collecting her thoughts, schooling her emotions, she pressed both hands to her lips. "It's just that . . ." She met Ben's gaze with one every bit as disappointed as his own. "You said it yourself, Ben. Just for today. And if any relationship between us is just for today . . ."

"Is that what's bothering you?" Ben laughed, his mood brightening. "And here I thought your qualms were the product of dark secrets."

Isabel laughed, too, the sound of it a little hollow, and her hand stole again to the pouch tucked into the front of her dress. She glanced at the chalk cliffs at their backs, then toward the water. "It really isn't a very good spot for a romantic rendezvous, is it?" she asked, stating a fact that would have been obvious to Ben had he been thinking with his head instead of with other parts of his body. "I do believe we could be seen from clear across the channel."

Ben couldn't argue with her there. Isabel was right. As much as he hated to admit it, she was as right as ninepence. Moving forward, he took her hand in his and squeezed it. Even now the warmth of her skin kindled an answering heat in him, and before she could remind him that it was far too public a place for far too private a matter, he pulled her to him and captured her mouth with his. He kissed her long and hard, until they were both struggling to catch their breath.

"We should be getting back." It wasn't at all what Ben wanted to do, but he knew he had to suggest it before the taste of Isabel's lips went to his head and robbed him of every one of his good intentions. "It will be past teatime by the time we get to London, and I think it best to be off the roads before the sun goes down."

"Yes. Of course." Isabel smoothed a hand over her hair and, bending down, scooped the shawl out of the sand. She tossed it over the back of the nearest chair and headed up the path that would take them to the top of the cliff and back to the waiting Phaeton.

Ben watched her walk ahead of him, savoring the gentle sway of her hips beneath the lightweight dress and the fact that her steps were every bit as unsteady as his. "Only, Bella . . ."

At the top of the path, he called to her and watched her turn, a question in her eyes.

"This may not have been the right time or the right place. But there are other times and other places." He took her arm and watched as her cheeks colored appreciatively. "Remember," he said, bending to whisper in her ear. "I am not the sort of man who gives up easily."


For the first time in four years, Ben and Isabel were at peace with each other. And with themselves.

It was about as surprising an outcome to the day's excursion as any Isabel might have foreseen, and thinking it through, she leaned back against the comfortably padded seat of the Phaeton and sighed, contented.

By the time they were on the road, she had calmed

her nerves and pushed her worries to the back of her mind. Ben had not discovered that she was carrying the recipe for Diamond Rain in the small silk pouch tucked into her gown, and for that at least, she was thankful. It was the one emotion tumbling through her that she could name.

The rest of her feelings swam through her head and heart the way the air streamed over them as they sped on toward London. They were clear one moment and the next blurred like the scenery that streaked by.

There was no denying the fact that she had been more than ready to surrender to Ben's sweet seduction. Four years ago—four months ago!—the very thought would have left Isabel wondering if she was mad. Today, she was ready to admit that only the fear of him discovering the secret in the silk pouch had kept her from yielding to the desires that had pounded through them both. But though she had not surrendered her body, she could not deny the fact that she had come a long way toward surrendering her heart.

The game of friendship they'd thought they were playing had been a revelation to them both. Ben had made her laugh. He'd made her ache with longing. He'd made her realize that for four long years she had been empty and wanting.

She never would have guessed that what she'd been wanting was Ben.

The very thought was so outrageous, it made Isabel smile. Ben noticed and reached over to pat her knee.

"We're almost home." He yelled above the noises of London traffic all around them. "We'll have dinner at Mancini's." He didn't ask if she was free, or even if she was hungry. A week ago the very thought would have sent Isabel's temper flaring like a rocket. Today, it made her realize that he didn't care if she was free, or hungry. Like her, he didn't want the day to end.

As amazing as it seemed, the thought lightened her spirits and burned through her body the way Ben's kiss had heated her through to the bone.

It was certainly not something on which they could

build a lifetime. It might not get them through the next weeks until the Jubilee. But for today it was enough.

"We've got a lot of work to do."

"Yes." Isabel's answer was snatched up by the wind. "I've given the Jubilee a great deal of thought. We'll open with an earth-shattering maroon."

"A maroon?" At the same time he negotiated a curve, Ben turned to her in amazement. How he was able to do both at the same time he avoided a dray that was stopped square in the street in front of them was a mystery to Isabel. She found herself clutching the leather upholstery with tense fingers and breathing a shaky sigh of relief when they came through the procedure unharmed. "We'll begin with a barrage of shells," he said. "Every color of the rainbow."

Isabel clicked her tongue and gave him a scathing look the potency of which was, unfortunately, lost behind her motoring goggles. Or perhaps it was not so unfortunate. She remembered the afternoon. And the way Ben had made her feel. She remembered their promise of friendship and disguised her skepticism behind a tight smile. "It's tradition to begin with a salute," she reminded him. "One giant maroon—"

"Yes, shells." Ben nodded vigorously. "I knew you'd agree."

"But I haven't. I—" Ben turned abruptly in front of an oncoming carriage and slammed to a stop directly in front of the De Quincy home, and the rest of Isabel's objection was lost in a shriek.

"We're here!" His eyebrows raised behind his goggles, he beamed at her. "I'll leave you to clean up and nip over to my flat to do the same. I'll be back in an hour. How's that? And we can—"

"You're doing it again!" The tender feelings Isabel had been contemplating only moments before melted beneath the rush of aggravation that stirred her blood every bit as thoroughly as had Ben's kisses. She bit back the words that were certain to convey her opinions and her annoyance, and hid the fact that her hands were trembling by carefully smoothing her fingers over her long dust coat.

"You are assuming that we are going to follow your plan for the Jubilee," she said, her voice as sweet as the look she gave him. "You're wrong, Ben." Refusing to let him know that the trip home had left her just as weak-kneed as had the trip to the shore, Isabel hopped out on the street and rounded the automobile to the pavement as quickly as she could. Bracing herself against the Phaeton, she stripped off her dust coat, hat, and goggles and tossed them onto the seat.

"No one begins a fireworks show with a barrage of shells," she said, and she congratulated herself. Her words were careful and measured. Her voice was calm. The voice of reason. "It simply isn't done. We carry an awesome responsibility. We are honor bound to design a show that is befitting of Her Majesty's—"

"The old dear will love it!" His legs apparently far steadier than Isabel's, Ben hopped out of the Phaeton and blithely discarded his goggles and coat. He came to stand with Isabel on the pavement. It was nearly evening, and what was left of the light settled in his eyes like the shadows that were building in the doorways of the houses around them.

It was the first clue Isabel had that he was every bit as annoyed as she was. The second was the smile he gave her, one that was every bit as stiff as her own. "The Queen isn't going to love a maroon. And neither is anyone else. The crowd is going to want sparkle. And brilliance. That is certainly more befitting the occasion than a little *pop*."

"But I'm not talking about a little *pop*. I am talking about a maroon." Isabel clenched her jaw until her muscles ached, but she'd be damned if she was going to let him see how angry he'd made her. She would explain reasonably. Logically. She would pretend as she had pretended all afternoon. She would pretend they really were friends. "I'm talking about a colossal maroon. One that is sure to make everyone sit up and take notice."

"And I am talking about shells." Ben crossed his arms over his chest. "Shells are much more interesting than maroons. They are colorful and—"

"Thank goodness you're home!"

The sound of Simon's voice from the front doorway interrupted whatever else Ben might have said. Isabel turned.

"You must come inside. Quickly." Simon waved them toward the house. His skin was far paler than it should have been. His breathing, far faster.

Isabel took the steps two at a time. "What is it?" she asked her brother. "What's happened?"

Simon shook his head. Whatever it was, he didn't want to discuss it out on the street. He opened the door and hurried inside, and Isabel followed him. The closest private room was the morning room, and that was where Simon headed. It wasn't until they were inside that Isabel realized that Ben had followed. He shut the door behind them and leaned against it, watching Simon carefully.

There was no time to argue, or to ask what he thought he was doing. Isabel went to her brother, her hands out. "Simon, what is it? What's happened?"

His eyes darting from Ben to Isabel, Simon ran his tongue over his lips. "It's the offices," he explained, breathless. "The offices of De Quincy and Sons. Isabel . . ." He looked toward his sister, worry shining in his eyes. "Isabel, we've been burglarized!"

# Chapter 13

Isabel might have done a dozen different things. She might have hurried to soothe Simon. Or demand an explanation. She might have asked if he'd informed the London Metropolitan Police. Or caught hold of his panic and felt as distraught as he looked.

What she did instead was laugh.

"Don't be ridiculous." Something about Simon's announcement didn't ring true, and Isabel rejected it with a decisive shake of her head and the kind of smile she used to give him when they were children and he was convinced there were dragons lurking beneath his bed. "There isn't anything at the offices anyone would want to steal. We don't keep any money around and—"

"It appears as if they weren't looking for money." Simon scraped both his hands through his hair. It stood up in spikes and left him looking rather like an agitated rooster. He flapped around the room, his arms slapping his sides. "They had a go at the safe, Belle. Got it opened, too. You know as well as I do what they were after. They wanted the recipe for—"

"Diamond Rain!"

Isabel's breath rushed out of her, and automatically her hand went to her heart.

Simon didn't notice, or if he did, he didn't understand the significance of the gesture. He massaged the back of his neck with one hand. "I came in to find the door of the safe wide open. I looked everywhere for the recipe, Belle. Tore the place apart. It's gone. Completely gone. Whoever broke into the safe—"

"Whoever broke into the safe was on a bootless errand." What Simon didn't understand, Ben apparently did. He stepped away from the door, and his gaze dropped from Isabel's face to where her hand was pressed to her bosom. "They didn't find it, did they, Belle?"

Was it Isabel's imagination, or did he sound as if his hopes had been dashed?

The question left her suddenly icy. It knotted her stomach and made her head spin.

Clutching a nearby table with one hand, Isabel pulled in a breath that stung her lungs. Suspicions rose in her mind, bitter as bile, and though she did her best to quell them, they would not be so easily silenced. She stood there, powerless, while the simple hopes that had brightened her afternoon faded before her eyes and doubts spread to fill all the places where only so short a time ago, desire had reigned supreme.

She struggled to hide her reaction at the same time she somehow managed to find her voice, and when she turned to Simon, she had smoothed every trace of her misgivings from it. "Would you leave us, please?"

"Leave you?" Simon could not have been more surprised. He flapped at her from across the room. "We have important things to discuss, Belle. Like where the devil the recipe's gone and what we're going to do now that—"

"Please, Simon." There was less pleading in Isabel's voice than there was determination. She gave the door a pointed look. "Ben and I need to talk. Alone."

Simon pulled to a stop. Offended by the dismissal and not above letting either of them know it, he pulled back his shoulders and headed for the door. When he was gone, Ben closed the door behind him and leaned back against it.

For a long time Isabel stood stock still, listening to the silence that closed around them. Disillusionment mingled with anger, leaving a taste like ashes in her mouth that made it difficult to speak. She glanced at Ben, at the lips that tasted of fire, at the arms that had clasped her to his heart, at the face, the one she was certain would haunt her dreams forever.

Steeling herself against the memories, she clutched her hands at her waist. "Disappointed?" she asked.

"Disappointed?" His brows dipping into a straight line over his eyes, Ben pushed off from the door. "What are you talking about? Why would the fact that your offices have been burglarized disappoint me? You can't think—" In the next second it was all clear to him. His expression grew thunderous. "You can't possibly think that I had anything to do with—"

"It was convenient, wasn't it?" As eager to escape from the sparks of anger in his blue eyes as she was to release the anxious energy that shook through her hands and made her knees quake, she turned away from him and went to stand near the mantelpiece. As always, the household staff had been in that morning to tidy up, and the photographs that were displayed there in their silver and enameled frames were dusted clean and aligned in precise order. Still, she rearranged them not once but twice, her fingers trembling though her voice was remarkably calm. "You made sure I couldn't go to the office today. Got me well out of the way. Then, when I was gone . . ."

Anxious to watch Ben's eyes and gauge his reaction, she turned to him. "Convenient, Ben. Too convenient. And a damned sight dishonorable. Even for you."

"Which is exactly why I didn't do it." Ben's voice reverberated off the crystal chandelier along with the profanity he used to emphasize his statement. "You don't really think that I'm enough of a fool to—"

"Oh, no. You're not a fool at all." Isabel congratulated herself. Somehow she managed to make it sound as if it didn't really matter. As if her heart wasn't broken in two. "I'm the fool. I've no doubt of that. I was skeptical at first, I'll admit that much. I doubted your sincerity. It didn't seem possible that you'd come out just to take me motoring. But after a while . . ." Her throat closed and she coughed away the sensation. "After the excursion to the sea and the delicious lunch, after we actually spent some time discussing the wedding without tossing accusations back and forth at each other . . ." She coughed again and covered the cough with a rough laugh. "You see, I am the fool. Even now I find it hard to believe I was gullible enough to think you actually meant any of it."

"Meant it? Of course I meant it!" Before Isabel ever saw him coming, he was only inches from her. He snatched her close, his fingers digging into her forearms. His eyes blazed into hers, blue as cornflowers and bright with fury. "What of our kisses, then, do you think they meant nothing?"

"As much as they did four years ago."

"That little, eh?"

Ben's words stung like a slap. He knew it. When Isabel flinched, a passing smile lit his eyes. It was gone as quickly as it came, and he dropped his hands and moved back a step. The inches between them widened into a chasm.

"Then I'm the one who's a fool," he said. "I thought what happened this afternoon was genuine. And you . . ." He looked her up and down and sniffed softly, as if dismissing her. "You must think I'm desperate."

"I know you'll do anything to get your hands on the Diamond Rain recipe. Just as four years ago, you would have done anything for Emerald Mist." Isabel hugged her arms around herself, absently rubbing the place where Ben's fingers had pressed her skin. Eager to make him believe the afternoon meant as little to her as it obviously did to him, she lifted her chin and bit back the tears that threatened to betray her.

"Burglary is a bit drastic," she said, "but not at all out of keeping with your character. It is probably not easy to find a burglar, and you probably paid dearly for the service. I'm only sorry to tell you that you've wasted your money. Though even Simon doesn't know it, the recipe isn't missing. It wasn't in the safe. It's with me, and has been since the day I learned you were back in the country."

"All that time ago!" Ben laughed quietly and shook his head, apparently baffled. "And here I thought I was making a good impression on you. And you—"

"Didn't trust you any more than I would trust the devil himself."

He acknowledged the fact with what looked to be begrudging admiration.

It was the only thing he could do. There was nothing left to say.

Her heart in her throat, her stomach clenched, Isabel waited for him to walk out the door. It would be infinitely better if he did. Then they could both get on with their lives.

But Ben didn't leave. He stepped back and his gaze slid over Isabel, from the top of her head to her face and from there down to her bosom. As if suddenly he understood her secrets, he nodded. "Well, if nothing else, it explains your reluctance this afternoon."

"Do you think so?" Eager to steer him clear of the subject, she tossed her head. "Had it occured to you, Mr. Costigan, that I may have realized how pointless any relationship with you might be? I admit, I was charmed. For a moment or two. Then I came to my senses."

"Yes. Just as I've come to mine." As quick as a cat, Ben darted forward. He had one arm around her before she could twist away, and with his other hand he reached inside the neckline of her dress.

His touch wasn't at all gentle and not the least bit sensual. His fingers were quick and sure. He had them wrapped around the silk pouch in an instant, and with a smile of triumph he snatched it out of its hiding place.

Outrage blocked Isabel's throat and heated her blood. She curled her fingers into her palms and wrapped her thumbs around them, bracing herself against the anger. "There. See how easy it would have been all along." Her voice was hushed, her words clipped and painful. "You could have saved whatever money you paid your burglar and had the recipe long ago, if only you'd realized where it was."

Ben didn't answer, and though he ran the silky pouch through his fingers, he didn't take his eyes off Isabel. "It's really in here, isn't it? The jewel of the De Quincy and Sons crown. Diamond Rain."

Anger and humiliation buzzed through Isabel's blood. She steadied herself against the onslaught of emotions and the sick feeling that churned her stomach, and bit her lower lip, fighting the tears. "Yes, it's there. You've got what you wanted. The only thing you've wanted since you came back to London." Her gaze snapped to the door. "Now take it and go. I hardly care. It may be a loss to the company, but I suppose it is a small price to pay for the satisfaction of knowing I was right all along. Right about you."

"Oh, you were right about me. No doubt of that." Ben tossed the pouch in the air and caught it in one hand. "You think I'm a rogue. And a reprobate. You're convinced that I'm a charlatan as well. I don't deny it. Not any of it. I also don't deny that I wanted this." His fingers tightened around the pouch. "I've always been curious about the recipe. Curious about what you've combined and what sort of effect you anticipate. Is it a billowy burst of color? Or a gentle sort of sparkling rain?" He looked at the pouch, and for a moment Isabel thought he would open it and read through the chemical formula right then and there.

He didn't. His gaze slid from the pouch to Isabel, and the fire in his eyes dimmed. "Oh, yes, Belle. I wanted it. But not as much as you think I did." Closing his fingers around the pouch, he pressed a kiss to it. His fingers were still warm from the touch of his lips when he gently tucked the pouch back where it had come from. His hand poised above her heart, his eyes touched Isabel's, but only for a moment, and his words reverberated after him as he backed away. "Oh, no, Belle," he whispered. "I didn't want Diamond Rain nearly as much as you think. Not nearly as much as I wanted you."

It might have been relief that blazed through Isabel. It might have been embarrassment. It might even have been the burning fire of the realization that if she let Ben go now, she would never see him again.

Whatever the emotion, it blocked her throat and robbed her of her voice. She cursed herself for not knowing her own heart well enough to understand the feelings that rocketed through her. She cursed Ben for not giving her the time to find the words she needed to say.

She was still cursing them both when he walked out the door.

Ben wasn't a man who was prone to regrets. He didn't grumble about mistakes. Or second-guess his past. Except in those rare instances when something he said or did inadvertently offended the sensibilities of someone who was too old, too young, or too inexcusable stodgy to fully appreciate his sometimes audacious sense of humor, he didn't apologize.

He liked that about himself.

He also liked the fact that he knew what he wanted out of life and he went after it full-out.

At least he always had before.

The thought intruded on what should have been an otherwise pleasant evening. He was at the theater, and tonight's crowd was responding to his fountain firework the way every crowd that had ever seen it responded.

They were delirious. Delighted. Enthralled.

And their applause rang hollow in Ben's ears.

Pushing off from the place in the wings where he'd watched the show, Ben headed for the door.

There was no use wasting another minute there. The theater wasn't working any more effectively than had anything else he'd done in the last three days. No matter how hard he tried, nothing seemed to work. Nothing he did could get Isabel out of his head.

As he had a hundred times since the day of the motoring trip to the shore and their picnic by the sea,

Ben replayed the debacle of their last minutes together over in his mind. Like the last time he'd thought through it, and the time before, and the time before that, he came to the same conclusions.

Isabel was hardheaded. Irrational. Too quick to make judgments. And far too slow to forgive.

She was also perfectly justified in her suspicions.

The very thought brought Ben up short, and he froze in the center of the narrow passageway. Of course Isabel thought he'd been behind the burglary at De Quincy and Sons. He couldn't blame her for that. A burglary wasn't any more outrageous than the lancework of Isabel in her frillies. Or any more bold than pushing Isabel out on stage in front of a boisterous music hall crowd. In fact, a burglary was just the kind of thing he might have done. Hell, two months ago he would have gladly done it, if only he'd thought of it.

But that was then.

And this is now.

And now he wouldn't dream of stealing a De Quincy recipe.

The thought settled in his stomach rather like a bad pudding, and at the same time he excused himself and moved out of the way of the chorus girls who were trouping through on their way to the stage, he chewed over it.

He wasn't prepared to examine the reasons behind his sudden change of heart. He wasn't even willing to admit he'd had a change of heart. He only knew that had he been the man he used to be—decisive, confident, determined—he would never have left Isabel without making sure that she fully understood that he had nothing to do with the attempted theft of the formula. Instead, he'd stood there with his tongue tied and his heart hammering like the dickens, unsure what to say, what to do. And when his indecision got the best of him, he'd taken the coward's way out. He'd walked away.

If he was the man he used to be—that decisive,

confident, determined Ben Costigan of old—he wouldn't be mucking about around the theater tonight. He wouldn't have tried to gamble away his troubles the night before at the gaming tables. Or pulverize them, the night before that, beneath elephantine Wagnerian melodies at the opera.

If he was that man, he'd be at Isabel's. If she wasn't at home, he'd find her. He'd convince her of his innocence. Even if it meant scooping her into his arms and kissing her suspicions away.

It was exactly what needed to be done. And he might be just the man to do it, if only it didn't mean admitting that four years ago she'd cracked his heart in two.

And that this time her distrust—deserved or not—had demolished all that was left of it.

No more comfortable with the thought than he was with his surroundings, he took his top hat down from the peg on the wall near the stage door and reached for his coat.

"Not goin' already, are you? It's far too early, and you'll leave a girl far too lonely if you do."

The voice was a woman's, and as sultry as sunlight. It raised Ben's hopes at the same time it brought him spinning around. The first thing he saw was a flash of pink, and for a second his heart beat double time. He took a step toward the shadows where the speaker stood at the same time the woman took a step forward that brought her fully into the light.

Ben's smile faded at the same time his hopes came crashing down around him like the burnt bits of shell casings that littered the ground after a fireworks show. He shouldn't have been surprised, of course. He'd just finished watching the show. He'd seen Lola dance to the middle of the stage and light the fountain. He knew she was the one in the frothy pink costume tonight. It was simply that . . .

It was simply that his imagination had run away with him as surely as had his reason. Reining in the one at the same time he called upon the other, he offered his hand and a smile. "Lola. It's good to see you."

"Is it?" Lola didn't look nearly as convinced as she looked just the slightest bit squiffy. She leaned forward a bit as if to see Ben more clearly, and the aroma of cheap gin rose around her, nearly as powerful as her gardenia perfume. "If that's so, why don't you look happy?"

"Happy? Of course I'm happy." Ben smiled. Briefly. Artificially. He glanced over his shoulder toward the door. "Always good to see you, m'dear, but I must be off."

"Not so fast." Lola sidled closer. Beneath the short-cropped pink costume, her hips swayed enticingly. Above the low-cut neckline, her breasts jiggled. She trailed one finger down Ben's arm. "Ain't nowhere you have to go that I can't come along. Make the night more fun. And a lot less lonely."

It would indeed.

"And Edward?"

Lola lifted one shoulder enough to make the pink costume dip. "Always busy, that one is. A meetin' here, an appointment there. He may have money, but money don't keep a girl warm in the dark of the night. Not the way you could, luv."

Ben didn't ask what Lola had in mind. He didn't have to.

What Lola was offering was mindless, exhilarating, and completely unrestrained sex with no strings attached except those that led directly to his purse.

Ben considered the thought, and discarded it so quickly, it surprised even him. He was at the door even before he finished wishing Lola a good-night.

Out in the cool night air, he reminded himself that he was probably as big a fool as had ever walked the earth. He was passing up the opportunity to smother his troubles and his memories of Isabel in the pillows of Lola's monumental breasts.

And he didn't even care.

Hailing a passing cab, Ben decided that there was

only one remedy both for his disturbing memories and for his wounded pride. The same remedy he always turned to when his thoughts were troubled. The only thing sure to lift his spirits and make him forget the ache in his head, and his chest, and his gut.
Fireworks.

Four days after watching Ben walk out of her house and her life, Isabel still wasn't sure what she should have said. What she might have done.

She only knew that with each hour that passed, she was more and more sure that she had made a mistake.

Her fingers tapping restlessly against the overstuffed arm of the divan where she sat, she thought over the problem as she had time and again. Still, she found herself no closer to working her way through it, and no closer to understanding what had happened between them.

She had been so certain she knew her own mind, and her own heart. Before Ben came back into her life, she had been calm, level-headed, at peace with herself and with the world.

And now?

Now the only thing Isabel was certain of was that Ben Costigan was implacable, imperious, and just contemptible enough to engineer the burglary at her offices.

She was also certain he didn't do it.

The air rushed out of Isabel with a sigh, and she slumped farther in her chair. Automatically, her hand went to her heart. Even now she swore she could feel the heat of Ben's touch against her skin. It was that touch—and the fact that he hadn't even glanced at the recipe when he'd had the chance—that had taken her opinion of him and turned it on its head.

One touch.

It seemed impossible, yet it was undeniable.

One touch from Ben had made her question her judgment and her reasoning. It had forced her to examine her disturbing feelings for him.

Disgusted with herself and what was proving to be a bothersome tendency to think about Ben morning, noon, and night, Isabel rose from her chair and paced to the other side of the room. There was a window there, and she pushed aside the draperies and stared out of it. With the electric lights lit in the room, it was impossible to see much of the garden beyond. Instead, she saw her own reflection: the worried frown that tilted the corners of her lips, the troubled gleam in her eyes. She stared at herself, wondering how she could have made such a mull of things. And what she was going to do about it.

It wasn't as if she hadn't already tried to do something. The day before, she'd screwed her courage to the proverbial sticking place and gone to Ben's London townhouse. She was not very good at apologies, especially when it came to Ben, and for more time than she liked to admit, she puzzled over what she would say when he finally appeared. She needn't have worried; he wasn't home, and if the grim-faced servant who stopped her at the front door was to be believed, he wasn't going to be home anytime soon. He'd gone to stay at his country home while he worked at his nearby fireworks factory.

And Isabel had yet to find the boldness to follow after him.

Irritated at herself both for her indecision and her inaction, Isabel dropped the drapery back into place and turned. She was about to talk herself into finishing up some of the work she'd brought home from the office when she heard a familiar noise coming from the street. It started softly, then grew louder, and by the time it was close to the house, she recognized it as the hum of an automobile engine. Before she could convince herself she was being hasty and perhaps even a little irrational, Isabel felt her pulse quicken and her cheeks grow hot. She'd already taken a step toward the door when she heard the automobile continue on, passing the house. Her heart plummeted along with her hopes.

# DIAMOND RAIN

Just as quickly they skyrocketed again. The front door slammed, and she heard footsteps racing down the passageway.

"Belle? I say, Belle, where are you?"

It was Simon's voice, and hearing it, Isabel couldn't help but be concerned. He sounded short of breath and frightened, and she headed for the door, eager to see what might be the matter. She got there just as Simon hurried by out in the passageway.

"Oh, there you are!" Simon's cheeks were flushed against skin that was as pale as fireplace ashes. His coat was open. His collar, undone. At the sight of her, the worry cleared form his eyes, but only for a moment. It was back in an instant, and he hurried over to where Isabel stood. "I'm so glad I found you. I thought you might be out and—"

"Calm down. Relax." Isabel forced herself to swallow down the panic that automatically infected her. Grabbing hold of Simon's hands, she pressed them between hers. "Don't tell me there's been another burglary?"

"Burglary?" Simon looked at her as if he hadn't any idea what she was talking about. The next second the confusion cleared from his expression, and he shook his head. "No. No burglary. But, Belle, dear . . ." He ran his tongue over his lips. "I must talk to you. Do you . . . would you like to sit down?"

It seemed as unlikely a suggestion as any Isabel might have heard, and she discarded it with an uncomfortable laugh. "No, I don't want to sit. I want you to tell me what's wrong."

"Well, I just heard about it. From Edward Baconsfield. Seems he was at some meeting or another where they were talking about it . . ." He gripped her hands more tightly. "It happened this afternoon, apparently, and no one knew, of course. Not right away . . ."

Simon's words trailed away. So, it seemed, did his thoughts. His eyes unfocused, his lips trembling, he stared over Isabel's shoulder.

"Simon." By this time Isabel was too distraught to be patient. She gave his hands a squeeze and he flinched.

"Yes. Of course." Simon squared his shoulders and looked down at his sister. "There's been an accident, Belle. An explosion. At . . . at Ben's factory."

The words settled like lead weights in Isabel's stomach. "Was he . . . ?" Unable to bring herself to ask the question, she ran her tongue over her lips. "Was Ben . . . ?"

Simon nodded. "Apparently, he was inside. No one's heard any more than that. No one knows—"

Isabel didn't wait for another word. Before Simon could stop her, before he could even react, she was out of the room and heading for the door. She hailed the first cab that passed, and within the hour she was at Victoria Station and on the first train headed to Surrey.

She didn't stop once to consider if what she was doing was rash. Or unreasonable. Or foolhardy.

For the first time in as long as she could remember, Isabel followed her heart. And she knew it was leading her in the right direction.

# Chapter 14

There were laws concerning fireworks factories. There had been for more than twenty years. As the person in charge of the day-to-day operations of the largest fireworks producer in the Empire, Isabel made it her business to know the wording of every one of them by heart.

She also knew that it was spontaneous combustion, not carelessness or incompetence that was the cause of nearly all fireworks explosions. That was the reason that, by law, the sheds where the gunpowder was mixed and the fireworks assembled, in hers and all other factories, had to be situated at least twenty-five yards apart. Far enough so that if there was an explosion in one, it would not cause the detonation of the others.

But though Isabel knew the law and saw to it that it was observed at her own facility, she had never before seen for herself the eerie consequences of following it to the letter.

It was dark, but against the lighter horizon Isabel could just make out the silhouettes of the work sheds all around her. They marched to the edges of her vision, spaced perfectly—and safely—at a distance from each other and from the main building near the front gate where, now that the excitement was over, Ben's workmen had gathered to exchange stories and wait for news.

Thanks to those laws and to the common sense that was as much a part of the manufacturing of fireworks as was a knack for the artistic and an appreciation of fiery beauty, the sheds around Isabel were undamaged. Everything was neat and intact. As if nothing unusual had happened.

It was a misleading sort of picture. Isabel knew it. And if she didn't, she only needed to take a deep breath.

The air was heavy with the biting smell of burnt gunpowder, and at a fireworks factory that could only mean one thing. Disaster.

The thought sat in Isabel's head and weighed heavy on her heart. Drawn by the smell of the black powder, she picked her way across the compound. After a minute or two, she didn't need her nose to guide her any longer. From up ahead, she saw all that was left of the spiking room, where the cardboard breaks were loaded with their stars. It was little more than a crater, blacker even than the night.

As did most of the buildings in a fireworks factory, the spiking room shed had a door at either end. They'd both been blown off by the explosion, and Isabel stepped over the broken remnants of one of them and skirted her way around what looked to be a piece of the corrugated iron that was used on the outsides of the shed walls.

The closer she got to the devastation, the harder it was to breathe. Weeks ago she might have convinced herself it was because of the acrid smell of the powder. Tonight, with no one to see and no one to try to analyze her response but herself, she admitted that the tension that blocked her breathing and pounded through her blood might have been for some other reason altogether.

Mesmerized by the tiny wisps of smoke that wafted by, Isabel stood at the edge of the charred pit and stared at the wreckage all around her. It was the first time since she'd raced out of the house that she'd had time to stop, time to think, and now that she did, she found her hands shaking and her knees rubbery.

For the first time since she'd boarded the train to Surrey and found a local villager with a dogcart who would bring her as far as the factory, she forced herself to face reality. If Ben had been in the shed when the gunpowder exploded . . .

Isabel dashed the thought away at the same time she swiped the tears that heated her cheeks. She needed answers. Information. And she intended to get it as soon as possible. She had already turned to head back to the main building when she saw a man coming her way.

"You there! What are you doing here?" It was John, the man who assisted Ben in loading and shooting his shows, and if he didn't look happy to see her, Isabel thought it no wonder. It had certainly been a difficult day for everyone at the factory, and John's face clearly showed its effects. Against the dark sky his skin was chalky. His coat was open and it fluttered around him, disturbing the pockets of smoke that had settled near the grass and sending them adrift, like dragon's breath.

John hurried over to where Isabel stood and pulled up at the spot where the grass was singed and damp from the water that had been poured on the fire to contain it. He bent forward for a better look, and when he saw that it was Isabel, his eyes narrowed and his top lip curled.

"So it's you, is it? Come to see if you finished the job?"

It took a moment to realize what he meant and another moment for the implications of his words to hit Isabel full force. She swallowed her outrage and fought for control.

"I'm here to see . . ." It was the first time since she'd purchased her train ticket that she had really tried to say anything and she found her voice remarkably unsteady. She pulled in a breath and started again. "I heard what happened," she said. "I tried to get information from the fellows in the main building, but they don't know a thing. I've got to find Ben."

"Do you?" John didn't look convinced. He settled his weight back against one foot and crossed his arms over his chest. "Seems more to me like you comed to make sure you done in Mr. Costigan right and for good this time. Just like you tried to do him in at the Crystal Palace."

Instinctively, Isabel defended herself. "Don't be ridiculous. I didn't try to do anyone in, I—" The full import of the words struck her.

"Dead?" John spat out the word. "Is that what you comed to see? Comed to see if he was dead?"

"Yes. No. I—" The world spun out of focus, and Isabel staggered back, one hand pressed to her lips to contain a sob. "You don't really think I would—"

"Maybe you would. And maybe you wouldn't." As if he was thinking about it, John chewed his lower lip and gave Isabel a searching look.

She didn't think it was her innocence that finally convinced him.

It was late. It was cold. The wet grass made the air clammy against their skin, and the smoke made it nearly impossible to breathe. It had been clear from the start that John was no more comfortable than was Isabel and, as the seconds ticked by, just as clear that he felt he couldn't trust her there alone.

"Come on." He didn't offer his arm. He turned toward the main building and, with a curt nod, motioned Isabel to follow. "Can't leave you out here in the dark, I don't suppose," he mumbled, glancing over his shoulder to make sure she followed behind. "May as well get you back to the offices and you can get yourself home from there."

"But I'm not going home. Not until I find out what's happened to Ben." Isabel's voice rang through the darkness. It was a little shaky perhaps, but it had an edge of determination that even John could not fail to notice. He stopped and turned back to her, and through the mist that clouded her vision, Isabel saw him take another look, another measure of her sincerity.

"You ain't tryin' to hoodwink me, are you, miss?" As if it was nearly impossible to believe, John shook his head in wonder at the same time his eyes softened with a concern that was as sudden as it was genuine. "You really are worried about the guv'nor." The gesture may have been made a bit begrudgingly, but he did offer her his arm.

Isabel took it, not because she needed the support but because now that they had forged even so fragile a truce, she was unwilling to do anything to break it.

She needn't have worried.

The moment John had a hold of her hand, his mouth dropped open. "You're as cold as death yourself!" he said. "You comed out without a coat on a night like this?"

Isabel had been far too worried about Ben to even think about collecting her coat on her way out of the house. She was dressed in a gray housedress with long sleeves and a high neck that provided little protection against the night's chill.

She didn't realize how cold she was until John stripped off his greatcoat and draped it over her shoulders. The coat was damp and smelled of gunpowder and smoke, but Isabel huddled into it.

"Lord, lumme!" With one hand John grabbed the sleeve of the coat and tugged her on toward the main building. "Got to get you inside. Get you a cup of tea and get you warmed up. He'll have my head if anything happens to you, that's for certain. Though I can't understand it myself. Not with you tryin' to ruin his shows and him tryin' to ruin yours. Don't make no sense to me at all."

His words penetrated her cold like no other warmth could. Her head suddenly clear, Isabel stopped. "What did you say?"

"I said, Mr. Costigan, he'll be madder than mud if he finds out you been wanderin' around here in the dark by yourself."

"You mean . . . ?" As afraid to ask the question as she was not to ask it, Isabel clutched John's arm with both hands. "You mean, Ben isn't dead?"

"Dead?" John laughed. "Lord lumme, Miss De

Quincy, but it would take more than a couple of pounds of gunpowder to kill a man like Mr. Costigan. He's as tough as a jockey's tail end, beggin' your pardon for sayin' it, miss. When they carried him out of there, he was swearing up a storm!"

"Carried him out. Did they?" The momentary exhilaration Isabel felt at the news that Ben had survived the explosion crumpled under a new measure of worries. She sped double time toward the front gates, stepping around what looked to be a piece of timber that had been blown from the spiking room. "Where is he?"

"Took him home," John called, hurrying to catch her up.

"And you'll show me the way?"

"Lord lumme, Miss De Quincy, I'll take you there myself."

Isabel wasn't sure why, but she expected her welcome at Ben's home would be much more gracious than the one she'd gotten from John.

She was wrong.

It was clear from the moment the door was opened to her that she would not have been allowed in at all if it wasn't for the fact that John vouched, if not for her sincerity, then at least for her right to be there.

The house was as splendid an example of the new, sinuous fin de siècle style as any Isabel had ever seen. It was large and airy, with an entryway complete with a curving wrought iron staircase and a gallery lined with windows that combined slim iron skeletons with translucent panes of colored glass. In daylight it must have looked like a fireworks extravaganza. Now, with only a few electric lamps lit to chase the shadows, the mood was decidedly more somber.

So was the reception Isabel received.

She was shown into the entryway by a sullen olive-skinned young man who looked far too uncomfortable with the duty for him to be a servant. And far too worried for Isabel's liking. When she explained she

# DIAMOND RAIN

was there to see Ben, she was told she would have to wait. The young man took John with him, and they both disappeared, whispering to each other. They left Isabel alone with her thoughts.

Shrugging off John's coat, she paced from one end of the long entryway to the other. From somewhere above stairs, she heard whispered voices, shuffled feet. But no one came to claim her. No one came to tell her where Ben was. No one came to explain to her how he had survived an explosion that, by all rights, should have blown him to bits.

The thought wedged up under Isabel's heart, and she pressed a fist to it, eager to dispel the feeling. When she heard someone coming, she sniffed back her tears.

The footsteps were strange and halting, each one punctuated by a thump. They echoed through the open gallery, closing in on her, until finally a door at the far end of the passageway opened and a red-bearded giant of a man clomped across the polished wood floor.

The man wore a white shirt that looked as if he'd lived a lifetime in it. It was stained with sweat, and there was something smeared across the front of it that looked enough like blood to make Isabel's stomach lurch. His sleeves were rolled up to his elbows to reveal beefy forearms that were covered with a network of nasty-looking scars and dusted with hair as bright and as red as that on his head. His collar was wilted.

His posture was anything but. The man was stiff-shouldered and tight-jawed, barrel-chested and, this close, as tall as one of the saplings planted outside the door of Isabel's home. He took another step toward her, and Isabel heard the now familiar clumping sound. She looked down to see that the right leg of the man's dark trousers was loose and rolled, revealing the stump of a wooden leg. He had the bleak expression of an undertaker, and a personality to match.

"What do ye want?"

The question caught Isabel as off guard as did the man's appearance, but she wasn't about to let him know it. "I'm here to see Ben," she told him. "I'm worried, naturally. I have to know what's happened."

"Do ye now?" The man was a Scot, and he bit through his words, chewing them with a distinctive burr that echoed in the air like thunder. "And who says ye can?"

"No one says I can. But I will." Tired of defending herself, and her worries and her every move, Isabel lifted her skirts and headed for the stairs. "He must be above stairs somewhere. I'll find Ben myself. You can try to stop me if you like," she called to the giant over her shoulder, "but you may as well know from the start, it won't work. You obviously know who I am, or you wouldn't be treating me this way. Well, then, if that is the case, you must know a great deal about me. If I have a reputation as a hellcat, I might as well live up to it."

For a moment she thought the man would try to stop her, or at least follow after her. He didn't. He stood at the bottom of the stairway, his impressive scowl marred only by the fact that, for the briefest of moments, Isabel swore a smile crossed his face.

She paid it no mind. Within moments she was in the passageway outside what looked to be a series of bedchambers. It didn't take long to find the one she presumed was Ben's. The others were dark; his had a light shining from beneath the door.

The door was partly shut, and quietly Isabel opened it the rest of the way and slipped inside. There was a single lamp burning on the table near the bed. It bathed the immediate area with warm yellow light but left the rest of the room in deep shadows, and she stopped just inside the door, both her hands on the knob at her back, and let her eyes adjust.

Ben was lying on the bed, a white coverlet pulled up to his shoulders. His arms were atop the blanket, and except for a crisscross of bandages that seemed to be covering an assortment of small cuts, they were bare.

Unwelcome images of the man downstairs rose in Isabel's mind, and instinctively she glanced over the blankets. From the outline of his legs, she could tell that neither was missing, and she breathed a sigh of relief and stepped forward.

It wasn't until she was nearly at the bed that she realized his eyes were bandaged.

Relief gave way to worry, and Isabel hurried to the bed. There was a chair pulled up next to it, and she dropped into it and reached for Ben's hand. It was as cold as death but not lifeless, and though she couldn't see his eyes, she knew he was asleep. His chest rose and fell at a steady rate, and the voice that scraped out of him was as soft as a sigh and as quiet as the whisper of a dream. He closed his fingers over hers.

"Bella," he murmured. "Bella."

It wasn't the sweep of sunlight touching her face that woke Isabel. Nor was it the gentle, half-heard sound of a clock chiming the hour from somewhere below stairs.

It was a crash.

Dazed and disoriented, she bolted out of her chair and scooped a curl of hair away from her eyes, fighting away the fog that clouded her head at the same time she winced against the pain in her neck and back caused from sitting upright in the chair all night.

For one sleep-dazed second she wasn't at all sure where she was or what she was doing there. She wasn't sure if she'd really heard the noise or simply dreamed it. But then she saw that the table on the far side of the bed was upended. The pitcher of water that had been on it was spilled across the floor. And the bed was empty.

Suddenly wide awake, Isabel rushed to the other side of the bed and found Ben facedown on the floor.

"Damn!" Ben's curse boomed through the room along with a string of oaths that would have done a sailor proud. From the waist down he was tangled in the blankets, and the more he tried to unravel himself, the worse the muddle became. It might have been a simple enough procedure had he been able to see what he was doing, but with his eyes bandaged tightly, it was more of an exertion than a man in Ben's precarious state of health should have to bear.

Her heart squeezing with sympathy, Isabel hurried to help him. She grabbed both his arms, and he clasped hers, a new and more inventive curse erupting from him with each attempt to get him back on his feet.

"Hell and damnation!" His hands clutched around Isabel's forearms, Ben nearly pulled her down to the floor with him. He gritted his teeth against the pain that shot through him and tightened his grip. This time he managed to struggle to his knees. "You'd think the bloody doctor would know better than to put blinking bandages over my damned, ruddy eyes. How's a man supposed to get up and find his way to the loo when—" As if it had been snipped with scissors, Ben's tirade ended abruptly. He ran his hands up and down Isabel's arms.

"Hello," he said. "What's this?" He slid his hands to her shoulders. "You're not John." With one hand he brushed the line of her jaw, and with his thumb he grazed her lower lip. "And it's a damned certainty you're not Hamish." He glided his hands across her shoulders. He fitted his hands against her waist.

"Belle?" Ben repeated the procedure in the opposite direction, skimming his hands over her waist and fingering her breasts. His lips were bruised, but he managed to lift them in a devilish smile. "Belle, it is you! How in the hell did you get here?"

"I might ask you the same thing." Isabel's mood veered sharply from concern to annoyance and back again. She was heartened to see that Ben was not, as she had feared the night before, on death's doorstep. She was annoyed that despite an assortment of injuries she could see and, no doubt, dozens more she couldn't, his questionable sense of humor had not been dimmed. Neither had his vital impulses. She was cheered for some unaccountable reason to find him acting very much like the Ben of old, and more relieved than she could say to see that he was hale. And hearty. And very much alive.

With a determined tug she returned his hands to her waist, and just to make sure they stayed there, she settled both of hers over his. "No one will tell me a thing, and I want to know what happened. You certainly sound enough like your old self, but your eyes . . ."

Ben was not a man who gave up so easily. Even before they were properly settled, he slipped his hands from beneath Isabel's. He slid them up her arms and back to her shoulders. He moved them up farther still and burrowed his fingers in her hair, and Isabel felt the shock of awareness that rocketed through him. It vibrated through her, too, and while he pulled in a sharp breath, she swallowed around the sudden knot of emotion in her throat and gave herself to the warmth that simmered in his voice.

"You haven't been here all night, have you?" Ben asked. "Not in that blasted uncomfortable chair next to the bed."

"It hardly matters." It was the truth. Isabel's aching muscles didn't seem the least bit important in the face of the assortment of cuts and scrapes that must surely be lurking under the bandages that dappled Ben's shoulders, his arms, and his bare chest. "It was a small inconvenience, and I am not the one whose life was in danger."

Ben dismissed the very idea with a grunt. "I was in no more danger than any of us is ever in when we mix the stars. Or shoot the shows." At the same time the corners of his lips lifted in a smile, he cupped the back of Isabel's head with one hand and slid his thumb forward, brushing her neck in a ceaseless, soothing rhythm. "No more danger than I am in now."

Isabel didn't dare ask what he meant. She closed

her eyes against the incredible heat generated by his touch, but it was impossible to give herself over to the pleasure. No matter how hard she tried to picture Ben's face, Ben's smile, the only thing she could see in her mind's eye was the devastation at the factory.

"I saw the spiking room, Ben." Isabel's voice choked on the words. "Or at least what was left of it. I was at the factory, and—"

"And someone should have given you a bed for the night. I'll sack the lot of them. Damn!" The final oath had less to do with the fact that Isabel had been left to sleep in the chair all night than it did with the fact that Ben tried to move too quickly. He flinched and grabbed his side, and when Isabel made to help him, he brushed her hand away as if it were nothing at all.

"Damn the lot of them." Ben's voice faded. So did what little color there was in his face. He sagged against the bed. "Imaging, them expecting you to sit here all night like a paid servant."

"It doesn't matter. Not any longer." Isabel's words were a mix of tears and laughter. She cupped Ben's face in her hands, and for the first time she realized that the skin around his bandages was red and raw. Gently, she touched a finger to his forehead and to the place above the bandages where his right eyebrow had been burned away by the blast. "What matters is what happened to you and—"

"And every muscle of your body must be aching." Ben tried his best to reach a hand toward Isabel's shoulder to caress it. The effort cost him dearly. He fell back and his hand dropped. "I've done it myself, you know. Fell asleep in that damned stiff chair. It must hurt like the devil and—"

"Not nearly as much as your burns. Please, Ben . . ." It didn't seem as if he would ever listen. To catch his attention, Isabel trailed a finger over Ben's cheek. "You've got to tell me what happened. No one has. All I know is that you must have been in the spiking room."

"Yes. Loading stars into the breaks. As I have a

thousand times before." Ben reached out and made a grab for Isabel's hand. He missed by a mile. Gently, Isabel guided his hand to hers and twined her fingers through his. It was a simple enough gesture on her part, yet it seemed to bolster his energy as well as his spirits. His voice gained strength, but the shadow of the memory darkened his face.

"I had just finished loading the tun-dish with the gunpowder," Ben said, "when all the world turned to hell. I remember the blinding flash of the gunpowder. The next thing I knew, the lads found me in a heap, ten yards from the place I'd last been."

"You were blown clear of the building." All the proof of it was there before Isabel's eyes. Even the places on Ben's body that weren't bandaged were bruised. His shoulders were blanketed in purple, and if she leaned over just far enough, she could see that there was at least one wicked-looking bruise on his back. It extended from his waist down to where his hips were hidden by the blankets that were wound about him. "You must have landed with a whacking good thump. You're lucky it was on your backside and not on your head."

Ben nodded grimly. "I don't remember much of anything. I woke up here with what seemed to be the entire household staff hovering around me, shuffling their feet and clearing their throats as if they were at a wake where the corpse wasn't quite dead yet."

"They care about you a great deal."

"Yes. Well . . ." Ben dismissed the very idea. "They had me all cleaned up by the time the doctor came. He says I'll be as right as a fiddle in a week or two."

"Really?" Another wave of relief swept through Isabel, this one tempered with disbelief. The bandages wound around Ben's head and bound tightly over his eyes looked to be hiding injuries she suspected were far more serious than the abrasions she could see on his body. "What about your eyes, Ben? Are you . . . ? Will you . . . ?"

"See again?" Ben gave a gruff laugh. "I'd better.

The doctor says it's the reason for these damned pesky bandages. Corneas are burnt. So he says. Should be fine in a week or two if I keep my eyes covered and then try to stay out of bright light for a while."

Softly, Isabel touched a finger to the dressing. "Does it hurt?" she asked.

"Like hell!" Ben admitted. "But it seems I'm lucky to be alive. And luckier still to wake and find you here waiting for me." His voice caught on the words. "You don't suppose I'm dreaming, do you? Or perhaps it isn't even a dream. Perhaps I'm really dead. This might be heaven."

Isabel laughed. "Don't be ridiculous. If you were dead, you most certainly would not be in heaven."

"True enough." Ben nodded. "But if I'm not dead and this isn't heaven, tell me . . ." He tightened his hold on her hand. "Why is there an angel here with me?"

This time it was Isabel who brushed away the compliment. "An angel wouldn't have had such a time of it getting here," she told him. "Simon heard the news from your friend Edward, you see, and he told me. I came as soon as I could. But when I got here, no one would tell me a thing. And then I ran into John and he brought me here. The man with the red beard—"

"Hamish."

"Hamish. Yes. He's a frightening chap, isn't he? He didn't seem to like the idea of me being here, but by that time I was so distraught, I hardly cared. That's the story, Ben, and I know it sounds like gammon and pickles, but it's true. That's how I happened to be here when you woke up."

"That may be true, but it's not what I asked." As if he could see it, he turned her hand over in his. One by one he smoothed her fingers open. His right hand was swathed in a bandage that covered his knuckles and reached as far as his wrist, but his fingers were free and they were gentle against hers. His touch was warm. It invited her to tell the truth. "What you've told me, that's how you got here. And I didn't ask you how you got here. I asked you why you came, Bella."

Even though Isabel knew he couldn't see her, she turned her eyes away. Apologizing to Ben had always been difficult. Especially this time, when she'd been so wrong.

About Ben and about the burglary at De Quincy and Sons.

About herself.

She swallowed her pride and her misgivings. "I had to come," she told him. "And do you know something? I never even stopped to think why. When I'd heard something had happened to you . . ." Isabel fell into Ben's arms. "All I could think was that I might never see you again, Ben. That you were hurt or even . . . even dead. I knew I had to apologize for the way I'd treated you. I know you had nothing to do with the burglary."

Ben's arms went around her, but he pulled back as if he could look down into her eyes. "And is that why you're here now?" he asked. "Because you feel guilty for the way you treated me?"

Isabel shook her head, then remembered he couldn't see it. "No." She skimmed a finger over his bare shoulders, and found herself uncommonly pleased when he shivered at the touch. There was a line of small abrasions and tiny spots of burned skin from his chin to his ear, and she kissed every one of them. "If that was the only reason," she told him, "I suppose I'd be on my way even now. And I have no intention of leaving. At least until you are better again. May I stay?"

He didn't answer with words but with a kiss. One that left Isabel breathless.

"You really shouldn't be exerting yourself." At the same time she knew it was true, she was hoping Ben would disagree.

"Shouldn't I?" He kissed her again. "Suddenly, I'm feeling better than I have in a good long time. Help me to my feet, will you, Belle? And let me welcome you to my home properly."

This time, with Ben's help and his cooperation, the procedure went much more smoothly. Their arms around each other, they managed to get him on his feet. It was a simple enough procedure, but it shook loose the blankets that had been wound around Ben's waist. They drifted to the floor, and as soon as they did, he shivered at the sudden scrape of cold air against his skin. He face went chalky. His voice took on that certain edge that told her, though he asked the question, he wasn't at all sure he wanted to hear the answer.

"Tell me, Belle," he said. "Am I wearing anything?"

Isabel stepped back and let her gaze drift from the top of Ben's head all the way down to where his toes peeked from beneath the blanket that was now in a puddle around his ankles, stopping along the way to admire those of his qualities she'd always thought the most noteworthy. She smiled.

"You're wearing an assortment of bandages," she told him, touching a gentle finger to each as she inventoried them. "On your shoulders. And your arms. There's another here on your thigh." She let her hand rest there. "But no. Not another thing. You're as naked as a worm, Mr. Costigan. And I must say, it is not at all an unpleasant sight."

"Hmmm." Considering the possibilities of the interesting predicament, Ben propped his arms on either side of her and back-stepped her over to the bed. He pressed her onto the mattress and sat beside her, wincing only a little at the effort. "That could save us a good deal of time, wouldn't you say?"

"Hmmm." Isabel pretended to be considering.

"You know I'm eager."

Isabel laughed, trailing her hand over him. "That is quite apparent."

"And you know I've been waiting for four long years."

"That is quite astounding!"

"And you know you have as well."

"That is quite true." Winding her arms around Ben's neck, Isabel brought her mouth to his. He pressed her back against the mattress, settling her and himself, and moaning only a bit from the pain.

The kiss was exquisite. Gentle. Leisurely. And when it was over, Ben propped his head in one hand and trailed the other over Isabel's body, from her chin to her waist and back again. "What's this?" he asked, his fingers tangling in the lace edging of her high collar. "Clothes? I say, Miss De Quincy, but that hardly seems fair. Here I am . . . how did you say it? . . . naked as a worm . . . and there you are all wrapped up like a Christmas gift. We'll need to take care of that." He undid the first button along the front of her gown. And the second. "It seems a frightful shame not to be able to enjoy the sight of you, but I'm convinced that what I can't see, I still might be able to enjoy by touch. And taste."

He had only begun to demonstrate when the door burst open and John and Hamish rushed into the room.

Isabel bounded to her feet.

"I'll go hopping to hell and pump thunder!" Ben slammed his fist down on the bed and grabbed a handful of blankets to cover himself. "Let me guess. It's you, isn't it, Hamish? And you, John? What in the name of—"

"Beggin' your pardon, sir." Hamish's face went as red as his hair. "We heard a crash, and we thought the De Quincy woman, she might be doing something to you."

Ben grumbled an oath. "She was doing something to me, right enough. Or at least she was about to."

"And now she is about to leave you in peace." It was far too late to rescue her reputation, but a quick retreat might still save her pride. Isabel bent and kissed Ben's cheek. "You need your rest," she told him. "And I need—"

"You need a bloody room! That's what you need.

And a damned hot meal. And someone to send for your things. Hamish! John!" Ben's voice rattled the windows. "Has anyone thought to give the woman a bloody room? She's been in that damned chair all night and . . ."

He was still raving when Isabel left the room. It was just as well that John and Hamish were too busy being cowed by Ben to pay the least bit of attention to her.

Something told her they would not have approved of the wicked smile that lit her face as soon as she was out of the door.

# Chapter 15

"I thought we might start with a maroon. You know, something bone-rattling. One big *boom* that will make everyone sit up and take notice."

"Really?" Her eyebrows raised in an expression of wonder, Isabel leaned forward on the blanket that had been thrown on the ground to accommodate the picnic supper she and Ben were supposed to be eating. They weren't. At least not yet. The hamper of food that had been prepared by Ben's cook and delivered personally to the picnic sight by Hamish was unopened. It had been all but forgotten in light of their discussion about the Jubilee.

Setting aside the paper where she'd been scribbling notes, she watched Ben raise a glass of wine toward the last of the light that hovered in the evening sky. He studied its mahogany depths against the darkening sky the way he'd been studying everything since the bandages had been removed from his eyes the day before, with new intensity and a very real appreciation.

Ten days ago it would have been cruel to tease him, Isabel knew. He'd been too sore, his burns too raw, his bruises too tender. But thanks to a doctor who'd insisted on a good deal of rest and regular doses of laudanum to assure it, Ben's health had steadily improved. He was feeling and looking more like himself by the hour, and one sure sign of that was his restlessness. He chafed at his forced inactivity, and especially at the fact that because the doctor had strictly ordered him to keep out of the sunlight, he had as yet been unable to visit his factory during the workday.

It was one of the reasons Isabel had suggested a picnic at this late hour. And a discussion about the Jubilee program.

But trying to cheer Ben's spirits did not, in her mind, mean permitting the kind of blatant and unmitigated bilge he was spouting. That was too much to ask.

"A maroon? Is that what you think?" She tapped her pen against the blanket, telegraphing her exasperation. "Wherever did you come up with an idea like that?"

"I've thought so all along. I've told you as much a dozen times. A maroon, I said, that's what we need to start the show."

"Rubbish! You wanted shells. A barrage of shells, you said. Every color of the rainbow." Isabel was already up on her knees with her hands balled into fists at her sides when she realized she was the one being teased. Grateful that Ben was laughing too hard to see the way her cheeks colored at being caught at her own game, she plunked back down again.

"You knew we'd start with a maroon all along," she told him, her words as clipped as the way she riffled through her notes and arranged them neatly into a pile. "It really is too awful of you to pretend otherwise. If I didn't know better—"

"What would you do, Belle? What would you do if you didn't know better?" Ben rolled to his side, and setting down his glass of wine, he grabbed Isabel's hand. He held on tightly, his fingers closed around hers, a smile lighting his face.

It was the first time since the morning she'd woken to find him on the floor that she had been close enough to touch Ben. It wasn't that she'd been avoiding him. On the contrary, when she wasn't busy contacting Simon to make sure her clothes and other personal items were sent on from London, and struggling to try and make some sort of peace with the household staff, she'd spent as much time with him as she could. But most of that time he'd been sound asleep. And when he wasn't, they were knee-deep in servants who were trying to help, employees who'd come to call, and the ever present John and Hamish, who, whether Ben liked it or not, watched after him like mother hens might a chick.

This was the first time they'd had the chance to be alone together, and if the smile on Ben's face was any indication, he was very much determined to use the opportunity and every ounce of his considerable charm to have his way with her.

It was not an unpleasant prospect.

Smiling to herself, Isabel scooted closer. "If I didn't know better," she said, "I might do a good many things."

"I don't suppose you'd like to demonstrate."

"Not an icicle's chance in Hades! The last time I even thought to do that, I found myself at the wrong end of one of Hamish's black scowls."

Ben looked back over his shoulder. Above a border of lilacs whose heavenly fragrance scented the air and an edging of rose bushes just coming into bloom, they could see the lights of the house a hundred yards away. "We're nowhere near the house," he reminded her. "And besides, I've warned every one of them. If they dare bother us tonight . . ."

"It's no good." Laughing, Isabel disentangled her hand from his. "I won't chance that sort of humiliation again. Not even for one of your kisses."

Always the actor, Ben put the back of one hand to his forehead in an exaggerated gesture worthy of a budding Bernhardt. "Then perhaps my kisses aren't as tempting as I thought."

"Or so tempting, I won't risk having them interrupted again." It was the truth, and Isabel wasn't ashamed to admit it.

Rather than looked pleased by the confession, Ben looked thoughtful. He tipped his head to one side and looked at her carefully, the way he'd been looking at her since his bandages were removed. "What do you think, Belle?" he asked. "If Hamish and John had not been the louts they are . . . if they hadn't interrupted us that first day I woke and found you in my bedchamber . . . If we had made love that day, would it have been the right thing to do?"

It was a question she'd asked herself more than once in the last days.

This time it was Isabel who took Ben's hand. She twined her fingers through his and noted with no small amount of satisfaction that the skin there wasn't nearly as red, his wounds not nearly as angry as they had been ten days before.

"It wouldn't have been wrong," she said.

"But it would have been a mistake."

"Do you think so?"

"Do you?"

Isabel sighed. It wasn't easy to fit the thoughts of four long years into a sentence or two that might explain everything that had happened in that time. Everything she'd said. And done. Everything she'd felt then. And now. "Making love was never our mistake," she said. "Our mistake was not loving in the first place."

"Of course."

Isabel cursed below her breath. Though there was a sliver of a moon halfway up the sky, Ben's face was in the shadow of the folly that stood in the center of the garden. She wished she could see it more clearly. She wanted to know if his eyes were twinkling or morose. Was he agreeing with her? Or brooding?

She banished the questions with a shake of her head. Her worrying about them wouldn't change a thing. She and Ben seemed doomed to be forever at the place where they had been much of the time they'd known each other. At an impasse. Frozen. Crippled by their pride and paralyzed by emotions neither of them had ever been willing to acknowledge. Or accept.

She settled his hand against the blankets and, collecting her papers, piled them to the side, next to the picnic hamper. "We need to decide the order of the shoot," she said, instinctively finding the one subject they could discuss without breaching the fragile wall each of them had built around their emotions. "Do you suppose we should start with Diamond Rain? Or end the show with it?"

Was she imagining it, or did Ben look as relieved at having the subject changed as she did changing it?

"Diamond Rain." He chewed over the words. "I've been thinking about Diamond Rain." With a grunt that told her he was not completely recovered from his injuries—no matter how much he liked to pretend he was—he got to his feet. She knew better than to try and help. In the last days she'd watched Ben reject offers of assistance from everyone from Hamish to John to Angelo, the young man who'd first let her into the house and who was, as it turned out, a stable boy who'd followed Ben from Italy.

When he was standing, he offered Isabel a hand up, and she took it and walked with him over to the folly.

The building was a replica in miniature of one of the ancient temples Ben had seen and admired in Italy. It was made entirely of white marble, and it gleamed in the moonlight, like a ghost. Ben sat down on the steps and, with a pat at the place next to him, invited Isabel to join him.

"This entire bit with the Diamond Rain recipe has me in a muddle," he admitted. "We both know I didn't engineer the burglary at the De Quincy and Sons offices. But if I didn't do it, who did?"

"Who indeed." It wasn't that Isabel hadn't considered the question; it was just that when she did, she found herself in as much of a muddle as Ben confessed to be in. Eager to dispel the uncomfortable feeling that something was going on around her that she didn't know about or understand, she smoothed her skirts and sat down. "I can't imagine who would want the recipe. It isn't any good to anyone. Not if they don't have the knowledge. And the chemicals."

"And the right factory to put them all together." Ben shook his head. The moonlight touched his hair, making it look more silver than golden. "It's damned befuddling."

"But I suppose it hardly matters. I have the recipe right here." Isabel touched a hand to her bosom. "And that's where it stays."

"Unless I remove it!" Ben sent her a smile that sizzled its way through Isabel and left her lightheaded. And filled with regret.

There was so much they'd missed. So many chances at life. And love. They'd mucked up their opportunities, and bumbled their chances, and Ben was a fool to think one heart-stopping smile would change anything.

Just as Isabel was a fool to desperately want to believe it could.

She disguised her uneasiness beneath the calm veneer of household talk. "I took a peek at what Cook packed us for supper. There's cold chicken and salmon and—"

"I hope she put in some strawberries."

"I certainly hope not." Though she tried to control it, Isabel couldn't help but shudder. "Strawberries give me spots!"

"Really?" Ben turned to see her better. "I never knew that. I used to send around big baskets of strawberries. You remember, when we were engaged and I owned that bit of land near the factory where they were grown."

Isabel hated being found out, especially after all these years. "Simon ate them all," she admitted. "If I had, I would have spent my days and nights itching."

"It's amazing, isn't it?" Ben captured her gaze and held it, the look as gentle as the laugh that rippled the air between them. "I've known you all these years, and I never knew that about you. These last ten days, they've been a revelation."

"They have, indeed." Isabel linked her hands around her knees. "But you're not the only one who's made discoveries."

She had Ben's attention now. He raised his eyebrows and waited for more.

"I've been talking to John," she told him. "And Hamish."

"Hamish?" This time Ben really did look surprised. "He doesn't frighten you any longer?"

Isabel hated to admit the truth, and she covered her discomfort with a self-conscious laugh. "I'm petrified of the man! But I've learned that he is devoted to you. It seems once John realized I wasn't going to murder you in the middle of the night, he turned into quite a long-winded chap. He told me all about Hamish."

Ben brushed away the comment with a wave of one hand.

"He told me Hamish used to be your chief assistant. He used to shoot your shows. Until the accident that maimed him."

Ben shrugged. "Damned inconvenient, that."

More bilge. And this time Isabel wasn't about to let it go by. "Most employers would have sent Hamish packing," she told him. "But not you. You gave the man a position and a place to live."

He twitched away what obviously sounded too much like a compliment for his comfort. "I built this great monstrosity of a house," he said. "And then I realized I had no butler. Hamish was available."

"As was Angelo. Is that why you brought him along with you when you left Italy?"

"Hell, no!" Ben dismissed the question with a groan. "Angelo might have been available, but he isn't a very good stable boy. He doesn't speak much English, and he's afraid of the horses. But he is mad about automobiles, and I'm hoping—"

"He never even saw an automobile until you purchased the Phaeton." When Ben looked away from her, Isabel prodded him further. "John says that during your visit to Italy, you found out that Angelo was having a love affair with a girl named Rosa. A girl who worked at the home where you stayed. You knew Rosa was going to have Angelo's child."

"You have been busy gossiping these last days,

haven't you?" Ben had done all he could to avoid the subject, but there was no doubt he recognized the determined tone of Isabel's voice. He surrendered, scratching a hand through his hair.

"Rosa's family found out about the child, of course," he said. "Damn, what a scene there was! Screaming and yelling and more talk of eternal damnation than any young girl should have to hear. After they reduced Rosa to tears, her father and brothers went after Angelo with a vengeance."

"So you brought them both home with you. And gave Rosa a job in your kitchen and Angelo—"

"Are you quite finished?" Ben threw his hands into the air. "Because if you're not, we'd better run out into the fields for some fresh air. The atmosphere here is getting a bit syrupy, wouldn't you say?"

"What I would say is that you are very kind." As touched by his stumbling efforts at humility as she had been by the stories of his generosity, Isabel wound her arm through Ben's.

He responded to the warmth of her touch, reaching for her and drawing her into the circle of his arm. "You won't tell anyone, will you?" He pulled a face, and his eyes twinkled. "I've worked long and hard to earn the reputation I have as a heartless bastard. I'd hate to have you ruin it for me."

"A promise!" Isabel laughed. It was a genuine enough laugh, but it stilled in an instant, disintegrating beneath the heat that simmered in Ben's eyes. Isabel's stomach clenched. Her breath caught. For one frightening moment she was afraid Ben would kiss her.

Afraid he wouldn't.

"Damn, but I missed seeing your face." He smoothed a hand over her cheek. "I lay in that bed, day after day. And I tried to picture every inch of you. And I prayed . . ." His fingers touched her eyes, her lips. They trailed down her neck. "I realized that dying in an explosion wasn't the worst thing that could ever happen to me. Or not salvaging my company's reputation with this ruddy Jubilee contract. The worst thing that could ever happen to me would be losing you, Bella." The corners of his mouth lifted in a little smile.

"There, I've said it." He looked infinitely relieved. And as nervous as Isabel felt. "You've promised me you'll never let anyone know . . . about Hamish, or Angelo, or any of the other rot you've no doubt found out about these last days. Promise me something else?"

Isabel's throat closed over her words. "What else would you like me to promise?"

Ben trailed his hand up her neck. He splayed his fingers through her hair. "I think," he said, "that I would very much like you to promise that you'll stay with me. Tonight. Always."

It was nearly impossible to think when he was this close. Nearly impossible to speak around the heat fueled by his touch. Isabel shook her head. "We've already tried for always," she reminded him. "It didn't work."

"We were fools!"

"Were?" She managed a laugh. "And we aren't now?"

"Oh, we're fools, right enough." Ben nuzzled a kiss against her ear. Another along the column of her neck. He touched his tongue to the hollow at the base of her throat. "Fools to let our happiness go up in flames, like the tail of a rocket. Fools not to hold on to it with both hands and not let it slip away, like we did four years ago."

"Four years ago we made a mistake."

"Oh, no." Ben looked into her eyes. "It was no mistake. You know that well enough. We loved each other. Damn, Bella, but I've always loved you. It seems what I've just discovered is how much I like you."

A ripple of happiness bubbled inside Isabel and escaped as a laugh. "Love? Is that what this feeling is? I hardly think it's what the poets talk of when they mention love. Yet it is what I feel." She sighed. "Even though I know we'll never live in peace."

"Good gad, but I hope not!" Ben laughed too. His fingers played with the top button of her white blouse, and even through the linen she felt the heat of his touch. "If we ever make peace with each other, I think our lives will be wretchedly boring." He slipped the button from its hole. His right eyebrow had only just begun to grow back in, and when he quirked it at her, it was a decidedly devilish expression that flashed through Isabel like an electrical current.

She gave her consent with a smile that trembled over her lips, and a flutter of delight that vibrated over her shoulders, and when he freed a second button, and a third, she caught her lower lip in her teeth. She glided a hand over Ben's knee and across his thigh. "I do believe we'll never have to worry about being bored," she murmured.

"I would agree with you there." Ben finished with the buttons and, one thumb under each of its edges, opened the blouse enough to see the skin beneath. He drew in a breath and, bending, made to dip a kiss into the soft shadow between her breasts.

He pulled back at the last second and with two fingers lifted the silk pouch from its hiding place inside her corset and tossed it onto the stairs next to him.

"There!" Ben rubbed his hands together. "That's better." This time the kiss found its mark. His lips were soft and warm. His tongue brushed her skin.

Isabel heard a noise that sounded very much like a groan. It might have come from her, or from Ben, and in a burst of clarity that was as stunning as the tremors of desire that were suddenly wreaking havoc with her breathing and unsettling her heart, she realized it didn't matter. They were one and the same, she and Ben. They always had been.

It was the reason they were only complete when they were together.

The very thought made her bold. And her daring heightened her desire. Her fingers quick and sure, Isabel removed the three studs from the front of Ben's shirt. She tossed them to the ground, and somehow she managed to pull his shirt out of his trousers and slip it from his shoulders at the same time she arched her back to allow him to deepen his kiss.

Isabel whisked her hands over Ben's broad shoulders. She trailed them over his chest. This time the sound that escaped her was a contented purr. It was a warm night, and like most men when the weather turned fine (or so she'd been told), Ben had dispensed with the usual undervest. His bare skin was smooth beneath her fingers. His muscles bunched at her touch. There was the finest sprinkling of golden hair on his chest, and she trailed her fingers through it, her palms flattening against his nipples.

"Crikey, Bella!" A shiver trembled across Ben's shoulders, and Isabel closed her eyes, enjoying the sensation nearly as much as she enjoyed the delicious tension building inside her. "You'll drive me mad." He stroked a kiss between her breasts. Another to her neck. He followed with one on her chin and ended the circuit at her lips. His mouth covered hers, hungry and determined.

Isabel met his lips with kisses as insistent as his own. She trailed her fingers through Ben's hair. She moaned when he parted her lips with his tongue, and when he pressed her back, she wound her arms around his neck, drawing him with her, until his chest was hard against hers and their hearts beat one with the other.

She moaned again, this time from the feel of the marble stairs poking her back.

Ben grumbled an oath and sat up. "I'm sorry, Belle. I wasn't thinking." But while Isabel looked toward the picnic blanket with undisguised anticipation, it seemed Ben had other ideas.

In one fluid movement he was on his feet, and in the next he reached for Isabel's hand and pulled her up beside him. His arms around her, he hauled her close. If Isabel had any doubts as to his intentions, they were dispelled in an instant. He was hard against her, and she skimmed a hand over him and murmured in approval.

"This is a most inconvenient place." Again, Isabel gave the picnic blanket a pointed look.

Ben might have noticed if he hadn't had his eyes closed. It was only after she moved her hand up to his waist that they drifted open again. His eyes were heavy with desire. Bright with enjoyment. He skimmed a look over her face and down to where her breasts peeked from the top of her corset. "Inconvenient, yes. But not impossible. Come on." He bounded up the steps toward the folly. "Come with me."

There was no question she would follow.

The folly was no more than twenty feet long and not nearly that wide. Its broad, shallow steps led to a short portico flanked by marble columns. There was an entrance between two of the columns, and Ben disappeared inside. Isabel stopped at the doorway. The folly had no walls, only the columns stood between its interior and the night, but without the glow of the moonlight, it was darker inside than it was out. She squinted into the blackness and listened to the sound of Ben's footfalls against the polished marble floor. A second later, she heard a rasp and a hiss. A match flared to life in Ben's hands, illuminating his face in a halo of yellow.

His bare chest glowing bronze in the light, his eyes reflecting the fire, Ben touched the match to a candle that had been set into a holder between the columns. There was another candle between the next two columns, and another beyond, and he lit each in turn. Soft light flowed across the floor and threw shadows between the pillars. It showed Isabel that the folly was not empty as she'd thought.

A kind of bed had been set out in the center of the floor: blankets piled one on top of the other and pillows thrown around them. There was a bottle of champagne to one side, and crystal flutes that winked the candlelight back at Isabel. Much like the devilish delight that winked in Ben's eyes.

Isabel looked from Ben to the bed and back, her face flushed, her heart suddenly beating double time with anticipation. And astonishment.

She propped her hands on her hips. She was well aware of the fact that the posture caused her blouse to gape. It was exactly what she intended. There was more than a bit of satisfaction in watching the way Ben's gaze dropped instantly from her face to her bosom. And more enjoyment still in seeing him swallow hard and exhale a breath that sounded to be ripped from the very heart of him.

She skewered him with a look that was convincing enough to make him squirm. "You're damned cocksure of yourself, Mr. Costigan."

His smile was fleeting and not at all the arrogant smile she was used to. This smile was small and anxious, the edges of it touched with yearning. It was all the more maddening for it. "I'm not at all as cocksure as I am hopeful." Ben stepped nearer. He was close enough to touch her. But he didn't. He let his gaze caress her—her face, her neck, her breasts—and when he was finished, he let his eyes drift upward again. He met Isabel's gaze with a smile. "You wouldn't want to disappoint an invalid, would you?"

She returned his look with one of her own, examining him inch by inch. Her gaze touched his eyes. It stroked his mouth. It drifted to his chin and from there to the place where his Adam's apple jumped when he swallowed around his anticipation. She stopped there for a moment, more to heighten his suspense than for any other reason, then resumed her leisurely inspection.

There was a V-shaped patch at the base of his neck that was pinker than the surrounding skin, and Isabel knew it was from a burn he'd received in the explosion. The very thought was too much to bear, and she ignored it and the rosy splotch, and concentrated instead on the well-muscled outline of his shoulders, and the dusting of golden hairs on his chest and the way it tapered at his waist. The slightest of smiles touching her lips, she looked down even farther.

"You are hardly an invalid," she said, and even to her own ears her voice sounded giddy with impatience. She let her fingers drift along with her gaze, brushing, stroking, caressing. "As a matter of fact, were I to judge, I would say that you are in fine working order."

"And you are temptress enough to drive a man mad!" With a sound halfway between a laugh and a growl, Ben snatched her into his arms. "You haven't run away, Bella. And you haven't demolished me with that deadly wit of yours. I take it that means you're staying?"

There were no words sufficient enough to answer him, and Isabel didn't even try to find them. She backed out of Ben's arms.

He looked bereft. But only for a moment. When Isabel slipped out of her blouse, his expression brightened considerably.

"You are an enchantress. There's no doubt of that." Ben's gaze caressed her bare arms and the narrow, lace-edged straps of her corset. It slid from the pink ribbon tie at the top of the corset to the matching ribbon at Isabel's waist. Eager to grab one of the loops of the ribbon and pull, he reached out one hand.

"Oh, no!" Isabel scooted back, opening a space between them that would allow him to see her to full advantage. "This is something I need to do myself. You, sir . . ." She met Ben's gaze and held it. "You may watch, not touch. At least not yet. Agreed?"

Ben sucked in a breath. "Damn, Bella!" He crossed his arms over his chest, and Isabel sensed it was the only way he could keep his hands from her. "You drive a hard bargain."

"Perhaps, but it's your forfeit for assuming too much. And don't try to deny it. You expected me to fall right into your arms. You must have, or you wouldn't have bothered with the bed. Or the champagne." With thumb and forefinger she grasped one end of the ribbon at her waist. She hesitated, looking at him for confirmation. "Do you agree?"

"Agree?" A smile lit Ben's eyes and traveled to his lips. "Oh, yes."

"Very well." Feeling suddenly shy under his smoldering look, Isabel was tempted to turn away. She was no blushing virgin, she reminded herself. No one knew that better than Ben.

She wasn't about to pretend to be. Sucking in a breath for courage, she cast aside her inhibitions and one by one she undid the buttons along the side of her dove gray skirt.

She stepped out of it and her shoes, and propping one foot against the foot-high wall on which the columns of the folly were built, she peeled away one stocking, then the other. Her petticoat was tied at the waist, a flimsy thing as fluffy and frilly as a wedding cake, and when she pulled at the ribbon tie, it fluttered to the floor.

She was left in her knickers and camisole.

"You're still watching." It was an understatement. Ben wasn't simply watching. He was hanging on her every movement, eyeing her with unmitigated delight. Desire burned in his eyes, but it was not the same desire she'd seen there four years earlier. That was passion at its most brazen. This was something else altogether. Passion tempered with longing. Desire burnished by love. It was that more than anything that tugged at Isabel's heart. That more than anything that made her fingers tremble against the ribbon tie at her waist.

"I could help." Ben moved forward, automatically reaching for her.

"Oh, no!" Another step back brought Isabel to the makeshift bed. She strolled to the center of it and, her eyes full on Ben, dragged the pins from her hair. It tumbled around her shoulders, and when it was freed, she shook her head and combed her fingers through it, smoothing it over her breasts. From there it was simple enough to unloosen the tie on her corset. She nudged the straps down around her shoulders, then slipped her arms from them. With a flutter like butterfly wings, the corset and her knickers joined her petticoats on the floor.

"Well, what do you think?" Isabel didn't really have to ask. She knew exactly what Ben was thinking. She could tell from the look in his eyes. And the delicious bulge at the front of his trousers.

"I think you've put me through just about all I can stand." In less than a minute, Ben was out of his clothes. He tossed them back over his shoulder and let them land in a jumble, and hurried to stand in front of her, keeping only far enough away so that their bodies didn't touch.

His skin was hot and the warmth flowed around Isabel, slow and delectable. He smelled musky and masculine, and the fragrance mingled with that of the soap he'd used for his bath. It sang through Isabel's blood and sent her head into a whirl. His voice was a whisper that made every inch of her skin tingle.

"Can I love you now, Bella?"

"It's all I've ever wanted." Isabel knelt on the bed, and when Ben knelt beside her, she wrapped her arms around his neck and gave herself to the fierce power of his kiss. He had been tried past his limit, his kiss told Isabel as much, and he proved it when he inched her back against the blanket and covered her with kisses. His mouth found one breast, then the other, and he nipped at her with his teeth and suckled her with his lips, coaxing out a groan that shimmered in the air like the opalescent moonlight outside the doorway.

"Oh, Ben!" Isabel's fingers flew over his skin, skimming his back, his chest, his waist. She traced the shape of his backside and smiled in answer to the murmur of approval that escaped Ben's lips. "It's perfect, isn't it?"

At her side, Ben propped his elbow against the blankets. His pupils were dark pools of desire, but a shadow crossed his face. "Perfect, yes." He looked away. The hesitation in his eyes was only momentary, but it was enough to make Isabel's stomach go cold.

"What is it?" She crooked a finger below his chin, forcing his gaze back to hers. "Is something wrong?"

"Well, it's just . . ." Ben pulled in a breath and let it out again. He squeezed his eyes shut and blurted out the question. "Was I really a mediocre lover? I mean, it is something I have to know. Something I should know, considering the circumstances and the . . . the situation we're in." He dared to open his eyes and gave Isabel a sheepish look. "Did you really only scream because you were so mightily disappointed?"

Isabel laughed. There was only one way to answer Ben's question. Stretching out against the blankets, she wrapped her arms around Ben and pulled him over on top of her.

# Chapter 16

It wasn't often that Ben had the leisure to stand idly by and watch his crew do the hundreds of things necessary for the setup of a fireworks show.

And he never had the inclination.

He was as willing as any to roll up his sleeves and get his hands dirty. Stronger than some and better able to dig the trenches where the mortars would nestle. More clever with his hands than others and more skillful when it came to the construction of the lanceworks. Just the smell of black powder made him itch to get to work, and he refused to issue orders and stand back while others carried them out. There was no challenge in that. No pleasure at all.

In all his years of designing, setting up, and firing shows, he'd never yet found anything that had the power to change his mind.

Until today.

From his vantage point on the shores of the lake that graced the center of the forty-acre gardens that surrounded Buckingham Palace, Ben stood back, his gaze following Isabel as she bustled about.

There was a certain odd contentment he found in simply watching her. A gratification that was comfortable at the same time it wreaked havoc with heart, mind, and body.

Isabel was a ball of energy encased in black trousers and a man's white shirt. A streak of light darting here and there, issuing orders in that no-nonsense voice he'd come to recognize, the one that sent a thrill through him as surely as did her whisper in his ear.

She was a cipher, that was for certain. A woman who could be as doughty as she was tender. A lady certainly, but one who, when she had the mind and the proper encouragement, had every bit as much appetite and fire (and imagination!) as the cream of the Covent Garden crop of adventuresses.

She was willing to work as hard as any of the men in her crew, or Ben's. She was at least as capable as any of them.

And, damn, but he did love her!

The thought shouldn't have caught Ben off guard. It was, after all, the same thought that had been buzzing its way through him these past, glorious weeks. The one that heated his blood and sent his head awhirl. Yet even now, after the days and nights he'd spent lost in the pleasure of Isabel's kisses and the paradise of her embrace, he couldn't quite get used to it.

Benedict Costigan and Isabel De Quincy.

Isabel De Quincy and Benedict Costigan.

It seemed daft. That was sure enough. It *was* daft. It was illogical. And unreasonable. It was incredible.

And it was, without a doubt, the best thing he'd ever done.

A smile tugging at his lips in much the same way as the beginnings of desire were pulling at his body, Ben watched Isabel show John and Tommy Eagan, her own crew chief, where they would need to mount the fireworks for the show that would take place after the Jubilee dinner. It should have been a simple enough task, but John and Tommy were not making it easy on her. Over Isabel's head they exchanged black looks, old rivals who'd been made to take part in an alliance that was at best uneasy.

If any of the workers were astute enough to notice the difference in Ben and Isabel's own relationship, they were wary enough of Isabel's reputation and of Ben's temper not to comment, and apparently disinclined to believe it would last. Old rivalries died hard, and this one was as old as they came. The crews of their respective companies kept their distance from each other, and more than once he'd heard a derisive comment tossed back and forth. They might have to work together, their words and actions told him, but they didn't have to like it.

For now Ben set the thought aside. There was nothing he could do to change their minds. At least not any time in the near future. Someday, they would get used to it. Just as they would get used to seeing Ben and Isabel work side by side. For now it was enough that they were working hard. The Jubilee festivities were the next day, and they would be ready.

Isabel finished with John and Tommy, and Ben watched her walk back toward the long line of fireworks that had been set on the ground in a part of the garden where columbine and violets grew in boisterous profusion.

Paying close attention, Ben took a few steps nearer, the better to see what Isabel was doing. Just as he'd hoped, she looked down the long line of shells and rockets that were waiting to be loaded into their mortars. One in particular caught her attention, and she stopped and stooped to retrieve it.

Isabel looked back over her shoulder, and catching Ben's eye, she held up the shell, which was no bigger than a Christmas cracker. The one with the note attached to it that said *Bella*. He gave her an innocent smile, and rubbing his hands together, he took a few more steps nearer.

A month ago Isabel would not have been so trusting. But that, like everything else about their relationship, had changed. Smiling a bit, she took the shell over to the table that had been set up along one side of the lake. Just as Ben anticipated, she grabbed the envelope fastened to the side of the shell, and just as Ben designed, the second she yanked it, the shell burst open with a satisfying *pop*.

Isabel squealed with surprise, and the air around her filled with the tiny red paper hearts that flew from the shell. Just as Ben had planned.

Laughing, he hurried over to where Isabel stood and found her gasping to catch her breath, her cheeks pink with astonishment.

"A nice little scream," Ben told her, keeping his voice down so that the workers who came running couldn't hear. "But I must say, I like the one I heard last night in bed much better."

"You scared me half to death!" Isabel gulped in breath after breath, trying to calm herself. In the afternoon sunlight her eyes were the clear blue of sapphires, and they flashed in irritation. "Imagine, doing that to someone!" When Tommy Eagan came huffing and puffing from around a corner, she waved him away with one hand. Tommy retreated, but he didn't look happy about it. Or about Ben. Before he signaled the other workers to get back to what they'd been doing, the big Irishman threw Ben a look that could have wilted the flowers that grew around them had he aimed it at them instead.

Isabel noticed, of course, and any other time she would have told Tommy what she'd told him and every other worker time and again these last weeks. They were all one crew now. All one side. The fact that she didn't say a word was a mark of just how rattled she was.

Cooling her flaming cheeks, she waved a hand in front of her face. It caused a breeze that sent a swirl of paper hearts drifting from her hair onto her shoulders. "I really can't imagine that after what happened to you in the spiking room, you have no appreciation of how frightening it is to hear the sound of an explosion during setup."

"That little *snap*?" Ben laughed. "If you were worried about that, then you haven't been in the business long enough to know what's dangerous and what isn't." He caught her eye and waited for her to admit the truth.

Isabel refused to accept she'd been bested, but Ben couldn't help but notice that there was a bit of a smile that tried to break free of the thin-lipped glare she gave him. "How can you even think to do something like that to me?" she asked, and now that her surprise had melted, the irritation in her eyes dissolved into a shimmer. "It was too cruel."

Love or no love, Ben wasn't about to stand by and be run roughshod over. He backed up a step. "As cruel as you removing the fuses on my rockets?"

"That was different." This time Isabel had to turn away to hide her smile.

"Different, was it?" Ben leaned over her shoulder. She smelled like lavender water, and he breathed in the scent. There was one paper heart caught just inside the collar of her shirt, and with a quick look around to make sure no one was watching, he plucked it out with two fingers and brushed it up and down her neck.

"Different. Yes." Isabel's breath caught. This time it had nothing to do with surprise. And everything to do with the same heart-stopping awareness that had suddenly begun to tingle through Ben's body.

"Different." Isabel tried again. "I was simply teasing," she said. She stuck out her lower lip in a little pout that made Ben want to kiss her right then and there. "And besides, I gave back the fuses as soon as you asked for them and even helped you attach them again."

"But not before I practically had apoplexy wondering what had become of them!" Ben laughed. Ten minutes before the start of a show at the Crystal Palace a few nights earlier, he'd discovered that the fuses on three of his best shells had been expertly removed. There was no question who the prime suspect was. His first reaction was instinctive. He was annoyed as hell, until he discovered that Isabel had only been teasing.

He leaned closer, his words soft against her ear, teasing in his own way. "I would say, my dear Bella, that we are even."

"You're right." She hated to admit it, but admit it she did. Isabel stuck out her hand. "A truce?"

Ben took her hand in his. "A truce," he said. His

fingers closed around hers, and his gaze skimmed the front of her shirt, his memory filling in the blanks, providing detail after detail about the delicious flesh that was hidden beneath. "I say, Miss De Quincy, has anyone ever told you that even in men's clothing you do not look at all like a man?"

She glanced up at him, a look that was as coy as it was confident. "I'm glad you noticed. Dare I ask what you intend to do about it?"

"Oh, what I'd like to do!" As if seeking strength, Ben looked toward the heavens. "I don't suppose the old girl"—he poked his chin toward the palace—"would mind if a couple of young lovers decided to use one of the empty rooms in the palace to—"

"Ben!" Isabel slapped his hand away, but it was clear from the start she was not as outraged by the suggestion as she was tantalized by it. "I hardly think that's fitting," she said. Though her words were decorous, something sparkled in her eyes that was anything but. "Especially when I know for a fact that Simon will not be home a good portion of the night. He's overseeing the setup of the shells along the parade route right now, but this evening he's going to the opera with Edward Baconsfield." She sidled closer, her breasts brushing Ben's arm. "No one will miss me. I could come over to your townhouse this evening and—"

The rest of what Isabel was going to say was smothered by the sound of a quick, sharp bang from the other side of the lake.

This was no innocent *snap,* no Christmas cracker pop. It was the sound of a good-sized shell exploding, and Ben's stomach pitched at the same time Isabel started off at a sprint. They ran neck and neck for a few hundred yards, but there was no question that Ben would outstrip her. By the time he got around to the other side of the lake, Isabel was far behind.

Ben pulled to a stop twenty feet or so from a scene of chilling chaos. It took him only a moment to confirm his worst fears. One of the shells had exploded. Thank God, it had not been one of the large ones.

The member of Isabel's crew who'd no doubt been placing the shell into its mortar at the time of the blast was injured, but not seriously. The man's face was rimmed with black powder, his eyes were closed, and if the tears that streamed down his face meant anything, they were stinging like hell. He was hurt enough to be flat on the ground. And well enough to be cursing like the devil.

Another of the crew members had gone over to attend to the injured man. Others of Isabel's crew, old hands at the fireworks business, had already sprung into action. Three of them rushed forward to get the remaining fireworks as far from the burning remnants of the exploded shell as they could.

A crew member who looked to be no more than a boy struggled by with an especially large shell, and Ben jumped into the fray. He grabbed one end of the shell and back-stepped his way over toward a tree along the shore of the lake. "Careful now. Easy." The young fellow's eyes were as wide as saucers, his hands trembled against the shell's cardboard wrapping, and Ben used his calmest voice to soothe him and slow him down. "We'll put it right over there. Right under that big oak. No hurry. Steady now. One step at a time."

By the time Tommy Eagan and the rest of Isabel's crew came running to help, the shells had all been moved a safe distance from the last of the flames. Ben turned to find three others of the crew busy dousing the area with the sand that was always kept at the ready in the event of just such a catastrophe. It took him a moment to realize one of those workers was Isabel.

Her face smudged with smoky stains, Isabel handled the crisis with the calm efficiency of a person who knew and accepted that the fireworks business was every bit as dangerous as it was exciting. She finished with the sand, ordered her workers to find the scraps of exploded shell and dispose of them, made sure the man who was injured was taken to a doctor, and, side by side with Ben, dealt with the representatives of the Queen's household who'd come running at the first signs of the commotion.

By that time every man working the show had arrived at the scene, not just Isabel's crew but Ben's as well. They arranged themselves in a loose circle around Ben and Isabel, each man keeping with his own crew. Costigan and Company on one side. De Quincy and Sons on the other.

It was not a subtle distinction. And it was not lost on Isabel. She glanced around the knot of onlookers, and whether she realized it or did it instinctively, she took a step toward the De Quincy and Sons crew.

Petty factions were the last thing they needed right now. Ben knew it. Right now what both crews needed was calm assurance. Level-headedness. He scraped both hands through his hair, scattering the tension that had built inside him while he fought to keep the minor disaster from turning into a major cataclysm.

"It's all right. All taken care of." Ben threw a smile around the circle.

No one smiled back.

"Everyone's safe. Everything's under control." He tried again, this time focusing his efforts on Isabel, knowing that at least with her he was sure to find an ally.

It seemed he was wrong.

Instead of the encouragement he expected to find in Isabel's eyes, he saw only disbelief and something that looked so much like suspicion, it made his blood run cold.

It was not the place to discuss Isabel's odd reaction. Ben was certain of that. It was not the time to rehash events, not when the smell of gunpowder was still so strong in the air. Emotions were running too high. So were fears. Something told him the situation was as explosive as their fireworks, and Ben knew better than to step into the middle of it.

But knowing what to do and doing it were two different things. And keeping his temper in the chill of the ice that suddenly filled Isabel's eyes was another thing all together.

"You can't be serious!" Ben's words boomed through the heavy silence, scattering those birds that had been brave enough to return after the noise of the explosion. "You don't think I had anything to do with—"

If Isabel had not had her back turned on her crew, they might have seen the tears that suddenly glistened in her eyes. She wiped them away with the back of a hand, smudging the grime on her cheeks, and pulled in a breath.

"I don't want to believe it. I can't believe it." Isabel's voice held something close to the contempt he'd heard crackle through it a hundred times before. Fool that he'd been these last weeks, he'd thought he'd heard the last of it. It seemed he was wrong. And a bigger fool than ever.

Isabel looked over the charred patch of lawn. "First the little Christmas cracker. Now this. I don't think you're malicious, Ben, and I'm sure you meant no harm but—"

"Meant no harm!" As much as he tried to control it, Ben's voice refused to do his bidding. It ricocheted over the lawn and reverberated back at him from the stately facade of Her Majesty's London home. "Of course I meant no harm, damn it. I didn't do it. Why would I—"

"Why indeed." Tommy Eagan stepped forward, arms folded across his burly chest. "And didn't I just hear you tell Herself you were trying to get even for that little prank she played on you at the Crystal Palace."

Ben let out a breath of frustration. "Trying to get even, yes." He turned away from Eagan, firmly refusing to let the man get in the way of what should have been a private discussion. "But—"

"So, you admit it, do you, boyo?" Eagan's words cut across whatever it was Isabel might have said.

Was it Ben's imagination, or did Isabel look cut to the quick by the realization? Her eyes filled with tears, but Isabel being Isabel, she refused to let them fall. She held her arms tightly against her sides, controlling the reaction and the shudder that snaked over her shoulders. He might have had a chance to explain himself, or at least to apologize for the whole, ridiculous muddle if behind Isabel her crew hadn't made a sound, like the rumble of approaching thunder.

Behind Ben the growl was echoed by his own crew.

He threw his hands into the air. His own good advice quickly disintegrated beneath the heat of the anger that built like a rock between his heart and his stomach. The accusations stung, and the only way he could think to deal with them was to fight back for all he was worth.

"I don't admit anything," he yelled. He glared at the men who had moved up behind Isabel, hands balled into fists, feet apart. "I don't have anything to admit. And you, madam . . ." He gave Isabel a scowl. "You are being as mulish and as difficult as ever. I thought you were over that. I really did. But I suppose even a good bit of loving—"

"How dare you, sir!" Isabel raised herself to her full height. Even that wasn't enough to bring her up to Ben's shoulders, but she made the best of it, lifting her chin for more effect. A muscle at the base of her jaw twitched. It was odd, Ben thought with the kind of lucidity that is born only in such moments, he remembered her chin as being well shaped, handsome, even adorable. He'd forgotten that she could tilt it stubbornly. Just as he'd forgotten how thoroughly illogical, emotional, and impossible she could be.

"I am not the one who started this." Ben poked a finger in Isabel's direction. "You've just confessed. You are the one who stole my fuses at the Crystal Palace. So if there's anyone to blame for this cock-up—"

"Blame? Me?" Isabel bit the words in half and spat them back at Ben. "You can't possibly blame me. It was my worker, after all, who—"

"Your worker who prob'ly didn't know what the hell he was about."

The comment came from somewhere behind Ben, from one of his crew. It was met with laughs and grumbles of assent from Ben's crew, and with stony silence from Isabel's.

It was the absolutely wrong thing for Ben's man to say, and more wrong still for his coworkers to agree with him, but Ben could hardly blame them. Some fireworks accidents were the result of carelessness. There was no denying that. The idea that the loader who was inserting the firework into the mortar had caused the accident, through oversight or neglect, was no less preposterous than was Isabel's theory. And it was a damned sight easier to believe than was the notion that Ben had somehow willfully planned the explosion.

"You think my workers ill-trained? You think them bungling? Or incapable?" Isabel thrust out her chin, each word challenging Ben. "At least I would never risk harming anyone. Even one of your crew. And the thought that you would, just to get back at me for a harmless practical joke, is too shameful to believe."

"But not nearly as shameful as damping a fellow's fuses."

This comment, too, came from somewhere behind Ben. He was about to ignore it. Discussing what had almost happened to his fountain firework at the Adelphi Theater so many weeks ago could have no possible bearing on what was happening here now. But when he saw John push his way to the front of the crowd, Ben's attention blossomed. John wasn't one to carry stories. And he wasn't one to hold grudges. He elbowed his way to where Ben was standing and held out a handful of limp, wet fuses.

"Damped," John said. "Every one of them."

For what seemed far too long, Ben could do little

but stare. "Are you sure?" The words grinded out of him, disbelief and disappointment mingling to fill all the places where only a short time ago passion had held sway.

"Of course I'm sure." John looked sheepish, or at least as sheepish as a man could look when he was gloating. He looked past Ben over to where Isabel stood with her mouth open, and Ben had the uncomfortable feeling that had he not been the employer and John the employee, John might have leapt up and down with cries of *I told you so!*

"I didn't want to bring it up, sir. We only just found them, you see." John looked up at Ben from beneath the shock of dark hair that hung over his forehead. "I ain't one to be telling tales out of school, but it seems as plain as Salisbury what's happened. It's the same thing what she done at the Adelphi, sir. Or what she would have done if you hadn't stopped her."

"Me?" It was Isabel's turn to express outrage, and she did it like she did everything else. Full-out and without reservations. By now her hands were balled into fists at her sides. Her neck was flushed with a red glaze of aggravation that traveled into her cheeks. She stepped forward, her virulent gaze aimed not at John but at Ben.

"You can't possibly believe that."

"Can't I? You believe that I ragged the shell to explode."

"I didn't want to believe it. I didn't believe it. Besides, that's different."

"Is it?"

"Yes. No." Isabel screeched in frustration. "I don't know! All I know is that I've never had these kinds of problems before. Not until your crew came along."

"And I've never had damped fuses before. It's unimaginative to the extreme, Belle. You could have at least come up with a different way to sabotage—"

"I didn't sabotage anything!" Isabel stepped up toe to toe with Ben. "I am not a scoundrel. Or a jealous, conniving, thieving—"

"Conniving, am I?" By now Ben wasn't at all sure if it was Isabel's face that was red, or just his view of the world. Anger pounded through his blood and throbbed inside his temples. "No more conniving than you, Belle. You're the one who lulled me into complacency. Not a bad ruse, that. When all the while, there you were damping my fuses. Are you really that desperate not to be embarrassed when the Costigan part of the show outshines the De Quincy part?"

Isabel didn't have a chance to answer. With a growl that rumbled back from one crew to the next, the two sides closed in on each other.

After that Ben wasn't certain what happened. He never knew who threw the first punch. He only knew that in a flash as quick as that of the shell that had exploded, all hell broke loose.

Isabel's head hurt. Her eyes burned. Her stomach felt as it had felt much of the afternoon and all of the evening. As if it were tied into a thousand Chinese knots, each one more impossible to untangle than the last.

Crossing the passageway into the drawing room of the De Quincy home, she winced and grabbed for the aching spot at her shoulder blade. That afternoon she'd been quick enough to disentangle herself from the heart of the melee and smart enough to keep well out of the way of flying fists and crushing boots. But still it was impossible to be that close to a brawl and come out without damage.

Not that any of her crew, or even Ben's scurvy lot, would have dared to strike a lady.

As angry as she was—at Ben, his crew, and life in general—Isabel knew that was next to impossible. Ben's workers might be as despicable as he himself was, but even they weren't that contemptible.

Dishonest, yes.

Devious, certainly.

As dishonest as their employer.

They had obviously learned that from a master.

Crafty. Treacherous. Two-faced. False hearted. Yes. Base and—

She might have gone on and on if she had the energy. Instead, she rubbed the bruise on her arm where Ben had grabbed her to hurl her out of harm's way and as far from the ruckus as he could, and tried to ease the pain in her back that wasn't nearly as excruciating as the one in her heart.

She should have known better.

The voice inside her head echoed the message of each painful heartbeat.

She should have known things would turn out no better this time than they had the last. She should have known Ben would betray her in the end.

But she hadn't.

Even now the thought dangled before her, like a carrot held out before a recalcitrant horse. It made her reexamine everything she'd come to believe these past weeks. About Ben. And about herself.

She wasn't sure where they'd gone wrong; she only knew it shouldn't have happened. This time they'd both been older. And supposedly wiser. This time they'd gone into their relationship with their eyes wide open.

Last time she'd only thought she was in love with Ben.

This time she'd been so certain.

Her heart as heavy as her footsteps, Isabel plodded to the drawing room and shoved open the door. Simon was home from the opera; she'd heard him come in some minutes earlier, and like it or not, she had to tell him what had happened that afternoon. Every last ugly bit of it.

"Simon?" Isabel stepped into the room. Her voice was hoarse, and she coughed away the roughness. "Simon, are you in here? I—"

Isabel pulled up short, looking from where her brother stood with his back to the sideboard and a glass of whiskey in his hands over to the large empty space between the two French windows.

"Simon, the piano's missing!"

"Is it?" Simon did his best to look as if this were news to him. His eyes wide, he stared at the bare spot. "I say! You're right! Imagine that. What do you suppose happened to—"

"Simon." Isabel was hardly in the mood for his tomfoolery. She ventured another few steps into the room and, with only the slightest wince of pain, managed to cross her arms over her chest. She raised her voice, not enough to be heard by the servants who might be lurking outside the door, but enough for Simon to know she was determined to put an end to his foolishness. "Simon," she said again. "The piano is missing."

"Er, yes." His face falling along with his jovial spirits, Simon deposited his drink on the sideboard. "It is."

"And may I ask what's become of it?"

"Only if I may ask why your eyes are red and swollen." His own eyes suddenly shadowed with worry, Simon took a few steps nearer. "Have you been crying, Belle?"

"Crying?" Isabel dismissed the very thought with a toss of her head and a smile pinched enough to make her cheeks hurt. "Don't be ridiculous. Why ever would I be crying? Just because I've found out that Ben Costigan is the lowliest, nastiest, most beastly—" Her words dissolved beneath a snuffle of tears.

"Belle!" Simon rushed over and stopped a foot in front of her. "It's true, isn't it?" he asked. "Everything I've heard about you and Ben. All the gossip, I mean. About you and Ben . . . Ben and you . . . being—"

"Lovers?" The very word was a mockery of everything that had passed between her and Ben that afternoon. Isabel's shoulders sagged. Her eyes filled with fresh tears. She swiped the back of one hand over her cheeks. "Oh, Simon!" she wailed. "It's awful. So very awful!"

"You really are in love with him." Simon didn't sound surprised by the realization. He didn't sound happy about it, either. He sounded rather disap-

# DIAMOND RAIN

pointed, and he looked as miserable as Isabel felt. "Do you think it's wise?"

"It hardly matters any longer." Isabel drifted to the other side of the room, across the empty space where only that morning the piano had sat square in the center of the floor. She was suddenly chilled, and she chafed her hands up and down her arms, chasing the cold and diffusing some of the nervous energy that had, all day, been building inside her. "It's over. For good this time. I don't expect you to believe me. After all, I said all this last time, didn't I? But this time ..." Isabel's vision blurred with tears.

"He nearly killed one of our workers." It wasn't the exact truth. Isabel knew it. Michael Gordon, the man who'd been injured in the explosion, had never been in mortal danger. Still, it might have happened. Others of the fireworks might have exploded at the same time. The entire palace could have blown sky high, damn it, and it was all Ben's fault.

"Ben ragged with one of the shells," she explained. "When Gordon was loading—"

Simon's face blanched. "He wasn't seriously hurt, was he?"

"No, thank God." Isabel dashed the thought away. It was hard enough to think about Ben using words like *treacherous* and *betrayal*. It was impossible to think about him associated with the word *murder*. "He knew what he was doing, I dare say. He made sure the shell went off so that the mortar, not the loader, received most of the percussion. Still, it doesn't change a thing. He risked causing a serious injury. All for the sake of getting even with me for a little practical joke. You'd think he'd know better after his accident at the factory."

It was another thought that deserved to be dashed aside, but this time Isabel could not get rid of it so easily. In spite of her best efforts, her head filled with thoughts of all they'd said and done in their days at Ben's country home. And all that she'd thought they'd meant to each other since.

"Damn, I never meant—" Simon realized he was speaking his thoughts out loud, and he reined them in, his face coloring sharply.

"Never meant what?"

"Nothing. Really. Nothing." He took a turn back over to where his whiskey glass was set next to the siphon and, lifting it, drained it down. His spirits bolstered, Simon squared his shoulders. "I didn't know you really loved the man," he said. His knuckles were white against the crystal glass. "I thought things would turn out as they had last time. You'd have your fling and—"

"Simon!"

"Oh, Belle, don't play the innocent with me." Simon's words were as airy as the way he brushed aside her objection. "There's nothing wrong with admitting the truth. I suppose I thought you were a lot more like me. You know, one casual affair after the other. I really can't imagine living any other way. Can't imagine . . ." He swallowed hard, and for a moment his face softened into an expression Isabel could only call wistful. "Can't imagine ever really loving someone. I thought you'd get Ben Costigan out of your system and—"

"I have." Isabel's admission was a little too quick even for her to believe. She held on fast to it, though, certain it was the only way she would get through the night. And the rest of her life without Ben. "I don't give a penny damn about Ben Costigan," she said. She scrambled to change the subject before she gave herself and her lies away by dissolving into tears. "There, you've gotten the truth out of me. I've been played for a fool. Again. And just like last time, I've lived to regret it. Now, Simon, about the piano . . ."

Simon looked up at the ceiling. He looked down at the floor. There was a still life in oils hanging above the sideboard just where it had been hanging since they were children, and suddenly interested in it, Simon turned to study it intently.

"Simon . . ." With the tips of her fingers Isabel

massaged her temples. "It hasn't gone the way of Papa's clock, has it?"

"I'm afraid so, yes." Simon twirled around and faced her, making excuses and pleading all at the same time. "I wouldn't have done it, Belle. Not if I'd known how you really felt about the fellow. When he showed back up after all these years, well, I knew you hated him, of course. And I could hardly blame you for it. I suppose, somewhere in the back of my mind when I was thinking clearly, which, I admit, I haven't always done, especially when I should have been . . ." He sucked in a long breath.

"I suppose that should have stopped me, but it didn't. Nothing could. No matter how hard I tried. I was in serious trouble with creditors, you see, but then, you knew that. And there were these chaps who offered me a way out, but . . . I know it's hard to believe that I thought anything at all, but I didn't think it the wisest thing to do. And then Ben, well . . . at least I knew him. Knew his character and such. And you weren't in love with him then. At least I didn't know you were. So I thought, well, what the hell! What difference does it make? But damn, Belle, he is a fine card player!"

It had been a long, eventful, and miserable day, and Isabel was tired. It was the only thing that would account for her thinking Simon had said what she thought he said. At least she thought so. Until she thought again.

Awareness dawned with all the subtlety of a train at full speed. Her voice was little more than a squeak. "Ben?"

Simon pulled back his shoulders and stood tall. "I'm afraid so. Yes."

"Ben and . . ." Isabel waved her arm toward the empty space where the piano used to be. "And . . . Papa's clock?"

"I told you he was a damned good card player."

Even before Isabel realized she'd made a move

toward the door, Simon came rushing after her. "You can't just go bolting off, Belle."

She paused at the doorway, but only for a moment. "Can't I?" Isabel asked, and as she had weeks earlier when she'd learned that Ben had been injured in the explosion at the factory, she hurried out the door and into the night. Only this time she wasn't on a mission of mercy.

She was in pursuit of vengeance.

Isabel had never been to Ben's London townhouse.

Though they had spent countless hours together in the past weeks, most of that time had been at Ben's country home. Once they returned to the city from Surrey, they'd met at Isabel's home a time or two and once at a charming hotel near Richmond, where the accommodations were as fine as the food, the setting as romantic as any Isabel had ever seen, and the wine from the hotel's famous cellars as heady as their lovemaking.

She had barely pushed her way past the sleepy-eyed footman who'd obviously pulled himself out of bed to answer Ben's front door when she realized why he'd gone out of his way to keep her at a distance from the place.

From somewhere not far away, Isabel heard a clock mark the hour with the Westminster chimes. Her heart sank and her throat went dry.

All the way over to Mayfair, she'd tried to keep herself from thinking the unthinkable. She'd told herself that she was imagining things. Eager to divorce herself from her feelings for Ben, she'd been ready to accuse him of every sin imaginable.

She'd tried to tell herself. But she'd never quite believed it.

"You can't go there!" When Isabel started down the passageway, the footman came after her.

She stopped him in his tracks with one withering look. Not knowing what else to do, the fellow raced up the staircase, apparently after reinforcements. Isabel continued on her way, following the sound of the chimes to a room at the side of the house.

She opened the door and with one hand groped along the wall. With his penchant for all things modern, she was certain Ben had electricity laid, and she was right. She found a switch and pressed it, and high above her head a chandelier sparkled to life.

The room was elegant, that was certain enough. With his usual flair for the expensive, not to mention the gauche, Ben had taken a space of classical proportions and added enough red velvet and gold gild to do a whorehouse proud.

But it was not the decorations that caught her attention. It was the fact that the place looked more like a box room than anything else. Crates and packing boxes filled nearly every inch of the floor. Furniture stood close against furniture. And some of that furniture looked disturbingly familiar.

Staring, Isabel swallowed around unwelcome tears.

Against the far wall stood a tall mahogany clock with the broad brass face plate and fat cherubs that sat one on each of its four finials.

For what seemed like a lifetime, she watched the clock tick away the seconds and scatter the last remnants of her hopes and dreams.

The piano was there, too, she realized, forcing her gaze from the clock. By that time she was hardly surprised. She was surprised, though, to see some other things that she hadn't even realized had gone missing. Her mother's collection of Spode was piled on a sideboard, and a painting propped against the mantelpiece was one that she'd last seen in her father's bedchamber, a room that had been unused and, she thought, untouched since his death.

Isabel pressed one hand to her lips. The other she held against her heart, as if that one pitiful gesture might prevent it from breaking further.

That is exactly how Ben found her.

He had obviously been in bed, though from the dark circles under his eyes, it didn't look as if he'd been asleep. He was dressed only in a shirt and trousers, and he had slippers on his feet. His hair stood up at odd angles, as if he'd been tossing and turning. His lower lip was swollen, and if the light wasn't playing tricks with her eyes, it was bruised as well. So was his left eye.

Ben pulled to a stop just inside the door. He looked at the clock. At the piano. At Isabel.

"Damn," he said. "You weren't supposed to find out about this."

## Chapter 17

Ben's face was an unreadable mask, cool and hard under the light of the electric lamps. The scuffle that afternoon might have left him with a blackened eye and a swollen lip, just as it had left her with every muscle aching, but, Isabel realized, it had done more than that. Much more.

It had raised barriers between them, insurmountable walls built of old rivalries and fortified with that most formidable of all obstacles, love that had turned into something else altogether.

Denying it would only make the pain last longer. Fighting it was futile.

The only thing Isabel could do was accept it, as she did the fact that all this time—the times when she'd hated Ben and the times when she'd loved him—he'd been playing her false.

"Your brother's an abominable card player."

It was a pathetic attempt at lightening the mood. Ben must have known it the moment the words left his mouth. He winced at the sound of his own voice. Or perhaps it was simply because with his lip split and misshapen, it was painful to speak. He ventured a step or two closer and gestured toward the offscourings of her home. "Simon told you?"

"Told me what? That he's an abominable card player? No, he didn't happen to mention that. He didn't have to." Isabel congratulated herself. When she put her mind to it, she could sound just as cold as he did flippant. Even when it felt as if her insides had been kicked out of her.

She strolled away from him, putting some distance between herself and the all too familiar heat of his body, and ran one finger casually over a mahogany table that, the last time she'd seen it, had been holding a dictionary in her father's library. "Or isn't that what you meant?" She whirled, her eyes finding his as surely as a magnet finds metal. The thrill was still there, as strong as ever. It was all the more painful for it.

Isabel bit back the stab of anguish that threatened to betray her. "I tried very hard this afternoon, Ben. I tried very hard not to believe the evidence against you. I couldn't imagine that you would put a workman in danger. Even one of my workmen. But after this . . . I might have known it was you. It was all along, wasn't it? It was you who had Simon writing draft after draft from the company funds. And when you'd nearly bankrupted De Quincy and Sons, even that wasn't enough. You decided to take our personal belongings as well. Papa's clock. Mama's piano." She looked around the room, cataloguing the damning evidence against him. "The paintings and the porcelain. The furniture. Even the crockery. Did you hate me so much that you wanted to see me a pauper on the streets?"

"No. It wasn't like that at all." Ben rejected her assessment of the situation with a swift shake of his head and a motion of a hand that sliced the air. His eyes lit with blue fire. His words rattled the crystal chandelier above their heads. "At least . . ." The fire died and his voice dropped. He scraped both his hands through his hair, and heaving a heavy sigh, he turned away from her. "At least that isn't how it was supposed to turn out."

"Oh?" Isabel couldn't help herself, she had to laugh. The sound was edged with hysteria—even she recognized that much—and she controlled it as best she could. She balled her hands into fists and pressed her nails into her palms, concentrating on the pain in her hands instead of the one in her heart. "And how were things supposed to turn out?"

"Not this damned badly." Ben shook his head. He leaned against the back of the nearest divan, his legs out in front of him, his ankles crossed. "Very well," he said, "I admit, at first I thought it was something of a lark. There I was playing cards with Simon De Quincy. Your damned brother. And there he was, losing like the devil. There was a certain power in it, don't you know? A certain thrill in watching him gamble away the De Quincy family fortune. All the while you were trying your best to damp my fuses and ruin my show at the Crystal Palace, you had no idea that your brother was draining the lifeblood out of your business. Losing it to me."

"You might have told me."

"Really? How would I have done that?" He fastened his gaze to hers, his voice as caustic as his smile. "I say, my dear Miss De Quincy, but you really must ask that brother of yours who he's meeting for cards. You know he's losing a bloody damned fortune." With a derisive snort Ben told her exactly what he thought of that idea. "You wouldn't have listened and, frankly, I didn't care. It was the perfect revenge. Simon would lose every penny you had." As if letting the money trickle through his fingers, Ben opened both hands. Just as quickly he curled them and brought them both to his chest. "And De Quincy and Sons would be mine."

It was one thing to be cool in the face of Ben's indifference. It was another to stand by and listen to him threaten the very existence of the one thing she had always held most dear. Before, that is, she'd given herself—heart, body, and soul—to Ben.

Isabel's temper soared along with her voice. "You wouldn't."

"I didn't, did I?" Whether he was proud of the fact, or disappointed by it, Isabel didn't know. Ben rose from his perch against the divan and paced around a packing crate that looked to be full of books from the

De Quincy family library. "Even when that damned brother of yours ran out of ready money, he wouldn't stop gambling. By the time I realized how very much I'd won from him, I knew I should have said something to you. But by that time it was too late. I didn't know what to say."

"I never thought I would find you at a loss for words."

"No. Well . . ." Ben jammed his hands into the pockets of his trousers. It was not a casual gesture. His anger was mounting. Isabel could tell as much from the flush that stained his neck. "When the money ran out and Simon couldn't pay me with a draft, he sent over the clock. Then the paintings. Then the piano. You see, he is determined that if he keeps gambling, his luck will change. It won't, you know. He is one of those chaps who will forever be ill-fated. Unlucky at cards. Just as I am at love."

Of all the things he'd said, and done, this hurt the most. Isabel wavered between anger and abject misery. The anger won. She knew it would. Just as she knew that anger was the only thing that would get her through the rest of her days.

"Even then . . ." The words escaped her, disbelief mingling with her fury, outrage and humiliation choking her voice. "Even then you couldn't say anything?"

"Damn it!" Ben brought one fist crashing down against the nearest table. "By that time I'd realized I was in love with you. I knew if you found out—"

"You mean *when* I found out." It was impossible to look into his eyes and not be swept away with the misery that filled every inch of her. Isabel spun toward the door. "So you took advantage of the situation. And of me. And you enjoyed yourself as long as it lasted."

"No!" Ben grabbed her arm and spun her to face him. His eyes sparked. "You know that isn't true. That's why I've held on to all this. Until I could find a way to tell you. Until I could explain."

"Or until I discovered what you were up to." Isabel

pulled her arm out of his grasp and rubbed the place where his fingers had been. "It's funny, isn't it?" she asked. "After all the fireworks there've been between us . . . Imagine us ending this way. With a whimper, not a bang."

With that, she turned on her heel and headed out of the room. She stopped only once, and that was at the doorway. She glanced back over her shoulder, toward those things that had been hers, and the man she thought she loved. Toward the ruins of her dreams.

"After tomorrow's Jubilee," she said, "I would like very much never to see you again."

On the morning of Tuesday the twenty-second of June, the sky above London was dull and overcast. Months earlier, the Queen had proclaimed the day a bank holiday, and with businesses closed, thousands of the city's inhabitants were free to join in the celebration of Victoria's sixty years on the throne. Though it was early and the weather was less than ideal, the streets were already beginning to fill with the throngs of people who were expected to watch the Jubilee parade.

Their voices drifted on the damp air. Their footsteps rang hollow against the gray pavement. It seemed as if every building along the route had been cleaned and adorned for the occasion, and even the lively decorations of paper flowers, electric lights, and signs that proclaimed GOD SAVE THE QUEEN! looked bleak and colorless in the hazy atmosphere.

But not nearly as bleak as Ben's spirits.

His fingers idly playing with the fat roll of banknotes in the pocket of his macintosh, Ben trudged up Piccadilly toward St. James Street, his footsteps echoing his thoughts.

Damn, bloody fool.

That's what he'd been. A damned, bloody fool.

There was no escaping the truth. And no denying it. He might as well get used to the fact here and now.

That way he would be free to spend the rest of his life regretting it.

The thoughts pounding through his brain, Ben stopped now and again to check with those of his crew who were positioned along the route to the north of the Thames, just as he supposed Isabel was even now checking with those of her crew who were stationed to the south of the river. According to plan, the main fireworks show would not be shot until that night, after Her Majesty and an illustrious group of royal guests were finished with their dinner at Buckingham Palace. But there would be no lack of fireworks until then.

The parade would begin precisely at a quarter past eleven, when the Queen would leave the palace in a carriage and travel a route that ringed the city. At midday, an abbreviated church service was planned for the steps of St. Paul's, a service that would begin with a brief but spectacular burst of fireworks. Her Majesty herself would send up the first volley with the flip of a switch. After the service, another barrage would follow her up the street and on toward the second half of the parade.

There would also be one shell fired every half mile on the seven-mile route. Of course, the fireworks would be shot well back from the crowd, but they were designed to streak over the street just as the Queen's carriage passed by.

With a grumbled word Ben looked up at the lowering skies. If the weather cooperated, they might still be able to proceed as planned. It was a good thing they had decided well ahead of time that each shell had to be not necessarily as colorful as it was dazzling, so that it could be seen easily enough in the daylight. The shells at St. Paul's also had to be spectacular enough to draw the attention of the thousands who would be watching.

Of course, Ben and Isabel had chosen Diamond Rain.

Though he tried to stop them, memories of the past

# DIAMOND RAIN

weeks crowded around him. He thought of the night two weeks earlier when he'd finally seen a Diamond Rain shell shot off. He remembered his initial skepticism. In spite of Isabel's promises, he was convinced that her Diamond Rain recipe couldn't possibly be all that much different from anything he'd seen before.

How wrong he'd been!

As they stood in the twilight gathering around the testing grounds of the De Quincy factory and the flame was touched to the Diamond Rain fuse, Ben remembered holding his breath. There was the familiar *harrumph* of the shell rising out of its mortar, and he tracked it into the sky. A few seconds later it burst two thousand feet over their heads, and Ben stood in awe.

By that time Isabel had shared the facts and figures of the recipe with him. He knew its chemical composition. He knew how much flash powder Isabel had included, how she'd decided to use less saltpeter and more charcoal to slow the burning, how she'd included aluminium in the mixture for bright, eye-catching sparks.

But he'd never expected anything like Diamond Rain.

To say the effect was spectacular was to do it an injustice. It was like nothing Ben had ever seen before. Like spangles and glitter and sweet tails of fire, and he and Isabel had celebrated afterward, with a bottle of the finest champagne money could buy and a night of lovemaking the likes of which he wouldn't trade for every coin in the Empire.

And now, instead of either every coin in the Empire or Isabel, he had nothing.

Nothing but a pocket full of twenty-pound notes, a head spinning with questions, a gut filled to bursting with remorse, and an ache in the place where his heart used to be.

"There you are, guv!" John waved from the steps of the National Gallery and called Ben over. "Been looking for you. That De Quincy bloke has, too. You seen him?"

"Simon?" Ben nodded. He sidestepped two matronly ladies who were collecting money to build hospitals in the name of the Prince of Wales Fund, and took the steps two at a time, meeting John halfway. "He found me right enough. And gave me this." He brought his hand out of his pocket and showed John the fist-sized roll of banknotes.

"Holy jumpin' mother of Moses!" John blew a soft whistle. "That De Quincy fellow gave you that?"

"He did. And damned if I can figure out where he got it." The familiar rat-a-tat of puzzling questions started again in Ben's head. "As far as I know, there isn't a bean left in the business. Simon's gambled it all away. But he said he knew he had to pay me. And this was his only opportunity to do it. Said it was so Isabel could get her things back." Ben sighed. "Said he never knew how much we meant to each other, Isabel and I. Thought this might make things right."

John pursed his lips. "Will it, guv?"

Ben shook his head, amazed that he could be so certain of what he wanted. And so uncertain about how to go about getting it. "Damned if I know. I would have returned the clock and piano and all the other things even without the money, you know. If only I'd known what to say to her. How to explain. But even with that . . ." He thought back to the afternoon before in the gardens of Buckingham Palace. To the accusations he and Isabel had thrown back and forth at each other. To the old doubts that had grown into new suspicions, and the new suspicions that had spread like a pox to infect their love.

"Damn." Ben thumped his fist against the granite balustrade. All night he'd wrestled with the emotions that played havoc with his heart. All morning he'd found himself right back where he'd been the night before when Isabel walked out of his life without so much as a backward glance.

He tossed the banknotes up and down, weighing

them. "I feel like I've been given thirty pieces of silver."

"More than that there, sure enough." As polite as he was trying to be, John couldn't help but stare, no doubt tallying the amount of money in Ben's hand. "You could give it back, I suppose, guv. You know, as a show of faith."

"I could." It was a thought Ben had already considered and discarded on his own. If Simon had the ready money, he would only gamble it away. And offering it to Isabel would only compound an already nasty situation.

"Or you could enjoy it as you should have your winnings all along." John made the suggestion half-heartedly, as if he knew before he said it that Ben would disagree.

"I could." Again, Ben tossed the money up and down. "Or . . ." Before John could stop him and talk some sense into him, Ben hurried down the steps. The ladies collecting for the Prince of Wales Fund were startled by his abrupt arrival, but not nearly as startled as they were to have a few hundred pounds thumped down on the table in front of them.

"Ladies." Ignoring their spluttered protests, Ben gave them a nod and a wink. Anxious to put questions about Simon and where he'd gotten the money as far from his mind as possible, he continued down the parade route.

It wasn't nearly as easy to put all his thoughts about Isabel out of his mind.

Once he'd told Isabel that theirs was the kind of love that had to be grabbed with both hands. Held on to at all costs.

And then they'd done their best to throw it away.
Damned bloody fools.
That's what they were.
Damned bloody fools.

At precisely a quarter past eleven, the clouds parted and the sun beamed down on London in all its glory.

The decorations that lined the streets gleamed, and for the first time since early that morning, when Isabel had begun her slow and careful inspection of the fireworks emplacements, the people in the crowd were talking not only about the weather but about its significance.

"Queen's Weather. That's what they're calling it." Isabel listened when someone came by, discussing the welcome change. "Blue skies and sunshine. Just what the old girl deserves and the best beginning to the best day ever!"

She wished she could feel so optimistic.

Her steps slowed by the thought, Isabel turned down a street that ran perpendicular to the parade route, then turned again to get to the place where a shell had been placed in its mortar and a shooter from her crew stood by ready to fire.

Just as all the others shooters she'd checked with that morning had been ready to do.

Distracted by the thought, Isabel nodded her greeting to the man, then bent over the mortar to examine the shell. There was something peculiar about the way it was positioned in the mortar, and with the help of her employee, she lifted it out and took a closer look. She stared at the fuse. It was twisted oddly into the break. Just like the last shell she'd examined, and the one before that.

Isabel didn't bother to ask the man if anyone had been by who might have tampered with the shell. She knew what he would say. Like the two other shooters down the road, she was sure he would swear no one had touched the shell. It hardly mattered now, at any rate, she reminded herself, and besides, she had her suspicions. Her fingers trembling with anger, her insides numb, she removed the fuse and replaced it with a new one. They had already returned the shell to its mortar when Isabel heard a voice call from across the way.

"You haven't mucked about with that one as well, have you?"

# DIAMOND RAIN

Isabel froze. There was no mistaking the voice. Or the fact that Ben was annoyed beyond measure. She straightened and smoothed the skirt she'd been obliged to wear rather than her usual trousers. As a show of gratitude from the Queen, both she and Ben had been invited to be seated in the stands erected in the churchyard of St. Paul's for the outdoor service, and in keeping with the occasion, Isabel had worn a navy blue skirt and matching jacket.

She carefully tugged both into place while she looked across Ludgate Circus to where Ben was coming at her at a pace that was somewhere between smart and out-and-out precipitous. His macintosh was open and flying, flapping out wildly behind him. In the glare of the sun, his hair was golden, but his face was gray with worry.

"I can't believe it. Even of you." Before Ben got to where she stood, he launched into a tirade. "Today of all days. To think that you'd rag with a shell and—"

"And I was about to say the same of you." Isabel's words were measured, and certainly not nearly as loud as Ben's, but they stopped him in his tracks. She brushed her hands together and looked back toward the mortar. "It's the third one I've found," she told him. "How many more have you altered?"

"Me? Altered?" He pulled up short and glared at her. "Don't be ridiculous. You don't think I'd put that kind of twist in a fuse. I'm not that careless. Or that stupid."

Isabel looked over her shoulder to where her employee was listening to their conversation with interest. There was no use worrying the help, she decided, and lowering her voice even further, she took a few steps toward Ben. "Then explain why you did it."

"Damn it, woman. That is what I am asking you!" Ben wasn't the least bit worried about the help or the crowd out on the street. His voice boomed against the nearby buildings.

It was not the first time he'd spoken to her as if she

were nothing more than day help, but Isabel swore it would be the last. Firmly ignoring the tiny flutter of excitement that seemed always to assail her when he was so near, she straightened her collar and pulled on her cuffs.

"There were two others on that end of the route," she said, pointing back toward the way she'd come. "Farther up the street."

"And three in that direction." Ben stabbed a finger toward St. Paul's. "Just beyond the church. The fuses were twisted on those as well and—"

"And do you have any idea what it means, Ben? If I didn't change them?"

"Change them? I changed the bad ones I found. And sent John to look over the ones you were supposed to check this morning. What will he find, Belle? Have you changed them? Or are you going up and down the street, twisting the fuses so that—"

"And I've sent Tommy Eagan to check the ones you were supposed to inspect."

". . . because if you are trying to ruin the grandest day the Empire has ever—"

"I? Try to ruin the Jubilee?" The accusation was enough to make her laugh. It was a pity there was no humor in the sound. "You know me better than that, and well enough to know I'd never risk anyone's safety. Not as you did yesterday afternoon at—"

"I didn't do a thing yesterday afternoon. Just as I didn't do a thing today. Nothing but change the fuses you'd put in wrong." Ben looked into her eyes, and where before, Isabel had seen nothing there but love, today they were filled with disappointment. And contempt.

The impact was staggering. Isabel reeled under it. A hand at her throat to try and ease the sudden tightness there, she shook her head in dumb protest.

"You do know what it means, don't you, Belle? If I hadn't fixed them?" Ben's words were stones, and his accusations hit and hurt. "Do you know what would have happened if I'd let those six shells be shot that way?"

"Of course I know what it means. That's why I can't believe it of you." As much as Isabel tried to sound as heartless as he did, she found she could not. Her eyes filled. "Those shells wouldn't have gotten ten feet off the ground before they exploded," she said. "You know that as well as I do, Ben. The only thing I don't know is why you'd risk people's lives. If it is simply to get even with me—"

Frustrated, Ben barked a curse. From up the street a chorus of cheers told them the Queen was drawing nearer, and from that direction they heard the quick, sharp report of a shell.

It was the last shell Isabel had checked, the last fuse she replaced, and she nodded, satisfied. She'd been around fireworks all her life, and she knew the sound of a good explosion. And the sound of a bad one. This one was good; her new fuse had worked just as it should have.

She knew Ben was thinking the same thing. "I told you I fixed it, Ben. Whatever you were planning—"

"Whatever *you* were planning, it hardly matters now. I've stationed my men along the route to make sure nothing else is touched. I dare say we can discuss this later, after the parade." He moved toward the street. "For now, I'm going to join Her Majesty at St. Paul's."

"And I will follow along," Isabel said, trailing after him. "Just to be sure you don't touch anything else."

Ben muttered something and Isabel didn't ask him to repeat it. Squeezing through the crowd, which by now was taking up every inch of the pavement, she shadowed him, heading toward the cathedral.

They were within a hundred yards of the place when Isabel spotted a familiar face in the crowd. Simon was supposed to be waiting behind the church, near the first shell of Diamond Rain that was to be shot. Why he was in the street at all was as much of a mystery as why he was headed in the wrong direction, away from the church.

Isabel pulled to a stop. Quickly, Ben was swallowed by the crowd. She stood on tiptoe and called out to her brother. He must have seen her. She could have sworn he looked her way, but Simon recovered in less than a heartbeat. His head down, he kept right on walking.

"Simon!" From every side the crowd pressed on Isabel. The buzz had started farther up the street; the Queen was near, and as one the people who were waiting to see her pressed forward. Someone crushed Isabel's foot beneath heavy boots. Someone else poked her with an umbrella. She flattened herself and continued through the crowd, heading toward the place she'd last seen her brother.

She caught him up just as he was about to turn the corner. "Simon!" When he pretended not to hear, Isabel grabbed his arm. It was only then she realized he was carrying a portmanteau.

"Simon, where on earth are you going?"

"Oh, Belle!" Simon acted as if he hadn't noticed or heard her calling, but he didn't look at all happy to see her. His brown eyes were wary. The corner of his mouth twitched. "Going? I'm not going anywhere, Belle. Just watching the parade, don't you know?"

"With your suitcase in hand?" Isabel gave him a long look. When he didn't respond, she tried a different tack. "Simon, you're supposed to be with the Diamond Rain shell."

"Yes. Well. Yes, of course." Simon ran his tongue over his lips. It was warm and sunny but not hot at all, yet there was a thin bead of sweat along his forehead. He flicked it away with one finger. "I was there, Belle. Yes. Of course I was. It's all set to go. I just thought I'd . . ." He pulled at one earlobe. "Well, I suppose I just thought I'd . . ."

"Damn it, Simon. Someone has to stand guard over that shell. Ben Costigan's been ragging with the fuses. Just as he messed with the shells yesterday at the palace." She started toward the place where the shell and mortar had been set up. "If you're not going to—"

"No, Belle. Don't!" With one hand Simon grabbed her arm. After he got a hold of her, it seemed as if he didn't know what to do. He shifted from foot to foot and his chin quivered. "It's best if you don't go over there, Belle," he told her. "No one's going to get hurt, of course, but—"

"What!" For a second it felt as if the pavement had been pulled out from under Isabel. She stared at her brother, her head suddenly in a whirl. "What did you say?"

"I said, no one's going to get hurt. At least that's what they've promised me. But you never know, Belle. You never do. And I really couldn't live with myself if anything happened to you. I only want you to be happy, you see. That's why I did it in the first place. That's why I paid back all the money I owed to Ben."

Simon was talking. But he wasn't making the least bit of sense. Her head more in a muddle than ever, Isabel held on to him with one hand and looked into his eyes. "Simon, you're going to have to start at the beginning. I don't understand."

"No. Well . . ." Simon looked toward the street. The vanguard of the procession was already starting by, representatives of Her Majesty's troops from throughout the Empire. "I never realized you really loved the man," he said, shifting his gaze back to Isabel and raising his voice to be heard above the cheers. "Ben, I mean. I never realized until last night that you really, truly loved him. If I had, I wouldn't have messed with those fireworks at the palace yesterday."

"You?" Isabel was wonderstruck. As if she might actually find him there and call him over to hear what her brother was saying, she scanned the crowd looking for Ben. Of course, he was long gone, and she turned back to Simon. "But why?"

Simon shrugged. "I thought he would break your heart again. You see, I did it for your own good, and I made sure no one was injured too badly. I didn't know you really loved him, and I thought you'd only end up hurt. Like last time. So I thought if I did something that would end the affair . . . well, better to see you hurt sooner and over it than wait until later when the hurt would only be worse."

"You ragged with the fireworks?" Isabel could hardly believe it. Her ears were filled with the sounds of cheering; her brain was in a spin. Through it all she tried to piece together the bits of what Simon had said. "But what does that have to do with paying Ben the money you owed him?"

Simon took a step away from her, but when Isabel tightened the hold on his arm, he stopped. "I didn't realize it would hurt you so much, Belle. I'm sorry. I should have known better than to gamble with Ben. I thought if I paid him back all I owed him . . . Well, I tried. I thought if I could get ahold of the Diamond Rain recipe, make it look like a burglary, I could sell it, maybe even to Ben. But first, well, the burglary didn't exactly work. And then when I took one look at you and Ben together, I knew he'd never buy it from me in any event. I told you before, Belle, there were these chaps who were willing to give me all the money I needed, but . . ."

The information was coming fast and furious, and Isabel wasn't at all sure she could work her way through it. She focused on something Simon had said earlier. "But you said—" A resplendent troop of scarlet-and-gold-clad soldiers went by, and another cheer went up from the crowd. Isabel waited for it to die down.

"You said no one's going to get hurt. What do you mean, Simon?"

"It is just to be a distraction, Belle. That's all. I twisted the fuses and—"

"You twisted the fuses!" By now Isabel was holding on to her brother with both hands. She shook him impatiently. "You ragged with the shells? This morning? You are the one who—"

"That's right. It was just to be a distraction, you

see. A couple shells gone off wrong. There would be some noise and a lot of smoke. I never asked why they wanted to do it, of course. But I'm not stupid. I think they must be planning to rob one of the banks along the way. The distraction would give them enough time to . . ."

Simon looked left and right. Another cheer went up from the crowd, and from somewhere toward the front of the pavement, Isabel heard someone call, "There she is! There's the Queen!"

Simon's face went ashen. "I really do have to go, Belle." He pulled away from her. "You obviously found the twisted fuses. I heard them go off, so I know you fixed them. If they think I haven't fulfilled my part of the bargain—"

"Simon!"

Simon started off in the opposite direction of the parade, and Isabel went after him. He'd already turned into a narrow snicket that ran between two buildings when Isabel made a grab for his jacket. She caught a piece of it, and she twisted her fingers, holding on tightly. "Simon, you've got to tell me what's going on. What people? Who are you talking about? What's going to happen?"

In the shadow of St. Paul's, Simon's face looked more pale than ever. He lowered his voice. "I needed the money, Belle. They'd approached me before, but I said no. I didn't like the kinds of things he was talking about . . ."

"He? He who? Simon!" There was something about the way Simon's voice broke over the words that told Isabel there was more urgency to the situation than even he would admit. She listened to the sounds of the Queen's carriage roll into the churchyard, the horses clomping in perfect meter to the furious pounding of her heart.

Simon looked toward the churchyard. "They gave me the money," he said. He yanked himself out of Isabel's grasp. "They paid me to do it, and I had no choice. I had to pay Ben. To keep you from hating him." He started down the alley. "We couldn't be sure those six shells would do the job, of course, so they asked me to do one more thing." Simon's eyes misted. "I didn't want to, Belle, but I had no choice. They said they'd hurt you if I didn't. Just listen to me, please. Stay away from the churchyard." With a last searching look Simon squirmed out of her grasp and took off at a trot. He called over his shoulder. "When she touches the switch . . ."

Simon turned a corner, and the last of his words echoed back at Isabel.

*When she touches the switch.*

What on earth was he talking about?

Like a lightning bolt, the truth struck Isabel. She spun back toward the cathedral. "The Queen! When she touches the switch . . ."

She could only imagine what would happen. And each thing she imagined was worse than the last.

Moving as quickly as she could through the press of the crowd, Isabel hurried toward the church. It wasn't easy. The pavement was packed six deep in spots, and there were people in doorways and perched on lamp posts, each one of them straining to get a look at the Queen. Isabel tried to excuse her way around them, but it was futile from the start. The cheering was far too loud, the crowd too thick, for anyone to pay the least bit of attention to one voice politely trying to clear a path.

There was nothing for it but to use her elbows, and Isabel did, bowling her way closer and closer to the churchyard, each step fueled by one frightening thought: if Simon's so-called friends were looking to cause a diversion, they had certainly found a way to do it.

When the Queen threw the switch that was supposed to launch the Diamond Rain shell into the sky, something else was going to happen. And if the way the fuses on the other shells had been twisted was any indication, she was very much afraid that it was something dangerous. And deadly.

Another thought struck and Isabel stopped, staggered.

If the Queen was in danger, so were those people who'd been invited to sit in the stands and watch the ceremony in the company of honored guests from throughout the Empire, ambassadors from every country in Europe and the royal family itself.

And one of those people was Ben.

# Chapter 18

There were thousands of people in the churchyard that day, five hundred alone on the steps of the cathedral and hundreds more in the two stands that had been erected to the right and left of the church portico. The place was resplendent with ambassadors, Indian rajahs, and nobility who had no official place in the procession, but whose presence was essential to the pomp and ceremony of the occasion. The entire procession had fanned out, and it filled the wide-open area in front of the church. Military representatives from throughout the empire were arrayed nearer to the crowd. Equerries, the royal children and grandchildren, were closer to the carriage that sat just at the bottom of the cathedral steps. It was an incredible sight, splendid enough to catch Isabel off guard and bring her to a standstill.

In the center of it all was a tiny woman with a grandmother's face. She was dressed entirely in black, her gown and cape embroidered with silver and trimmed with ostrich feathers.

Close enough to the front of the crowd to see around the people who stood firmly between her and the ceremony, Isabel watched the Queen accept the welcome of the Archbishop of Canterbury in his purple robes. There were other bishops on the steps of the cathedral with him, and their robes of yellow and green and gold and white flashed in the sun.

Her breaths coming in short, sharp gasps, Isabel scanned the crowd, desperately searching for Ben. It was no use. There were hundreds of men present, and even if she could find him, she was too far away to attract his attention. Too far away to warn him.

Panic filled Isabel's throat. It blocked her breathing. Ignoring the outraged comments from the people who, no doubt, had spent the night in the churchyard to assure their superior place, she pushed her way forward. But even when she broke through to the front of the crowd, there was still a solid line of New South Wales Mounted Rifles and their horses, a contingent of Indian Imperial Service Troops, the Lord Mayor, and a sea of aides-de-camp, attachés, and gentlemen-in-waiting between Isabel and the Queen.

Above the hum of the crowd she heard the Archbishop's voice. She saw an equerry approach the royal carriage, carrying a pillow on which was set the electrical switch that would shoot the Diamond Rain shell into the sky.

Or blow them all to kingdom come.

Isabel sidestepped along the front of the crowd. Closer now, to the church and to the Queen, she maneuvered through a company of Australian soldiers in their distinctive slouch hats and past a column of tall, fine fellows in scarlet coats. It wasn't until she dodged a man in state robes and an elaborate chain of office that anyone noticed her. The man barked in outrage and ordered Isabel to stop, but by that time she didn't have a second to wait.

"The Queen!" She looked toward where the man with the pillow and the switch moved closer and closer to the queen, desperately trying to convey what she had no words to explain. "I've got to stop her, I—"

"Oh, no, you don't!" The man clamped a hand down on Isabel's arm. "Guards! Guards!" He tried his best to keep his voice down so as not to distract from the ceremony, but he was apparently enough of a personage to draw attention. From the corner of her eye Isabel saw a bobby come running and she knew she didn't have a second to waste. The Queen had already acknowledged the man with the pillow. Her hand raised, she reached for the switch.

"No!" With a shout Isabel tore herself out of the man's grasp and lunged for the Queen. "No, Your Majesty, don't! Don't touch that switch!"

Her eyes bright with surprise, Victoria looked at Isabel.

It was the last thing Isabel saw before three burly bobbies tackled her from behind and she landed in a heap at the Queen's feet.

It was amazing how a man's mind could play tricks on him.

Even though Ben had told himself in no uncertain terms that he had no choice but to put all thoughts of Isabel far behind him, he could have sworn he saw her face in the close-packed crowd arrayed in front of St. Paul's Cathedral.

That was ridiculous, of course.

Isabel had been invited to participate in the ceremony from the steps of the church, just as Ben had been, though he'd be damned if he'd allow himself to look around for her. It was the last thing she needed to see, some sign that he was far weaker than he was pretending to be. It was the last thing he needed to do, for it would only serve to confirm that weakness to himself, and he didn't need that. He felt bad enough already.

Now if only he could keep himself from seeing Isabel's face everywhere he looked.

Ben sighed. At his side Edward Baconsfield caught Ben's eye and nodded toward the fringes of the crowd, indicating that he was about to leave. It was a damned inconvenient time for the fellow to decide to depart, but Ben had better things to worry about. He stepped back to allow Edward by, all the while scanning the spectators, looking toward the place where he could have sworn he saw Isabel only a few moments earlier, slipping in and out of sight, weaving and bobbing her way through the crowd.

There was no sign of her, of course. He didn't think there would be, and he shifted his gaze to the Queen.

# DIAMOND RAIN

The old girl looked as chipper as he'd ever seen her and as bright as a new penny under the adoring eyes of thousands of her subjects. She was, of course, too old to climb the steps into the cathedral. It was one of the reasons the service had been planned for outdoors. With her daughter-in-law the Princess of Wales next to her, and her sons on horses around her carriage, Victoria sat and waited for the equerry who was to bring her the switch that would send the Diamond Rain shell roaring into the sky.

Diamond Rain.

The words set Ben's teeth on edge. The last thing he needed was a reminder of Isabel's betrayal. Too disturbed by the thought, he looked away from the Queen and the switch and back to the crowd.

There was a rustle from somewhere behind the New South Wales Mounted Rifles, some horse that had chosen the wrong moment to shy, he imagined, and he concentrated on the ripple that went through the throng, forcing his mind back to the occasion and away from the memories he knew would haunt him the rest of his days.

He saw the Queen acknowledge the man with the pillow with a nod. He watched her raise her hand and reach for the switch.

"No!"

A voice rang out from somewhere along the front edges of the crowd. At least Ben thought it did. He shook his head, eager to dispel his fantasies. Now he wasn't simply imagining he saw Isabel. He was hearing her, too.

A buzz fluttered through the crowd, and at the end of a long row of spectators, Ben saw Edward pull to a stop. All around him people leaned forward, eager for a better look. So did Ben, and what he saw made him catch his breath.

As if she'd been shot from a mortar, Isabel bolted out of the crowd. Her face was pale. Her hair was tousled. Her eyes were wild. With a shout she lunged for the Queen. "No, Your Majesty, don't!" she screamed. "Don't touch that switch!"

Ben rushed forward at the same time three muscular bobbies threw Isabel to the ground.

By the time Ben fought his way past the tangle of equerries and footmen who scrambled to the Queen's aid, Isabel had already struggled to her feet. A beefy bobby had hold of her right arm; a thinner but no less determined fellow had hold of the left. The third policeman hadn't fared as well in the scuffle. He sat on the pavement, nursing what was sure to be a black eye, and one look at the stubborn tilt of Isabel's chin left no doubt in Ben's mind that she was the one who'd given it to him.

"No! Don't!" Isabel continued to shout, this time at the equerry with the pillow who, apparently determined to continue the ceremony and ignore the unpleasant incident, had decided to approach the Queen again. "Don't let her touch the switch. Don't let anyone—" A wave of relief washed over her face when Isabel spotted Ben.

"Ben!"

He had the distinct impression that Isabel would have liked nothing better than to throw herself into his arms. She fought against the hold of the policemen, and lowered her voice so that only those closest could hear.

"Ben, tell them not to touch the switch. I found out . . . found out what happened yesterday at the palace. And this morning. I'm not sure, Ben. Not at all sure. I know it sounds insane, but I think the shells may be wired to explode."

Coming from anyone else, the allegation would have been ridiculous. Even mad. But Isabel was not a woman given to hysterics. And Ben was not a man who trusted to chance. Not when it came to the lives of thousands. Or the love of one woman.

Waving off the police who came running to accompany him, he took a few slow steps toward Isabel. "Who?" he asked. "And how did they do it?"

Isabel bit her lower lip. She looked at the bobbies who had hold of her. "I . . . can't . . ." She was torn between telling the truth and protecting someone, and that could only mean one thing. She didn't want to implicate someone. Not here in front of thousands. That someone could only be Simon.

Ben nodded in understanding. He looked to his left, over to where the Queen sat in her carriage, her back ramrod straight, her keen eyes taking in every bit of the drama that swirled around her. With a nod he asked permission to proceed, and when Victoria gave him the slightest of nods in return, Ben took another step toward Isabel.

"What's going to happen?" he asked.

"I'm not sure." A single tear slid down Isabel's cheek. "He said . . . he told me to stay away. He said no one was supposed to be hurt but . . . You saw the twist in the fuses, Ben. You saw what he did along the parade route."

"Of course." It made so much sense, Ben could hardly believe they'd both been too blind to see the truth. "And yesterday? At the palace?"

Isabel nodded. "I don't think he meant to hurt anyone." She looked toward the Queen when she said it, explaining, excusing her brother's excesses as she always did. "He was lied to, I think. He thought . . . he thought they wanted to rob a bank, but, Ben . . ." She looked back at him. "You know as well as I do what will happen if the switch is thrown."

"She's right, of course."

It wasn't until Isabel's gaze slid over Ben's shoulders and her eyes went wide that Ben registered the voice that came from behind him. When he finally turned, he didn't see the man's face at first. All he saw was the barrel of a pearl-handled pistol aimed straight at his gut.

Instinctively, Ben took a step backward at the same

time he let his gaze slide up to the man's face. "Edward!"

Edward Baconsfield smiled. At Ben. At Isabel. At the Queen. "I'm sorry to ruin the festivities, Your Majesty," he said, his top lip curling over the words, "but it seems things haven't gone quite as planned. If Miss De Quincy had chosen to be a little wiser and a little less meddlesome, none of you'd be here right about now. The way it is . . ." Edward gestured toward Isabel, and the two bobbies, not knowing what else to do, dropped her arms and moved away from her. "The way it is now, Miss De Quincy . . ." Edward grabbed Isabel and yanked her to him, and when Ben made a move, he poked the pistol into his stomach.

A startled gasp went up from the people who were closest, the only ones who could clearly see what was going on. Edward silenced them with a look, then instructed Ben to back off. He did, but not before a look he hoped told Isabel all he was thinking.

He meant it to say he was sorry, for doubting her and for ruining the one chance at happiness they had left.

He needn't have bothered.

The look Isabel gave him said all the same things.

His arm around Isabel's throat, Edward dragged her over to where the equerry stood with the pillow. He raised his hand above the switch. "It looks as though if you want something done right, you have to do it yourself."

"No, Edward. Don't!" Hoping for the chance to grab Isabel's arm and haul her out of Edward's reach, Ben darted forward. He stopped cold when Edward pressed the pistol to Isabel's forehead. "Edward . . ." Ben lowed his voice. Slowly, he took another step toward Isabel. "You don't want to throw the switch, Edward. We'll all be blown to bits."

"Yes, well . . . that's the idea, isn't it, old man?" Edward laughed. "I was hoping that idiot brother of yours could take care of all this, Miss De Quincy, but it seems he's botched this as he's botched everything else in his life. No matter. We'll all die together. You." He poked the pistol toward Ben. "Her." He looked at Isabel, and a smile slowly lifted the corners of his mouth. "Her." He stabbed the pistol at the Queen and looked around at the other royals assembled around them. "And all the rest of you parasites who live off the blood and sweat of the working people. I'll gladly die for my comrades, what about you?"

One of the royal princesses fainted dead away. Another two had already started to cry. Ben saw the situation slowly slipping out of his grasp, and he scrambled to salvage it. At least until someone stepped forward who had enough courage—and enough lunacy—to do something.

"And here I thought your journey to Russia had done little more than given you an appreciation for vodka and a taste for caviar. Really, Edward." Clicking his tongue, Ben slid closer. "You might have told me you'd taken up with the Bolsheviks. It's sure to make you a pariah, you know. You'll never be invited to Ascot again. And you can forget the Henley Regatta. Damn, Edward, but this is sure to make a shambles of your social life."

"Shut up!" Edward raised his hand above the switch. "And say good-bye."

It was the first thing Edward had said all day that made any sense.

"Good-bye, Bella," Ben said. He gave her a wink and the smallest of smiles at the same time he threw himself at Edward Baconsfield.

The gun went off with a roar that exploded next to Isabel's ear. She didn't think she screamed, but it was quite honestly hard to say. All around her, women shrieked and men shouted and cursed. Her feet went out from under her, and she landed facedown on the pavement. Someone landed with a thud square on top of her. It was someone heavy, and the weight made it difficult for her to catch her breath. All around her she saw feet; black boots that ran forward and rose off the ground, as if their owners were jumping, grabbing, fighting.

As quickly as it all started, it was over. Silence settled in all the places where only moments before all had been chaos. From the crowd Isabel heard the sounds of crying. She tried to move, but it was nearly impossible with the heavy weight atop her. She reached around her back, eager to shake whoever it was and get him to his feet, and her fingers met something hot and sticky.

Isabel pulled her hand in front of her eyes and stared at the blood that glistened on her fingers. Looking up, she saw that the burly bobbies who'd had hold of her had changed their quarry. They had Edward Baconsfield firmly in hand, and as they dragged him away, he spouted something about the people's rights and the end of the aristocracy. When he was gone from the churchyard, a deadly silence fell over the scene. All around her Isabel saw people's boots as they gathered around. She felt their eyes staring.

"Ben?" Again, Isabel reached toward the body lying on top of hers. She shook the man's shoulders. She struggled to turn over, and the first thing she saw was Ben's golden head. His eyes were closed. His face was colorless. Isabel's stomach lurched along with her heart. "Ben!" Her voice was edged with panic and tight with tears. She scrambled to slide out from under him and sit up.

The movement was enough to accomplish what her gentle shake had not. Ben groaned and shook his head. His eyes popped open.

"What the hell!" His voice boomed across the churchyard. Glaring at Isabel, he sat up. His face was dirty. His jacket was torn. His shoulder was wet with blood, but when someone offered to hold a handkerchief to the wound, he pushed the hand away.

"What the hell is wrong with you, woman!" Ben pulled himself to his feet and scowled down at her. "You could have gotten yourself killed!"

"Me?" When someone offered her a hand up, Isabel gladly took it. Her legs feeling like they were made of India rubber, she stood and faced Ben. "I am not the one who threw myself at that madman," she yelled.

"No. But you came charging over here to warn everyone. When you knew there was danger." Again, someone made a move to help Ben. He sent them scurrying for cover with a look. "Damn it, Isabel, you should have run the other way!"

"And done nothing while you were blown to bits?" It was too ridiculous for words, and it only went to prove what she'd known about Ben all along. The man was as mad as a hatter, that was for certain. He was an arrogant, egotistical, self-centered lunatic. "If you think I would ever stand by and let that happen to you, you don't know a thing about me, Ben Costigan. And besides, you are hardly one to criticize. You might have been killed yourself, jumping on Edward that way."

"The bastard might have hurt you." A man whom Isabel recognized as the Prince of Wales seemed a more determined soul than the last one who'd tried to help Ben. With a no-nonsense look and a scowl of epic proportions, he held a handkerchief to Ben's shoulder. Ben winced, but he accepted the help readily enough. He pressed the handkerchief in place and nodded in thanks even as he turned his attention back to Isabel. "I can't believe you could even think that I might stand by and not come to your assistance. You think I could go on if something happened to you? Now, there's an absurd notion if there ever was one."

"No more absurd than the fact that I couldn't live without you!" Bleeding or not, he was being totally irrational, and it was Isabel's duty to tell him so. She stepped up to Ben and raised her chin. "You have absolutely no right to sacrifice yourself for me and—"

"My dear young people."

The sound of the voice stopped Isabel cold. As one she and Ben turned to face the Queen.

Not a hair or an ostrich feather out of place, Victoria looked down at them from her perch in the royal carriage. She was holding the red velvet pillow with the switch atop it, her fingers tight around the gold braid that decorated its edges. With a look, a gentleman-in-waiting came and relieved Her Majesty of the pillow, and Ben signaled John to disconnect the switch.

The matter taken care of, Victoria brushed her hands together. "It seems to me," she said, "that you two are at cross purposes. And it isn't the first time, is it?" As if to refresh her memory, the old lady looked at her daughter-in-law, who nodded in return.

"Yes. Yes. Just as I thought." Victoria smoothed a hand over her skirt. "I was invited to the wedding. Four years ago, wasn't it? And I must tell you, I was mightily disappointed when it was canceled. Ah, well . . ." She sighed a sigh of regal proportions. "It seems nothing changes much. Unless . . ." She looked from Ben to Isabel, her gaze penetrating. "Unless you two have something you need to say to each other?"

Ben reached for Isabel's hand. "Do we, Bella?" he asked.

Isabel smiled, a smile that started from somewhere deep inside her and bubbled into a laugh. "I love you, Ben Costigan!" She shouted the words, as loud as she could, and her statement was met with applause.

"And I . . ." With the help of the Prince of Wales, Ben got down on one knee. "I love you, Bella," he said, his voice a murmur that touched her heart and warmed her soul. "Will you marry me?"

Isabel tipped her head, considering the suggestion. "Will you arrive at the church this time?"

In a second Ben was on his feet. "I? Arrive at the church? You are the one who—"

"Mr. Costigan! Miss De Quincy!" Again, it was the Queen who interrupted them, and again Ben and Isabel turned to her, chastised. "*We* will be there," she said, and there was no question about it, it was the end of the discussion.

\* \* \*

# DIAMOND RAIN

Diamond Rain exploded in the night sky, reflecting in the lake that graced the gardens of Buckingham Palace. From the balcony of the palace itself, applause rose, and Ben smiled over at Isabel.

"You're a success, Miss De Quincy."

Isabel returned his smile. "No. *We* are a success, Mr. Costigan." She watched a flight of rockets light the night sky. "And I . . ." She gave Ben a sidelong look. "I am feeling quite as happy as I ever have."

"That makes two of us." Ben came up from behind her and wrapped his good arm around her waist. His shoulder had been bandaged, and he was wearing a sling, but it didn't stop him from hugging her close.

Isabel sighed. "What will happen to Simon?"

"Simon may be gullible, but he is not vicious. I explained that he didn't know what was planned. Sir Digby assures me that he will be handled gently."

"I'm glad." Isabel smiled. Colors spread across the sky, blue and purple, pink and white. They danced on the breeze and drizzled to the ground, and when she looked up into Ben's face, she saw that he was smiling at them, too.

"We'll make quite a team, I think," he said, settling her tighter against him. "I can see it now. Costigan and De Quincy, Purveyors of Penultimate Pyrotechnics."

Isabel could hardly believe her ears. Being careful not to move too quickly against his injured shoulder, she spun in his arms. "You have it wrong, sir. It is to be De Quincy and Costigan, surely."

Ben's lips thinned. "Costigan and De Quincy."

"De Quincy and Costigan. It has to be. We are the oldest fireworks manufacturer in the country and—"

Ben's laugh stopped her cold. "We'll never be bored, the two of us."

"No." Isabel sighed. "And we'll never be in agreement, either."

Ben grinned. "I hope not! If we stop fighting . . ." He nuzzled a kiss against her neck. "We'll have to stop apologizing. And if we stop apologizing . . ." He glided his lips all the way up to her chin. "We'll have to stop making our peace with each other. And making our peace . . . well, Miss De Quincy . . ." He tightened his good arm around her, pressing her close. "It seems to me, that is quite the most pleasant thing I can think of!"

Happiness bubbling through her like the *pops* of the shells exploding high over their heads, Isabel laughed and brought her lips to Ben's.

It was the first time in as long as she'd known him that she had to admit, he was absolutely right.